"Tell you what," he said,
giving Lila a sidelong glance.
"I'll take Rick and you get Ted."

Lila passed him a towel and they patted down their charges. Paul tried not to stare at her chest, but it was like having a front row seat at a wet T-shirt contest during spring break in Daytona. Bath water had soaked the front of her, outlining her generous breasts and causing her nipples to jut against the fabric.

He busied himself by wrapping Rick like a mummy while she did the same to Ted. Standing, they each picked up a boy and brought them into the bedroom.

Relieved they'd left the confines of the small bathroom, Lila heaved a breath. She'd been doing fine until Paul knelt down beside her. Once that happened, she'd thought all the oxygen had been sucked from the room. They were side by side, up to their elbows in suds and water, and all she could think about was sharing the tub with him while his big, capable hands lathered her skin . . .

Avon Contemporary Romances by
Judi McCoy

WANTED: ONE SPECIAL KISS
WANTED: ONE PERFECT MAN

JUDI McCOY

WANTED: One Special Kiss

AVON BOOKS
An Imprint of HarperCollinsPublishers

AVON BOOKS
An Imprint of HarperCollins*Publishers*
10 East 53rd Street
New York, New York 10022-5299

Copyright © 2004 by Judi McCoy
ISBN: 0-06-056080-0
www.avonromance.com

First Avon Books paperback printing: December 2004

Avon Trademark Reg. U.S. Pat. Off. and in Other Countries, Marca Registrada, Hecho en U.S.A.
HarperCollins® is a registered trademark of HarperCollins Publishers Inc.

Printed in the U.S.A.

10 9 8 7 6 5 4 3 2 1

For Karen Moser, Janice Boot,
Donna Robacker, Debbie Williams,
Dolores Reiter, and Marilyn Skaggs,
staunch supporters of my work
from the beginning.
Thanks, ladies,
I couldn't have done it without you.

Prologue

Lila followed her mother and father up the entry ramp to the transporter. Rila, her twin sister, was leaving today on a mission so vital to their world that only nine women had been deemed intelligent and courageous enough to take part. Her family was there to say good-bye.

Hugging her carryall to her chest, Lila followed demurely. She too had been selected from the first wave of volunteers. The sisters had gone through a period of training, until the group had been whittled to eighteen. Rila the Perfect, as Lila often secretly referred to her twin, had made the final nine.

Lila had not.

Everyone who knew their family assumed Rila would be selected. More humiliating was the fact they all seemed shocked that she, Lila, had gotten so far. Though no one had expressed their misgivings out loud, she knew that even her parents had been surprised to learn she had made the prestigious group of eighteen. She was here today to alter their opinion.

She was younger than Rila by only a few moments, but as they'd reached adulthood the short amount of time had grown until it seemed they were separated by a chasm. Rila had found a place in their world, while Lila was still searching. She was sick to death of coming in second to Rila the Beautiful, Rila the Brilliant, Rila the Perfect.

After today, she would be Lila the Free.

Each of the group's nine participants waited in a private chamber that led directly to a traveling pod, in order to say farewell to their loved ones in private and ready themselves for the journey. At a signal, they would slide down the entry chute to their pod, where they would stay until they reached their destination. On the trip, they would prepare by reviewing Earth history and customs one final time.

Lila was clever; she knew the drill. She could study the data that explained her sister's ideal match and learn the last of the lessons in the review. After her pod hit ground, she would complete enough of the mission to integrate fully into life on a new and exciting planet. She would become her own person, not a shadow of Rila. This quest was the chance to succeed at *something,* and begin her life anew.

She waited, thinking positive thoughts, while her twin bubbled with enthusiasm as she chatted with their parents. It wasn't Rila's fault she was intelligent and brave. If this mission went as planned, she would get chosen for the next one.

Finally, their parents left and she and Rila were alone.

"Wish me luck, little sister?" said Rila, her expression glowing.

"I love you, Rila," said Lila. "I know you never meant to make me feel less worthy. I want you to always remember that."

"Less worthy? Oh, Lila, I apologize if I gave that impression. I too hoped you would be chosen. You love children so much, you were made to be a mother. This mission would have been perfect for you." A bell rang, then an announcement blared from the speakers, telling Rila it was time to prepare for launch. She pulled her twin close. "We've shared so much. I'm truly sorry you weren't chosen."

Too choked to speak, Lila wrapped her arms around Rila's neck and returned the hug. She'd thought for days about her decision. If there were any other way . . .

Moving swiftly, she pulled an injector from her bag and pressed it against her sister's neck. "Please, make them understand, this is something I have to do for me."

Catching Rila when she collapsed, Lila propped her in a chair, removed the chips from her sister's earlobes and the bracelet at her wrist, and tucked them in her carryall. Struggling with Rila's dead weigh, she tugged off her flight suit and quickly donned the one-piece garment. Then she placed a note for her parents on the table. The second warning bell came with orders for the travelers to climb into the entry chute, which Lila quickly obeyed. Once she was safely in the pod, no one on the mother ship would know she'd stowed away.

At the next signal, she closed her eyes. Sliding down the chute, she said farewell to all her yesterdays, and set her sights on tomorrow.

One

"I'm sorry, Dr. P, but it's just not working out. Your boys are too big a handful." Rose Sweeney passed Paul Anderson his twin sons, then took a step back and folded her arms. "My Phil needs his sleep, and little Teddy and Rick aren't always cooperative when it comes to nap time."

Keeping his smile intact, Paul sighed inwardly. Rose Sweeney was a friend and, until this moment, his babysitter. His waiting room had been full from the first day he'd hung his shingle in this tiny eastern shore community, but he was still adjusting to his surroundings. He had patients by the dozens; friends here were as scarce as a cup of Starbucks. He didn't want to lose Rose as either.

"If it's a question of money—"

The young woman held up a work-reddened hand. "You pay me plenty. I'm hurt you'd think I want more."

Great, now he'd insulted one of the few people in

town close to his own age. He was batting triple zero for the day.

"I'm sorry if I offended you, Rose. I can't tell you how grateful I am that you've kept the twins this long." He hefted a two-year-old in each arm. "I just finished with my last patient, so I'll take the boys upstairs and give them their dinner."

Rick stuck a finger in his father's ear. "Dinna! Dinna! Dinna!" he yelled at the top of his lungs. Teddy smacked Paul on the side of the head, slapping in time to his brother's chant.

"They sure are loud," said Rose, wincing at the racket. "About frightened my little Sally to death this afternoon when Rick threw one of his temper tantrums."

"Sorry, I'm trying to break him of that habit." He set the boys on their feet and, as if on roller skates, they headed for the pile of magazines he'd just straightened. "Could you do me one favor? Keep them for me until someone answers my ad?"

She eyed the twins as if they were puppies let loose on a newly laid carpet. Teddy tossed magazines like chunks of confetti, while Rick continued his call for supper. "I don't know . . . You've been running that ad for a while now. How much longer before you find the right person?"

Paul shrugged as he raised his voice over the racket. "I have an ad in the *Eastern Shore News* and the *Beacon*. They come out today. I'm sure someone will respond by Monday or Tuesday."

"So I'd only need to have them for two more days?"

"Tomorrow, Monday, and maybe Tuesday," he

agreed, mentally crossing his fingers. "Wednesday at the latest."

"I play Scrabble at the firehouse on Wednesday mornings," she reminded him. "And I have to attend a few of the Founders' Day meetings. You still take that day off, remember?"

It was Paul's day off unless old man Painter's arthritis acted up, or Mary Barton's new baby had another bout of colic, or Pete Starrett fell off a ladder again. But he was sure of one thing. If no one answered the ad this week, he was going to the city council to demand they live up to another of their contractual agreements: help with the care of his sons.

He avoided giving her a direct answer. "I'll do my best to have a full-time nanny by Wednesday."

Rose raised a brow and he knew she was thinking that she'd heard this song before, as had a host of other women in Preston's Ferry. When he'd accepted the city's offer of town physician, they'd promised to supply him with some modern equipment, as well as lend a hand with the boys until he found a full-time nanny. So far, the townsfolk had kept their word about the office supplies and were supposed to order a portable X-ray machine as soon as they completed the Founders' Day budget. They'd tried to elicit help with the twins too, but everyone who'd spent more than a few days with his energetic sons had run screaming for the Chesapeake faster than a seagull with its tail on fire.

"Okay, drop them off tomorrow morning and I'll explain it to Phil." Rose gave the twins a final once-over, wincing when Teddy shrieked out a laugh.

" 'Bye, now, fellas. You be good for your daddy, hear?"

Paul locked the door immediately after Rose left, fearful she'd change her mind. Then he turned and focused on his boys. Rick sat on a split vinyl chair, the one with the stuffing peeking out, munching happily on the front cover of *Reader's Digest*. Teddy, the deep thinker of the two, methodically tore page after page from the newest *Eastern Shore Life* and set each sheet neatly beside him in a pile.

Paul loved his children, but times like this he really wanted to hunt down his ex-wife Melanie and kick her to Canada and back. He'd collected a truckload of sympathy when word leaked that she'd left him for the electrician who'd come to repair their wiring after a power outage. But deep in his heart, he knew she'd been right. He had shamelessly neglected her and their sons. He only wished she'd clued him in before she'd run off, and given him a chance to change. If that had happened, they might still be married and he might still be the most sought-after plastic surgeon in Baltimore.

"Dinna! Dinna! Dinna!" shouted Rick, beating his fist on what was left of the *Reader's Digest*.

Paul sighed as he studied his shambled office. It wasn't much, just a small waiting area with mismatched tables, a ratty sofa and chairs, and a desk for the receptionist he'd yet to hire. The single door alongside the desk led to three tiny examining rooms, a makeshift kitchen that doubled as a lab, a patient bathroom, and a closet-sized office for him.

He'd taken the place sight unseen when he'd accepted the position, and now he wished he'd had the brains to check it out more carefully. But he'd been desperate at the time, trying to balance his hectic profession with his newer parenting duties. When his third housekeeper quit, he realized it was time for a change—and a new schedule that would give him the freedom to raise his sons, as his ex-wife had suggested in her farewell note. He'd gone through their separation in stages—anger, denial, self-pity, and pain—but in the end he realized Melanie was right. He had lost touch with the important things in life, including his children. It was too late for him to be a good husband, but he still had time to become a real father. The ad for a doctor to tend the citizens of Preston's Ferry, a small town on Virginia's eastern shore, had sounded like the perfect way to make that happen.

"Okay, guys, dinner it is." He hoisted Rick in his arms and did the same with Teddy. "I'll take care of this mess after the two of you are in bed." He carried them through the door to the back stairs that led to their second-floor apartment. "What do you guys feel like eating tonight? We've got macaroni and cheese or hot dogs and chips. There might even be some chicken nuggets we can nuke. Does any of that sound good?"

Teddy kept mum, as usual, while Rick spoke for both of them. "Mac and *sheez*, Da."

Paul hugged both boys tight. Rick had only started saying Da a few days ago, and the single syllable was music to his ears. Teddy often followed his brother's development, but it sometimes took a while. He'd brought them to a speech therapist for an evaluation in the month right after Melanie left, and they had tested normal. The therapist assured him that once they grew comfortable with their father and formed a bond, their speech would improve and they'd be fine.

He couldn't wait until his sons learned to talk in full sentences. Then he could hold a conversation with them instead of the aging population of Preston's Ferry or the smattering of younger couples who'd moved in because the chicken processing plant was hiring.

Because it was a sure bet his children were all he was going to have in the world to keep him company as he grew older. He was damn certain he would never get involved with a female again.

Lila's pod hit ground with a bone-jarring thump, knocking her senseless. Lying still, she caught her breath, then staggered to her hands and knees, crawled out of what remained of her craft, and rested on the soggy earth. She'd been warned the touchdown would be rough, but landing the pod was part of the training she'd taken. If the tutorial was correct, the pod's remains would disappear with the first heavy rain, and the harmless residue would be absorbed into the soil.

She trusted that she'd landed somewhere near her target, but since it was the middle of the night, she had little to verify the data. May was supposed to be a beautiful time in this section of Earth, a month when the azure sky was clear, the single sun warm, and the myriad plant life vivid in its awakening.

Arriving under the cover of darkness was part of the master plan, but the surrounding area seemed dangerous—not friendly, much less inviting. Sniffing the damp air, she recoiled at the noxious scent of stale water intermingled with decaying plants and aquatic life. Stifling a gag, she recalled that most of the planet's human population consumed animals. She'd never eaten any creature with a heartbeat, but if it was necessary to her survival, she would find a way.

A breeze rustled the vegetation surrounding her and Lila shivered. She'd learned from the training hologram that her sister's match lived somewhere on the Delmarva Peninsula. She'd also learned that the area was sparsely populated and surrounded on three sides by water, which made it a perfect place to carry out her goal. The fewer humans who knew of her existence, the easier it would be to blend into her new world.

Peering into the darkness, she inched away from the pod and found herself up to her knees in cool, sludgelike water. A glance at the surrounding landscape told her she was in a swamp or marshy grassland. She viewed the remains of her vehicle, now scattered on a mound of sodden earth, and trudged doggedly through the mire. Heading toward a stand of trees, she found a spot of drier ground and settled into the natural bed of pine needles.

Opening her carryall, she gazed at what was left of her old life: a favorite childhood toy and a paper image of her family. Her decision to stow away had been made in haste, and now she wished she'd prepared better for this trip. Her enthusiasm had often gotten her in trouble back home, causing her to attempt several fields of study, all with disastrous results. Now that she was on Earth, she'd run out of options. This was her final chance to rise from under Rila's shadow and succeed at a life that would be hers alone.

She removed the translator and memory chip from the bag and inserted each into an earlobe. She should have no problem using the devices, because her biological makeup was an exact match to her twin sister's. Unfortunately, she needed to carry out Rila's mission for the chips to continue working properly. She had thirty Earth days to become pregnant by her sister's perfect match. When the hormonal changes in her body were made within that time frame, the new language pattern would imprint itself into her brain, thus discontinuing the need for the microchips.

She retrieved the bracelet inset with nine gems and enclosed it about her right wrist. She'd had ample training in its use. The three clear stones were for self-preservation; the three emeralds would aid her in locating her target and the mother ship; the three ruby stones would enhance her mental capabilities.

But the ruby stones had been specially tuned to aid Rila, not her. Rila was a healing empath, someone who could feel another's pain and take it into herself. Lila was adept at telekinesis, the movement of inanimate objects. She had little hope of using the ruby stones to bolster her own gift, but selling them might come in handy if she failed to earn a living on the planet. The candidates had been warned that the stones were highly valued here, and had to be guarded carefully. It was best, she'd been told, for a traveler to never remove the ear chips or the bracelet, and she vowed to follow that rule.

The call of a bird startled her. An owl, she thought, thrilled she'd remembered its name. They had similar birds on her planet, just as there were similar plants and animal life. The comparison submerged her in a wave of homesickness. Sighing, she leaned back against a tree trunk. A tear escaped and she brushed it away, but it didn't stop the torrent that followed. Her mother, her father, her sister—she would never see them again. Fighting the loneliness rising in her chest, she recited in her mind her own personal mission. Each traveler had been sent to Earth to become pregnant. She would prove that, had she had been chosen, she would have succeeded. Driven by pride, she swore to complete the task before she set out on her own in this new world.

Her sister had been matched to a man named Paul Anderson. During descent, the pod's locator had tracked him to this peninsula. If the instruments had been accurate, she'd landed within a few miles of the man. She had to meet Paul Anderson, have sex with him, and become pregnant before she could be free. Once that occurred, she could go about the business of becoming human.

Paul penned his findings in Mary Gray's folder, noting his diagnosis. The older woman had arthritis, brought about by age and the type of work she'd done for the past forty years. He scribbled his prescription, a standard dose of medication he'd read up on that seemed to have good success with the over-seventy crowd, then closed the chart.

Walking down the hall, he set her folder on top of a filing cabinet and proceeded to examining room number two. He'd dropped Bill Halverson's file in the plastic pocket holder tacked to the door when he'd led the man inside. He'd never seen Bill as a patient before, and thought it wise to prepare for the exam. Especially if the man was still wearing on his head what Paul thought he'd been wearing.

Seeing nothing unusual in the chart, he knocked, then opened the door. Bill sat in a paper gown on the edge of the table, bony legs crossed, reading a magazine. Paul tried not to stare.

"Mornin'." Bill set the journal aside and gave a toothy smile. "Saw you around town a time or two. Nice to finally meet you."

Paul nodded and accepted Bill's outstretched hand. Doing his best to ignore the aluminum foil contraption on the older man's head, he sat on a stool and rolled it to the table. He'd seen a few of his neighbors wearing identical caps while walking around town the past few days, but every time he thought to ask Rose about them something came up with the boys or his practice and the question flew from his mind.

"What seems to be the trouble?"

"Having a hard time falling asleep at night," said Bill, resting his elbows on his knees. "Used to be, my head would hit the pillow and, bam, that was it until six. Now I lie awake for hours before I manage to grab a few winks."

"I see." Paul made a notation in the chart. "Has

anything changed in your personal habits lately? The way you exercise, or what you do to relax?"

"I'm on the Founders' Day committee and we're counting down to D-day. This year I'm still on the setup squad, but I'll be running a booth of my own for ESAW."

"The fair's next weekend, right?"

"Yes, sir, and I'm gonna be busier than a mouse in a grain silo. That's why I need my rest."

"Have you noticed any change in eating, urination, bowel movements, or the like?"

"Nope."

Paul tried not to smile, but he had to ask. "How about your sex life?"

"Let's see." Bill scratched his temple and the aluminum cap shifted to the left. "Me and the missus are still doin' it regular as clockwork, every Wednesday morning and Saturday night, so I'd hafta say no to that one, too."

Impressed, Paul made a note in the seventy-one-year-old's chart. Maybe it was something in the sea air. Then he stood and did a heart and lung check, took Bill's blood pressure, and continued the routine exam.

"Lie down, please."

The man flattened his hand over the foil cap, presumably to keep it from falling off, and complied while Paul palpated his abdomen. "Any aches or pains you haven't told me about?"

Bill sat up and straightened his gown. "Not a one."

"When was the last time you had a screening for rectal or colon cancer? Diabetes?"

Bill shrugged. "A year ago. Right before he re-tired, Doc Jensen made a bunch of us seniors take the bus over the bridge to Virginia Beach. Went to a clinic where we all got head-to-toe physicals, even Doc. That's how they discovered my Ellen's ovarian cyst, and Albert Fielding's prostate cancer. Far as I know, anyone who had a problem got it ironed out."

Paul gazed up at the man from his stool. The alu-minum foil cap sat at a jaunty angle, reminding him of something he'd seen in a movie not long ago.

"Mind if I ask about the hat?"

Bill shifted on the table and pointed to his head. "This?" he asked, his expression serious.

"Uh, yeah."

"Put it on a few days ago, and I ain't about to take it off."

Paul thought about Bill and his wife *doin' it* while the old gent had his head wrapped in silver, and bit the inside of his cheek. "Even when you're . . . in bed?"

"Especially when I'm in bed. Talked Ellen into wearing one too, but she's not as religious about it as I am."

"And you wear it for . . ."

"Protection."

"Protection?"

Bill stared as if he thought Paul was the one who needed an exam. "From the aliens. Eustace figures they won't be able to read our thoughts through the foil."

Paul blinked. "Aliens?"

"Well, sure. We've been on high alert all week. Haven't you heard?"

In between seeing patients, doing laundry, cleaning, cooking, and making an attempt at potty-training Teddy and Rick, he'd had little time to gossip with the townsfolk. "Sorry, no," Paul confessed. "I've been kind of busy with my sons."

"Oh, yeah. Ellen met them when Millie Entwhistle took a turn watching them. Said they was cute kids."

"I think so. Now, why don't you tell me about this high-alert thing?"

"Might take a while."

"Unless someone's come in since we started this exam, I have the time."

Bill gave him a once-over, then raised a brow. "You ain't gonna laugh, are you, or tell me I need to go see one of them psychiatrist fellas? 'Cause if you are, I'll leave right now."

"No, no." Paul folded the chart and set it on the counter next to the sink. "I'm interested. Really."

His expression still wary, Bill nodded. "I belong to ESAW, that's short for the Eastern Shore Alien Watch. We got us a president and a treasury—the whole nine yards. I'm district commander of the Preston's Ferry watch committee."

"I see." Paul stood and propped himself against the sink cabinet. "And why exactly have you been on high alert?"

"Eustace Carter, he's the president, lives up in Exmore, and he's got one of them high-powered telescopes on his roof. That's the reason we elected him leader, you know."

"Because of the telescope?"

"That's right. Well, anyway, he's the one who first spotted the lights. He called a meeting and a bunch of us went up there last Saturday and took turns checking them out. Let me tell you, in all the years I've lived here, I ain't never seen a prettier or more compelling sight."

"What kind of lights?"

"Started out tiny, but they got bigger every night, until they seemed to jump right outta the sky. And they twinkled, like that old poem my kids used to recite—you know the one. 'Twinkle, twinkle little star, how I wonder,' and all that."

Logic, Paul told himself. Maybe the man could be swayed with logic. "Did anyone think to call the NASA station out on Wallops Island? I hear they monitor everything in the sky from radio waves to weather balloons."

"We did. All they yammered about was a meteor shower."

Paul didn't know much about the stars or aliens, but NASA's version made sense to him. "I take it you didn't believe them?"

"Hell, no." Bill straightened his shoulders. "Couple of us have studied up on this stuff. The lights had a definite pattern, and they lasted way too long to be a meteor shower, or shooting star residue, or anything else those stiff-necked scientists suggested."

"Did you give them your theory?"

Snorting, Bill shook his head. "Called 'em every evening, sometimes two, three times, and told them what we thought. Last few nights, they just hung up on us. Eustace even called an old buddy of his up in Washington, D.C., but the man never returned his message."

"I see." Paul raised his brows. "So, what else was

it about the lights that made you think we'd, um . . . been visited by aliens?"

"First off, the lights split up two nights ago, each of 'em headin' off in a different direction. But one of 'em stayed right on track for the peninsula. Winked out of sight south of here, out near the wildlife refuge, which puts Preston's Ferry smack in the middle of the target area. A couple of us tromped the swamp yesterday, found some trampled grass but not much of anything else. We're on the lookout, though."

"You and your buddies all came to the same conclusion?"

"Sure did. Alien spacecraft is the only answer. The ship coulda taken off after dropping a spaceman or sunk into the swamp. But don't worry none. We'll find 'em."

Paul ran a hand over his mouth to keep from laughing. "And when did you first start to have trouble falling asleep?"

Tugging at his chin, Bill moved his lips as if counting to himself. Awareness dawned and his face flushed pink. "About six, seven days ago." He frowned. "Shoot me for an idiot, Doc, but I see what you're getting at. My subconscious is flustered about these lights, so my mind can't rest." He set his hands on his spindly thighs. "Did I get it right?"

"I'd say yes," said Paul, grinning. "And I'd bet that as long as you and the rest of your gang are on *high alert,* you'll continue to have trouble. Do you want me to prescribe a mild sleeping pill or suggest something over the counter?"

Bill slid off the table and dropped to his feet. "Heck, no. Medication would just make it harder

for me to wake up for my watch. I got to stay alert."
He stepped into his underwear, then his baggy
trousers, and removed the paper gown. After slip-
ping an undershirt over his head, he said, "Think
I'm gonna start taking a nap in the afternoon, like
Ellen does. That way, I'll be rested up for Founders'
Day or the big showdown, whichever comes first."

"Showdown?"

He stuffed his arms in his flannel shirt and did up
the buttons, then tucked both shirts into his pants.
"Once we find them spacemen, we're gonna capture
'em and take 'em to Washington. We'll show them
government boys how to defend our country from
extraterrestrial attack."

Paul escorted the older man from the examining
room into the front office, collected his fee, and did
the necessary paperwork. Then he walked to the
door. "Let me know if the naps work. If not, I can
still prescribe something."

Bill shook his hand. "Say, ESAW is always looking
for folks to join the group. Just say the word and I'll
get you a membership form. It's only five bucks to
sign up." He tapped a finger on his head, and his cap
dipped to the right. "I'll even make you one of these.
And one for each of your boys."

"Thanks," said Paul, determined not to laugh.
"I'll let you know."

He escorted Bill to the door. Heaving a sigh, he
picked up his home delivery copy of the *Eastern
Shore News*. Aliens. Just what he needed to make his
day. He'd thought this little town was too good to be
true, peaceful yet with enough population to have a
post office, bank, restaurants, grocery and drug

stores, and a few other shops. If he needed more in the way of civilization, all he had to do was pay a hefty toll and drive the Chesapeake Bay Bridge Tunnel. He could be in Virginia Beach in less than an hour. Too bad the mayor hadn't told him about ESAW *before* he signed the contract.

Glancing at the wall clock, he noted it was lunchtime. If he was lucky, he'd have a light afternoon. He could spend his time catching up on the laundry, then start a decent supper before Rose dropped the boys off. He took the paper to the kitchen, made a peanut-butter-and-jelly sandwich, and ate it while he read over his ad in the employment section.

> Housekeeper/Nanny needed for professional man and two toddler sons. Generous compensation, all benefits plus room and board. Days off by arrangement. Apply in person at . . .

The ad finished with his address, no phone number. He didn't believe in wasting time talking to curious people who wouldn't pan out. If someone was truly interested in the position, they'd show up and he'd do the first interview face-to-face. Then he'd let the boys meet the candidate. If his sons liked the woman—he'd naturally assumed it would be an older woman—and her references checked out, he'd hire her on the spot.

He heard the office door open and pushed back from the table, wondering if his next patient would be wearing aluminum foil on his head or sporting a full-body suit of the shiny stuff. If nothing else, another conversation like the one he'd had with Bill would make for an interesting afternoon.

Stepping into the waiting room, he stopped in his tracks. A woman, looking rather bedraggled and a bit confused, stood with her back to the door, the very picture of contradiction. Wild, curly red hair and translucent skin gave her an aura of fragility, but her tall, generous form reminded him of an athlete, maybe a tennis player or skier, or a track star. With her long legs and full bust, Paul imagined her magnificent figure would bring a monk to his knees.

She raised her gaze and blinked through large green eyes, and he pointedly ignored the stirring below his belt. She didn't look sick, so he doubted she was here for a checkup. She didn't smile, simply stared as if taking in each and every detail of his person, no matter how insignificant.

His gaze moved from her full lips to her impressive bustline and down to her clenched fingers. When he got a look at the newspaper she held, everything fell into place.

Walking farther into the room, he extended his hand. "Hi. I'm Paul Anderson. I see you've come about the ad."

Two

Lila held her breath, fearful if she spoke she would make a fool of herself. Before her stood the most wonderful man. Tall, with wavy light-colored hair and a welcoming expression, he wore dark pants and a blouselike shirt. The sight of him made her knees weak. She could almost feel his virility from across the room.

His blue-eyed gaze darted over her, warming her from head to toe. Hoisting her carryall over her shoulder, she raised the hand in which she held the newspaper. The man shifted his stare to the paper and charged toward her. When he clasped her palm and introduced himself, she tingled all the way to the soles of her feet. Shocked, she couldn't think of a thing to say. This human had to be the one she was searching for. Rila's perfect match. Paul Anderson.

Still holding her hand, he continued talking. "It's nice to meet you. Have you had lunch?"

Lila's tongue stuck to the roof of her mouth. "Lu-lunch," she managed to stutter.

"You know, the noon meal? Have you eaten yet?"

She focused on the dimple in the center of his square jaw. "Um . . . no, I've not eaten since this morning."

"Then let's go upstairs so we can get acquainted in more comfortable surroundings. Hold on a second."

He took a step toward her and she skittered out of the way. Opening the door, he turned over the sign hanging on the outside. "That should do it. If anyone needs me, they'll know to ring the buzzer, and I'll come down."

He crossed the office and disappeared through the same doorway. Overwhelmed, Lila breathed a sigh of relief. She'd spoken briefly to several human males on her journey to Preston's Ferry. The men varied in age from young adult to the elderly, and not one of them had made her insides tremble and her heart hammer the way Paul Anderson had just done.

She'd spent the past day walking the main highway, stopping at the roadside stands she found along the way while she made an effort to blend in and learn what she could of this new world. With no Earth currency to pay for shelter, she'd slept outdoors and drunk water from the many streams running through the surrounding forests. This morning, she'd cleared and carted trash and vegetables from a market stand, and the owner had given her a bag of fruit for her work, but that had been long ago.

It was then she'd realized she would need money to continue the quest for her target. The man had also given her a newspaper, and she'd been drawn to an announcement on the second page. Dr. Paul Anderson, specializing in family medicine, was open for business in the town of Preston's Ferry. The announcement also gave his address and hours of operation. Certain it was *her* Paul Anderson, Lila set out to find him.

He stuck his head around the corner. "Hey, I thought you were following me. You are here about the job, right? You're not a patient, are you?"

A patient? Lila smiled to herself. The scientists of her world had eradicated most diseases generations ago. She was in excellent condition, as were each of the women on this mission. Besides the guaranteed physical compatibility with their targets, they'd been chosen for their intelligence, ingenuity, and exceptional health.

"I'm very well, thank you. I never get sick."

"That's good to know. My boys are healthy too, at least as much as can be expected for two teething toddlers. Of course, they have their share of scrapes and bruises. Right now, Rick is nursing a hurt finger. I wasn't paying attention a few nights ago, and he burned himself on the range. I try never to take my eyes off of them, unless the baby gate is up, and even then they can get in trouble."

Lila sucked in a breath, trying to assimilate all he'd just uttered. She'd tugged her left earlobe a moment ago, and the translator chip had kicked to life, but she'd lost the first half of his speech. It sounded as if he'd said he was healthy too, which she already knew. He'd been a sperm donor in college, when he'd been tested and selected by her planet's scientists. And he had exactly what the earthmen chosen as targets needed: an unusually high ratio of the XY chromosome.

"You want to come upstairs? I'd like to show you the nanny's quarters and the rest of the setup."

"So that I can live here? With you?"

"Like the ad mentions, the job comes with living quarters and a salary. It's not much by big-city standards, but it should be more than enough down here. Once I get my finances sorted out, I'll be buying a house and there'll be more room."

"Are you offering me a job?" she asked, finally in tune to what he was saying.

"I want Teddy and Rick to meet you, then we can decide, but I have to be honest. That ad ran in two papers every week for the past two months, and aside from one elderly lady who could barely make it up the stairs, you're my first viable applicant."

"I see," said Lila. "How old are your sons, exactly?"

"Twenty-three months."

"Then they're twins?" Her heart gave a rapid thump. Twins, like her and Rila. "Are they identical?"

"They're mirror twins. Ted's a lefty, parts his hair on the left and all. Rick is the opposite, right-handed with a right side part. It's the only way I can tell who's who, except for their personalities, of course. Once you get used to them, you won't have a problem."

Paul Anderson was the man she'd been searching for, and he was offering her a job, exactly what she needed. To learn she'd be taking care of twins was more than she hoped for. It would be almost like home.

"You're not saying anything. Don't tell me I've frightened you off already." His smile wavered. "At least come upstairs and let me explain things before you decide."

Lila nodded and followed him through the door.

Paul heard her footsteps behind him on the stairs. She was a timid thing; the way she stared through those wide green eyes reminded him of Little Red Riding Hood gazing warily at the big bad wolf. She'd find out soon enough he was harmless. He planned to stay female-free for a long time for a variety of reasons: he had to learn how to be a father and do a good job raising his boys; there were few women in the area of the proper age to interest him; he had a practice to establish and a professional duty to his fellow man. How would it look if he hit on the woman he hired to care for his sons? Groping the Nanny was definitely not a game he intended to play.

He arrived on the landing and turned to let her enter ahead of him, and she bumped smack into his chest. He grabbed her by the elbows to steady her, and she colored beet red. Quickly, he dropped her arms.

"Um . . . sorry. I didn't realize you were so close."

She blinked up at him, and he felt that same earlier stirring in his groin. Maybe this wasn't such a good idea. This young woman *was* of the proper age, and she wasn't his patient. If he got this flustered with innocent body contact, *don't grope the nanny* was going to become a damned mantra before too long.

The landing led to the kitchen. Fairly modern, with white-painted cabinets and white appliances, it had a pale yellow countertop and black and white tile floor. He'd arranged a farmhouse table with four ladder-back chairs, and added two high chairs without the trays under the lone window.

"Have a seat and I'll make you a sandwich." He opened the refrigerator and peered inside. "I've got peanut butter and jelly and . . . peanut butter and jelly. But it's filling and tasty. You want milk or soda with the sandwich?"

When she didn't answer, he turned to find her tugging on an earlobe again, her expression one of confusion. "Um, the peanut butter and jelly sounds fine, and I'll have milk, thank you."

Paul wanted to whack himself in the head. He chattered when he was nervous, and right now he felt like a kid at his first confession. His guest was the only woman to answer the ad. If he stopped talking, she might walk out the door and never return.

He glanced over his shoulder and found her scanning the newspaper. She looked intelligent, but seemed reserved. Of course, since he'd been rambling like an idiot, what choice did she have? Her clothes were stained and her shoes looked ragged, but his biggest worry was that she hadn't smiled once since she walked through the door. Anyone who took care of his boys needed a stellar sense of humor if they wanted to survive with their sanity intact.

He brought her sandwich to the table, then poured

a glass of milk, set it in front of her, and took a seat. "I've introduced myself, but I don't know your name."

She met his eyes and touched her earlobe—again—calling attention to her earrings. Diamond studs, at least a karat each, caught his eye. Then he noticed her bracelet. His wife had bought enough expensive jewelry for him to know the metal was either white gold or platinum, set with beautifully faceted gemstones the size of dimes. He was so busy staring at the near fortune in jewels, he almost missed her reply.

"It's Lila." Her gaze dropped to the newspaper and back up to him. "Lila Shore."

"Shore, eh? Okay, Lila Shore, welcome to Preston's Ferry. Have you ever been to the Founders' Day celebration?"

"You mean the festival I saw announced on the billboards on the way into town?" She took a bite of her sandwich.

"The very one. It'll be my first time. I'm running a booth that will screen citizens for high blood pressure and offer advice on a few other tests. Most of the proceeds of the fair will go toward paying for a portable X-ray machine for my office."

"Where are your boys now?"

"With a temporary sitter. Rose Sweeney has a little girl a few months younger than Teddy and Rick. Due to a change in circumstances, she's unable to continue babysitting, but she is willing to help out in a pinch." He cringed inwardly at the half-truth.

"A pinch?"

"You know, an emergency. With a live-in nanny, I won't need to bother her anymore."

Lila chewed daintily, and he found himself staring at her lush, pink lips. As a plastic surgeon, he'd met thousands of women, and rarely had any of them been confident enough to face the world without a trace of makeup, as Ms. Preston did. Her flawless skin placed her age at anywhere from twenty to thirty, and she had a glow about her that brought the phrase *timeless beauty* to mind.

Questions, Paul reminded himself, concentrating on the moment. He had to stay focused, ask questions, and request a reference or two. Nutcases were a dime a dozen these days. She'd be with his children more hours than he would, and a parent needed to be careful, even if his sitter seemed pure as new-fallen snow.

"So, tell me a little about yourself. Are you from the peninsula?"

She gave another tug on her ear and Paul chalked the odd gesture up to a nervous habit. No biggie. Like him, some people talked a blue streak when they were anxious, others stammered or wrung their hands. His roommate in med school had hurled before every exam.

"Yes, I came from here," she answered, after she'd downed the last of her peanut butter and jelly sandwich.

"You need another one of those?" he asked.

"Please," she answered demurely.

He stood and made a second sandwich. The downstairs buzzer rang as he set her plate down. "Hold that thought. Someone needs me. Take a look around. I'll be back in a little while."

* * *

Lila walked the spacious apartment, proud of the fact that she was figuring things out for herself. She inspected the cold box—refrigerator—and, as Paul had said, found it sadly lacking in wholesome nourishment. The kitchen led to a short hall and a closet stocked with boxed and canned food, and a top shelf filled with cleaning supplies. One entire center section was devoted to a product labeled macaroni and cheese. Thinking it a dietary staple, she read the box and frowned. The contents would do *in a pinch,* but she doubted it was terribly nutritious. There were more chemical additives listed than natural ingredients, and none of them sounded palatable.

The hall brought her to a central room with comfortable-looking furniture, a wall of bookcases, and a television, along with a huge box of toys. From there, she walked through another hall that opened onto a full bath and three sleeping chambers. The first and smallest had two cagelike beds, identical dressers, and more toys. The next was larger, with bookcases filled with medical texts, dark wood furniture, and a big bed. Next to that room was another full bath.

Tucked in the back corner was the chamber she supposed would be hers. The furniture seemed new and the bed, when she sat on it, felt firm yet inviting. There was a dresser with mirror along one wall and a chest of drawers on another. One door led to the bath she'd just passed, the other to a spacious closet. She grinned, thinking that soon she'd have money to buy clothes to store there.

She set her carryall on the bed and returned to the room with the comfortable furniture. Sitting on the largest piece, she used the remote control to turn on the television. She'd learned from the instructional hologram that the area with the television was usually the center of the American home, so she thought it must be important. Studying the offerings, she spent a few minutes watching a news program, but it didn't hold her interest.

She turned off the television and went to the bookcases, where she found a set of alphabetized books. She chose the volume marked A and brought it to the sofa. Before opening it, she gazed about the room.

The box of toys was so full, its contents formed a mound of trucks, games, and unidentifiable plastic pieces that spilled onto the carpet. Toys for little boys. Besides her father and a few of the researchers at Project Rejuvenation, it had been forever since she'd interacted with an adult male. She'd watched children at the government-run care center, but the numbers had dwindled until she was no longer needed. Her world had simply stopped making children of either sex after they realized they couldn't repair the damage they'd done.

The biological breakthroughs of their scientists, once thought to be the answer to a perfect race, had weakened the physical makeup of their male population, causing future generations to be born either sterile or impotent. The Elders no longer trusted cryogenically stored matter and were, in fact, leery of all male genetic material on their planet. An infusion of new sperm was the only way to regenerate the species.

Once earthlings were deemed the closest to their

kind, they'd sent several of their scientists to work in sperm banks across the country. Paul Anderson and the other targets had sold their sperm while in college, and were implanted with an infinitesimal chip behind their left ears that marked them for future identification. When the Elders began the selection process, the travelers were chosen and matched to the perfect human.

The nine women who'd been sent here had a single goal: to be impregnated by a human who would give them the best chance of conceiving a male child. Right now, Project Rejuvenation seemed the only logical way to save her race.

The thought that she was betraying her people brought tears to Lila's eyes, but she refused to be swayed. She needed to be her own person, not a shadow of Rila. Her parents loved her, but they'd never understood her inability to conform. How could they have, when she didn't fully comprehend her sometimes rebellious nature herself?

There were plenty of competent women on her planet; there would be a second mission and a third. In a few generations, her race would be human enough that her planet could introduce itself, and the two worlds would come together. In the meantime, she would prove she could succeed at something. Even if no one remembered Rila's twin sister—the girl who stowed away—Lila would have a child to love and encourage.

Sighing, she sank back against the sofa cushions. So far, things were going well. She'd found her target, he'd given her a job and a reason to be near him, and she would be taking care of twin boys. Once she interacted with Paul, she would be free to begin a new life with her son.

Comforted by those facts, Lila closed her eyes. She'd gotten scant hours of rest, as sleeping in the woods had been disconcerting. She'd wondered about the personality quirks of humans. The travelers had been warned that some earthmen were untrustworthy, but the man selling produce had been pleasant. Paul Anderson was a healer; someone who cared for others. And it sounded as if he loved his sons.

It boded well that she felt a churning deep inside of her whenever their gazes locked or she'd caught him staring. Earlier visitors to this planet had often joked that earthmen were easy. Having sex with Paul would be fulfilling and pleasant. A way to spend her time while she learned and grew into a human being.

After she knew she'd conceived, she would leave. She would make a new life for both of them.

Paul collapsed against his desk chair and rubbed his tired eyes. What had started out as a light afternoon had grown to a deluge. He'd seen ten patients in four hours, treated a host of minor complaints, written prescriptions, and been privy to enough gossip to fill the Baltimore yellow pages. If things continued like this, he'd soon be able to afford a house. After that, he'd look into a few more pieces of equipment to upgrade his pitifully inadequate lab.

He'd sold his home and put every penny of profit into a college fund for the boys. Melanie had informed him through her attorney that all she wanted in the divorce settlement was her clothing, jewelry, and Mercedes, which was fine with him. He had a healthy 401K he'd been advised by his accountant not to touch. The city paid the utilities and the rental on this house, as well as half his health and malpractice insurance. All he needed to stay afloat was money for food, clothing, and entertainment.

And enough to pay a nanny/housekeeper.

He ran a hand through his hair. Christ, he'd forgotten completely about Lila Shore. She'd been alone upstairs most of the afternoon. What if she'd managed to rob him blind or—

Smiling to himself, he put a lid on his thoughts. Besides the fact that he had very little of value to steal, he no longer lived in an area where he needed to worry about getting mugged or burgled. Preston's Ferry was as safe a place as you'd find in today's world—sort of the Mayberry of the new millennium. From what he could tell of the gems on Ms. Preston's wrist and ears, the last thing she needed was the paltry few dollars he kept in his sock drawer for an emergency.

Still, he'd been incredibly rude to leave her alone all this time.

The thought that she might have sneaked down the stairs and left the building while he'd been with a patient fluttered through his brain. Nah! Wouldn't have happened. She seemed too nice a person to simply disappear without a good-bye. Besides, she'd acted pleased at the prospect of being offered the job. She'd even looked happy that she'd be caring for twin boys.

That thought made his smile broaden. Of course,

she could always be an escapee from a mental hospital. Once the Thorazine wore off and she realized what she'd gotten herself into, she would probably run screaming from the town. There wasn't much else to explain why an attractive young woman would want to shut herself up in this backwater burg just to care for toddler boys.

He heard the front door open and checked his watch. It was suppertime, so he doubted it was another patient. It had to be Rose with his sons. He couldn't wait to see the expression on her face when he told her about Lila.

"Da, Da, Da."

Rick's singsong voice greeted him as he walked into the waiting room. Rose had set the boys down and they were marching around the room as if on parade. It took Paul a few seconds to figure out what they were wearing on their heads.

"Here they are, Doc, safe and sound. And Phil says it's okay if I keep them for the week, but next Friday's B-day."

"B-day?" Hunkering down, he opened his arms and the boys ran to him for a hug. Squirming like puppies, they patted his face as they squealed their delight.

"Babysitter day. Phil says you have to have one by then."

Paul hoisted his sons up as he stood. "Not a problem. I've found someone."

Rose opened and closed her mouth. Then she grinned. "Well, that is good news. Who is she? Do I know her?"

Attempting to keep the boys quiet, Paul perched

on the edge of the desk and rocked them in a jostling rhythm. "I doubt it. I've never seen her before today."

"Is she young? Old? What's her name?"

"Lila Shore. Ever heard of her?"

Cocking her head, Rose folded her arms. "Sorry, it doesn't ring a bell."

"She's young, early twenties is my guess. I haven't gotten her references yet, but I doubt there's going to be a problem."

Rose walked to the boys and dropped a kiss on Rick's cheek, then did the same to Teddy. "I'm gonna miss these dynamos. It sure will be quiet without them tearing around the house."

Paul set his sons on the tile floor and followed her to the door. She turned to give the boys one final wave, and he had to ask. "I guess you saw Bill Halverson today?"

"Yes, I did, but how do you—oh—" Rick removed his aluminum foil hat and crumpled it in his pudgy fists. Giggling, Teddy did the same. "Then you've heard his . . . um . . . theory?"

"He came in for a checkup wearing identical headgear. Kind of hard not to notice."

"Bill is making it his personal mission to protect the good citizens of Preston's Ferry from aliens. Told me he's going house to house, offering to fashion a hat for each person in town for the very modest fee of two dollars. Millie's thrilled because she's selling him aluminum foil by the caseload. Says she's going to buy the next lot at a big discount and pass the savings along to Bill. I swear, they're all Looney Tune."

"I take it you don't buy in to this alien-watch

thing?" Rick crawled under the desk, with Teddy hot on his tail. Paul squatted to take a peek and was met by two pairs of smiling blue eyes. Things looked safe, so he stood. "I believe he called it ESAW."

"ESAW is nothing more than a bunch of retired men with too much time on their hands, thinking up ways to look important." Rose opened the door. "Couldn't you tell that when you talked to him?"

"I'm a medical doctor, Rose, not a psychiatrist. And from the sound of it, they're harmless."

She stepped onto the porch and turned. "I suppose so. Just don't be surprised if he tries to sell you a hat. He'll cut you a deal, three for five bucks, at least that's what he offered Phil and me." She waggled her fingers. "And good luck with Miss Shore. Bring her around this weekend so I can meet her. It'll be nice talking to another young person. New blood is just what this town needs."

Paul shut the door and locked it. Rose was dead on with her last comment. Sighing, he went around the desk and dropped to a squat. The sight that greeted him sent him into parental shock. Grabbing a broken pen from Rick's smiling mouth, he huffed out a breath. Blue ink covered his son's forehead, chin, cheeks, and arms. Rick grinned, showing a gray-blue tongue, and pointed to his brother as he gurgled out a laugh.

Rolling his eyes, Paul moaned. Teddy's face resembled a Salvador Dali canvas. Both boys did a belly flop and started to crawl away, but he scooped them up before they escaped.

"Oh, no, you don't." Rising to stand, he whacked his head on the underside of the desk, plopped flat on his ass, and let go of his sons. For the first time in his life he knew what it meant to literally *see stars*.

Dazed, he held a hand to the back of his head, muttering a curse when he felt the rapidly growing lump.

"Da?" Rick toddled into the kneehole and sniffled as a fat tear trickled down his cheek.

"I'm okay, buddy, but you and your pal are in deep doo-doo."

Teddy grinned when Rick smacked Paul on the shoulder and began to chant, "Doo-doo-doo!"

Paul rolled to his hands and knees and used the desk chair to lever himself to his feet. A dull throbbing had already started in his head. His sons needed dinner, he had a mountain of wash to do, and he doubted that ink would come off without a sandblaster.

Then he remembered his upstairs guest. Lucky for the three of them, Lila had stopped by. He'd give her a choice: make dinner or clean up his kids. If she was efficient, maybe she could do both while he fixed an ice pack for his head and popped a couple of ibuprofen.

Sighing, he tossed the pen into the trash and bent to retrieve the boys. The throbbing intensified and he grimaced. "Come on out from under there, you two," Paul ordered, trying not to shout.

Rick emerged first, then Teddy. Gingerly, he tried again to lift them in his arms, and this time he succeeded. Blowing out a breath, he made it to the back stairs and the second floor landing. In the kitchen, he kicked the door closed with his foot and set the boys down. They took off running in the direction of the living room.

Three

*H*ot breath tickled Lila's cheek. She inhaled a sweet scent that reminded her of . . . lunch? Still half asleep, she opened her eyes and focused on two miniature humans. One had a finger in its frowning mouth, the other had a digit buried in its nose. And both beings were streaked blue, as if some crazed artist had dipped a brush in paint and used their faces and arms for a canvas.

Scooting backward on the sofa, she swung her feet to the floor and gave them a closer inspection. Both had light-colored hair and square chins set with a dimple in the center—exactly like Paul Anderson. Identical grins broke out simultaneously on their faces, and Lila realized they were the twins. Leaning toward them, she mimicked the usual Earth greeting and held out her hand, but the boys simply stared.

What were their names again?

"Do you two know you're blue?" She really wanted to ask the whereabouts of their mother, something she'd thought of before falling asleep, but from the way they were staring she decided neither one was capable of answering.

The child who had his finger in his nose removed it and slapped her palm, leaving behind a slimy smear.

She cringed as she wiped her hand on her thigh.

Still holding his finger in his mouth, the other boy giggled. "Da." His voice was surprisingly deep. "Da, da, da."

"I'm Lila," she said in response. "What's your name?"

"Ee-poo-too-ka."

She tugged at her earlobe, but the odd sounding syllables didn't register. Was there a glitch in the program, or was there a problem because the chip had been synced to Rila's brain waves?

"I see you've met the boys." Holding a hand to the back of his head, Paul Anderson stood under the kitchen archway. "Rick is the one saying Da-da. He's got it down pat, but I don't have the heart to tell him most everything else he spouts is gibberish. The other guy is Teddy."

"Gibberish?"

"Baby talk." He walked to the sofa and sat down. When the twins climbed onto his lap and settled against his chest, he grinned. "You two are scary-looking." He glanced at her. "Rick found a pen under the desk in the waiting room. Before I knew it, he'd decorated himself and his brother. Sorry to hand you such a mess your first day on the job."

Lila couldn't believe things were working out so well. She had to ask, just to be sure. "Then you've decided to give me the position, even if we don't know that they like me?"

"We'll have to wait and see, but since they haven't run screaming from the room, it's a good bet they do," said Paul. "Do you think you can clean them up and put supper on the table inside an hour?"

Highly doubtful popped into her mind, but Lila didn't think it was the answer he wanted to hear. "I'm willing to try."

"Great, because when I crawled in to get them, I banged my head. Now it feels like a steel drum band decided to play a concert in my brain. The ice should help with the swelling and I took a couple of ibuprofen, but I have to lie down before I fall down."

"Do you think they'll go with me?" Lila asked, her gaze resting on the boys.

"They're friendly, once they get used to you." He gestured to the child on his right. "Try picking up Rick first. He's more outgoing. Teddy's still a little shy."

Rick and Teddy. Lila stored their names for future reference, then stood and held out her arms in welcome. Rick gurgled a laugh, but didn't accept her offer.

"This is Lila," said Paul. "She'll be taking care of you instead of Rose. Can you say Lila?"

"La, La, La!" Rick bounced on Paul's knee.

"That-a-boy." He gave her a pleading look. "Care to try again? I really need to close my eyes for a few minutes."

"Is there anything I can do for you—besides taking them so you can rest?"

"Nope. They need food and a bath, probably in that order. Once they eat, you can hose them down and get rid of the ink, grime, and food residue at the same time. I'll eat later."

Hose them down? Lila thought her world's linguistic scientists really needed to do a better job with American slang the next time they programmed the translator chips. Surely he didn't expect her to water his children as one would flowers in a garden?

"I usually let the dirt soak off while they play with their toys. The hard part is shampooing their hair without starting World War Three."

Bending forward, she again offered her arms to Rick. "Would you like to come to the kitchen for some food?"

"They know snack time, breakfast, lunch, and dinner. Try one of those," suggested Paul.

"Would you like dinner?" Lila asked.

"Dinna, dinna, dinna!" Rick practically jumped at her. "Ee-wa-mack'n sheez."

"Uh, that's macaroni and cheese," Paul explained. "You'll find boxes of it in the pantry. Think you can handle it?"

Hoisting the little boy onto her hip, she remembered the shelf she'd found in the closet devoted to the stuff. "I'll be back for Teddy."

She carried Rick into the kitchen and set him down. Half a second later, he dashed to the archway. Snatching him up, Lila spied a gate attached to the doorframe and figured out what it was for. She set

Rick down again, sprinted to the gate ahead of him, and hooked it to the locking mechanism.

Telling herself this shouldn't be a difficult job—she'd watched several children at a time when she worked at the care center—she opened the pantry and removed two boxes of what Paul asked her to make for dinner. While reading the directions, she saw Rick climbing one of the tall chairs at the table.

"Oh, no, you don't," she said, quickly whisking him to safety. "Sit." She pointed to the middle of the room and the boy dropped to his seat with a squishy-sounding splat. Focusing on dinner, she searched the cupboards, found a pan and filled it with water, then turned on the heat. When she looked for Rick, she spotted him back in the pantry, on his hands and knees digging at the floor. By the time she got to him, he'd upended a bucket full of rags and emptied an open bag of paper napkins.

Lila scooped him up a second time and scanned the room, searching for a safe place to deposit him.

Rick patted her face. "Dinna!"

She thought the shriek would break her eardrum. Wincing, she eyed the tall chairs again, each pushed up against the table. She carried Rick there, slipped him into a seat, and used the straps to anchor him in place.

"Stay put, and don't move. I'm going to start your food, then get your brother."

Rick began beating on the table. "Dinna! Dinna! Dinna!"

She opened the two boxes of macaroni and cheese and tossed the small round noodles into the now-boiling water. Then she stepped over the gate and searched for Teddy. When she found him methodically removing books from the bookcase, she picked him up and went to the sofa to check on Paul.

Lila signed inwardly. Paul Anderson was a handsome, virile man. At rest, it was plain to see how much his sons resembled him. Many women from her world had applied for the privilege of making this quest, each with the intention of saving their species. If they'd known the men involved looked like Paul, they would have fought for the position with greater vigor.

She came from a world of peace, duty, and order. But it was that very order that had gotten her people into their current predicament. For Lila, it was too late to wait for change. Rules, laws, regulations, and requirements had been constructed, and lives carefully monitored in the Elders' desire to create perfection, and it was that very choreography that had been her downfall. Individual choice and personal freedom had been so planned out, her planet was now as sterile as its males. Self-expression, the right to choose a career, even the joy of selecting a mate, had all fallen under scrutiny. Unless things changed, upheaval would follow, and she didn't want to be there for the battle.

Now that the Elders had authorized this experiment, things were sure to get better, but she wanted freedom and adventure now. She needed to step from her sister's shadow and live her destiny. In her heart, Lila sensed she could do all that and more on Earth.

When she'd gotten the particulars of her match, her sister had talked about the man until Lila wanted to scream. She'd wondered how a woman could be so enamored of someone she had never seen. Now that she'd met Paul, she thought she might be a bit distracted by him as well.

If Rila ever caught sight of him, Lila was positive she would never be forgiven.

Teddy squirmed in her arms and she snapped from her daydream. Paul was a compelling man, but he was also a means to an end. An end she needed to reach before she could make a beginning.

Paul woke with a clear head. The sounds of childish laughter echoed from the bathroom and he grinned. Sitting up on the sofa, he gingerly inspected his skull and felt a still-tender quarter-sized knot on the back. Good thing he'd put ice on the bump or it might have swollen to the size of an egg.

Standing, he carried the soggy mass of plastic bag and wet paper towels to the kitchen. Used glasses, silverware, and plates lined the sink. An open package of Twinkies sat on the counter. He checked the stove and found a saucepan of lukewarm macaroni and cheese. Unable to resist, he retrieved a clean fork and ate directly from the pot. He was hungry, and this would hit the spot.

Except for the dirty dishes, the kitchen was neat and orderly—a first point in Lila's favor. He chewed on the macaroni, swallowing down its creamy texture and cheddary taste. Point two, she made an okay batch of comfort food.

He'd been a little worried when he'd come upstairs and found her asleep. Frail and delicate wouldn't get the job done where the twins were concerned. Besides the need for a firm hand and a sense of humor, the person who cared for them had to be wide awake from sunrise to sunset. Wilting violets and fainting females wouldn't do for his boys. Or him either, he thought with a shake of his head.

One of three sisters, his ex-wife had come from a genteel family—no loud voices or roughhousing allowed. Melanie had been in a panic from the first moment she learned she was carrying twin boys. Paul knew she'd tried to be a good mother, but the money he made in his practice gave her an out. She'd hired a nanny before she'd given birth. If he'd been home more often, he might have sensed she was bored and restless, but at the time he'd been too busy building his business to notice.

She'd played tennis and bridge, become a driving force on the charity circuit, even belonged to a garden club, but he sensed she was never really happy. When she'd left him for a hot-shot electrician who'd come to do work on their house after a power outage, he wasn't shocked as much as wondering what had taken her so long. He remembered how lousy he'd felt the first time he'd heard her call Jerry Goldberg her soul mate. It hurt that she'd never referred to him in such a tender manner, but he'd gotten over it. For all the years he'd spent with his wife, Paul had never thought of Melanie that way, so she and the electrician were probably perfect for each other.

He was glad she'd found the other half of her whole, and happy she'd given Paul custody of his sons. In a way, he owed her a huge thanks for forcing him to see the light where his children were concerned. He had them to fill his time; medicine and the boys would be his life from here on out.

Shouts and screams brought him back to the present. The cries sounded a little frantic, so he scraped out the last of his dinner and swallowed it down while he headed for the main bathroom.

Turning the corner, he stopped, not to spy, exactly, but because he wanted to see how Lila handled bath time without him breathing down her neck. He almost laughed out loud at the upheaval, then thought better of it.

The new nanny was half in the tub, her shapely rear raised in the air while she worked at pinning a squirming Teddy in place. Rick, who had a head full of soap suds, was rubbing his eyes and crying to wake the dead, even though Paul bought tear-free shampoo. The little stinkers were giving her a hell of a bad time.

"Come on, hold still," said Lila, her voice firm but low. "I've heard little boys enjoy being dirty, but you have to get clean. If you don't, your father might not hire me, and then where would I be?"

He and Rick made eye contact and the child stood. Quick as a blink, Lila grabbed him and sat him back in the water.

"There will be no escape until I rinse that shampoo."

"I think I'm the problem," said Paul, taking pity on her. He knew firsthand that bath time could be a frustrating experience. He knelt at the side of the tub and ran a stream of warm water from the faucet. "I'll get Rick, you finish up with Teddy," he told her, filling a small plastic bucket. "Heads up, big guy. You know the drill." He snagged a washcloth and squeezed it dry with one hand, then place it over the kid's eyes. "Hold on to that, like I taught you."

Rick did as he was told, and Paul poured the water over his hair. Then he pushed back his son's dripping locks with one hand and squeezed a rubber duck with the other. When he turned, he found Lila staring through wide green eyes.

"I'm sorry. I didn't mean for you to help. Did we wake you?"

"Nah. How are things going?"

She pursed her lips. "The boys are slippery. It's like trying to hold on to—to—"

"Twin greased piglets?"

Not exactly sure what he meant, she turned to Teddy, who was back to sniffling. "Let me try it your way." She wrung a washcloth dry, then tipped up the boy's chin and put it over his eyes. "Hold tight," she ordered when he put his hands on the cloth.

Stretching across him, she filled the bucket. Paul leaned back to give her room, but her breasts grazed his arm, sending a jolt to his gut. Wow, what a rush. *No groping the nanny,* he reminded himself. But, God, it was tempting.

She copied his actions with the bucket, then removed the cloth and wiped Teddy's face. "Better now?"

Without a word, the boy grabbed the cloth and shoved it in his mouth. Paul inched to the edge of the tub and inspected his son's face and arms, then did the same to Rick. The ink had faded to a pale blue, but they looked clean enough.

"Tell you what," he said, giving Lila a sidelong glance. "I'll take Rick and you get Ted. We can dry them off and go through their nightly routine together."

Lila passed him a towel and they patted down their charges. Paul tried not to stare at her chest, but it was like having a front-row seat at a wet T-shirt contest during spring break in Daytona. Bathwater had soaked the front of her, outlining her generous breasts, which caused her nipples to jut against the thin fabric.

He busied himself by wrapping Rick like a mummy, while she did the same to Ted. Standing, they each picked up a boy and brought him into the bedroom.

Relieved they'd left the confines of the small bathroom, Lila heaved a breath. She'd been doing fine until Paul knelt down beside her. Once that happened, she'd thought all the oxygen had been sucked from the room. They were side by side, up to their elbows in suds and water, and all she could think about was sharing the tub with him while his big capable hands lathered her skin.

"I enjoy getting them ready for bed," he said in a cheerful tone, setting Rick on a padded, waist-high table. "Tonight, I'll take care of Rick and you can do Teddy."

He placed a hand on the boy's shoulder while he reached into a lower drawer with the other and pulled out a one-piece suit patterned with airplanes.

Then he took a plastic-covered rectangle from a pile, set it on the table, and guided Rick to his back.

Rick grabbed his feet and giggled, rolling on the table.

"They're getting big, so I'm thinking of buying twin beds for their second birthday. Now that you're here you can give me your opinion. I hate the idea of pushing them into growing up too soon, but getting them potty-trained would be nice."

Potty-trained. Lila tugged at her translator chip. When nothing surfaced, she could only guess what the words meant.

He lifted Rick by the ankles, neatly sliding the diaper underneath. Reaching up, he grabbed a container from an overhead shelf and gave the boy a liberal dusting of white powder. Rick slapped at the snowy stuff, then let his hands wander to his male parts.

"Hey, hey. Not in front of a lady. You guys need to learn manners with your new nanny."

Heat raced to Lila's cheeks. Glancing at Paul, she found him coloring as well. "Do they . . . um . . . do that often?"

His face grew bright red as he pulled the diaper up, undid the tapes, and pressed them along the top of each side. "I guess you don't have any younger brothers?"

She shook her head.

"Well, little boys like to—to—touch themselves," he stuttered. "It's what they do until they're old enough to know better. I've been told that when they start school and get with other kids, they stop, at least in public."

"I see."

He wrestled Rick into his bedclothes, then picked him up and took a brush from the shelf. "Time to make you presentable." Rick sat with surprising patience while his father carefully smoothed his hair to the right. Taking a step back, Paul admired his handiwork. "And there you have it. One little guy, clean and ready for bed."

He picked up his son and moved aside. "Your turn."

Lila swallowed. Almost all of the children she'd dealt with had been female. If these two were any indication, little boys were a more demanding lot. Copying his efficient manner, she tried to sit Teddy down, but his legs didn't want to bend; instead he squirmed and rolled, reaching for his father.

"Hang on a second." He deposited Rick in a crib and returned to her side. "You have to be firm. Teddy, lie down so Lila can put on your PJs."

Staring through big blue eyes, the boy did as he was told.

She unwrapped his towel and was reaching for a diaper when she felt something warm and wet hit her arm.

Paul grabbed the towel and tossed it across Teddy's middle.

"Hey, enough of that. You do your business in your diaper or the toilet, you understand?"

She swiveled her head, positive her face was on fire, while she dabbed at her arm with the edge of the towel. "How often does *that* happen?"

"Not too often, honest," he answered with a chuckle. "Though it is another frequent hazard with boys. It's gotten much better since we've started potty-training. I think they're just excited tonight, because you're a stranger."

Lila used something called a *baby wipe* to wash Teddy off, then mimicked Paul's actions with the diaper. He handed her clean pajamas and she tugged them on Teddy without incident, then used the brush to sweep his hair to the left. Teddy giggled and tried to grab the brush from her hand, but she grew wise to his antics and kept it out of reach.

"All right," said Paul. "I think that does it."

Teddy smiled at her, showing a smattering of pearly teeth. Lila held out her arms and he dove into her chest, snuggling near. She carried him to the crib, and his eager affection squeezed at her heart. The young girls she'd spent time with at the government-funded center had never been this warm and loving. Her joy of children was one of the reasons she'd signed on for Project Rejuvenation. Soon she would have a baby to care for and love. If she was lucky, her little boy would be very much like this one.

"Let's switch, so they both get used to you. I'll cover Teddy and you take Rick," suggested Paul.

She walked across the room and found the child already on his side, clutching a fuzzy orange-and-black-striped animal. "Ah, he's got Tigger, so everything's okay," commented Paul as he stood by her side.

"Tigger?" She draped a blanket over Rick's sleeping form.

"You know, from *Winnie the Pooh*. Teddy likes Pooh, but Rick here is a Tigger man all the way. I sometimes read them a story before bed, but you and I should talk, so it won't happen tonight."

He smoothed the boy's forehead, then headed for the door. Lila gave a last wistful glance at the cribs and followed him from the room.

"Would you like a cup of coffee or some tea?" Paul really wanted a cold beer, but didn't think that would impress the new nanny on her first night on the job. "I have decaf."

"Decaf?"

"Decaf coffee or herbal tea. The regular stuff keeps me up this late at night."

"I'll have whatever you're having," Lila answered.

He filled the kettle and turned on the heat, then brought down mugs and tea bags. Balancing everything, including an open bag of cookies, he carried it all to the table.

"So, what do you think?"

She tugged at her earlobe. "Think? About what?"

He grinned. "The job. The boys. Me. Still interested?"

"Yes!"

Her answer, so eager and forthright, made him wonder. Every other woman in town had been up front about the fact that his sons were a challenge they didn't intend to conquer. When he'd stood in the bathroom doorway and overheard her talking to the boys, it sounded as if she really needed a job. How much did he know about Lila, other than she had no brothers?

The kettle whistled and he strode to the stove, using the time to think. Pouring hot water into her mug, he asked, "So, where did you live before you came to the eastern shore?"

She used her spoon to stir the tea bag. "Here and there. Is it important?"

Paul sat down across from her. "Have you been in school or have you been working?"

She kept her focus on the tea bag. "I've held a variety of positions, but only recently decided to try my hand at something completely different."

"What were you doing before you got here?" He mentally crossed his fingers, hoping she didn't say trapeze artist or mud wrestler.

"Trying to find myself—I guess you might say I was a work in progress."

A polite way of saying she had yet to choose a career, he thought. And that was okay by him. "Just as a reference point, I was wondering what kind of experience you have caring for small children."

Her expression wistful, she blew at the steaming liquid. "I spent time working at a care center for children. It was an activity I enjoyed until I had to leave."

"Budget cuts? Or didn't the job pay enough?"

"The pay was—wasn't the problem. I do love children."

Paul nodded. Now they were getting somewhere. "That's good. What about siblings?"

"I have a twin sister."

"Really? Are you identical?"

"We are. I'm the lefty, like Teddy. Rila is right-handed like Rick."

"Where's your sister now, and the rest of your family?"

"Um . . . away. Far away. I'm on my own here."

When she puckered her lips and sipped at her tea, Paul's groin came to life. *Don't grope the nanny,* repeated the nagging voice in his head. Annoyed, he took a drink of his own tea and felt the burn on his tongue.

"You're sure no one is looking for you? Your parents? An angry boyfriend?" He forced a casual tone. "The police?"

"The police?" She set down her mug with a thump. "I am not a criminal. I just need a job."

"What about luggage or a car? Do you have to move out of the place you've been staying?"

Lila ducked her head. "Everything I own is with me," she muttered. "I left most of my things at home when I decided to come here." She ran a hand over her shirt. "I don't have much in the way of clothes. That's why I need to work."

From the sound of it, she needed a lot more than a job. So why didn't she just hock one of those gems she wore and get money that way? *Her jewelry is none of your business, pal,* Paul told himself, putting on the brakes. He was in a bind, and she didn't act like a liar. All he needed to know was that Lila didn't have a criminal record and she'd take good care of his kids.

He took another swallow of tea. "How about this? I give you a trial period—say one week. I'll pay you three hundred, plus your room and all you can eat. If it works out and we agree you'll stay on, I'll raise it to four hundred. Your days off will be Sunday and Wednesday, because I don't have office hours then, and a half day on Saturday, but I might

need you in an emergency. We can play the rest by
ear until we get a routine in place."

When she didn't answer immediately, he said,
"Take tonight to think about it, and let me know in
the morning."

Smiling at him, Lila raised her head. Paul winced
inwardly at what that megawatt grin did to the area
below his belt. He'd been using the catchphrase
don't grope the nanny as a joking reminder to keep
things strictly business. Now he thought he might
need to carve the mantra into his office desk, or
make a tape and play it every night before he fell
asleep. He was too old, she was too young; he was a
doctor and she his employee. Lila was being hired to
take care of his children, not him.

"How old are you, by the way?"

"Um . . . does it matter?"

"Not really, but tell me anyway."

"I'm twenty-seven."

He nodded, holding his surprise in check. He'd
pegged her at twenty-one, tops. Since he was thirty-
three, the answer made him feel marginally better.
At least he wasn't lusting after a teenager.

Four

Lila awoke disoriented. The small room was dark, its lone window showing only a glimmer of gray light. She recalled her spacious quarters back home, with a skylight and open views that looked out onto the lake and mountains. She'd been raised in an agricultural area, nothing like this small waterside city, but Preston's Ferry was home for the moment. It was important she come to terms with her surroundings in order to build her new life.

When Paul had escorted her to her room last night, they'd shared an awkward moment. First, he'd explained that he would move his personal items from the bathroom between their bedrooms over the weekend, because a private bath came with her position. Then he made space on a shelf in a mirrored cabinet for her things. When she gave him a blank look, he searched a bottom cupboard, found a toothbrush still in its box, and set it on the sink. After that, he'd walked out and returned with a soft white shirt. Mumbling something about staying decent, he'd thrust the garment at her and stumbled backward from the room.

Puzzled by his actions, she'd undressed, slipped on the shirt, and snuggled into her bed. Then she'd realized how strange it must have seemed, showing up with nothing but a small carryall and the rumpled clothes on her back. Unfortunately, the pod that brought her to Earth wasn't much bigger than its passenger, and was meant to dissolve with the first heavy rainfall. Except for a handful of items, everything the Elders thought they might need was built into their earrings and bracelet. Perhaps one of the women who returned would make a list of suggested necessities for the next group of travelers.

But that was no longer her worry. It was time she got to work. She walked to the window and pulled up the shade, happy to see that it had rained overnight, which would aid in the dissolution of her pod. In the bathroom, she ran a comb through her tangled curls and brushed her teeth. The cabinet held a few interesting items, but she decided to investigate later, when she had more time.

Hungry, she headed for the kitchen. If her duties included making breakfast, she had to get started. When she rounded the corner she found Paul at the table, sipping from a cup and reading a newspaper. "Good morning," she said, keeping her voice cheerful.

He gazed at her over the paper and smiled. "Good morning. Did you sleep well?"

"I did. I guess I was more tired than I realized, or I would have awakened sooner."

"No problem. The boys are rarely up before eight. Sit down and let me make you something to eat." He pushed from the table. "Bacon and eggs? Toast? Or would you rather have cereal?"

"I assumed meal preparation was part of my duties. I don't want to be any trouble."

"As a housekeeper, it is, but you're the nanny first, so Teddy and Rick are your main concern." He brought over a cup filled with dark liquid and set it down. "I drink my coffee black, but there's milk in the fridge and sugar in the bowl if you take it light and sweet. We might even have some of the pink stuff, if you like that better."

Lila had studied coffee in the lesson on "Earthly Habits to Avoid" she'd monitored on her journey. Her world once drank a similar beverage, and used substances that resembled alcohol, nicotine, and other so-called recreational drugs still found here. Due to their addictive properties, they'd all been banned from her planet after the first Citizens' Unification Summit. She'd come here to experience new things, and Paul didn't seem bothered by the liquid, so it had to be safe. Raising the cup to her lips, she inhaled the unfamiliar aroma.

"It's quality stuff," said Paul. "I order it online from a specialty house and they ship it direct. There's not a Starbucks for miles, and a good cup of coffee at breakfast is one of my passions."

The not-quite-bitter liquid burned her tongue, causing her to frown her displeasure.

"Try it with a little milk," he suggested. "Unless you're not a coffee drinker."

Lila took a carton from the cold box, added milk, and tasted it again. The flavor was not unpleasant, and she found it hard to believe the drink was addictive. Raising her head, she met Paul's open gaze. "Um . . . I'll have to learn how to make coffee for you in the morning."

"I don't mind doing it. Besides, I enjoy getting up early, so I can read the paper and spend a few minutes planning my day while I have my first cup. You might want to do the same once you realize how little time you have when the twins are awake. Now, how about that breakfast?"

"Please sit. If you don't mind my exploring, I think it's better I find things for myself."

Shrugging, he took his seat. "No problem. Most mornings the boys have toast with peanut butter or cereal and milk. There are a couple of boxes in the pantry, including a heart-healthy oat bran. Help yourself to whatever you find. If we're running low, just add it to the board."

Doing her best to follow his rapid-fire instructions, she took note of the white slate hanging on the pantry door, then opened the closet and chose the only cereal box not decorated with a childish drawing. She told herself she had to act more like a normal earthwoman or Paul wouldn't trust her with his children. If that happened, she'd have no reason to be near him, which would ruin her future here.

Standing at the counter, Lila filled a bowl with cereal, then added milk and carried the bowl and her mug to the table. She tasted the cereal and swallowed. "This is good."

It had been an effort for Paul to concentrate on his paper. From the moment he'd seen Lila in the doorway, looking bewildered yet incredibly sexy, he felt compelled to follow her movements. It wasn't just her tall, curvy figure that had him mesmerized, but her very presence. Her few guarded smiles had warmed him with a heat that flowed straight to his zipper. He enjoyed the way her eyes met his when he spoke, as if she were hanging on his every word. That she seemed in awe of ordinary items like coffee or cereal only added to his confusion.

Don't grope the nanny beat a warning tattoo in his brain, and he told himself his unprofessional reaction was simply one of a man who'd gone too long without the companionship of a willing woman. Lila was here to take care of his boys and his house. Not him—at least not in the way he was thinking.

He'd fallen asleep flummoxed by the notion she had no clothes and no personal items, not even a toothbrush. While there were women who didn't wear makeup, they were rare. Not that she needed cosmetics. She had a clear, unlined complexion and lovely green eyes fringed with dark lashes. From her mannerisms and the jewelry she wore, he assumed she came from a moneyed background, so why would she settle for an unexciting and menial position? Where had she lived before coming here?

Embarrassed to be caught staring, he drank the last of his coffee before he spoke. "I'm afraid I let nutritious meals fall to the wayside after we moved.

I had to get my practice up and running, and find a capable sitter for the boys. I'm hoping you'll see to it they eat healthy and get more attention."

"I understand. I was just wondering about my duties."

He blinked, relieved at least one of them was clear-headed enough to be practical. "Right, we do need to clarify your position. I'll work on a job description today, in between patients. Did you get a chance to think about the salary offer I made last night?"

She bit her lower lip, as if still considering, and Paul held his breath. If Lila wanted more money, he would be hard-pressed to come up with it. The agreement he had with the town covered his living space, partial health and malpractice insurance, and some much-needed equipment, but he had to earn his own living. He figured once the folks in neighboring cities knew about his practice it would grow, but until then . . .

"I'm sure it will be sufficient."

Filled with a sense of accomplishment, he smiled. "I thought you might want to take a stroll through Preston's Ferry this morning. I could pay you in advance on your salary. In case you wanted to . . . um . . . buy some . . . personal things."

"Personal things?"

"You know, some clothes and makeup or a few . . . female necessities." Clinical, he had to stay clinical and matter-of-fact, if they were going to make this work.

"I see." Lila sipped at her coffee. "And where in town would I find those?"

"For clothing, there's a family store at the end of Main Street that carries clothes for infants all the way to adults. They even sell sneakers and shoes. The styles are out of date, but that's to be expected for this town. The drugstore has a selection of whatever else you'll need." He folded his paper. "I have to open the office. After you feed and dress the boys, bring them down. I'll write a check for the trial week, and you can cash it at the bank, but they close at noon so you need to get moving. How does that sound?"

"It sounds . . . acceptable."

Paul felt as if he'd just begun a momentous journey, almost as important as the day he'd decided to go to medical school. He finger-combed his still-damp hair, then realized he was grinning like a fool. No wonder Lila kept staring at him as if he were one fry short of a Happy Meal.

"Great." He sidled toward the door that led to the stairs. "I'll wait for you in my office. Take a left at the bottom of the stairway. It's the last room off the hall."

Lila held her breath until she heard Paul's footsteps fade. The Elders had warned there would be a connection, an intimate pull between the travelers and their individual matches, but she'd thought that only referred to Rila. The infinitesimal chip planted behind his right ear was meant to activate if she used her locater, but she'd already found Paul, so that hadn't been necessary. What was it about the man that made her knees weak and her stomach react as if she were still in her pod hurtling to Earth?

She shrugged. She had no time to sort out her emotions when there was more important work to be done. After clearing the table, she washed the dishes and left them to dry. Then she headed for the boys' room. Hearing the twins' happy laughter made her smile. Teddy and Rick were the key to pleasing Paul Anderson. If he approved of her, it would be all the easier to convince him to have sex.

Turning the corner to the bedroom, Lila stopped in her tracks. Slapping a palm over her nose and mouth, she stared at Rick, who was standing in his crib with a wide wet grin and a drooping bottom.

"Pooh-pooh!"

Cringing at his shout, she crossed to the window and opened it in hopes of circulating a bit of much-needed fresh air. Then she glanced at Teddy, who was also standing. His bottom swayed as he jumped up and down, and she realized what it was that poisoned the air.

Lifting the boy from his bed, she held him at arm's length and carried him to the changing table. After wrestling him to his back, she unsnapped his sleep suit, peeled it off, and pulled at the tabs on his diaper. Greeted by a mass of noxious fumes, she cringed. It had been a while since she'd cone in contact with baby waste.

"Do you do this every morning?"

Teddy grinned at her and grabbed his male equipment.

"Oh, no. Your father said that wasn't allowed." Lila *tsked* as she tugged his hands away. "Keep your fingers to yourself while I do my job."

She took down the wipes and began the cleanup

process, amazed at Teddy's ability to squirm. The potty-training Paul had mentioned couldn't come soon enough for her.

After scrubbing him off, she dressed him in a fresh diaper and clothes, then brushed his ringlets. Satisfied he was respectable, she deposited him in his crib and went to Rick. The little boy hung on to the railing and danced in place as the evil smell wafted around him.

"Pooh-pooh!" he shouted again.

Lila grimaced, doubting the words would enhance her earthly vocabulary. Steeling herself for what she knew lay ahead, she picked up Rick, held him in front of her, and brought him to the table, where she began an identical wipe-down.

The little boy gurgled out a laugh when she opened his diaper, and she frowned. *How could these tiny humans produce such an incredible amount of toxic waste?*

"I wish I knew what was so funny," she told him, holding his hands to stop him from squirming. Rick kicked his chubby legs and she sighed. Children were important, not only for the necessity of continuing a species but for the joy and love they brought to the world around them. This distasteful job was a minor hindrance when compared to the wondrous things having a child encompassed.

When finished, she set him on the floor and lifted Teddy from his bed. They walked into the kitchen, with the boys pulling at her as Rick chattered at the top of his lungs. Unfortunately, "Dinna! Dinna! Dinna!" was the only word she understood.

Lila set the twins in their chairs and strapped

them in, then took breakfast fixings from the refrigerator and assembled the meal. Once she figured out the toaster, she found identical cups in an upper cupboard, filled them with milk, and brought them to the table.

Before she knew it, Rick upended the contents on the floor. Quickly, Lila grabbed Teddy's drink and set it out of reach, then mopped up the mess. By the time she finished, the toast had popped. If she divided herself in two and gave each half four hands, it wouldn't be enough to manage a simple meal with these small boys.

Back at the counter, she spotted two plastic circles with spouts and realized they were made to snap onto the top of the cup to prevent spills. After refilling them, she capped them, then spread peanut butter on the toast, cut the bread into quarters, and brought everything to the table. She found rectangular pieces of fabric with strings and pockets hanging off the back of their chairs, and tied one firmly in place around each boy's neck before she served their food.

Suddenly hungry again, she sat between the twins and ate a piece of toast while they smeared the peanut-butter-laden bread with their fingers or took bites of their meal. Rick banged his cup on the table and she stilled his hand. Checking, she saw that the cup was empty.

"Do you want more?" she asked him.

"Ee-ba-ma." He held up the cup. "Ee-ba-ma."

She poured more milk and he gurgled in satisfaction.

"Next time you're going to ask nicely," Lila told him.

"Pee-ba," said Rick, licking his fingers.

"Pee-nut but-ter." She enunciated each syllable clearly.

"Pee-ba! Pee-ba! Pee-ba!"

She turned to Teddy. "You know, we'd get along a lot better if you both spoke so I could understand you. How about it? Can you say peanut butter?"

"Pee-ba!" yelled Rick, as if angry he was being ignored.

"How about milk?" Lila asked Teddy.

Teddy buried a peanut butter-covered-finger in his nose and gave a solemn stare.

She shook her head. "Okay, you're going to make me wait, but your brother"—she turned to Rick—"is just dying to tell me what he wants. Aren't you?"

His eyes glinting mischief, Rick beat his feet against the bottom of the table.

"Pea-nut but-ter," said Lila.

He stuck out his lower lip.

Not to be thwarted, she did the same. "Pea-nut but-ter."

Rick gave her a grin. "Pee-na butta."

"That's much better," she declared. She added two more slices of bread to the toaster, waited for it to pop, and brought another helping to the table.

Soon the boys had their fill of the gooey toast and milk. Lila gathered the remains of breakfast and began the wash-up process all over again. When finished, she set them on their feet and gave them an order.

"Do not move." She turned to the sink. "I have to rinse off your dishes and—" At the patter of tiny feet, she spun on her heel just as the twins disappeared through the door leading to the stairway. She arrived at the landing in time to see them crawling backward down the stairs.

Stepping between them, Lila placed a hand on each child's back and guided them to the lower level. As soon as their toes touched the floor, they turned left and raced down the hall.

Paul grinned at the sound of footsteps rattling the ceiling. Rick and Teddy were up and running. Lila seemed agreeable, even eager to take on the task, but only time would tell if she had the stamina to handle his sons. The boys liked her, but he was still worried about her bewildered expressions and occasional bouts of confusion, not to mention her lack of humor. Though pleasant, she rarely smiled. And he'd never heard her laugh.

He tried to work a half day on Saturday. If Lila hadn't accepted the position, he would have followed his usual routine, with the boys playing in the waiting room while he sat behind the front desk. When a patient walked in, he gated the twins in the examining room reserved for children, which he'd already childproofed and filled with toys. They screamed up a storm while in there, but short of begging Rose to watch them or cajoling some senior citizen into lending a hand, it was the only way for him to have office hours for part of the weekend. Now that he had a nanny, he could do his paperwork in peace.

Paul remembered he owed Lila a check and pulled his ledger from the side drawer. He wrote the check to cash, figuring she could use the money to buy necessities. Rifling through a folder, he found the employment papers his accountant had sent and removed an application. Once Lila filled the papers out, he'd mail them to the CPA and they'd be good to go.

He heard squeals and a commotion on the stairway. Bracing himself, he pushed from the desk as his sons rushed headlong into the room. Teddy and Rick scrambled onto his lap and he held them close. They smelled of baby powder and peanut butter. Drawing back his head, he took in their neatly combed hair, shining faces, clean clothes, and Velcro-strapped sneakers.

"Did you two have a good breakfast?"

Teddy patted his face while Rick said proudly, "Pooh-pooh, Da. Pooh-pooh."

Oh, boy! Paul met Lila's green-eyed gaze and caught the glimmer of a smile. "Sorry about that. I forgot to warn you it's the way they usually start the day."

She wrinkled her nose. "I can't wait for tomorrow."

He thought she might be joking, but her serene expression gave nothing away. "I assume you found the trash can?"

"I did. It needs emptying, but I wasn't sure where things went. I was hoping for a tour of the house and some guidance."

Paul set the boys down and handed her the check. "Here's your money, as promised. Follow me and I'll show you around the backyard. You can take the boys to the bank in their stroller and have a look around town. By the time you get back, they should be ready for lunch and a nap. I'll give you the full tour then."

Lila stared at the check, folded it, and put it in her pocket. He wanted to assure her it was good, but she'd find out soon enough. Clasping each boy by the hand, he led the way through his makeshift lab to the rear porch. When they stepped onto the spacious landing, the twins crawled backward down the stairs and ran into the yard.

"This is the other downstairs exit," said Paul. He gestured to the rolled-up chain ladders hanging from windows in the second floor of the house. "The only way out from upstairs is the steps you've been using, so I had the city council install fire ladders in each of the three bedrooms." He walked into the fenced yard. "The back is pretty much baby-proof. The twins are too small to climb into the swings by themselves, and the seats have built-in safety straps. Never leave them alone when they want to play on the swing set. They can manage the slide if you stand behind them while they go up the ladder. I've taught them to stay at the top until someone comes around to catch them. Just tell them to wait, and they usually do."

"Usually?"

He realized he was talking at warp speed again and flashed her a grin. "Sorry, am I going too fast for you?"

"A little." She stared at the turtle-shaped sandbox he'd bought just last week. Teddy had climbed on top and was attempting to stand on the rounded slippery surface, while Rick tried to pry off the lid. Seconds passed before he started beating on the shell and screaming at the top of his lungs.

"What is that thing Teddy's on?" asked Lila, wincing at the piercing shrieks.

"A sandbox. It keeps them busy for hours, but it has to be closed in case of rain, like last night, and to discourage the neighborhood cats from making it their own personal litter pan." He walked to the wailing toddler, with Lila trotting behind. Teddy was easygoing, but Paul still wasn't certain which ancestor he had to thank for Rick's aggressive temperament and sometimes too-rough behavior. Scooping the boy into his arms, he spoke in a firm but gentle tone. "Take it easy, little guy. Enough with the tantrums."

He stood Rick on his feet and told Teddy to come down. Instead, Teddy dropped to his fanny, gazed at his furious brother, and chortled his glee. When Rick screamed in frustration and kicked at the sandbox, Lila fell to her knees. Wrapping him in her arms, she held him in place.

"Calm down," she ordered in a soothing tone. "There's no reason to be so angry."

Rick heaved a gasp, and she continued her litany until he stopped howling. Staring at her as if she'd spoken Swahili, he stuck a finger in his mouth, and she wiped at his tears. "It's okay. I know it's hard to share, but he's your brother. No one else will ever be as close to you as Teddy. Now ask him nicely to please come down."

Paul opened his mouth to tell her there was no way the kid understood word one of what she wanted, then closed it just as fast when he heard Rick's baby voice.

"Teddy, peas dow."

Lila smoothed the hair off Rick's sweaty forehead. "That was very good." She gave Teddy her hand. "Now, you slide off there and we'll open the top so you can both play."

Immediately the child did as commanded. She raised the turtle shell and the boys climbed inside to claim their shovels and buckets.

"How did you do that?" asked Paul, in awe of the way she related to his boys.

"Do what?" said Lila, rising to her feet.

"Get Rick to say what he said, and make Teddy listen?"

Her smile vied for brightness with the morning sun, and Paul felt as if he'd been sucker-punched. Good thing she didn't grin often, or he'd never have another coherent thought in his head. He figured she'd caught the idiot gleam in his eyes, because she dropped her gaze to her feet.

"I didn't do anything except talk to them clearly, and tell them what I wanted."

"Yeah, but Rick's been jabbering for months and I could never make heads or tails out of it. And when he's in a foul mood, his temper goes haywire." He realized he was getting a bit too boisterous himself and lowered his voice. "Are you sure you didn't grow up with little brothers?"

She raised a brow. "Does that mean I have the job?"

Paul swiped a hand across the back of his neck. How could he argue with her logic when it seemed so . . . so logical? And did it really matter how often she smiled, when his boys were content and obedient in her presence? Hell, he'd been happy enough thinking he'd finally found someone to rely on. He never dreamed he'd hire a nanny who would actually share a connection with his kids. Right now it looked as if Lila was the right woman for the task.

"How about we discuss it after you've been here a few more days? I have employment papers you need to fill out. Once I check your references, which I'm sure are fine, we can make it official."

He could tell by her concerned expression she was disappointed, but he wanted to be sure this was going to work. "Let's go to the porch so I can show you how use the stroller."

Five

As soon as Paul wheeled the huge blue contraption with dual seats and a rear basket from the storage area under the porch, Rick and Teddy lost interest in the sandbox and raced to the steps. With their father's assistance, they scrambled into the carriage and bounced, eagerly anticipating their ride.

Now on the sidewalk with the twins strapped in their traveling pod—or stroller, as Paul had called it—Lila headed farther into Preston's Ferry. Walking slowly in order to absorb all the sights, she thought about his comment on checking her references. If she was lucky, she would be gone before he had a chance to do whatever needed to be done. If not, she'd have to come up with a way to distract him from the task.

Making her way into town, Lila got her first real glimpse of a community so small it didn't need a traffic signal to monitor the flow of vehicles or pedestrians. Paul's home and office, a white-painted, two-story frame dwelling with a wide front porch and dark green trim and shutters, was located in a residential section that gradually gave way to several blocks of businesses in various stages of repair. A few of the buildings were boarded up, but signs in the murky windows announced the opening of future shops with apartments overhead.

She passed two restaurants, a small grocery, an arts center, and a combination hardware store/real estate office before arriving at the stately gray stone building that housed the bank. Pushing the stroller past the edifice for a few more blocks, she saw that the abbreviated town center again turned into private homes facing a large body of water.

Unfortunately, when Lila crossed to the opposite side of the street, she found nothing more to recommend it than a series of abandoned stores and parking lots, a cement factory, and a dilapidated railroad turnaround. The only bright spot came a half block farther with the appearance of a well-kept public beach on the bay.

During her travels, she did her best not to stare as she returned the nods of smiling people ambling the walkway. So many older citizens wore silver helmets atop their heads, she thought the shiny crowns might be a badge of honor or a testament to their longevity.

Traversing the street again, she headed for the business Paul had said would turn her check into currency. After maneuvering the cumbersome carriage through the double doors of the bank, Lila waited in line while the boys busied themselves with miniature steering wheels attached to the front of the vehicle. She hadn't been inside long before she locked gazes with two women in the next line, neither of whom wore the odd silver hats.

"Rose told me Dr. Anderson finally hired a nanny," said the first woman. Dressed in red, white, and blue, she had a round cheerful face and short gray hair. "I'm Millie Entwhistle. Welcome to Preston's Ferry."

Comforted by the warm greeting, Lila introduced herself. "I'm Lila. It's nice to meet you."

"I own the Shop and Bag. You probably passed it on your way here. Dr. P has an account there. If you stop in with the boys, I'll be happy to show you around."

Before Lila could answer, her line moved forward and she drew even with the second woman.

"Sheila Jackson. My husband Fred and I own the business center." She pushed long brown hair behind her ears, emphasizing her thin face. "It's not much, just a copy machine, fax, and Federal Express pickup, with some office staples and computer gadgets for sale, but we do all right. Dr. P buys supplies there, as does most of the town. Hope you'll stop in and visit sometime, or maybe you, Millie, and I can meet for lunch at the Harbor Café. I'm sure the twins would love it."

All Lila could do was smile, because she'd arrived at the front of her line. Pulling the check from her pocket, she handed it to the woman behind the counter. "Dr. Paul Anderson said you would exchange this for three hundred dollars."

The woman smiled, her brown eyes crinkling

with pleasure, and Lila read the name on a tag attached to her plentiful chest: Eleanor Sweeney.

"You must be the new nanny. I'm Rose Sweeney's mother-in-law. Rose told me Dr. P finally hired someone."

"Rose is the woman who used to watch the boys, I believe?"

"Sure did. She took over after Rick and Teddy exhausted about a half dozen of Preston's Ferry's seniors. Those two are a handful, and with my son a fireman and all, well, he needs to sleep some days, and the boys aren't exactly quiet." She peeked over the counter and waved at Teddy and Rick, then pulled out two sticks with colorful plastic-wrapped balls on top. "Here's a couple of lollipops for the little guys."

Lila assumed they were edible, but didn't want to give the twins something Paul might not approve of. "If you're sure it's all right—"

"It's okay. Dr. P's let's 'em have a treat every now and then. Go ahead."

She unwrapped the plastic and handed one to each child. Faces wreathed in smiles, the boys stuck the candy in their mouths and sat back to enjoy.

Eleanor glanced at the check. "If you want to open an account, I'll need to see some ID."

"ID?" Lila tugged on her ear. Why did so much of what she heard fail to translate into words she understood?

"A driver's license is best or a Social Security card, but we'll take a credit card, even a library card if that's all you have. I know who you are, but—"

"I . . . I hadn't planned to open an account." And

she had no access to any of the things Eleanor just mentioned because, with only thirty days to spend on this planet, the Elders hadn't thought it necessary. She made a mental note to investigate obtaining some identification to aid in her adjustment here, and fixed her gaze on the older woman.

Eleanor hunched forward. "Not a problem, but you should always save a little for a rainy day. When you get the time, stop by and open one. I'll take care of it for you and nobody will be the wiser."

Lila used common sense to intuit the woman's confusing explanation. Currency institutions had disappeared from her world long ago, and they now used an automatic debit system, while identification was taken care of with a microscopic chip implanted into each citizen's skull at birth.

Opening an account didn't matter, because she had no intention of allowing the bank to hold funds that would be needed for her departure. "Thank you," she said, giving the impression she would do what the woman asked.

Moments later, Eleanor handed her a stack of green-colored paper. "It was nice talking to you. I know Rose is dying to meet you. If it's on my day off, we could all get together at my house for morning coffee and a play session with Sally and the twins."

Contemplating the suggestion, Lila tucked the money in her pocket. Meeting with Rose Sweeney would surely help her assimilate into life on Earth. The former babysitter could explain pertinent facts about toddlers, so Lila wouldn't continue to flaunt her ignorance in front of Paul. She might even pick up a few mannerisms and speech patterns of younger earthwomen. Getting to know Rose would be the same as having a mentor, something that would come in handy in her life as a human.

Intrigued, she smiled. "Tell her I'll look forward to it."

Lila guided the stroller onto the sidewalk and inhaled the brisk sea breeze. Brilliant sunlight sparkled on the slim stretch of water visible between the silos of the cement factory and the sand dune that marked the start of the beach. She crossed the street and headed for the public area, steered the stroller down a long wooden walkway, and sat on a bench, where she watched birds fly overhead.

She'd studied the history of Earth, and knew that unlike her home, this planet was haven to many cultures, most of which had their own language and government. Her old world had gone through much turmoil before it had united as a single people. Project Rejuvenation would benefit them all. By now the Elders knew what she had done. She only hoped they wouldn't come after her and force her to return. The frightening possibility was one more reason why she had to leave Preston's Ferry as soon as she conceived.

When the twins grew restless, she retraced their steps until she was back at the bank. Looking up at the large clock, she noted it was almost noon, the time Paul said he finished office hours. The carriage began to sway and she glanced at Teddy and Rick. Both boys were rocking in place, their faces grinning wetly.

"Dinna! Dinna! Dinna!" chanted Rick, while

Teddy slapped at his steering wheel with sticky fingers.

Lila sighed, again amazed at the difference between boys and girls. Did either of them ever stay clean for more than a few minutes at a time? And did they ever think of something besides food? At this rate, she would spend all her time feeding them just so they could produce more of the toxic waste she'd cleaned up that morning.

She turned the stroller in the direction of Paul's home. She had to prepare lunch and put the boys down for a nap in order to experience the one bright spot in her day. Paul had promised her a tour of the house and property . . . without the twins.

Six peanut butter and jelly sandwiches and a carton of milk later, Lila and Paul were alone. When she returned to the house, she'd assembled the midday meal while he'd diapered and washed his sons. After they'd eaten, she and Paul had switched chores. He'd straightened the kitchen while she cleaned up the twins and prepared them for their nap. When she'd removed their socks and shoes and placed them in their cribs, Rick and Teddy had laid down, clutched a fuzzy toy, and closed their eyes without a bit of trouble. In a few minutes, they were asleep.

Now in the living room with Paul, she told herself to breathe. His close proximity made her stomach flutter and her brain feel as if it were on sensory overload. Throughout lunch, she'd found herself drawn to his large competent hands and wondered how they would feel skimming her body. When he gazed at her through his clear blue eyes, she thought he could see into the heart of her, almost as if he could read her mind.

"I guess we'll start in the kitchen."

He walked into the hallway and she followed, secretly admiring his wide shoulders and taut behind. Knowing she had to be intimate with him froze her tongue in place.

"You've already figured out where most things are," he began, oblivious to her wayward musings. "I don't know about you, but I'm getting sick of macaroni and cheese and peanut butter and jelly. Your job includes the grocery shopping, so feel free to buy whatever you think appropriate and charge it to my account. I want the boys to taste a variety of fruits and vegetables, though brussels sprouts and beets aren't high on my list. I enjoy a good steak or burger, but chicken, pork, and fish are okay too."

Lila swallowed down a lump of disgust. Her planet had many plant foods similar to those grown on Earth, but she'd forgotten about humans and their penchant for devouring animal flesh. She'd often cooked at home, but her expertise would not help with his request for meat. Her first trip to the grocery store was sure to be interesting if not difficult. Perhaps she could convince Rose to share a few simple recipes along with her advice on Rick and Teddy.

Still pondering the possibility of a meeting with the former sitter, Lila rushed after Paul and found him outside her bedroom, peering through the doorway as if he didn't dare invade her private space.

"I take it you found things to your liking?" he asked. "The bed . . . er . . . the room is okay?"

Walking past him, she sat on the mattress. Sex was a topic their women talked about continually. She'd discussed the act in detail with her sister, and knew it often took place in the prone position. Rila had colored red when she'd reiterated the instructions the travelers had been given for convincing earthmen to indulge in the procreative act. Unfortunately, it was *after* Lila had been released from the program, so she'd never had a chance to tell her sister that she too was looking forward to experiencing passion with the right man.

"The room is fine, and the bed is quite comfortable," she said, hoping Paul would join her.

"That's . . . good." He averted his gaze. "I want you to feel at home here, so if there's anything you need—your own phone or television—"

"I don't think I'll have a use for either of those amenities." Concerned she wasn't getting her point across, Lila leaned back on the pillows. "You really should try the bed."

Instead of taking the hint, he retreated into the hall. "Um . . . no, thanks, and please feel free to use the house line to call your family and friends."

Paul's reticent attitude perplexed her. She'd been told most earthmen enjoyed sex at any time, whether or not they were married to the woman. She remembered that she had not yet asked Paul about his wife. It was obvious the woman didn't live here; perhaps she had died and he was respectful of her memory.

Rising to her feet, she met him at the door. "How long will Rick and Teddy sleep?"

"A couple of hours." He stared at the floor as if

his shoes held more appeal than she did. "I'll clean my stuff out of the medicine cabinet when you go to shop, so you can have the bathroom to yourself. You ready to go downstairs?"

"I was just wondering . . ."

"Yes?"

"If you want to continue using the space, I won't mind. It's convenient to your bedroom and you're obviously settled in. With a bit of planning, I'm sure we can share the room to your satisfaction."

Paul stuffed his hands in his pockets. When Lila made that crack about him trying out her bed, he'd panicked. Now he knew she was joking, because no sane woman would volunteer to share her bathroom with a man when she could have it all to herself. He and his sisters had been forced to share, and Sandra and Sherry used to lock him out of their joint bathroom whenever they could. He and Melanie had a huge bathroom with dual sinks, separate showers, and private commodes, and even then he'd felt as if she were merely tolerating him in her personal sanctuary.

Besides, sharing a bathroom with Lila would open up a million opportunities for disaster. It would only take one time for him to barge in on her while she was naked, and he'd never get the image out of his mind. Of course, if he confessed that to her, she'd probably laugh her head off or accuse him of being a pervert. Once she heard what he'd been thinking, she'd quit, and then where would he be?

"No, no. The room is yours. I advertised the position with a private bath, and I won't go back on my word. Not to mention, it'll be easier potty training the boys. It will give us an excuse to . . . ah . . . bond and do . . . um . . . guy things." Paul wanted to kick himself for stammering, but her suggestion about the bed still made him feel sixteen all over again. "Plus I'm a slob. I'll keep our bathroom up to snuff, and you won't get grossed out cleaning it."

Lila wrinkled her forehead, then flashed him a smile. "All right, and thank you."

"Follow me downstairs and I'll show you the washer and dryer." Breathing a sigh of relief, he walked through the living room and kitchen and took the stairs to the first floor. At least she'd found her sense of humor and slipped him a full-blown grin. Though a little off kilter, the bed joke had to mean she was getting more comfortable around him, which would help with their professional relationship.

When they reached the first-floor hall, he inclined his head. "You already know where my office is. These three rooms are for patient examinations, and the laundry is off the lab." He went to the last door on the right. "It's really a kitchen, but I refer to it as the lab because that's what the last doctor used it for."

Walking to the refrigerator, he explained. "I never keep food in here, only blood and urine samples and throat cultures, as well as medications that require cold storage. When needed, a delivery service stops by, picks up the samples, and takes them to a laboratory for testing." He rested a palm on an upper cupboard. "These cabinets are always locked, because of the drugs and medical supplies, which can be a temptation to some. A cleaning service comes in once a week, so you don't have to worry about anything on the lower level, but you should still know where things are in case there's an emergency of some kind and I'm not around."

Her confused expression told him he'd been talking too fast again. "I know this is a lot to absorb, so feel free to ask questions."

She shook her head and the puzzled look disappeared. "I'm just overwhelmed . . . it's not a problem."

He continued into a small room they'd walked through earlier on the way to the back porch, and stopped in front of the washer and dryer. "Sorry about the laundry being located way down here, but that's the setup. I'm hoping to find something more convenient when I buy a house, but for now it's all we have."

Lila ran a hand over the top of the dryer, then opened the lid on the washer and glanced inside.

"The soap, stain remover, and dryer sheets are up top in the storage area. I send my dress shirts and slacks to the cleaners, so you'll only have to do my casual clothes and under—um—my personal things."

Suddenly Paul wished he was anywhere but here in this cramped space talking with Lila about his boxers. Maybe it would be better if he sent out all his laundry or did it himself, because the idea of her fondling his underwear was making him sweat. If he kept this up, he'd be back to doing the chores instead of her, which totally defeated the need for a housekeeper.

Thankfully, Lila seemed lost in her own world. She'd turned the dial that started the washer, and was now peering in the opening while the machine filled.

"This is probably a good time to put in the load I brought down from the boys' bedroom yesterday."

She moved back and he dumped in the basket of clothes, then added soap, set the temperature gauge to warm and the cycle on normal. "Would you believe my mother had to teach me how to do this? She kept the boys while I got settled in, then drove here from Philly to deliver them."

He closed the lid and rested his backside against the wall. "Anything else you need to know right now?"

Lila gave the washer a once-over, then copied his pose on the opposite wall. "Yes, but it doesn't have anything to do with my duties. I've been wondering what happened to your wife. Unless it's something you'd rather not talk about."

Paul had been waiting for her to ask the question, because almost everyone he'd met in Preston's Ferry had hinted at the same. He hadn't given out the details, so he imagined there were plenty of stories circulating. Better she heard the truth from him than an embellished tale from the town gossips. The sooner he got Melanie's defection out of the way, the sooner Lila could go about the business of taking care of his sons.

"The divorce was final a month ago, but we'd lived apart for a while. It was during that period I went through enough scheduling problems and nannies to recognize it was time for a change. When I decided to start fresh with Rick and Teddy, and Melanie approved, I answered the ad that brought us here. She may show up to visit from time to time, but I doubt it will happen soon." He cleared his throat. "If people ask about it, that's all you have to say."

"Isn't it unusual for a father to get the children when a marriage is dissolved?"

"It's not the norm, but it worked for us. I had to make a few serious life changes, but my goal from here on out is to do what's best for my sons."

The genuine compassion in her eyes kicked Paul's heart rate up a notch. It was bad enough she sometimes stared at him with an adoring gaze; her look of total understanding damn near jump-started his entire body. If she kept it up, something serious was going to happen between them, and he was pretty sure that wasn't a good idea. He was still trying to get used to the last upheaval in his life. He didn't need another.

He pushed from the wall, signaling the end of the discussion. "You about ready to start shopping? I thought we'd go out to dinner tonight to celebrate. We can talk about the twins' schedule then."

Lila strolled the town at a leisurely pace, pondering everything Paul had just said. When he'd talked about divorce, he'd made it sound as if he'd divested himself of an unwanted pet, but his eyes had told a different story. He wanted people to believe love for his sons was all he needed in life, but she hadn't been fooled. Inside, Paul Anderson was hurting.

And knowing that he hurt touched her in a place she was supposed to ignore, a spot deep inside she knew she had to stay away from if she intended to survive.

The travelers had been warned to keep their emotions separate from their mission. Sex was to be more a scientific experiment than an act of desire and commitment. Their goal was clear: have intercourse with the target as many times as was necessary to conceive, then meet with the mother ship at the appointed place and time.

If they failed, they would be welcomed home just the same, because no matter how things progressed they were expected to return. Their world would reveal itself to Earth, but only after they knew for certain the two species could mate successfully.

Now in the final block of shops, she stopped in front of Mary Lou's Clothes Closet. Gazing into the window, she viewed a variety of apparel on mannequins or artfully draped across wicker chairs and brightly colored benches. Certain she would find something to her liking, she opened the door and bumped into an older man wearing one of the shiny silver helmets she'd noticed earlier.

"Hey, little missy," said the man. "You okay?"

"I'm fine," said Lila, backing away. Her focus shifted to his silver hat, now tipped at an angle over his ear.

He bent to retrieve the paper bag he'd dropped in their collision, then glanced up and followed her gaze. "I'm Bill Halverson. And who might you be?"

"Lila," she answered, reconnecting with his blue eyes.

"Ah, the new nanny."

She frowned. Paul had been correct about the gossip in town, yet it didn't seem fair that everyone knew about her while she knew almost nothing about any of them.

As if sensing her apprehension, the man shook his head. "Word travels fast in Preston's Ferry. Everyone likes Dr. P, so we want to know what's up with him and the boys. A lot of folks had a hand in helping with Rick and Teddy. They're curious to see if you'll do a good job."

"I'm going to try." She shuffled sideways to pass him.

"I'm sure you will," said Bill, intent on talking. "I see you admire my cap."

Admire wasn't the correct word, but she was curious. "Um . . . yes. It's very . . . unusual."

"Might be unusual, but it's a necessity right now. You and Dr. P and everybody else in town need to be protected."

"Protected?"

Bill grasped her elbow with his free hand and led her to a bench in front of the store. Taking a seat, he placed his bag on the bench. "Sit a minute and let me give you the scoop."

Lila glanced at the other pedestrians and realized no one thought it odd she was speaking to a man with a crown on his head. If anything, the number of shiny hats and the people who wore them had increased since her visit to the bank. Sitting beside him on the bench, she waited to hear what he had to say.

"I belong to ESAW and this headgear is our symbol, so to speak. Course you can wear one even if you're not a member, but then you gotta pay."

"I see." Things were becoming clearer. ESAW was the name of a society or club, and the silver helmets showed membership. "And those who wear the hats know each another? You have meetings?"

"That's right, and we're having our first get-together in a couple of nights. I'm hanging flyers on the telephone poles, and a few teenagers are gonna deliver them to everybody's house. We got lots to talk about, ya see."

At one time, her world had held public gatherings to discuss local politics and criticize or compliment the government, but those meetings were no longer allowed. For the past several generations, people had been told what to say and how to think. Open forums were sometimes approved, but only when the topic was deemed harmless by those in charge.

What Bill suggested thrilled Lila to her marrow. It sounded as if the atmosphere here was unfettered, with each citizen welcome to voice his or her opinion. Freedom of thought and expression were a few of the reasons she'd longed to leave her planet, and this town seemed to encourage that very idea.

"How much does it cost to join?" she asked. If the money in her pocket wasn't enough, perhaps she could get Paul to advance her pay for next week.

"It's a bargain at five bucks, little missy, 'cause you get one of these"—he pointed to his hat—"with your membership." Bill pulled a rectangular board holding a sheaf of papers from his bag. "Want me to sign you up?"

"Yes, please." She proceeded to give him her full Earth name. After automatically filling in Paul's address, he handed her the sheet.

"Put your John Hancock at the bottom," he advised.

Lila wasn't certain what Bill meant until she met his amused gaze. When she took his pen and wrote her Earth name for the first time, pride swelled in her chest. She'd just taken an important step in becoming human.

"You're all set," said Bill. "Give me a minute and I'll make you a hat." Digging in the bag, he pulled out a long narrow box imprinted with the words ALUMINUM FOIL and tore off a sheet of the shiny stuff. Working quickly, he formed a cap and set it on her head. "That's quite a pile of hair you got there," he commented, pressing the foil onto her skull.

"Is it too much?" Lila asked, patting her crown. If cutting her hair would make appear more like an earthwoman . . .

"Nah, but you might need a pin or two to hold it in place. Mary Lou probably has some. Just ask her when you're inside."

She remembered that she was supposed to be buying new clothes and had yet to pay her membership fee. Pulling out her money, she handed him a paper with the number twenty on it. In return, he gave her three with the number five imprinted in the corner. She did a quick computation in her mind, noting the way the system worked.

"Say, how'd you like to buy a hat for Dr. P? He didn't want to join, but now that you're a member maybe you can convince him."

Paul had probably been too busy with his practice and his sons to attend meetings. Now that she was here, he would have the time. They could even go to-gether and bring Rick and Teddy.

"That would be wonderful. How much are they?"

"Three for five," said Bill, plucking one of the pieces of paper from her hand. "I already gave Rose one for each of the boys, but I'm betting they need another. They have to be measured to fit, so you come find me when you're out walking the twins. We'll figure a way to get Dr. P his hat later."

Standing, Bill picked up his bag. "It was a real pleasure meeting you, Lila. And thanks for joining ESAW. I'll mail in your membership application first thing Monday morning."

Lila nodded, then thought of another question. "By the way, what does ESAW mean exactly? I'm not familiar with the word."

"Stands for Eastern Shore Alien Watch. The group tracked them stars that came down to earth a few days ago. Now that we're fairly certain we've been invaded by beings from another planet, we're on a mission. Find, catch, and apprehend—that's our motto."

"Could you repeat that, please?" Lila tugged at her translator chip. "Did you just mention aliens?"

"Damn straight, I did. The Eastern Shore Alien Watch is on the hunt for creatures from outer space."

Six

Lila clutched her bracelet, desperate to subdue the frightening scenarios clashing in her brain. Was Bill saying people were aware of her existence, or merely suspicious? And what did he and his friends know of the other traveling pods? Until now, he had seemed harmless. Was it all a ruse to catch her off guard?

With an expression devoid of suspicion, the older man raised a brow. "Where'd you come from, anyway? Somewhere up north, I bet, 'cause you don't have the eastern shore twang. My Ellen's from New York, but she's been down here so long she talks just like one of us. Our sons moved to New Jersey and Atlanta, so they sound strange when they visit. I swear, most times I don't even understand the grandkids when they . . ."

Lila inhaled a calming breath as Bill rambled. She'd already drawn attention as a newcomer; she couldn't afford to expose herself to the entire town.

If that happened, she would be captured and disposed of, or given to Earth's scientists for experimentation. She would never live the life of a human.

The rational part of her mind told her that Bill was simply a senior citizen with a friendly nature and an urge to share his opinions with anyone who would listen. ESAW was his pet project of the moment, and therefore his current topic of conversation.

Slowly, she let go of her bracelet and removed the hat, setting it beside her on the bench as if it were an incendiary device about to explode.

"Say, now," said Bill, "you'd best keep that on, at least when you're outside."

"What . . . what is it supposed to do, exactly?" she stuttered. Had she somehow harmed herself by wearing the aluminum headpiece? Would it prove to be her downfall?

"Keeps the aliens from reading your thoughts or penetrating your brain, for starters," he said in a solemn tone.

Mentally deciphering his unscientific explanations, Lila ordered herself to stay in control. He and his fellow *alien hunters* didn't have a clue as to the particulars of her species. True, many of the inhabitants of her planet did have the ability to read minds, but the explorers had done so generations ago and found the human brain both primitive and immature. The idea that any of the travelers would probe an earthman's mind was ludicrous.

"Least ways, that's what Eustace Carter says," Bill added.

"Eustace Carter?"

"Our leader. President of ESAW and the man who chairs the main meetings."

"I see. And what is Mr. Carter's background?" Lila expected him to extol the man's credentials as an astronaut or government investigator, or one of the leaders of America's space program; at the very least, an astronomer with expertise in UFO sightings.

"United States Navy, retired, with a nose for sniffing out extraterrestrials. He's done some fieldwork for NASA, too. He's into all kinds of important stuff, still has friends in D.C. who keep him in the know on what few folks realize is a secret government project for the detection of alien life forms. He even has a computer connected to that organization searching for extraterrestrial life in the universe.

"Most nights he sits and watches the sky so he can keep informed on what's happening, because the government won't." Bill stood and picked up his bag. "Our first public meeting is gonna be right here in Preston's Ferry after the Founders' Day discussion. I'll introduce you when he comes to the meeting."

She sucked in a breath. Between landing in the swamp, which she now realized was a wildlife refuge, and last night's rain, she was certain the pod was history. Still, if Mr. Carter and his crew decided to go exploring . . .

"Then he's not employed by your—the government?"

"Nope, but he talks to the scientists on Wallops Island couple of times a day. His buddy in Washington is looking for a man by the name of Lucas Diamond, but the guy is hard to pin down. Seems he's the head of an agency that's so secret the yahoos in charge won't admit it exists."

Lila had no idea where Wallops Island was or what took place there, but if Eustace Carter was retired, he had to be close to Bill's age. And it didn't sound as if the people in charge had much faith in his observations, which put her further at ease. But she couldn't afford to drop her guard. She started to ask another question, when a distant rumble caught her attention.

Bill peered to the right and she followed his disgruntled gaze as a huge metal box on wheels rounded a corner, veered back and forth across the yellow center lines, and aimed for town. The vehicle lumbered as if too large for its many wheels, but it moved at a steady pace.

"Damned tourists. Don't have the sense God gave a duck, steering that monstrosity like it was a Volkswagen Beetle."

The huge vehicle drew closer, and Lila saw that it was inhabited by a man and a woman, and the woman was driving. "It looks like a traveling house," she said aloud.

"That's what a Windcruiser is, and my guess is it's heading for the empty lot in front of the cement factory. The mayor thinks it's good business for the town to allow trailers to park there. Charges 'em for a permit and the right to hook up to the city's water and electric lines, instead of sending 'em to the campgrounds down the road. Crazy birders."

"Birders?"

"Bird-watchers is my guess. We get dozens of 'em tromping through Preston's Ferry this time of year.

Tend to gravitate toward that wildlife refuge. Folks come from miles to kayak or hike the trails and catch sight of the migrating waterfowl." He shook his head. "The bird-watchers like it better in town, 'cause there are more amenities. If you ask me, all they do is block our view of the Chesapeake."

If she hadn't been so unsettled, Lila would have laughed. The only way someone could see the body of water from the empty lot was to walk to the very edge of the pavement and climb onto one of the mounds of abandoned cement, and even then the *view* would be minimal.

"I have to go." Vowing to keep her fears in check, she stood and offered Bill her hand. "It was nice meeting you, and I hope to see you again when the twins are with me."

Bill nodded. "Same here. And don't forget to wear your hat. Oh, and tell Dr. P you joined the group. Maybe he'll decide to do the same." Continuing to mutter disparaging remarks about tourists and their danger to the town, he shuffled away without a backward glance.

Lila heaved another calming breath and picked up the aluminum cap. It didn't sound like Bill and his group were going to look for her downed pod. Instead, ESAW was concerned with what the pod had brought to Earth—her. If she were here legally, she could contact the mother ship, tell the commander to warn the others and ask for an emergency pickup, but that was impossible.

She had no business on this mission. If she revealed herself to the ship, she might be tracked by her own people and returned to her planet for justice. She would be branded a traitor, instead of a woman seeking freedom and a new beginning to her life.

Which only made it more imperative she assume completely the guise of a human.

Peering through the window of the Clothes Closet, Lila focused on her goal. Several changes of costume would go a long way in making her appear fully human.

She opened the door to the shop and inhaled the scent of musty fabric and a pungent odor reminiscent of the coffee she'd had with breakfast. Inspecting the interior, she recalled the shopping experience on her planet. Retail stores frequented by the public were so large they had to be traversed by a system of automated walkways. All items were displayed behind clear panels, and shoppers simply touched their personal debit code into a keypad, then noted the desired size, number, and style of the goods they wanted. The objects were bagged and waiting at the walkway's end, which made the visit efficient but uneventful, and one of the reasons so many of her fellow citizens shopped on her planet's equivalent of the Internet.

Hoping to hide her amazement, she strode to a rack and began sifting through the offerings. After a few seconds, she sensed a presence at her side.

"Can I help you find anything in particular?"

She gave the woman a sidelong glance. "No, thank you."

"Are you looking for yourself?"

"For me, yes," she answered, not used to assistance while she shopped.

"Well then, you might want to inspect the racks on the other side of the store. This is men's clothing."

Heat rushed to Lila's cheeks. She'd made another mistake, and given a human cause to wonder about her. Now she was forced to initiate damage control. After scanning the sign on top of the display, she sent the woman an apologetic smile.

"I guess I didn't read carefully enough. I'm in a bit of a hurry. I have to get back before the twins wake up."

Appraising her through shrewd brown eyes, the woman folded her arms. "You're Dr. P's new nanny."

"Yes."

"I'm Mary Lou," said the woman, the lines in her face crisscrossing like an interstellar road map. Stepping back, she focused on Lila's silvery headpiece. "I see you've met Bill Halverson."

"He convinced me to join his organization." Lila fingered the foil on top of her head. It only made sense to wear the hat. With it, she could hide safely, certain no one would suspect an alien of using something made specifically to keep them at bay. "How well do you know Bill?"

Mary Lou snorted. "Shoot, known the man all my life, just like most everyone else in town. Last year, for his and Ellen's forty-fifth wedding anniversary, a bunch of us women got together and sent her a sympathy card. Ever since the man retired, she's put up with more horse pucky than a stable hand. This alien watch thing is simply the latest pecan on the nut tree of her loopy husband's imagination."

"But I saw quite a few people wearing them," Lila informed her. "Surely they can't all be . . . pecans?"

"Not all. Some folks are doing it to humor him, and my guess is the younger ones are just plain having fun. Without using my thumb and pinkie, I bet I can count on one hand the number of people in this town who actually believe we had an alien landing."

"I see." Lila eased out a breath. Things were sounding more promising than she'd thought.

"Does Dr. P know you joined ESAW?"

"Not yet," she admitted. "Why?"

"Just wondering, but don't be surprised if he laughs his fanny off. Big-city folks don't have the same sense of humor as we eastern shore natives do." Mary Lou put her hands on her ample hips. "Now, how about you tell me what you need?"

Lila shrugged. "I'm not sure. I lost my clothes, so . . . everything, I guess."

"Lost your clothes?" Mary Lou's harsh *tsk* echoed in the store. "You poor thing. Did you report the theft to the police?"

Amazed at how quickly the people she met offered assistance, Lila shook her head. "It happened a couple of days ago, and not in Preston's Ferry. Paul gave me an advance on my salary so I can buy replacements."

The store owner rubbed her hands together as if ready to roll up her sleeves and get to work. "This could take a while. We'd better get started."

Bill Halverson was a man on a mission, and he didn't care who knew it. He wasn't as stupid as some people thought. He'd been retired from his job at the cement factory for five years now, and every day since had been as boring as the last, until he'd met Eustace Carter and joined ESAW.

Ellen still worked part-time at the Harbor Café, God bless her, and she accepted her husband's need of an outlet for his energy. Retirement was a bitch, especially if a man was sharp-minded and willing to work. He was lucky enough to be both.

So what if his fellow citizens called him and Eustace and the rest of the leaders of ESAW fools? And so what if they laughed behind his back, or in some cases to his face? It didn't bother him a bit. Because this wasn't like the time right after he'd retired when he'd tried to convince folks they needed to stock up on duct tape and bottled water to protect themselves from the possible disasters of the new millennium.

This was different.

He could feel the anticipation in the pit of his stomach, much like when he'd been waiting in line to ride a roller coaster at a theme park in Williamsburg. The foreboding of disaster was so strong, bile rose in his throat at the very thought of what might be out there waiting to pounce on him and the decent men and women of Preston's Ferry.

Aliens stalked the eastern shore, and he was going to find them.

Striding toward the center of town, he smiled at folks who wore his tinfoil creations. A few of the older men already belonged to ESAW, so there'd been no problem convincing them it was time to don the silver helmets. The women were a harder sell, Ellen included. His wife would only wear her protective headgear at home—and never to bed.

He'd sold a few hats to teenagers, too. They thought it was cool, an inside joke meant to shock, like shaving their head or piercing their tongues or navels. But he refused to stop, because every once in a while he met someone who understood the importance of his message. Like that new housekeeper of Dr. P's. Now, there was one sweet young woman, well mannered and polite, with a serious attitude and a whole lot of common sense. And she was a real looker, too, with all that curly red hair and those big green eyes.

He could hear the biddies at the tea parlor, wagging their tongues about what might happen between Lila and Paul because the two of them were sharing the same house and all. Hell, he didn't care. A man in Dr. P's situation needed a good woman, and those rambunctious boys needed two parents to be raised right. He had more important things to worry about than what went on in private between consenting adults. He had citizens to protect.

Plus, he was earning extra cash. Eustace let him and the other district commanders keep two dollars of every five they collected when they signed up a new member. The money he made selling the protective headgear to nonmembers was his free and clear, minus the cost of the foil, of course. It felt good to be contributing to his and Ellen's living expenses with more than his measly Social Security check.

He'd covered the entire downtown today hawking his wares, and tomorrow he'd do the same outside a few of the local churches. He still had to stop by Sheila's and pick up the flyers for the meeting and deliver them to the Gibson boys, then hang the rest on telephone poles around town.

He stopped at the edge of the vacant parking lot attached to the abandoned grocery and gazed at the Windcruiser parked at an angle across six spaces. Scratching his jaw, he wondered if it was too soon to pay the folks inside a visit. Not only because it would be prudent to sell the occupants a hat *before* they heard the naysayers discredit him, but because he'd always believed in the adage "strike while the iron is hot."

And damn if it could get any hotter than now.

Scrutinizing the mammoth trailer, Bill walked across the asphalt. He'd thought about buying a similar vehicle when Ellen officially retired, in hopes the two of them could travel, but nothing this large or showy. The darned thing probably got five miles to the gallon and needed a lot of expensive permits and inspections, though it was hard telling. Circling the Windcruiser, he noted there were generic Virginia license plates on the front and rear, but no stickers in the windows, not even the kind used for registration.

What it did have was an odd-looking antenna on top, more resembling old-fashioned radar gear with a periscope attached. He'd never seen anything like the ornate metal configuration, and figured it was some type of fancy viewing device birders used to scope out their quarry without being detected.

Striding to the vehicle's side, he put his ear to the door, then knocked a jaunty rhythm and waited.

And waited.

Well, shoot, the trailer just got here; the passengers couldn't have had time to disembark. Besides, he heard voices. The owners had to be inside . . . unless the sound came from a television or radio. Frowning, he rapped again, then peered into the nearest window and found it blocked by a curtain. Glancing around, he checked the sidewalk, but didn't see any strangers. The town hall was closed today, so he doubted the owners were buying their permit. Besides, if they knew what was good for them, they already had one, or George Gibson, Preston's Ferry's chief of police, would have been here by now to write the parking ticket.

Maybe they were getting supplies in the Shop and Bag. Or they'd gone to the Harbor Café for a late lunch. If so, Ellen would know all about them.

Whistling, he stuck a hand in his pocket, picked up his bag of supplies with the other, and crossed the street to the café, one of Preston's Ferry's three restaurants. He'd promised to walk his wife home, and her shift was over at four. He had time for coffee and a slice of pie, maybe a friendly conversation with the Windcruiser's owners. Once he told them about the alien landing, how could they not want protection?

"Hey, Mom." Paul spoke into the telephone, relieved he was talking to his mother's answering machine. "Just wanted you to know I found someone to care for the boys. She's here for a week on trial, and it looks like she's going to work out, so it's okay if you can't make the Founders' Day celebration. Talk to you later. 'Bye."

Paul hung up, grateful fate had cut him some slack. His overly protective mother was probably puttering outside or walking a mall. Leaving a message saved him from answering questions about Lila, but gave him points for being thoughtful by letting her know her grandsons were in good hands. If he was lucky, it would even delay her planned visit while the four of them settled into a schedule.

He sorted through the jumble of papers and magazines on his desk, tossing out the catalogues and flyers that made up the bulk of his daily mail. At the bottom of the stack was a small white envelope with no return address and a foreign stamp in the upper right corner. Immediate recognition of the handwriting wiped away all thoughts of his mother, and caused his stomach to clench with a variety of emotions.

Melanie had sent him a letter.

Exhaling a frustrated breath, he stared at her neat round script. She and Jerry had taken some time to relax and get to know one another better. At least, that's what she'd said they were going to do when she called after the divorce was final. She'd wanted him to know where she was, in case the twins needed her, but Paul suspected her intention was selfish. She simply wanted to gloat because she'd found someone else to take her on that trip to the Mediterranean they'd always planned but never managed to accomplish.

He speared rigid fingers through his hair. Why the hell hadn't she just sent a postcard?

After tearing into the envelope, he waited a few seconds to center himself. He'd told his ex-wife to keep in touch, hadn't he? No reason to assume Melanie was bragging about her new and perfect relationship, or the fact that Jerry loved her enough to devote himself to making her happy, instead of running one of the most successful electrical firms in Maryland.

Unfolding the heavy cream-colored paper, Paul read the name of an expensive-sounding resort printed in gold at the top of the page. The letter was short and to the point. She and Jerry Goldberg had married, and Melanie thought it best Paul find out from her before he read it in the society page or was told by one of their old friends.

He crushed the paper into a ball before he realized what he'd done. He'd figured she and Jerry would marry . . . someday. He just hadn't thought *someday* would come so soon.

And he'd never thought it would hurt this much when it did.

He tossed the note into the wastebasket under his desk, then leaned forward on his elbows and ground the heels of his palms into his eyes. Christ, he'd been an idiot. Money didn't buy happiness and it never would. So why had he worked so hard to build his career, instead of his marriage? When had he lost sight of the things that were important in life? Why hadn't he tried harder to keep his family together?

It's too late now, pal, he chided himself. *You have a new life and a new perspective on what's important, so wish Melanie luck and move on.*

Bolstered by his self-lecture, he sorted the remainder of his mail into two piles, pulled a large envelope from a side drawer, and slid the invoices that had to do with his practice inside. His accountant wanted all professional documents mailed to him weekly. Dave had been his accountant for years, and Paul always did what the man suggested.

Straightening the desk blotter, he found the blank employment papers he'd set aside earlier. They were one more thing to add to Dave's envelope, after he got his new nanny to fill them out. And speaking of Lila— He checked his watch and saw that two hours had elapsed since she'd left on her shopping spree. Maybe she'd lost track of the time, not uncommon for a woman in the throes of replenishing a wardrobe. Considering how little she'd owned in the way of personal items, she probably needed this much time just for the basics.

Pushing away from his desk, he stood and headed upstairs. The boys might be awake. If not, he could move his personal care items out of her bathroom and into the one he was going to share with Rick and Teddy.

"Da! Da! Da!"

Paul heard Rick's demanding shout as he climbed the stairs. Thinking this might be an opportune moment to continue his foray into potty training, he went to the bedroom and snatched Rick from his crib before the twin woke his brother. Arriving in the bathroom, he slipped off his son's coveralls and fairly dry diaper, and stood him in front of the toilet.

"Okay, buddy, pay attention to what Daddy's doing." He pulled down his zipper and took care of business.

Rick eyed the proceedings with interest, then grabbed his penis and giggled. By the time Paul realized what had happened, the little guy was standing in a puddle. So much for lesson number 227.

"That's okay," he said with a positive inflection. "You'll get the hang of it." He went to the linen closet, took out a clean washcloth, and wiped down the chubby legs. "Let's go find a fresh diaper and check on your brother."

Rounding the corner with Rick at his heels, Paul saw his other son standing in the crib with his arms raised. "Hey, Teddy. Hang on a second, and I'll be right there."

He made quick work of getting Rick changed and dressed, then set him down and crossed the room. "Did you have a good nap?" He hoisted Teddy from the crib and brought him to the bathroom while Rick trotted behind. Diligently, he repeated the potty-training exercise . . . with the identical result.

Repeating the cleanup process, Paul figured it might be time to take a ride across the bridge and hit a bookstore. There had to be books on the topic, maybe *Potty-Training for Dummies* or something else equally simple for inept parents. Especially since he'd had no luck.

He led the boys to the kitchen and strapped them in their high chairs, intent on staving off hunger. He didn't want to make dinner plans until he spoke with Lila, but he and the twins needed a little something to tide them over. Searching the pantry, he found an open bag of cheddary, fish-shaped crackers and placed a handful in front of each boy.

After swallowing a few himself, he filled the kettle and put it on to boil. Checking the cupboard, he took down two mugs and two tea bags, certain the nanny would arrive soon.

Her arms laden with packages, Lila climbed the stairs. Compared to her harrowing experience with Bill, the time she'd spent in the Clothes Closet had been a fortifying adventure. She'd used most of her money, but she'd received lovely things in trade. She couldn't wait to bathe and change into one of her new outfits.

After crossing the landing, she stopped in the doorway, took off her foil headpiece, and tucked it into one of her shopping bags. Before she told Paul she'd joined ESAW, needed to find out what he knew of the organization. If he thought it was a joke, she could rest easy. If he believed the group and their idea had merit . . .

Entering the kitchen, she spotted Paul at the sink. Rick and Teddy saw her and began to bounce, pounding on the table with one hand while they stuffed bits of orange-colored food into their grinning mouths with the other. Paul turned and her heart fluttered in her chest. His blue eyes smiled a welcome, as did the twins', warming her from the inside out. She'd only been here a day, and she felt so close to these three men.

The memory of the family she would never again see tugged at her heartstrings. If she'd been able to fit in, find a usable skill, and make her parents proud, she would still be with them, even though she'd been rejected for this mission. Maybe someday she'd find a way to send them a message or plan a visit.

"You're back. Let me help with that." Rushing to her side, Paul grabbed the bags and set them on the end of the table. "Looks like you single-handedly helped the Clothes Closet turn a profit for the month."

She removed her favorite purchase, a bright yellow shirt, and he quirked up a corner of his mouth. "That color will look good on you."

Lila almost laughed out loud. Clothing on her planet was usually a one-piece fitted suit in muted colors of black or gray, composed of a material that repelled stains. Only the very boldest wore bright colors, if they could find them. She'd thought about voicing her displeasure with the government's ridiculous dress code by wearing something outrageous, but hadn't wanted to embarrass her parents or her sister, nor ruin her chances at being a traveler. In the end, it hadn't mattered, because she'd been overlooked anyway.

"I even bought three pairs of shoes. Sandals for the beach, athletic shoes for daytime, and a pair for evening."

"Only three pair? Sounds to me like you restrained yourself."

Should she have bought more? "I can only wear one pair at a time," she reminded him. "But Mary Lou said I would get use out of all three."

"When it comes to shoes, I guess you just can't argue with a woman's logic." He set a cup down at her place at the table. "I thought you'd be home soon, so I made tea. It's the same brand we had last night. Sit and tell me what else you bought."

Lila put her bags on the floor. Teddy reached for

her cup and she held it away, then pushed his two-handled mug toward him. "I found pants, shirts, a skirt, and a dress with a jacket, and these. . . ." Reaching into one of the bags, she pulled out a handful of silky white panties. "Mary Lou called it lingerie."

Paul's gaze darted from her face to the lingerie and back again, then moved to Rick. Handing the boy another cracker, he said, "Uh . . . yeah, that's what it is, all right."

Lila caught a glimmer of surprise in his eyes before he turned away. Stuffing the lingerie back in the bag that held other frilly things, she refused to let his odd reaction dampen her delight. Instead, she sipped her tea and smiled when he again glanced her way.

During the seconds that passed, Lila thought she'd been put under a microscope. Paul's jaw clenched, his gaze grew intense. Her eyes were drawn to him, yet she was unable to speak. Standing, she carried her empty cup to the sink, while she explored whatever was pulsing between them. Returning to the table, she picked up her packages.

"I'm going to put everything away and get ready for dinner." At the pantry, she stopped. She was the hired help, a woman who should be taking orders, not giving them. She worked for Paul and he could get rid of her at any moment, for any infraction, including insubordination.

Meekly, she peeked around the doorframe. "I'm sorry, I didn't mean to sound so . . . so . . ."

Looking more relaxed, he leaned back in his chair. "It's not a problem. I don't want us to be uncomfortable with each other, Lila. This is a small apartment. We'll be living in close quarters until I can afford a bigger house. It's important we work together, for Rick and Teddy's sake."

She nodded. "Are we still going out to dinner, or would you like me to cook?"

"Dinna!" squealed Rick. Paul patted his son's head. "In a little while." He cleared his throat. "I thought we'd go to the truck stop on the highway south of town, unless you want to stay in Preston's Ferry."

"I'll be happy to go wherever you and the boys want."

"In that case we'll go to Croakers. It's a little rustic, but the food's good and the atmosphere is definitely eastern shore. I can get the boys cleaned up and ready while you put your clothes away."

"I can do it. I'll leave my things in bags and—"

"I don't mind. Besides, tonight is officially your first night as the nanny, so you're entitled."

"But—"

"Go on. Take a shower and change, and do whatever else you need to do. I'll handle the twins."

Seven

*T*o Lila's knowledge, nothing like Croakers existed on her planet. Part of a gas station and truck stop complex that sold an assortment of eastern shore items, the business so fascinated her she found it difficult to follow the line as it snaked toward the dining room. Several types of eating establishments were available on her world, but they sold only food. Compared to this restaurant, the experience was staid, formal, and boring.

She scanned the lobby, as curious of it as she'd been of the clothing store. Displayed on one wall was a honeycomb of cubbyholes, each filled with bottles of wine, one of the substances forbidden on her planet ninents ago. Hanging on the opposite wall were colorful T-shirts ranging in size from infant to adult, each decorated with a drawing or slogan. A variety of seashells and hand-painted wood carvings occupied space next to magnets, candles, and homemade birdhouses. Hanging prominently in the center of the shelves was a sign that read YOU BROKE IT, YOU BOUGHT IT.

The area to the left of the entry featured chewing tobacco and cigarettes, plus tickets for something called a lottery. They also carried peanuts in the shell, specially cured ham and smoked bacon, all touted as Virginia delicacies. Mixed in with those items were cookbooks, canned crab chowder, candy bars, water and soft drinks, maps and travel guides, a selection of hunting knives, hand-crafted jewelry, and fireworks.

Now second in line inside the restaurant, Lila drew her attention to the blackboard menu, where she hoped to find a meal that didn't include the flesh of a once-living creature. Crab was the specialty of the night, and one could order it broiled, stuffed, or in a cake. Then came grouper, drum, and snapper, which she assumed were fish, and scallops or oysters, each prepared several ways. They also served chicken, fried or with dumplings, veal in a tomato and red wine sauce, pulled pork—she refused to contemplate the origin of such a distasteful-sounding dish—and prime rib. She had to read all the way to the bottom of the four-foot-long board before she found a list of vegetables.

Paul held a twin in each arm, too busy keeping them occupied to notice her awe of Croakers. "So, what sounds good, fellas? You want to share a plate of spaghetti and a side of green beans?"

"Hey, Dr. P," said the girl waiting to take their order. "How are you and the boys?"

Lila heard the cheerful lilt and gave a sidelong

glance. Pretty and petite, with white-blond hair pulled into a tail at the back of her head, the cashier gazed at Paul through black-rimmed eyes shadowed in purple. Her low-cut red blouse and hip-hugging pants made Lila feel as if her new outfit, a pale pink shirt and plain beige slacks, were something one of her planet's Elders might wear if they came to Earth.

"Ashley, I didn't know you worked here. How's your mom?"

"She's fine, and this job's just for now. I've decided to try something more challenging once school gets out, and I've been meaning to ask—have you found a nanny yet, because maybe I could—"

"All taken care of, but thanks for thinking of us," said Paul. "I hired Lila yesterday."

A flicker of surprise, then disdain sparked in the young woman's brown eyes, just before she offered Lila a sullen sounding hello.

Lila kept her expression polite. "It's nice to meet you." *And don't get any ideas about Paul,* she added in silence.

"Ashley babysat for Teddy and Rick a few times when I was called out on an evening emergency. She's a sophomore at the local high school."

"Actually, I'm finishing my junior year. I'll be a senior in the fall," the girl corrected, flashing Paul another grin. "So, what are you having?"

"Ladies first," said Paul.

Ashley tapped her pencil on the counter in time to the piped-in music blaring overhead. "Ma'am?"

"The vegetable platter," said Lila, shocked at her reaction to the young woman's attitude. Where had that thought about Paul come from?

The girl's smug smile turned impatient. "You get a choice of four items from the bottom list."

Disconcerted, Lila read the board again. Mentally crossing her fingers, she hoped at least one dish would be familiar. "I'd like the baked potato, sautéed spinach, green beans, and . . . and . . ."

"Their corn casserole is a specialty," Paul offered.

"The corn casserole."

"And to drink?"

"Water, please."

"How about a glass of wine?" He nodded toward a bottle displayed on the counter. "I usually have the house merlot."

Wine? Did she dare? Then again, she'd had no ill effects from coffee or tea. "That would be fine."

Paul ordered meals for himself and the twins, and led them to a table in the nonsmoking section. A waitress brought over tall wooden chairs and he settled the boys, while Lila took her seat and placed the diaper bag she'd been carrying on the floor.

Free to observe the room, she fought back a wave of panic when she saw several guests wearing the distinctive headpiece that marked them as a member of ESAW. Was there anything about her that would cause them to suspect she was from another planet? If so, would they follow Bill's advice to *catch and apprehend*?

She'd left her foil hat on her dresser, but she hoped to bring up the subject of ESAW with Paul when the time was right. Even if he scoffed at the idea, Lila planned to continue wearing the silvery helmet when in town. It would keep Bill and his compatriots from suspecting her, and she would rest easy knowing Paul thought the alien theory a joke.

"Would you mind getting the twins' cups from their bag?" Paul asked, not batting an eye at the foil headgear. "And their bibs?"

Relieved at his disinterest in the ESAW diners, Lila found what he asked for, then realized she should be the one preparing the boys for their meal. The waitress arrived with a tray of drinks, and he quickly commandeered the cups and milk, while she took care of the bibs.

"Since this is a celebration of sorts, maybe I should give a toast." He picked up his wine. "I really want this to work, Lila, not only for Rick and Teddy's sake, but mine too. We like you, and I hope you like us."

His comment sounded so sincere. For generations, her planet had condemned lies and the people who told them. Deceit was foreign to her. She still mourned the fact that she'd cheated her world in order to fulfill a purely selfish goal. She'd taken this job under false pretenses, as well, which only added to her guilt. But she'd sworn an oath to herself, and was bound to uphold it. She had to remember that living with Paul and his sons was merely a way to make that happen.

Paul touched his glass to hers and she mimicked his action. "Here's to the start of a long and happy relationship, for all of us."

He sipped his drink and Lila did the same. The wine tickled her senses, its rich, fruity flavor burning a trail as it slid down her throat. Pondering the odd sensation, she evaluated her reaction to the heady liquid. She'd grown warm, but the restaurant was crowded and—

Paul set down his glass and folded his arms. "May I ask you a question?"

As long as it isn't about where I came from, how I got here, or my reason for staying. "What would you like to know?"

"I couldn't help but notice what you ordered. I didn't realize you were a vegetarian."

"If that means I don't eat anything that once had a heartbeat, I guess I am. I hope it's not a problem?"

"Not if you don't mind cooking meat or eggs and dairy products."

Would she? Only time would tell. "The idea of killing and eating living creatures unsettles me. None of the animals used for food are as predatory as the humans who consume them."

"Goes against your principles, does it?"

"It's the way I was raised. But I could give you a list of reasons why a diet composed of vegetables, fruits, and grains is more sound for humans than animal flesh, and more correct for their body's physical well-being."

"No, thanks. I realize the middle to lower section of the food pyramid is better for you, but I enjoy the taste of a good steak, and fried chicken is a favorite of mine. Who knows, with the right recipes you might be able to convert me. And I don't mind if you try it out on Rick and Teddy—as long as they get the proper nutritional requirements."

A server took that moment to bring their meals to the table, and Lila breathed a sigh of relief. All the items on her plate looked familiar. She picked up her fork, then noticed Paul's struggle as he dodged four tiny-but-determined hands each grabbing for the extra plates, two dinners, and dish of green beans lined up in front of him.

"Hang on, give me a minute," he said as he juggled the plates and food.

Teddy banged his cup hard on the table, and Rick gave his usual ear-splitting dinner chant, then threw his fork and began kicking the underside of the table. Setting down her own utensil, Lila inhaled sharply at the bad behavior.

"Excuse me." She took away Teddy's cup and grabbed Rick's offending hand. "Your behavior is impolite. If you eat dinner in a proper manner, I'll read you both a story when we get home. If not, it's a bath and straight to bed. Is that clear?"

With their lower lips set in identical pouts, the boys stared at her so seriously Lila couldn't stop the corner of her mouth from twitching. They giggled and she rolled her eyes. "You two don't fool me with that innocent act."

She returned Teddy's cup, accepted the clean fork Paul offered, and handed it to Rick. After dividing the spaghetti and vegetables, she passed a meal to each toddler. Soon they were munching contentedly, and she was able to concentrate on her own food. Taking a bite of what she guessed was corn casserole, then one of spinach, she gave a blissful sigh.

"Good?" asked Paul.

"Delicious."

He glanced at his sons, eating as efficiently as could be expected for two-year-olds, and raised a brow. "Are you sure you don't have a younger brother?"

"Positive."

Leaning back in his chair, he raised his glass of wine and gave a second toast. "Way to go, Lila."

"I'd like to get up early tomorrow morning and go for a run," Paul told her as soon as he closed the boys' bedroom door for the night. "I'll make coffee before I leave, but I was hoping you'd take care of the twins and see to breakfast."

Not wanting to disturb Teddy and Rick, Lila stepped into the living room and turned to face him. "Isn't that what I'm supposed to do?"

"Sunday is your day off, remember? I don't want to start taking advantage your first week on the job." He ran a hand through his honey-colored hair. "I thought after that I could show you the sights, maybe take you across the bridge to the mainland. I want to go to a bookstore with the boys, and figured you might like to come along." He walked past her and opened his bathroom door. "You don't need to give me an answer now, just think about it. I'm taking a shower and going straight to bed, but feel free to stay up and watch television. The place is your home too. Please do whatever makes you comfortable."

Before she had a chance to speak, he shut the door in her face. Confused by his contradictory attitude, she frowned. He'd issued her an invitation and a dismissal almost in the same breath, and she had no idea what to make of it. Did he want to be with her or didn't he?

After they'd come home from the restaurant,

she'd given Rick and Teddy their bath and prepared them for bed on her own. Then she'd sat in the large stuffed chair in front of the bookcase and settled the boys on her lap with a book Paul had said was one of their favorites. The antics of Christopher Robin and his good friend Pooh, a small, yellow bear with a life full of interesting ups and downs and a penchant for honey, had delighted her as well as the twins.

Halfway through the story, the boys had fallen asleep nestled against her chest, and she'd lost herself in their contentment. Holding them close, she'd inhaled their baby-fresh scent, and hoped her own child would be as sweet and loving as these two. When she raised her head, she'd found an even more fascinating scenario. Paul seemed to have been listening as carefully as his sons. And this time, when their eyes locked, she didn't look away. Instead, she met his curious gaze and smiled warmly, her invitation clear.

A long moment passed before he walked to her chair, lifted Teddy, and carried him to bed, while she did the same with Rick. She'd planned to sit with Paul in the living room and speak with him first about ESAW, then issue a more pointed request for him to join her in bed. Contrarily, Paul hadn't given her the chance. His desire for a good night's sleep and a visit to a bookstore had taken her by surprise, but the message had been clear. He didn't want to be alone with her.

But had he meant just for tonight, or at any time in the future?

In her bedroom, Lila undressed and removed one

of her new nightgowns from the dresser drawer. When she'd been in the Clothes Closet, the gown had caught her eye immediately, and she'd asked Mary Lou to find one in the proper size. She'd also purchased two others made of soft cotton, but this cream-colored swath of material was silky and so transparent she could see her fingers through the fabric when she held it to the light.

What would Paul say, she wondered, if he found her wearing this gown? Would he notice the way it dipped low over her breasts and caressed her hips? Would he follow the line of her leg as it disappeared up the slit that ran from her ankle to her thigh? Would he peel the narrow satin straps from her shoulders and take her to his bed?

Prepared to sleep, she turned off the light and lay on the mattress but found it impossible to relax. Her every thought was about Paul and how she might lure him to her side. If only she knew what enticed him, or what would make her so desirable he would forget his plan to take an early morning run and come to her instead. What did she have to do to have sex with Paul?

Images of the two of them partaking of the seductive and sensual things Rila had described flickered in her brain. All hope of slumber fled as heat bubbled through her veins, itching at her skin from the inside out.

Lila dragged herself from the mattress to her bathroom, where she splashed cool water on her face, but it didn't take away the tremor that ran through her whenever she thought about what she needed to do with Paul. Reminded of the fact that humans seemed to have a remedy for every kind of ache or pain, she opened the cabinet and found several medicines, but none of them described her symptoms or sounded right for the parts of her that needed attention at this moment.

Thinking food might help, she left her room for the kitchen. Once there, she opened the refrigerator and retrieved a container of milk, the liquid she'd drunk with her peanut butter sandwiches. Tugging on the memory chip in her right ear, she recalled the properties of the creamy beverage.

When the information revealed that the liquid was sometimes warmed and used as a sleep aid for humans, Lila took a cup from the cabinet, filled it partway with milk, and carried it to the microwave. The primitive cooking tool seemed so simple she didn't bother searching her chip for instructions on its use, but merely set the cup inside and started the appliance.

The prospect of mating with Paul crept into her brain, sending another shiver up her spine. When she'd first decided to take her twin's place on this mission, she'd relegated him to a necessity with whom she had to interact in order to achieve her final goal. Paul was meant for Rila, not her, and there was no reason to think otherwise. After she became pregnant, she would move on without a second thought for the earthman.

But once she'd met him, everything had changed.

The moment she'd walked through his office door, he had touched something deep inside of her, a secret hidden place where she kept her hopes and dreams. Then she found out he had twin sons;

adorable little boys with distasteful bodily functions and impish grins that had her shaking her head and grinning with amusement at the same time.

She'd only been with them a short time, yet she knew Paul and his boys needed her, not only to cook, clean, and do chores, but to share in their life. And if this was another place, one where ESAW didn't exist, she might be tempted to stay and do exactly that. But every day she spent in Preston's Ferry put her at risk of being found out and hunted down.

The microwave sounded and she bent forward to retrieve the warm milk. Taking out her drink, she rested her elbows on the counter and blew on the liquid to cool it, then sipped at the contents. Tamping back the feeling of guilt, she sighed. Humans had learned to harden their hearts ninents ago. They were known throughout the galaxy to be a selfish race that thought little of their own kind, squandered their planet's resources, and warred with their neighbors at the slightest provocation.

Just because she hadn't found the proper place in her world didn't mean she couldn't fit in here, once she chose what she wanted to do. She had to take what she needed from Paul, forget about him and his sons, and do whatever was necessary to make her personal mission a success.

Paul focused on the clock on his nightstand. Unhappy with the late hour, he turned and punched his pillow. Tomorrow was Sunday, so he could sleep as long as he wanted. He'd already informed Lila he was going for a run and expected to come home to a breakfast he hadn't fixed himself. It would be a nice change from his normal rush to feed the boys before they destroyed the kitchen, and she'd been agreeable to the request.

Rolling to his back, he stared at the ceiling and the glittering pattern thrown by the moonlight creeping through the blinds. Things were finally coming together. His office was thriving and, contrary to an earlier worry, he was actually beginning to enjoy doling out medication for aches, pains, and allergies, as well as giving children their yearly physical or stitching up a cut. Even listening to his more senior patients who stopped in to make sure their minor memory loss and slower reflexes were a normal part of the aging process didn't bother him.

General practice might not be as glamorous as performing eyelift surgery on a Washington society maven or sculpting a debutante's nose, but it was a hell of a lot more satisfying. Less prestige, less pressure, and less money weren't for every doctor, but now that he realized what was truly important in his life, that suited him just fine.

Stymied by his inability to sleep, he decided to ponder his predicament logically. As he'd deduced with Bill Halverson, an inability to fall asleep was usually precipitated by some change in schedule or lifestyle. So what else besides his practice was different? What had happened in the past forty-eight hours that hadn't happened last week?

The only thing he could come up with was Lila. She had to be the reason for his insomnia. Her touching story time with the twins must have affected him more than he'd realized, as had the way she'd handled Teddy and Rick at the restaurant. His children were good kids, but when they were with the new nanny he'd swear they sprouted invisible wings and halos. He was a sap where his sons were concerned, and her firm-yet-gentle discipline and caring manner got to him almost as much as her provocative green eyes and joking innuendo.

And that was a problem. He was the father of two boys he'd vowed to put first in his life. He wasn't ready to become involved with a woman, let alone date, even if Lila made his heart race and his blood run hot. The fact that they had to live together, practically on top of each other, was something he hadn't taken into account in his hunt for hired help.

It was his responsibility to see to it Lila's reputation stayed pristine. She'd said she was twenty-seven but her innocent attitude made her seem years younger. From the moment he'd seen her with her back pressed against his office door, his emotions had ping-ponged like a tennis ball. At first, her vague answers to his questions and serious manner had given him doubt that she could do the job. But after careful observation, he decided she was perfect. Teddy and Rick's welfare was the important thing, and they couldn't like her more. Lila of the wild red hair and Amazon princess body was the only choice.

Now he wondered if he needed to rethink the entire setup. Was having the woman in his apartment truly in the boys' best interest, or had he hired Lila because of what she did for him?

Don't grope the nanny!

To his credit, he'd never cheated on his wife, though there'd been plenty of opportunities. In his old practice, he'd seen women all day long, and many had made it clear an affair would be welcome, but he'd deflected the offers and stuck to business. So why did Lila's comments about sharing the bathroom, testing out her mattress, and buying new lingerie tie his hormones in a knot? How come the mere thought of her made his body ache and his brain burn until she was all he could think of?

He knew the apartment was less than spacious, but with Lila living here, it had become downright claustrophobic. Their rooms weren't connected, yet he swore he could hear her breathing, could smell her sweet-yet-spicy scent as it somehow seeped through the wall dividing their bedrooms.

To put it simply, the woman was driving him crazy.

He huffed out a frustrated breath. Now that he'd identified the cause of his insomnia, there were only two things that would help him fall asleep—sex or alcohol. Since the first cure wasn't available, and he wasn't totally comfortable with the second, his best bet was to heat a cup of hot chocolate in the microwave and add a splash of brandy in hopes of easing his sexual tension.

Throwing off the covers, he fumbled for his robe, then stepped into the living room, where he spotted a pale glow coming from the kitchen. Carefully threading his way so as not to wake the boys, he rounded the door—and stopped in his tracks. As he'd suspected, the utility light over the sink was on, but not because he'd forgotten to turn it off.

Lila, shrouded in shadow and leaning forward on the counter, was gazing into the softly humming mi-

Eight

What the hell was the woman wearing?

A nightgown, you idiot, came the silent reply.

Releasing a pent-up breath, Paul cursed his stupidity. If he had half a brain, he would have better prepared himself for awkward moments such as this. The last thing Lila needed was to catch him ogling her from behind. He had to get to his room—fast—because he didn't want to be here when she turned around.

Before he could make his escape, Lila straightened and spun on her heel. Placing a hand in the center of her chest, she gazed at him through wide solemn eyes.

And damn if the gown did exactly what he feared it might. Cut low in front, it settled across her generous breasts and clung precariously to her distended nipples, then hugged her waist and curved over her gently rounded belly, where it showcased the hollow of her navel and the dark thatch of curls at the apex of her thighs.

"Paul?"

He swallowed, hoping to dredge up enough moisture to speak.

"I . . . um . . . didn't realize you were awake. I don't want to disturb you, so I'll just—"

"I couldn't sleep and thought to warm some milk." Lila raised her glass. "I'd be happy to heat some for you."

He gave a silent, mirthless chuckle. Never mind heating things up—what he needed was a bucket of ice water. "I had the same idea, but I was going to use cocoa mix and a shot of brandy to take care of it."

She took a sip of her drink and pursed her lips. "Will it taste better than this?"

Hoping to camouflage his arousal, Paul tied the belt on his robe and stepped into the kitchen. There was no need to be rude. They were both looking for the same thing—something to help them fall asleep. "I would hope so. I don't know many adults who enjoy plain warm milk."

She set her cup on the counter. "That's a relief. I'd heard that hot milk helped you relax, but it tastes like—"

"Liquid cardboard?" Averting his gaze from the front of her gown, he hoped his attempt at humor would convince his erection to take a hike. "Because even Rick and Teddy aren't crazy about warm milk unless there's chocolate in it."

"Chocolate?" Lila realized she'd voiced her question out loud and tugged at her ear. The description of chocolate was unlike anything grown on her planet. Better still, it sounded tasty and decadent, exactly the type of thing she'd hoped to find on Earth.

"Do you need help?"

"Nah," said Paul, who had walked to the pantry. "I don't make it from scratch, just a packaged mix. You want it with or without marshmallows?"

Lila pulled at her ear a second time, but the word marshmallow garnered no response. Another Rila-related glitch, she decided when she saw him waiting for her answer. "I'll have whatever you're having."

He returned to the counter with two packets, opened and emptied them into the cups, added water, and stirred. Then he placed them in the microwave. "This stuff's made from powdered milk, a poor substitute for the old-fashioned kind. You know, like your mom probably made, where you mix cocoa and sugar, stir in the milk and let it cook on the stove. We'll use a little of what you warmed to make it taste more homemade."

Throwing Paul a sidelong glance, Lila refused to move. He wore a dark-colored robe over pajama bottoms, and before he'd belted and tied the wrap she'd caught a glimpse of dark hair covering a well-muscled chest. She'd come to the kitchen in hopes of finding something to help her relax. Instead, she felt exhilarated and very much awake.

"Do you normally have trouble sleeping?" he asked, his gaze trained on the microwave.

"Not usually."

"Me neither. Most nights my head hits the pillow and I'm gone until sunrise, but tonight . . ."

The oven signaled and they reached for the door at the same moment. His touch, so fleeting she thought she'd dreamed it, sizzled up her arm. When she jerked away, Paul took out the cups, stirred again, and set one in front of her.

"Try it and let me know if it's warm enough."

One sip of the delicious liquid ignited her taste buds. "It's wonderful."

"How about a splash of brandy?"

Lila knew he was suggesting alcohol, and grew brave. There had been no adverse effects from the wine she'd had with dinner. How could this be any different? "Yes, please."

He opened a cupboard above the stove, revealing an array of bottles in different shapes and sizes. After choosing one, he poured a small amount into each cup, then raised his drink. They brought the warm liquid to their mouths at the same time. She sipped cautiously, inhaling the rich, intriguing scent, made more complex because of the brandy. The creamy concoction caused her tongue to tingle before it burned a path down her throat and lower. Deciding she enjoyed the sensation, she took a second, longer swallow.

Paul stared at her over the rim, his eyes hooded, his mouth set in a line. "Good?"

She nodded. "Very."

Before she could say more, his gaze lowered to her chest. Glancing down, she saw that her nipples had turned to turgid peaks just below the edge of her gown. A rush of heat she suspected had nothing to do with the warm beverage claimed her and she raised her head, meeting Paul's hungry stare.

The scent of chocolate and brandy surrounded her. The ticking of the kitchen clock, its insistent noise loud and rhythmic, beat in her brain. She drained the liquid in a few gulps when she realized the pounding was that of her own heart.

His face was pale in the dim light, his eyes dark and shining. "Lila, I—"

She raised her hand to his lips to stifle any negative response, and he caught her fingers. She took his cup with her free hand and set it on the counter.

He sighed, his breath a flutter of heat as it caressed her fingertips. "We can't do this, Lila. It's not right."

She curved her mouth upward, pleased to learn that he felt it too, this drugging desire to merge as one. "Do you love another?"

"I divorced my wife. There's been no one for a while."

"I'm not seeing anyone either."

"I'm your employer. I'd be taking advantage of you—"

"You can only take advantage if I let you. And if I let you, then you're not."

His expression turned thoughtful, and she took a step closer. Rising on tiptoe, Lila wrapped her arms around his neck and breathed in the scents of soap, musk, chocolate, and brandy, a feast for the senses. She closed her eyes and brilliant colors swam behind her eyelids. Leaning forward, she brushed her lips across his waiting mouth.

At first, Paul simply stood there, failing to cooperate. Determined, she tasted, nibbled, and teased, learning the contours of his mouth. Heartened when his muscles clenched against her pliant body, she took the kiss further, until it led where she wanted them to go.

He growled low in his throat.

Pelvis to pelvis, she felt his erection under the cotton of his robe, and moved her trembling fingers to unfasten his belt.

His hands cupped her bottom to raise her up and she pressed against his chest, clutching at him as if he were a buoy on a dark and dangerous sea. He released her and she slid slowly down his front. His chest hair grazed her breasts and rasped against her nipples, causing her entire body to ache.

Paul pulled away and the sudden separation ripped her back to the present. His eyes burned with a strange inner light, his jaw seemed set in stone.

"Lila, stop." His gaze softened. "We—I can't do this. You just started to work for me; we don't know each other. This isn't the way things are supposed to be." He stepped back. "I'm going to bed now—alone—and I suggest you do the same. We have to forget this happened."

Lila woke from a fitful sleep, her mind a muddle and her heart disappointed. She was still in a fog over what had transpired—or rather what hadn't—between her and Paul in the kitchen. If she was doing something wrong in this man-woman thing, she had no idea what it might be. He'd mentioned they'd be going to a bookstore today. Perhaps she could find a book on luring a man to her bed.

Bright light spilled from the edges of her window, telling her it was time to rise. Swinging her legs over the mattress, she stretched, then remembered that Paul had asked her to watch the boys in the morning so he could go running. This was the start of a new day. Never one to give up, she told herself his rejection was merely a minor setback in her mission. It had taken gentle persuasion, but eventually he'd responded to her kiss and she'd felt the proof of his desire.

As long as she had this job, she had the opportunity to continue in her quest. Time was her only enemy. Paul was single and he'd admitted there was no other woman in his life, so that wasn't the problem. If he'd refused her offer because of scruples, she would simply have to be more persistent.

After washing her face and brushing her hair, she dressed in another of her new shirts and a skirt, then peeked in Paul's room and found it empty. The sound of childish babble drew her to the twins' bedroom, where she greeted them with a smile.

"Good morning." Wrinkling her nose, she steeled herself to tackle their usual morning activity. When Teddy stood and reached out his arms, Lila took care of him first, then changed and dressed Rick. Finished, she set them down and squatted in order to be on their level.

Teddy stared soulfully, while Rick squirmed his delight. Unable to help herself, she opened her arms and they snuggled close. Gurgles of contentment sounded in her ears, tugged at her heart. Ignoring the flutter of emotion building in her chest, she retreated from their affectionate greeting. But oh, how she wanted to rock them in her arms and tell them she would be here always.

"Are you two ready for breakfast?"

"Dinna! Dinna!"

Rick bounced on his feet, his elation clear, and

Lila grinned at Teddy. "What about you? Can you say breakfast?"

Teddy gave her a toothy laugh and patted her face.

"Fine." She sighed, determined to get him to speak, or at least attempt a few nonsensical words. "Don't talk, but I'm wise to you. You're going to have to make an effort to speak or starve."

The twins followed her into the kitchen, where she immediately latched the gate, put them into their chairs, and did the straps.

"Dinna! Dinna! Dinna!" Rick shouted again, slapping the table in tandem with his brother.

Lila filled their cups with milk and brought them over, then put bread in the toaster. Next, she poured herself coffee, grateful Paul had kept his promise to make the brew when he woke. Carrying her drink to the refrigerator, she dosed it with milk and sugar before inspecting the contents of the box. Eggs, butter, and cheese helped her recall a recipe her mother had made using similar ingredients.

The toast popped up and she gave each boy a slice, then assembled the first dish. After cooking it thoroughly, she divided it in half, cut the food into bite-sized pieces, and carried their plates to the table.

"Careful, it's hot," she warned, giving them each a fork. When they dug in with gusto, she returned to the stove and began a second serving for herself. By the time the mixture was finished, Paul's footsteps thundered on the stairs. Bounding into the kitchen, he filled the room with his presence.

"Hey, you're up." Grinning appreciatively, he

sniffed the air. "It smells great in here, and I see the boys agree."

Lila smiled over the rim of her cup as she took in his utterly male persona. He wore shorts, a white T-shirt, and athletic shoes. The damp shirt clung to his broad chest, outlining every ridge and sinew of his well-toned body. Sweat beaded his forehead, dampened his sun-kissed hair, and trickled down his chiseled jaw. His shorts showed his long legs, dusted with hair and roped with muscle, to perfection.

"Just cheese, eggs, and toast," she answered, positive he was the reason she suddenly found it difficult to breathe.

"Sounds good. I love omelets." He walked to the door that led to the living room. "I'm going to take a shower. I'll be back in a few minutes."

Heat suffused her cheeks as she took in his taut buttocks and confident stride. If the men on her planet had even a quarter the virility of Paul Anderson, their women would be a contented lot.

After refreshing her coffee, she assembled his omelet, poured it into the pan, and added more bread to the toaster. Carrying her cup to the table, she checked on Rick and Teddy, who had devoured every morsel.

"I am impressed," she said in a tone of approval. "I don't know where you two put all that food, but I do know what happens when you finish the processing job."

She cleared their plates and checked the refrigerator for something else they might enjoy. Finding a lone apple, she cut it into pieces and set it in front of them. She had to buy food supplies or there would be nothing to cook for their next meal. She buttered Paul's toast and slid his breakfast onto a plate, just as he walked into the room.

Rick garbled to his father while Teddy gnawed on his apple. Lila concentrated on her omelet, pleased to find it palatable. Between bites, she observed Paul's interaction with his sons. It was obvious he loved them. He'd told her a bit about the reason for his divorce, but she couldn't imagine why any sane woman wouldn't want him as a father for her children.

The twins reminded her of herself and Rila, and happier times with their parents. Suddenly the urge to make this family her own overwhelmed her and she set down her fork. Visions of Bill Halverson and his explanation of the Eastern Shore Alien Watch filled her with trepidation. She was already under scrutiny because she lived here with Paul. It would take only one incorrect word or suspicious action for her to be found out and revealed to the community.

"Here's the paperwork I need filled out."

Lila realized Paul had spoken and raised her eyes. He set the papers in the center of the table. "The sooner you answer the questionnaire, the sooner I can get it to my accountant. He'll take care of the references and give me a call. Of course, I'm sure everything will check out fine," he added, almost as an afterthought.

Unable to take her eyes off the paper, Lila's brain shifted into worry mode. More than likely, a few of those questions would involve the identification items Eleanor Sweeney had described when she'd gone to the bank. Names and numbers that Lila hadn't a clue how to obtain. If there were some way to take Paul's mind off the document until she left town . . .

"So, are you up for going to the mainland and visiting a bookstore today?"

She dragged her gaze from the table and tried for a smile. "Yes, I think I'd like that."

"Great. What say I clean up these guys while you tackle the kitchen? We can pile in the car and make a day of it."

Paul took care of Teddy, while Lila helped Rick out of his high chair. He disappeared through the doorway with the twins at his heels. Glancing at the papers, she picked them up by her thumb and forefinger and walked to the trash can, where she proceeded to tear them into tiny bits and hide the pieces under the apple peelings. If things went according to her plan, she wouldn't see such papers again.

The next twenty-four hours were the apex of her first fertile period on Earth. She had to conceive immediately and leave before the subject of references came up again.

Bill Halverson gazed at his pitifully small supply of ESAW flyers. He'd spent the morning handing out the notices at the Episcopal church, Catholic church, and finally the Baptist church. There were a few more religious congregations in town, but the services overlapped and he couldn't be in two places at once. He had to save the rest of the flyers for the booth he was manning on Founders' Day, and hope that word of Wednesday night's meeting got to those folks via the flyers he'd posted around town or the ones hand-delivered by the Gibson boys.

Ellen was home making Sunday dinner, so he was free for the next couple of hours. He could spend the time sticking the extra flyers under the windshields of cars parked on the street or over by the public beach. So what if nonresidents heard of the meeting? If they were staying at one of the town's bed and breakfasts or motels on the highway, they were welcome to stop by or even join ESAW.

The association could use the membership fees, and the newsletter Eustace Carter published would help get the word out. It was important for the whole country to know it had been invaded by aliens. Besides, the spacemen might have set down in other places not as savvy as the eastern shore. Spreading the news was his patriotic duty.

Speaking of duty, tonight was his turn to host the monthly—now bumped up to weekly—meeting of the district commanders. He had a list of snacks he wanted to serve, and this was as good a time as any to take himself to S&B. Ellen had suggested cut-up fruit and a vegetable platter—rabbit food for a garden party, as far as he was concerned. None of that female cru-dee-tay crap for him, and no chips and dip either. He wanted canned wieners and spicy mustard, hot wings served with ranch dressing, and a few of those bite-sized pepperoni pizza thingama-jiggers. Hot chili with chopped raw onion and grated cheese might be nice, and beer on ice in that big galvanized tub he kept on the back porch would complete the menu.

He opened the door to the grocery and took in the Sunday crowd. The lunch counter was packed with regulars chowing down on the special of the morning: two eggs any way, three strips of bacon or sausage, home fries, and toast, with a cup of coffee or juice. Millie didn't want to compete with the restaurants in town that offered lunch and dinner, so she served breakfast from six to eleven; after that, it was ice cream only.

Bill chose a cart and started down the aisle, greeting neighbors as he shopped and giving a wink and a nod to the folks who wore one of his tinfoil helmets. A couple with three children—tourists, he guessed—blocked his way and he made to go around them, but his polite "Excuse me" was drowned out by one of the little boys.

The child, who might have been eight, pointed a finger. "Dad, look, there's another man wearing one of those funny hats, just like in that movie we saw—the one with the space guys. Remember?"

The kid's father inspected Bill's hat, then covered his mouth and hid his smile behind a cough. "Peter, how many times have we told you, it's not polite to point?"

"Don't bother me none," said Bill. "And you're right, son. This hat is exactly what you saw in that movie, and for the same reason too."

"For protection against aliens?" Peter's eyebrows shot to his hairline. "Wow, are there really aliens around here?"

"That's enough, son. I'm sure this gentleman—"

"Not yet, but they're out there," Bill said, interrupting the still-grinning father. "About a week ago, a few of my friends tracked 'em from the sky until they landed on the eastern shore. Here, have a flyer." He pulled a folded page from his back pocket. "If you and your family are in town on Wednesday, you're welcome to attend our meeting and hear the whole story."

I've done my duty and spread the word, thought Bill with a shrug of satisfaction. If he got a few more tourists to attend, one of them might be interested enough to start a satellite branch of ESAW. From there, the message would catch on. Eustace and the gang were aware only of their little corner of the world. Who knew how many more landings had taken place across the country or around the globe?

"Morning, Millie," Bill said when he wheeled his cart to the checkout.

"Bill." The store owner took in his silver hat before she rang up his order. "Seeing you in your aluminum finery reminds me, that extra case of foil arrived. You want me to include it with this sale?"

"Sure do," said Bill, helping Millie pack his goods. Then he took a look at the four bags of groceries. Added to a case of foil, he'd be hard-pressed to get everything home without losing bits and pieces along the way. "Think you could keep all this for me in the back freezer? I'm gonna have to walk to the house and get my car, then come pick it up. Do you mind?"

"Not at all," Millie answered. "By the way, a couple stopped in today and asked about the flyer in the window. Came from that Windcruiser in the lot across the street."

"Did you tell them the meeting wasn't just for locals?"

"I did. They seemed real interested too. Asked me a lot of questions."

"Questions?" Bill scratched his head, then righted his headgear. "About what?"

"Oh, you know," said Millie. "Who made up the flyers, what did I know of ESAW. Asked if I'd seen any strangers around town." Nose in the air, she put a hand on her hip. "As if I have nothing better to do than check on the tourists who come in and out of Preston's Ferry."

"Hmm." Bill tugged at his jaw. "I woulda bet my last nickel they were birders."

"They are," she said knowingly. "Had binoculars hanging around their necks and everything."

"How many of 'em were there?"

"A man and a woman. The woman talked with me about the meeting while the fellow did the shopping. After they paid for the order, they left for the Windcruiser. Right about that time, a car pulled next to their trailer, and another man climbed out and followed them inside."

"Maybe I'll stop by and see if they want to buy a couple of hats," said Bill, never one to miss a monetary opportunity.

As if on cue, Harley Fogg, the grocery's sizable jack-of-all-trades, came to the counter. "Want me to help you carry these home, Bill?"

Bill smiled at the genial man-child who often accompanied him on walks. "How about you just take the bags to the freezer? I'm gonna stroll across the street and visit those tourists, then go home and get my car. And thanks."

After leaving the store, Bill looked both ways before he stepped off the curb, and was lucky that he did. Maude Pelter literally flew past him down Main

Street as if her tail were on fire. His hat rattled with the rush of air trailing in her wake. He had to admit, for a woman who claimed she could barely climb a flight of stairs, she was a spry old bird.

Stepping lively, he crossed to the Windcruiser and took note of the muddied Jeep Wrangler parked beside it. The behemoth looked as forbidding and empty as it had yesterday, but now that he knew curious folks resided inside, he was determined. If they wanted information on ESAW, he was the man they needed to talk to.

Raising his hand, he knocked three times in rapid succession. When no one answered, he put his ear to the door and held his breath. The sound of muffled voices caught his attention, but like yesterday, he couldn't be sure if he was hearing live speech or a television or radio.

Straightening his spine, he knocked again, this time with a bit more vigor. The door swung open and he blinked.

"Yes?"

Bill smiled at the middle-aged man with the potbelly and walking shorts. "Name's Bill Halverson. I heard from Millie over at the Shop and Bag you had questions about the meeting we're having at the town hall Wednesday night."

The man raised a brow. "That's right."

"Well, I'm the fella with the answers."

His eyes hostile, the man's gaze rested on Bill's hat. "Oh, really? And why is that?"

"Because I'm the district commander of ESAW."

The surly birder gave a snort, and before Bill realized it, slammed the door in his face with such force he was practically blown backward off the steps. Not to be deterred, he righted his shoulders and knocked again, but he failed to receive a response.

Nine

Paul kept his speed steady as he crossed the Chesapeake Bay Bridge Tunnel toward home. Situated at the tip of the Delmarva Peninsula, the huge expanse, with its lead-in ramps, tollbooths, two tunnels, and series of bridges, covered over twenty miles and was touted by many to be a modern marvel. Since the demise of the ferry, it was Virginia's only link to its eastern shore, unless one traveled north on the inner coast, crossed into Maryland, and drove back south down Route 13.

The volume of cars and trucks would increase with the coming of summer, but right now it was almost traffic-free. Four pelicans flew over the waves in a precise line, while raucous seagulls filled the air, cutting through the crystalline blue sky and dive-bombing their next meal from the storm-gray waters of Chesapeake Bay. Fishing boats of every shape and size dotted the horizon, while in the distance tankers, barges, and destroyers returning to the naval base in Norfolk made the pass-over from the Atlantic.

Paul had always enjoyed this area of the country. During his teen years, his family had rented a house in the ocean front community of Sandbridge, just south of Virginia Beach. His father spent weekends there, and drove up to their home in Philadelphia early on Monday mornings to take care of his general practice. He'd always thought he and his family might do the same someday, even though he'd opted for plastic surgery, and opened his practice in Baltimore.

In the middle of the divorce and feeling down on himself, he'd begun to think Melanie was right—he was a selfish bastard who couldn't relate to his kids and worshiped prestige over family. Then he'd read the ad Preston's Ferry had placed in a medical journal and, determined to prove his wife wrong, applied for the job of general practitioner. The town couldn't pay a salary, but they could supply him with lodging and help with his insurance costs while he built a practice that would encompass many of the village-sized towns on the shore. Where better to make a life with his sons than a sleepy little burg in a sparsely populated area where he could set his own hours and still be close to civilization? His dad always said being a GP gave him more time for his family. Paul figured if it was good enough for Dr. Theodore Anderson, it was good enough for him.

Now through the second tunnel, he glanced in the rearview mirror. Teddy and Rick were still fast asleep, worn out from their trip to a Barnes and Noble, a visit to Kids "R" Us, lunch, and a stop at a mall. After buying two books on toilet training and skimming them in the bookstore's coffee shop, he realized he needed a different type of diaper and a special toddler-sized chair if he was going to succeed at this potty thing.

During lunch, he'd determined that Lila hadn't been to a real shopping center in a long while, so they'd spent a few hours walking Lynnhaven Mall, where they purchased the boys a summer wardrobe and new sneakers. It had been a productive day.

Slipping a sidelong glance at his front-seat passenger, he heaved a breath. With her hair a lustrous waterfall of red and gold, Lila slept as soundly as the twins, apparently as exhausted as they were. She'd lost herself in the bookstore, been in awe of the Kids "R" Us, and had a field day in the mall. Her enthusiasm had spread to Teddy and Rick, who had gurgled with glee at whatever they saw or whoever stopped to comment on the uniqueness of twins.

Lila had been so enamored of each experience, he'd spent more time watching her than his sons. Her curious nature and obvious delight at the most simple of situations made him think she'd been hidden away in an institution since birth or maybe was visiting from another planet.

Unable to help himself, Paul's gaze skimmed her legs. Her skirt was modest enough when she stood, but barely came to the middle of her thighs when she was folded into her seat. She breathed a sigh and he caught the movement of her breasts under her form-fitting yellow shirt. So much for trying to keep his thoughts on the straight and narrow. Lila had been appealing in a bedraggled kitten sort of way in her old clothes. In the new ones, which he admitted were nowhere near provocative, she was not only appealing but desirable.

Dragging his gaze back to the bridge, he drummed his fingers on the steering wheel. He had to be desperate if he was starting to think a plain khaki skirt and cotton T-shirt made a woman sexy. It had to be his subconscious recalling her in the peekaboo gown she'd worn last night, and projecting those impressions into his immediate thoughts.

Sweat beaded his brow at the memory of their kiss. Lila's body, so different from Melanie's model-thin figure, was a heady temptation that fit perfectly in his arms. Her chocolaty sweet lips had been as potent as the brandy he'd added to their drinks. He'd been hard from the moment he'd seen her backside through that darned swath of silk, and couldn't seem to erase the sight from his memory bank.

Still taken aback that she'd been the aggressor, he'd realized from the confused look in her eyes that his reasons for the rebuff made no sense to her. Hell, they'd hardly made sense to him, especially when compared to his body's reaction, but she'd taken the rejection in stride. She'd been cheerful and attentive all day, even when the sales clerks and a few strangers had referred to her as the boys' mother.

Don't go there, buddy, Paul warned himself. His kids didn't need a mother, and he didn't need a wife. His use of a nanny was temporary, more like a cast for a broken leg, until the twins started school full time. He stopped at the traffic light that led from the highway into town, and Lila opened her eyes.

Stretching, she smiled in his direction, then

checked the rear seat. "I'm guessing this ride will take the place of Rick and Teddy's afternoon nap."

"I'm afraid so," he agreed. "I was wondering, do you have any plans for dinner?"

She sat up straight and tugged at her skirt, removing her shapely thighs from view. "Not exactly. But I did do an inventory of the refrigerator and found it . . . lacking. I should go to the grocery store."

"It's still your day off, and I'm not sure how late the S&B is open on Sunday. There's probably some chili in the cupboard or—" Paul remembered she was a vegetarian. "We could go back to Croakers."

"Why don't I help get the boys settled, then walk to the market and buy the ingredients for supper? While I'm there, you can unload the car. If the store's closed, we still have time to make a decision."

"Okay, you talked me into it." Paul pulled into the driveway at the back of the house, and he and Lila extricated the twins and carried them to the second floor. After laying the boys in their cribs, Paul shut the bedroom door and he and Lila returned to the SUV, where he popped the rear hatch.

"I'll be home in a little while." She glanced at the overladen cargo area. "Unless you want help?"

"I can do it, but I might need a hand later putting it all away." Maybe unloading diapers and assembling the potty chair would give them something to do besides lusting after each other, at least on his part. "Or you could still take advantage of the little time left of your day off. If the S&B is closed—"

"We'll figure something out." She tossed him a wave and headed down the driveway with her hips swaying.

Paul rubbed the nape of his neck. He had to get a grip and see his nanny through more practical eyes. Maybe if he asked her to wear a uniform or stick to baggy slacks and an oversized shirt or—

Who was he kidding? He'd be attracted to Lila if she wore sackcloth, support hose, and bowling shoes. It was up to him to come to terms with his libido and make it clear there would be no hanky-panky. A strictly business relationship and the well-being of the twins—that was the rule.

All he had to do was obey his new mantra: *Don't grope the nanny.*

Lila walked into the Shop and Bag, still thinking about the mall. The shopping center might not have been as large as the sales establishments on her planet, but each store had been a tactile delight. People were free to touch and try on clothes at will, and there were thousands of styles available. Unlike her world, Earth encouraged its inhabitants to be individuals.

Even the bookstore had been unique. While she and her fellow citizens learned from efficient microdots of information that were linked to the chips in their brains, people on this planet continued to read books. She'd enjoyed story time with the boys, but had no idea the informative objects with their pleasantly pungent aroma of paper and ink were such a mainstay in this world. Now she understood why Paul had so many books displayed on the walls of his home. If only she had the time to read them all.

Right now she had a more pressing matter: to buy something she could eat that would also win the approval of Paul and the twins. Following the lead of the other shoppers, Lila pushed a cart as she inspected the aisles. Even though the market was small, she found many choices for carnivores. Sadly, the array of vegetables and fruit was slim.

Standing before a display of corn in the husk, or on the cob as explained by the sign, she tugged at her ear, hoping to dredge up more information about earthly edibles. Long seconds passed before she realized someone stood beside her. A young woman with brown hair and a cheerful face gazed at her while trying at the same time not to be noticed.

"Hello," Lila said, fingering her translator chip. She'd tugged on her ear so much today it ached.

"Hi. Sorry for staring, but I'm Rose, Rick and Teddy's last sitter. My mother said she'd met their new nanny yesterday in the bank, and I'm guessing you're her."

Lila's face broke into a grin. This was the very person she'd been hoping to befriend. "I'm Lila. It's a pleasure to meet you." She gave Rose's hand a shake. Where should she begin? "I'm trying to find something for dinner, and I'm still not sure what Paul or the boys enjoy eating."

Rose scanned Lila's empty cart. "I see. Well, what do you like?"

"Lots of things, but nothing Paul mentioned. I'm afraid meal preparation could get difficult, because I don't eat meat, and I have to find food that appeals to all of us."

"Then you're a vegetarian? That's great, because I am too," chirped Rose. "There are a few of us in town, so Millie makes sure she carries what we need."

Lila smiled her pleasure. She had found a human who understood her eating habits, and she was young and a woman, too. "And Teddy and Rick enjoyed the meals you prepared?"

"Not always," Rose admitted. "But they ate enough of what they liked to stay satisfied. I fed them mushrooms, tomatoes, green beans, corn, pasta, and fruit—but not too much because it does terrible things to their bowel movements. And cheese and eggs, because I'm ovo-lacto." Walking as she talked, Rose approached a display of tubers in various shapes and sizes. "And potatoes. I supposed you've heard the joke—it's the only thing a vegetarian eats that has eyes."

Lila was still thinking about the comment Rose made regarding the twins and fruit. Could their morning diapers get any more disgusting? But the saying about not eating anything with eyes was amusing.

Rose pointed to a basket of large, spongy-looking disks. "Try these tonight. You can make delicious Portobello mushroom sandwiches with sautéed onions and Paul will think he's eating a Philly cheese steak." She filled a plastic bag with mushrooms as she continued her commentary, unconcerned that Lila had yet to agree to her suggestion. "This should be enough—" She set the bag in the cart and added another of onions. "Just heat a little olive oil and butter in a fry pan, cut up one of the onions, add the sliced mushrooms, and cook until soft. Serve it over a roll with some cheese on top."

In awe of the one minute cooking lesson, Lila asked, "Do you ever prepare animal flesh?"

"If I have to, but I'll let you in on a secret. Millie carries a selection of frozen products that taste almost exactly like meat, especially the hot dogs and burgers. I serve it to my Phil, and as long as it's tasty and filling, he can't tell the difference. As with most men, food is like sex; give them enough of it and they'll do anything a woman asks. I just throw him a real steak once a week, and he's a happy guy."

"Do you think Paul would agree to have—would be all right with—" Rose's comparison of sex to food had Lila stumbling over her words. "I mean, do you think he could tell that it wasn't meat?"

"I'm not sure, since I've never been able to get him to our house for dinner," Rose babbled, oblivious to Lila's stutter. "I invited him, of course, but he always wanted to do for himself." She set her hands on her hips. "If he complains, just dump a couple shakes of hot sauce on his food. Men usually go for that too."

"Hot sauce?" Lila tugged at her ear, but no reference appeared. "Could you recommend a brand?"

"I'd be happy to, but first let's get you some salad fixings to go with the sandwiches." She continued to toss produce in Lila's cart as she spoke of various ways to prepare the vegetables, then stood back to appraise her handiwork. "That ought to keep the guys happy for a couple of nights. Now let's see about that hot sauce."

Rose led the way to the condiment aisle and advised Lila on several different brands. Then they headed for the frozen food section, where she introduced a dozen products made with a combination of ground vegetables and textured vegetable protein.

By the time the shopping lesson was over, Lila's brain was as overladen as her cart.

They wheeled their items to the checkout just as Millie was turning the CLOSED sign on the door.

"I thought you two would never finish." The grocer eyed Lila's order. "Looks like Rose did my job today. Helped you buy out the store."

"Paul said you would put it on his account."

"Not a problem." She began ringing up the sale. "How are you doing with those boys, by the way?"

"Fine." Lila watched the number of bags grow. How was she ever going to carry it all home?

"And Dr. P? How are you getting along with him?"

Distracted by the mounting pile of parcels, she blurted her frustration. "Not as well as I'd like."

"Dr. P's a sweetheart," said Rose. "He and I always got along great."

Millie tossed the young woman a look of impatience. "I don't think she means it quite that way, Rose," she said, as if reading Lila's mind.

Embarrassed anew, Lila felt heat flooding her chest and she gazed at her shoes. When she heard Millie's chuckle, she raised her head and caught Rose blushing too.

The younger woman smacked her forehead with the heel of her hand. "Oh, gosh, I am so sorry, always talking before I think." She gave a fluttery smile. "But I don't blame you. Paul is one heck of a hunk. Hang in there, he'll pay attention eventually."

"Do you think so?" Lila asked, unable to confess that if *eventually* didn't come soon, she wouldn't survive on Earth.

Millie finished bagging the order. "You're a presentable young woman, and the doc's a healthy single man. If there's chemistry between you, things will happen. But here's a word of advice."

As one, Rose and Lila leaned across the conveyor belt, each eager to hear the pronouncement. "The way to Paul Anderson's heart is through those boys. Get Teddy and Rick to love you, and he'll follow." Millie lowered her voice to a whisper. "Of course, a dab of vanilla behind your ears and a sexy nightgown couldn't hurt."

A dab of vanilla?

Rose giggled. Confused, Lila joined in the laughter. If this was the way earthwomen bonded, she had to do the same.

"You need help with those bags?" asked Millie.

Before Lila could answer, someone banged on the front door and Millie hissed her annoyance. Marching to the door, she opened it to Bill Halverson. "I'm closed."

"I see that, but I forgot the ranch dressing. Can't serve hot wings without ranch dressing."

"Oh, all right, but hurry it up. I got a life, you know." Millie shook her head as he sauntered down the aisle, then rang up Rose's order. "Looks like the Tinman from the Wizard of Oz with that danged hat on his noggin, don't he? Poor Ellen. I'll bet she wishes she had a husband with a real job."

Lila was still trying to figure a way to get her groceries home when Rose asked if she needed a ride.

"That would be very kind—"

"Don't bother. I'll see Lila home," said Bill, who now stood in the checkout lane with a cluster of grocery bags in front of him. He passed Millie money for his dressing. "I got to drive right by Dr. P's to get to my house, so it's no trouble."

Rose said good-bye and promised Lila she'd call to arrange a play date. Lila gathered her bags and followed Bill out the door and to his car.

Bill was all business as he loaded his rusty sedan. "Mind if I ask why you're not wearing your hat?"

"My—? Oh—my hat."

"Remember what I said about them aliens? I wasn't joking."

"I'm sorry. I was in a rush when I left the house—"

"I got a meeting tonight," continued Bill, steering the car into the empty street.

"A meeting? What kind of a meeting?" Lila asked, fearful of what he was going to say.

"Eustace and the other commanders are coming to my house to discuss the next phase of our plan. And we're going over the articles for our first big newsletter since the touchdown. Once folks get a gander at our stories, they'll be believers for sure. Eustace says his man at NASA gave him the names of a few other cities that had sightings. We're gonna out all of 'em."

Lila wished there were some way to warn the other travelers, but there was simply nothing she could do. As a stowaway, she hadn't been privy to any of the drop sites, so she had no way of telling if ESAW's information was correct.

Besides, she had her own personal mission to take care of.

Tonight.

* * *

Lila tugged at her ear for the third time in as many minutes to make sure she understood the definition of vanilla correctly. If she'd been thinking straight at the S&B, she would have purchased a bottle of the mystery potion before she'd checked out. She couldn't imagine why the odor of a baking ingredient would make a human think of sex, but Rose had implied the same: to men, sex and food were equivalent. According to the explanation from her ear chip, vanilla was a food source, so maybe the shopkeeper's statement was true.

Walking back into the kitchen, she took inventory of the cupboards, but found nothing of interest until she got to the one above and to the right of the stove. Recognizing baking ingredients, she carefully checked the contents. Flour, sugar, salt, and baking soda were dry and powdery, and therefore not close to vanilla. Oil was liquid, but not sweet. Chocolate chips were sweet, but not liquid. There were a few small bottles labeled food coloring, but one taste told her they weren't right either.

She dug further and found honey—sweet but too sticky—and a container of mint flavoring that reminded her of toothpaste. Stretching, she removed a bottle wedged in a corner. After opening the top, she inhaled a scent that reminded her of a fruit she enjoyed back home. The flavoring was used in foods on her planet, and had a sweet yet refreshing scent. Orange essence wasn't vanilla, but it might be an adequate substitute.

Propping her bottom against the counter, Lila tucked the container into her pocket and surveyed the kitchen. The sandwiches had been a success.

Paul had made a single comment about how much he enjoyed mushrooms of any kind, splashed a dash of hot sauce on his food, and ate heartily. The twins were so hungry, they'd eaten with their hands and clamored for more. When she'd served dishes of chocolate ice cream for dessert, Paul had led them in a round of applause.

After dinner, he'd continued to insist it was her day off, at least where Teddy and Rick were concerned, and taken over their bath and story time while she tidied the kitchen. Then she'd begun her search for the unfamiliar ingredient Millie said would be a plus in implementing the next phase in Paul's seduction. Lila only hoped orange essence would work as well.

Walking into the living room, her eyes were drawn to the pale light of a lamp standing behind the overstuffed chair near the bookshelves. The sight of Paul, holding a son in each arm with the tale of Winnie the Pooh propped on his chest, so unnerved her she took a step of retreat.

All three were asleep, their faces shadowed, their features relaxed. With a child's head on each shoulder, Paul looked the very image of a fatherly protector, yet seemed as young and boyish as his sons. His golden hair, just a few shades darker than the twins', tumbled over his forehead. His strong, square jaw appeared vulnerable, his chiseled lips gentle with the promise of his kiss.

Overwhelmed by a wave of guilt, Lila stifled a gasp. The emotions swelling her chest were both familiar and forbidden. She'd only been on Earth a few days, and the three men had already taken the place of her family in her heart. Her goal, her very existence, seemed in jeopardy whenever she allowed herself to see Paul and his sons in this light. Until she left here, she was in danger, and not only from Bill Halverson and the members of ESAW.

As if reading her thoughts, Paul opened his eyes, sat up straight, and clasped the twins to his chest. "Sorry. Guess we fell asleep."

She bent and gathered Teddy in her arms, dismayed at the fuzzy warmth settling in her chest when the boy nestled into the hollow of her neck. "How about if we get these young men to bed?"

"Good idea," whispered Paul, standing.

Together they walked into the twins' bedroom and lay the boys down. Teddy puckered his mouth and made a little sucking noise, and Lila gripped the crib rails, mesmerized by the innocent baby motion. She imagined putting her own son to bed, watching over him while he slept, nurturing his mind, and encouraging his accomplishments. And if she had twins . . .

Teddy and Rick closely resembled each other, but their personalities were vastly different. She and Rila had been the same. Like Rick, Rila had been the first to talk, the first to charm and impress their parents. Teddy seemed more like her, a quiet child, content to let the older sibling lead the way and take the bows.

Before she realized it, Paul was at her side. "I worry about them both, you know. But Teddy more than Rick."

"Oh? And why is that?"

"He's a quiet little guy, who likes to keep to himself unless his brother sways him. He has yet to say a word, while Rick babbles like a parrot. I've had them tested and been assured they're both normal, even above average in intelligence using the criteria available. It's just that Teddy sometimes seems to be in his own world."

He's making plans, thought Lila. *Plans to fly free from under his brother's shadow when the time is right.*

"If the tests are normal, all you can do is give him time to develop. He'll come into his own when he knows it's right."

"You think so?" Paul reached down and brushed a curl from the boy's forehead.

"I know so."

Straightening, he focused on her face. "For a woman who claims she doesn't have any younger kids in her family, you sound pretty sure of yourself."

"I'm a twin, remember? I know how it feels to be overshadowed by a sibling."

Understanding dawned in Paul's eyes. "Then you're the perfect person to help Teddy come out of his shell and gain confidence in himself. I just wish . . ." He ran a hand through his hair, ruffling the golden locks. "Aw, never mind. It doesn't matter."

Lila sensed that it did matter, or he wouldn't have brought it up. "What do you wish?"

Paul grasped her by the elbow and guided her into the living room. "I'd like to hear him say Da-da, like Rick does. And if not that, then one coherent word so I know he can talk. It would be a load off my mind."

"I have the feeling he'll talk, when he has something to say," she said, hoping to allay his fears. "It's very easy to take a back seat when your twin is dominant and demands center stage."

Lila thought of all the years she'd emulated her sister, and allowed Rila to make their decisions. Now that she'd removed herself from the situation, she realized her sister hadn't had a thing to do with her problems. When the call went out for volunteers, Lila had signed up in secret, positive she would be chosen. They'd both done their best, but Rila was the one they'd wanted. That final humiliation had prompted her to take action in the only way she knew how.

Now that Lila was on her own, she had no one to blame but herself if she failed.

"Is that how it was with you and your sister?"

"Sort of. And now that I'm farther away from her and thinking more clearly, I can see that it was my own fault I followed instead of leading, especially after I became an adult. I now realize I can be or do whatever I want."

"And you decided to become a nanny because . . . ?"

Lila could tell by the inflection in his voice that he didn't think too highly of her aspirations. "I decided I had options. If things don't work out here, there's a big world I've yet to explore, full of opportunities waiting for me."

His eyes narrowed, and she knew instantly he didn't approve of her answer. Well, fine. If she planted the seed that her leaving was a possibility, it wouldn't be such a shock when she did. "Right now, taking care of Teddy and Rick is my only concern."

She concentrated on his mouth, a potent reminder of her reason for being here. "Do you need help with the things you bought today?"

Paul seemed to drink in her gaze. She inched closer and he scanned the room, focusing on the television. "It's all taken care of. I'm going to watch a little TV, then get ready for bed."

She fingered the bottle hidden in her pocket. "I'm taking a shower. After that I'd like to join you."

Paul's jaw clenched as he swallowed. His eyes narrowed as he licked at his lips. Was he remembering their last kiss and recalling the heat they'd found in each other's embrace? Or was he trying to forget?

"Uh, sure. Fine. But I doubt I'll be up long. To-morrow is Monday, a busy day at the office."

Smiling, Lila took a step back. "In that case, I don't want to waste any more of what's left of my time off," she murmured, using his words to get her point across. "I'll see you in a few minutes."

Ten

Paul's gaze followed Lila as she turned the corner into the rear hall. What the hell had just happened? He had a hard on stiff enough to pound nails, and he'd swear the temperature in the room had just shot up twenty degrees, all because she'd sent a clear invitation with those luscious lips and sultry green eyes.

One second they'd been discussing Teddy's problems as a twin and talking about Lila's past experiences, the next . . .

He heard the shower run and took a deep breath. His first thought was to skulk to his bedroom and lock the door, but it would be cowardly, not to mention impolite, to call it a night after Lila told him she was coming back, even though he had a feeling he was going to be in a lot more trouble if he stayed. Her dreamy-eyed stare and seductive smile had held a promise no red-blooded man in his right mind would want her to break. After his reaction to their kiss, she had to know what those hot and heavy glances were doing to his libido.

Then again, maybe she wasn't aware of the effect she had on him. Could it be he was taking her subtle come-ons the wrong way? If that was the case, he was going to look like a grade-A fool when he told her he wasn't interested. Even worse, he might upset her so much she'd walk away from her job.

Frustrated, he picked up the remote from the top of the television, sat on the sofa, and started to channel-surf. He needed a rousing action adventure movie or maybe a sci-fi film—anything to drown his thoughts of sex and help him speak with Lila in a calm and rational manner.

Unfortunately, it was a minute before the hour, which meant every station was in commercial mode. And damn if they all weren't running a spot for shampoo or body wash, or some kind of need-to-be-nude skin cream. Not only was every woman cavorting in the shower—one even looked as if she were having an orgasm while she washed her hair!

He closed his eyes and Lila came into view, but instead of wearing her demure T-shirt and skirt, she was naked under a spray of streaming water. Thanks to the sheer gown he'd seen her in the other night, he could imagine each droplet as it inched down her skin, rolled over her breasts, and clung to her distended nipples. The trail of undulating water led lower, to the indentation of her navel, over her stomach, and down to the mahogany brush of her sex. . . .

Ticked at his lack of self-control, Paul slammed

the door on the vision. He was an idiot to be thinking about his housekeeper like this. If he didn't learn to control his hormones, his sons were going to have another upheaval in their lives. He couldn't lose Lila now, not when the little guys were finally getting comfortable with her; not when she seemed to care so much and was making a real effort at fitting in.

If she left them, he'd be high and dry again, forced to run another series of ads and wait for someone to answer, then be disappointed when weeks passed and no one did. His only recourse would be to attend a meeting of the town council and demand their help. Next thing he knew, his boys would be crawling around Mayor Hickey's office, or learning to play gin rummy at the fire hall, or getting stuck with a geriatric citizen who had no idea how to care for two active toddlers.

Paul cursed as a second, more fantastic thought came to mind. What if he had been reading her signals correctly?

What if having sex with Lila was the only way to get her to stay?

Lila slipped her nightgown over her head, then dabbed a drop of orange essence behind each ear and another in the center of her chest. After brushing her hair until it fell in a sweeping curtain of copper, she stood back and surveyed her reflection in the bathroom mirror.

She still had no idea why she hadn't been chosen for this mission. She was tall, well proportioned, and soundly built, as were all the travelers. Her breasts were large, her hips generous, and her legs long and strong. She had perfect teeth, excellent hearing, and a sturdy heart. Her clear green eyes spoke of intelligence, wit, and a positive outlook. The superior physical and mental attributes were necessary, as the Elders had wanted only the most fit to mother the children who would save their race.

Tonight was the apex of her first fertile period. Her body's physiology was close to that of an earthwoman in every respect except reproduction. Females on her planet were fertile in blocks of time, rather than once an Earth month. Her time frame for conception, as it was with all the travelers, was a forty-eight-hour period now, with two more to come in the next twenty-eight days. Failure this evening wouldn't ruin her plans, but it would be cause for concern.

When she'd volunteered for this quest, the Elders had warned of two possible dangers. This country and several others on Earth were actively seeking contact with beings from other planets, so the chance of detection and capture was high. And human males were touted throughout the galaxy as an aggressive lot. Both problems made for a volatile situation.

The females of her world discussed sex—what it was like, how it would make them feel, the impact it would have on their lives—on a daily basis. Most had never experienced intercourse or even mild flirtation with a male, and were hoping this mission would improve the situation for future generations, as well as ensure the propagation of their species.

All of the travelers were honored to be chosen, but according to Rila several of the final nine found the concept of masculine aggression a perfect fantasy. The idea that a targeted male would view his intended as so desirable he could think of nothing else while in her presence was a bonus their planet's women imagined would only intensify the pleasure.

Lila understood that Paul had been destined for her sister, which might account for some disinterest on his part, but she'd been accepted for the program because she had the correct features and personality to attract an earthman. Inexperience aside, she should have been able to entice him by now. Her failure was exasperating as well as annoying. Did she have an unsuitable personality trait or physical flaw that repulsed him?

Why did Paul continue to reject her?

She'd felt the proof of his potency when they'd kissed, so she knew he had to be mildly interested. Perhaps it was time she became more encouraging— or more demanding. If he requested she give up her position, she would be forced to find another reason to be near him, but from the way Paul had described his search for a nanny she doubted that would happen.

His children needed a caretaker. She had to make him believe he needed her as well.

After a final inspection in the mirror, Lila walked to the entryway of the living room. From there, she saw the back of Paul's head as he sat on the sofa, as well as the program on the television. Portrayed on the screen was a great hulking insectlike creature with gaping jaws and a drooling mouth, creeping with menace toward a terrified woman. The screen flashed to a commercial, but not before she read the name of the movie: *Alien.*

She recoiled at the distasteful title. Ever since meeting Bill Halverson, the word depicted a monster, a reprehensible being who wanted nothing more than to destroy the human race. No wonder other intergalactic life-forms had decided against making full contact with the people of Earth. If they thought all species from another world were so heinous, earthmen would never accept them as allies.

Which was her second reason for leaving here once she conceived. Paul kept rejecting her as a human. What would he do if he found out she was from a different planet? How would he treat a child who was only half human?

She released a breath and he stiffened on the sofa. Did she offend him so much that he couldn't bear looking at her?

Refusing to give the idea credence, she tiptoed into the room.

Paul heard Lila's sigh, a gentle expulsion of air that sent a silent message he hoped he was interpreting properly. He could tell she was relieved to find him waiting; and she was going to try to seduce him. Again.

Her footsteps whispered on the carpet as she came into the room, walked around the sofa, and stood to the side of the television. The glowing screen outlined her form, shading the peaks and valleys of her voluptuous body, reminding him once more of the bounty that might be his for the taking.

Fully aroused, he hit the off button on the remote and stood. Without a word, he strode into his bedroom, returned with his bathrobe, and thrust it into Lila's hands.

"Here, put this on."

She clutched the garment to her chest. "Why?"

Training his eyes on the floor, he began to pace. If she quit because of what he was about to say, he was going to kick himself around the block and back again.

"Because I'm not going to be able to concentrate with you standing there half dressed."

"I am clothed to my ankles. I believe that makes me *fully* dressed."

Paul fisted his hands and gazed at the ceiling. "Put the robe on, Lila, or I'm going to leave the room."

"I'll wear it, but only if you tell me why."

Meeting her expression of challenge, he narrowed his gaze. Could she really be so naïve, so clueless? "Don't play games. You know why."

"Lower your voice or you'll wake the boys," she hissed, her voice tinged with indignation.

"Fine," he muttered back. "Now put on the robe."

She stuffed her arms through the sleeves and shrugged the garment over her shoulders. Glaring, she shoved the sleeves up to her elbows. The robe gaped open down the front, but at least he couldn't see straight through to her skin.

He sighed, determined not to let her rattle him.

When the sleeves slipped down her arms and hung over her wrists, she gave them another angry push. "Are you going to act like an adult, or shall I prepare to stand here and be bullied?"

"Bullied? Is that what you think I'm doing?"

She raised her chin. "What else can I think? I came in here planning to have a pleasant evening and you immediately started to give orders."

"I'm your boss, remember?" Paul winced at his threatening tone. He'd done his best to be friendly and charming all day, and now, when he made one tiny suggestion, she decided to be assertive. Talk about being sensitive.

"Might I remind you this is my day off, which I willingly gave up to spend with you and the twins? I should think I'd get to wear what I want for the last few hours."

He ran a hand through his hair. She made a good point. They had to live together on a daily basis. If he couldn't handle the way she dressed, it was his problem. Worse, if he kept being argumentative she could be gone by morning. Then where would he be?

He took a place on the couch and pointed to the opposite end, praying she would obey and put him out of his misery. "Okay, fine, wear a straitjacket if you want. But stay on your side of the sofa."

Instead, the perverse woman plopped down at his side, just close enough for him to detect the elusive aroma of something sweet, citrusy, and supremely alluring. "This is a big couch," he grumbled. "Don't you want more room?"

"I like it here. This cushion is quite comfortable."

Groaning silently when the robe parted to reveal her shapely thighs, Paul inched over until he was glued to the sofa arm. Damn if he couldn't feel the warmth of her skin enveloping him with the heady scent of desire. He cleared his throat. "Was there anything in particular you wanted to discuss?"

Lila leaned back and inhaled. Mesmerized, he watched her amazing breasts rise up through the lapels of the robe. His body began to throb and he crouched over, resting his elbows on his knees.

"My work performance, for one. How do you think it's going? Have I been doing a good job?"

He stared at his hands. "It's a little soon to tell, but I—the boys—Rick and Teddy seem to like you. And tonight's dinner was passable—"

At her silence, he gave a sidelong glance, easily reading her arched brow and teasing smile. "Okay." He forced out a grin. "Breakfast and supper were delicious. I never knew an omelet or mushrooms could taste so good. And I—I mean we—the boys and I—really enjoyed the ice cream. Even if you didn't make it, you did think to buy it."

Why was he having such a difficult time arranging simple words into cohesive sentences? *And what in the hell was that smell?* Giving his brain a stiff mental shake, he added, "How about us? Think you enjoy the work well enough to stay?"

She rearranged herself on the sofa, but didn't speak. Paul turned to find her waiting, as if she weren't going to answer until they made eye contact.

"I don't have a problem with the chores, and the boys are a delight. There's just one more thing that will make my position here complete."

Paul stared at her mouth. Her lips turned up at the corners and he began to sweat. The expectation was killing him. He clenched his hands to keep from touching her. If he didn't kiss her soon, he was going to explode.

Steeling himself for her answer, he gritted his teeth. "Care to clue me in on what that might be?"

Lila rose up on her knees and swayed toward him. Off balance, she fell forward and conformed to his chest like a blanket. She captured his jaw in her hands and bent near, brushing her mouth against his in a blatant caress.

The kiss intensified until Paul thought he'd swallowed a stick of dynamite and the wick was burning down inch by agonizing inch. He clasped her rib cage and let his hands drift upward until he cupped her breasts and thumbed her hardened nipples through the wispy material.

Moaning, she shrugged off the robe. He gazed into her eyes and she gave him a full-blown smile. "This is what I want."

Nestling her hips into his, she leaned down to kiss him again, and he raised a shaking hand. "Lila, stop and think a second. Are you sure you know what you're doing?"

Biting at her lower lip, she frowned. "Definitely." His erection jerked to attention and she snuggled closer. "A part of you knows too."

Betrayed by his body, Paul struggled to sit up straight. How could he tell her she was wrong, when she felt so good plastered to him like a full-body Band-Aid? Nuzzling the soft skin behind her ear, he catalogued the elusive aroma of oranges. Damn if the woman didn't smell good enough to eat.

He sighed. "Unfortunately, it's the part a man can't always trust. I don't want this to be a decision

made by our hormones. Having sex is serious business. I'm not into one-night stands or casual affairs.
I believe there has to be a modicum of respect and
genuine caring between partners before they take
the next step."

Again she bit her lip, and he swore he could feel
her teeth sinking into his own skin.

"You don't respect me?"

"Of course I do."

"Then you don't care about me?"

"I care, probably a little too much at the moment."

She wrinkled her nose and a worry line formed between her eyebrows. "You're not making sense. You
just listed the two things you thought necessary for
us to have sex, then agreed we have them. Now
you're saying we can't perform the act." Huffing out
a breath, she deepened the frown. "Please explain
further."

Before he could come up with an answer, she began to unbutton his shirt. "It's more than that," he
muttered, stilling her busy fingers. "It's—it's—"

"You're not attracted to me?"

"Oh, sweetheart, I'm attracted, all right." Frustrated in both mind and body, he realized she was
correct about him not making things clear. "It's the
boys. I don't want them to be hurt if what we—what
you want to do—doesn't work out."

"Why won't it work out?"

Paul focused on her eyes, those beautiful green
pools that reminded him of a sea of spring grass. "I
have no intention of ever getting married again,
Lila. That means I can't commit to anyone. I don't
even intend for your position to last past when the

twins start school full-time. Then I plan to bring in someone to cook and clean a few days a week."

Inching up his chest, she grazed her teeth over his chin. "Fine, but until then I see no reason for us not to take pleasure in each other."

She ran her hand to his ear, cradling the back of his head, and he swore a switch flipped on in his mind, turning his already engorged penis into a missile with her as the programmed target. The flare-up so shocked him, he jolted upright and they rolled off the sofa and onto the floor in a tangle of limbs.

Paul scrambled to his feet while Lila did the same. He was rooted to the spot, and his chest rose and fell with the force of a sexual need so intense it boggled him. What the hell had happened to his self-control? His ability to say no and walk away?

As if reading his confusion, Lila smiled and took a step closer. Reaching out, she encircled his neck with her arms and fused her mouth to his. He groaned and she levered herself against him, hoisting herself up and anchoring her legs around his waist as if she wanted to crawl inside of him.

Powerless to resist, he grabbed her bottom and walked them to his bedroom. Heaven help him, he had no other choice.

The joy threatening to break free inside of Lila was so intense she thought she might explode. Paul clutched at her buttocks and sucked her tongue into his mouth, joining them from chest to belly to hips as he brought them into his room. Kneeling on the bed, he lowered her to the mattress and gazed at her through hooded eyes.

His focus never left her as he finished unbuttoning his shirt, slipped it off, and tossed it over his shoulder. Then he unzipped his pants and stepped from the rest of his clothing.

The beauty of his form, an obelisk of polished marble, held her enthralled. Before she reached out to touch him, she drew her eyes from his engorged shaft and met his steely gaze. Now she understood why Rose had equated sex with food. Paul was staring as if he wanted to devour her in a few frantic bites. Growing brave, she inched her gown up and over her calves, knees, thighs, and chest, until she lay bare before him covered only in the moonlight slanting across his bed.

"You are incredible," he said, his voice a ragged moan.

"So are you," she answered, her words a reverent whisper. His penis, long and thick and potent, rose from a nest of dark curls, and she automatically spread her legs and raised her arms in invitation.

Dropping to his hands and knees, he caged her between his arms and settled into her thighs. "I can't remember the last time I wanted a woman this much."

"Then take me." She grabbed his shoulders and drew him near. "Make me a part of you."

Their lips joined as their tongues danced in a rhythm as ageless at the universe. Lila ran her hands across his back, delighting in the play of corded muscle and sinew trembling under her palms. Sliding her fingers to his taut buttocks, she pressed him down until she felt his arousal probe the center of her core.

Without warning, Paul reared back. "I need a condom."

She clutched his hips and pulled him into her. "You don't need birth control."

"Not just for birth control—"

"I swear to you I'm healthy."

"Lila—"

She stopped his protest with a demanding kiss. Clasping his penis in her hand, she cupped his sex, urging him inside. Stroking herself with the tip of his shaft, she moaned encouragement and he slid into her, breaking the barrier of her innocence in one powerful thrust.

She stifled her cry, but it was too late. Time stood still as Paul stiffened and raised himself up to gaze into her face. Clenching his jaw, he bit out the words.

"Why didn't you tell me?"

Fluttering her fingers over his hardened mouth, Lila ignored the searing pain. "Because it didn't matter. All I could think of was how much I wanted you."

He hung his head and she moved beneath him, searching for something she couldn't name, something . . . more. "I've waited a lifetime for you, Paul. Please don't stop now."

When she lifted her hips, he blew out a strangled breath. Easing back inside of her, he rocked slowly as he ran his lips from her jaw to her collarbone to her breast. Clasping the mound in his palm, he took the nipple into his mouth and sucked in tandem with the rhythm of his pumping hips.

Finally, the movement made sense, and Lila followed his lead. Rising and falling with the motion, she whimpered as a tingle built deep inside, overriding the burning ache. The sensation rose to a crescendo of need, a tremor of wanting that drove her faster, harder, higher in his arms, as if she could fly back to her world on the wings of this one man.

Paul drove into her, determined to make this experience one Lila would always remember. He'd never been any woman's first, and the knowledge gave him a sense of fulfillment he'd only dreamed of achieving. Lost in desire, he ignored the insistent warning his overtaxed brain was sending. Sex with Lila was more powerful than his imagination, more potent than what he'd ever thought it could be.

His only goal was to please her, to bring her to completion and start pleasing her all over again as a thank-you for giving him the incredible gift of herself.

She wrapped her legs around his waist, and he shifted his weight to penetrate her more deeply. Her frantic whimpers turned to ragged moans, then muffled screams as she clamped her teeth onto his shoulder and rode the crest of his frenzied thrusts.

Colors blazed behind his eyelids, taking him higher than he'd ever gone before.

Lila spasmed beneath him and Paul stretched the moment, riding her orgasm like a wave crashing to shore. When she trembled in his arms, he caught her up and kissed her, drinking in her fading cries.

Breathing heavily, she opened her eyes, her face a mix of joy and amazement. "I never—that was—"

She shook her head and he grinned. He felt like a runner who'd just won his first hundred-yard dash, and he'd yet to cross the finish line. He didn't want

Eleven

$\mathcal{P}$aul rolled over and groped his nightstand, sending the ringing telephone crashing to the floor. Stumbling out of bed, he located the receiver and groaned when he found the line dead. Puzzled, he sat on the edge of the mattress. It was too early for his mother or a telemarketer to call, and the only other person who bothered him at this hour was old Maude Pelter, usually with a litany of complaints.

Dragging both hands through his hair, he waited for whoever it was to try again. When that didn't happen, he stood and retrieved his jeans from the pile of clothes at his feet. As he tugged them on, he frowned. Since when did he toss clothes on the—

Squinting through the gray morning light, he focused on Lila, fast asleep with her hand fisted under her chin and her face snuggled into the pillow. The sight of her, looking so perfect in his bed, sent a shock wave through his system. Gut-wrenching de-

sire and the memory of several mind-blowing or-
gasms rushed over him, nudging his morning erection to full mast.

He hadn't been driven to such intense passion
since his honeymoon, and even then—

He groaned again. What the hell had they—he—
done?

He heard a voice downstairs call his name, then
frantic pounding and intermittent buzzing. There
was someone at the front door, and from the racket
it had to be an emergency. Unconcerned with his appearance, he slid naked feet into a pair of loafers and
shrugged into a clean T-shirt.

"What's happening?"

Drawn to Lila's sleep-sexy voice, Paul turned.
"Someone's at my office door. I'm going to check it
out."

As if on autopilot, he bent to kiss her, then
stopped short. A show of affection would only com-
plicate things; not a bright idea when he was sure
last night had been a stupid move on his part. He
and the nanny had to talk. Unfortunately, now
wasn't the time.

He headed through the hall, down the stairs, and
into the waiting room, where he flung open the door.

"Thank God you're awake." Millie Entwhistle
stood on the porch gulping air, her fisted hand
poised to knock. "I called but got disconnected, so I
thought I'd do better in person. It's Harley. He was
opening cartons and damn near sliced off his thumb.
He's bleeding like a stuck pig."

The woman's last sentence cleared his mental fog.
Paul shouted over his shoulder while he raced to the

makeshift lab. "Get back to the store and have him sit with his hand up and bent at the elbow. Wrap the wound in clean towels, apply pressure, find a few more towels, and wait for me. I'll be there in a minute."

After unlocking a cabinet, he grabbed his bag, grateful he'd taken a page from his father's book of family medicine. He even had his dad's battered black medical bag to show for it. He didn't have to check inside to know it held sutures, tape, gloves, bandages, stethoscope, blood pressure cuff, local anesthetic, syringes prepped for a variety of drugs, and whatever else was practical. Years ago, his father had advised him it would come in handy and, as usual, the man had been right.

He jogged through the office, down the front porch stairs, and into the rising dawn in time to see Millie, about three blocks ahead of him, disappear into the alley next to the grocery. It was too early for the S&B to receive customers, so she had to be going to the loading entrance, which made sense if Harley had been opening boxes to replenish the inventory.

Imagining the worst, he charged down the alley, pushed in the first door, and found himself in a warehouse area. Peering through stacked cartons, he heard Millie's call.

"Doc, is that you?"

"Where are you?"

"Come straight back and turn right at the cleaning supplies. And hurry."

Doing as ordered, Paul rounded the corner. Harley, who stood six-foot-four, weighed in at about 350 pounds, and normally wore an affable grin, was so pale he resembled an oversized Pillsbury Dough Boy viewing a bake-off disaster. As instructed, he sat on a folding chair with his left arm bent and wrapped in a blood-soaked towel.

Paul knelt next to the patient, popped the latch on the bag, and snapped on sterile gloves. "Hello, Harley, I'm Dr. P. We've met a time or two, remember?"

"Here's more towels," said Millie. "Anything else?"

He unwrapped a large absorbent pad and laid it on his knee, talking as he worked. "Get me a chair. And I'll need better light." He set the clean towels on top of a cardboard box, intent on using the area as a surgical tray. "Call Chief Gibson and tell him to stand by. If this is bad, he'll have to transport Harley to Shore Memorial."

"It hurts, Dr. P," grunted Harley.

Paul tried to remember all he'd been told of Harley's past. He was a gentle giant with the mind of a child and no family to speak of. He'd lived in town his entire life, doing odd jobs to help support his widowed mother, but Millie had taken him on full-time after he buried the woman three years earlier.

"I know, and I'm going to take care of it. How did it happen?"

"I was cutting boxes and being real careful, just like Millie told me I should," said Harley, "but the knife slipped." He moaned. "I don't wanna lose my thumb, Doc."

"I'm here to make sure that won't happen." Paul carefully laid the patient's left hand on his knee. "Just relax, okay?"

"Yes, sir."

Millie carried in another folding chair and what looked to be a desk lamp. "This is from my office, but I can get a flashlight if it isn't bright enough." She found a plug, turned on the lamp, and held it above and behind Paul's head.

Paul eased into the chair. "Keep it steady," he said in an even tone. When Millie didn't answer, he gave her a sidelong glance, then shifted his gaze to his patient, noting each face was set in a grimace.

"Don't either of you dare faint on me."

"No, sir," gulped Harley, but Millie remained quiet.

Paul shrugged. He'd worry about the shopkeeper if she hit the ground. Right now, he had an injury to assess. He peeled away the toweling and swiped the base of Harley's thumb with sterile gauze. The inch-long cut appeared deep, but it wasn't as bad as he'd first thought. The tendons and nerves were intact, and the bleeding had slowed to a trickle, though it still needed stitches.

Digging through the bag, he found a Betadine swab and cleaned the wound, then reached for a syringe of lidocaine. "This is going to sting, so hang on. Millie, you and Harley might want to maintain eye contact and talk about the weather while I work."

He injected the numbing agent, and felt Harley flinch. Taking out a suture kit, Paul willed his hands to keep steady as he concentrated on his task.

"Thought we might get rain this morning. Does it look that way to you, Millie?" asked Harley in a little-boy voice.

"No," said Millie, whispering the word.

"Maybe this afternoon?"

"Nu-uh."

At Harley's heroic effort, Paul hid a smile. There weren't many people who could watch themselves get sewn up like a button and keep their composure. Unfortunately, his assistant didn't sound nearly as together as his patient.

"Hang tight, both of you. I'll be done in a few minutes."

Eight stitches later, the trio breathed a collective sigh of relief. "Harley, do you remember the date of your last tetanus shot?"

"Tet'nus what?"

"Ooo-kay. I want you to come to my office after I'm through here." He smiled at Millie. "You can call Chief Gibson and tell him we won't be needing his squad car."

The woman wiped a hand over her sweat-beaded brow. "Is his thumb gonna be okay?"

"I think so." He wrapped Harley's wound with gauze and taped over it. "Think you could find a disposal for the trash while I finish?"

Paul added a set of tongue depressors to the bandage, taped them to the thumb, and wrapped the hand until it resembled a mitten. After packing his bag, he stood, as did Harley. Millie rushed in carrying a drawstring garbage bag, and he deposited the remnants of the mini-surgery.

At the sight of the bloody towels, Harley swayed on his feet. Paul caught him and helped him back in the chair. "Take it easy while I talk to your boss."

He and the grocer walked to the door that led into the S&B. "Does Harley have workman's comp or health insurance?"

Millie set her hands on her hips. "I pay him off the books, so I doubt he'll be getting anything more than his monthly Social Security check from the government."

"Then it's a good thing he didn't need a trip to the ER. Does he live alone?"

"In a double-wide on a lot at the edge of town. Why?"

"Because he won't be able to do much work for at least a week, and I'm not sure he can handle the responsibility of caring for his injury." Paul glanced at Harley, who was staring openmouthed at his bandaged hand. "I'll bring him to the office for a tetanus shot, then he needs to stay with someone who can keep an eye on him."

Millie sighed. "I'd let him stay at my house, but I don't have a free bed right now, what with my niece, her husband, and three kids in town for the festival. How about if he hangs out here and sleeps on a cot in the storeroom until you say it's okay for him to go home?"

"That'll do, but remember, he's not to use the hand. In the meantime, make up that cot. I want him in bed for the rest of the day."

Lila stretched, wincing at the twinges that assaulted muscles she didn't realize she had. She heard agitated voices, thudding footsteps, and the slam of a door, and knew Paul had left the house. Someone needed him. As a physician and a caring man, it was only logical he go.

But oh, how she wished he was still beside her in the bed.

Last night had been the most wonderful of her life, filled with warm sighs and even warmer caresses. She and Paul had done things to each other she'd never imagined a man and woman might do. He'd kissed and stroked her in places so sensitive and intimate, she'd swear she still felt his lips and fingers against her flesh.

If she was very lucky, they had made a child.

And if they hadn't . . .

Rila had told her that in order to avoid emotional attachment, the travelers had been instructed to discontinue mating with their targets once they became pregnant. But the rule had been made for those returning home, not her. She was here to escape the Elders' stifling restrictions and fly free. If she was pregnant, she could have sex with Paul as often as she wanted, until she decided to leave. In fact, she could make love with him as many times as it took, for as long as it—

The thought made her bury her head under the pillow. Flights of fancy were not to be tolerated, not now, when she had a goal to attain. If they'd made a baby, their intimate contact was over. If not, they would mate until she accomplished her mission. Meeting her personal mission would give her the courage to forge ahead with her plan. She'd assessed her predicament a hundred times before last night, and it was the only solution. Once she conceived, she had to leave Preston's Ferry and begin life anew.

Lila checked the clock on the nightstand. The twins weren't due to wake for at least an hour. She had time to take a shower and ease some of the aches plaguing her body as well as her mind. She stood to straighten the sheets, and spied a rust-colored stain. Virgin no more, she was now enlightened as to the sighs and whispers she'd heard from the older women on her planet, as well as their forlorn expressions. Her mother had tried to explain it, but never seemed able to get the words out.

If her parents felt this way each time they had sex, Lila now understood their difficulty in recounting the feelings.

In a rush, she stripped the linens from the mattress, found fresh sheets, and righted the covers. After walking to her bedroom, she deposited the sheets in a basket, then used the shower. Once dressed, she thought about linking into the pregnancy test built in her bracelet, then realized it was too soon. She needed twelve hours before her body registered a positive or negative reaction.

Lila had just finished drying her hair when she heard a cry. Rick, she thought, hungry for breakfast, which meant Teddy was awake as well, though he wouldn't be shouting. She really needed to do something about the child's silent state.

Entering their bedroom, she waved a hand in front of her face and opened a second window. "You two are dangerous." She tossed them each a grin. "Who's going to be the first to get cleaned up this morning?"

"La! La! La!" Rick chanted, while Teddy merely held out his chubby arms.

Raising a brow, she went to Teddy. "Can you say Lila? Or maybe breakfast?"

The little boy stuck three fingers in his drooling mouth.

"How about wishing your brother a good morning?"

Giggling, Teddy bounced on his toes.

Lila sighed. Getting the child to talk was going to be another personal goal, one she hoped to accomplish before she made her way in the world. Not wanting to dwell on the idea of leaving, she lifted Teddy from the crib and promptly wrinkled her nose.

"Pee-uuu."

Teddy's blue eyes sparkled. Still laughing, he patted her face as if apologizing for what he'd done.

She made quick work of the full diaper and dressed him in clean clothes, then did the same to Rick. With a child's hand in each of her own, she led them to the kitchen. While the boys ate their usual breakfast of peanut butter on toast, she fiddled with the coffeemaker, hoping to surprise Paul when he returned. The machine started the drip cycle, and she sat at the table with her own meal.

Minutes later, her heart tripped in her chest when the downstairs door opened and closed. Paul had left so suddenly, she was sure he would come up to eat, which would enable her to gauge his reaction to the night they'd shared.

Footsteps pattered on the stairs, then he stood in the doorway. "Good morning. Everything okay?"

Rick and Teddy rocked in place, waving crumbling toast and grinning at their father.

"We're fine. Are you going to have breakfast?"

He flashed the boys a smile, but failed to look her in the eye. "First I'm going to get cleaned up, but I need a favor."

"I made coffee," Lila answered, hoping to entice him.

"Great. I'll have a cup after I shower." He edged toward the hallway. "Can you take the twins to the waiting room and sit behind the desk for a while? Harley's down there and he's feeling woozy, so I sat him on the sofa, but he shouldn't be alone. Grab a few toys from the smallest examining room for Teddy and Rick, and answer the phone if it rings."

"Who's Harley?"

"My emergency," came his reply as he disappeared from view.

Lila sighed. So much for a discussion on passion or their special evening. If the detached expression on Paul's face was any indication, he barely recalled they'd shared a bed, never mind what they'd done in it. Which meant there was little chance he would want to do it again.

Standing, she wiped down the table and stacked dishes in the sink. Then she made the boys presentable and set them on their feet, muttering the entire time. "He wants me to keep an eye on Harley, whoever that is, and I'm supposed to answer the phone." The twins scrambled to the stairway and she followed. "What do I say when I take a call? Does he want me to make appointments?"

The boys dropped to their hands and knees and scooted backward down the steps. "Be careful, you two," she admonished. "And don't disturb Harley."

Rick and Teddy scampered into the waiting area while Lila found the room with the toys. Choosing a picture book and a set of stacking blocks, she carried them to the front office, where she came to an abrupt halt. Sitting on the sofa was one of the largest humans she had ever seen, which didn't seem to bother the twins, because they had climbed onto the couch and taken a seat on either side of the mountain.

"It hurts pretty bad," said the man she presumed was Harley. He held up an oversized hand wrapped in white. "But Dr. P stitched me up real good. Used a needle and thread, the way my mama used to do when she sewed a tear in my pants."

Rick and Teddy gazed at Harley's hand, while the giant assessed them. "Say, you two look just alike, don'cha? How come I ain't met either of you before?"

Babbling, Rick struggled into a sitting position on Harley's knee as Teddy patted the man on top of his head. Lila held her breath, not sure what to think. The twins weren't in danger, that was certain, but there was something about Harley that wasn't quite . . . right.

"Hello."

She blinked, focusing on his friendly face. "You must be Paul's emergency." Walking into the room, she thrust out her hand. "I'm Lila."

His dark brown eyes grew wide at her gesture, as if no one had ever bothered to shake his hand before. Then he eased Rick from his knee and stood to accept her offer. Holding up his bandaged hand, he said, "I got hurt."

"I see that," said Lila, meeting his awed expression. When he didn't let go of her, she pulled from his grasp. "But Dr. P fixed it."

"Yes, ma'am." His cheeks turned pink. "Are you married to Dr. P?"

"Married? N-no," she stammered.

His complexion flushed red. "That's good. 'Cause I'm not married either." He took a step closer, gazing at her through adoring eyes. "Maybe you'd like to marry me?"

Lila tugged on her ear, sending out a silent question. A burst of clarity parted the clouds when the program pinpointed Harley's diminished mental capacity. Since her planet had found a way to take care of this type of impairment—and any other flaws they felt detrimental to their species—generations ago, first in the womb and later in a test tube, she'd never met a being who wasn't physically and mentally perfect.

Then she realized what he'd just asked her. "Oh, well, I don't think so. I have to take care of Dr. P's twins."

His confusion obvious, Harley's brows met at the bridge of his nose. "You're their mama, but you're not married to Dr. P?"

"I'm their nanny—you know—a babysitter. Only I'm with them all the time," she explained. Harley, she could tell, was a bit like Teddy and Rick in mind, only older and more sizable. And he could talk, which made communication easier. "Dr. P pays me to care for them."

"Then you could still marry me," he insisted. "I got a job and a house, and I—"

Paul strode into the room and spoke pointedly to his patient. "Well, I'd say you're feeling better. Come into an examining room and let me give you that tetanus shot, then I'll walk you to the Shop and Bag."

"Could Lila bring me back?" Harley shot her a pleading grin. "Please, Lila. The little guys can come too."

Lila figured looking after two boys was almost the same as caring for three. It would keep her and the twins busy and give her time to consider her next move with Paul. Besides, Harley was sweet, and he had to think she was special if he wanted to marry her.

"That would be fine," she said, ignoring Paul's impatient expression. "You go with Dr. P while we get the stroller. Meet us out front when you're through."

Lila and the twins pushed through the door of the S&B while Harley held it open with his good arm. Millie glanced up from the register.

"Morning. You the new delivery girl?"

"Delivery girl?" Lila followed Millie's gaze to Harley. "Oh, I guess so. Paul had patients to see and Harley—"

"Dr. P gave me a holder for my arm, see?" He raised the sling supporting his injured hand. "He says it'll help my thumb feel better."

"Good for Dr. P," Millie said, nodding.

"And Lila's thinkin' about marrying me. She said so."

Grinning, the grocer raised a brow. "Is that right?"

Lila shrugged, certain Millie realized her predicament. "Paul told me to remind you that Harley has to rest for the day." She passed over a small packet. "This is a sample of the medicine for his pain. He's already given Harley the first dose and wants you to give him two more tablets every six to eight hours until they're gone."

Millie tucked the packet in her side pocket. "I'll see to it. Just let me get this big guy settled in the storeroom and I'll be right back."

Latching on to Harley's good arm, the store-keeper propelled him through an aisle. " 'Bye, Lila," he called over his shoulder. "Tell Dr. P I'm coming to see him tomorrow."

Lila breathed a sigh of relief. Conversing with Harley on the way over had been a lot like talking to Teddy and Rick, only more frustrating. She'd made a mistake when she thought he wouldn't be any trouble, because he'd somehow gotten the idea she was actually considering his proposal.

The bell rang and Bill Halverson walked in, carry-ing his ever-present bag of aluminum foil. Marching up to her, he zeroed in on her head. "Where's your protective headgear, young lady?"

Trying her best not to bolt, she said, "Um . . . at home. I keep forgetting to put it on."

"Well, you're in luck. Got me a new roll of foil and a couple of extra minutes." He set his bag on the checkout counter and pulled out the box. Tear-ing off a sheet, he quickly shaped it and sat the hat on Teddy's head. "Owe you one for each of the boys, remember."

Teddy giggled, slapping at the hat. "Leave that right there, young fella," warned Bill. "Don't want no aliens suckin' up that itty-bitty brain of yours, do ya?"

Before Lila knew it, he'd fashioned a cap for Rick

as well. Satisfied with his handiwork, he began a third. "This one's for you. And I won't even charge you for it, if you promise to stay after the Founders' Day meeting and attend the one for ESAW."

"You mean the one you and your friends are holding?"

"That's right. And see to it Dr. P stays too. The more new blood comes, the better." He fitted the aluminum dome to her head, pressing it into her mass of hair. "I got these just for you," said Bill, pulling a handful of what looked to be clips from his pocket. He anchored the foil in place. "You got no excuse now."

Lila's shoulders sagged. No excuse—and no way to explain to Paul why she wore it. When he learned she'd become a member of ESAW, she'd never get him back into bed.

Millie eyed both of them as she returned to the register. "Still selling those tinfoil fedoras, I see."

"Damn straight. Heard you had a bit of excitement this morning. Harley all right?"

"How did you hear about Harley?" asked Millie, echoing aloud the question in Lila's mind.

"Talked to one of the deliverymen unloading in the lot, and he mentioned it. Where is he?"

"Back in the storeroom. Why?"

"Because I promised him a hat. Course, it don't matter much whether he wears one or not." Bill ambled down an aisle, talking as he walked. "Ain't nothin' in his head an alien would be interested in, but it's good advertising just the same."

"Old fool," Millie grumbled. Reaching under the counter, she pulled out two lollipops, unwrapped them, and handed one to each twin. "So, how are you and Dr. P getting along?"

A wave of heat shot from Lila's chest to her neck. She was sure her face was on fire.

Millie's lips lifted in a smile. "That good, huh?"

"Please don't say anything to Rose or Bill," begged Lila, wishing she'd been able to control her emotions.

"Secret's safe with me." Millie puckered her lips and used two fingers to pantomime a key turning in a lock. She took in Lila's hat. "Does Dr. P know you joined ESAW?"

"Not yet, but—" The door to the S&B opened, and three people Lila didn't recognize walked in.

"Morning," said Millie.

"Good morning," responded the woman in the group. The two men with her requested that Millie take care of them at the deli counter. When the trio left, the woman gazed first at Lila's foil crown, then Teddy and Rick. Finally, she said, "I hear you're new in town."

"I am," said Lila.

"And you've already joined that group of renegade alien hunters?"

"Renegade?" Pulling at her ear, Lila tried to keep her voice even. Her mind zeroed in on the definition, and she huffed out a breath. "Are you accusing them of doing something illegal?"

"Do you believe in beings from outer space?"

Swallowing, Lila jutted her chin. "It doesn't matter what I believe. I thought people here were free to think whatever they wanted as long as they didn't hurt anyone."

The tall thin woman stood ramrod straight, an expression of suspicion etched in her frowning face. "Where, exactly, do you come from?"

When Lila didn't answer immediately, the woman seemed to locate her good manners. "Sorry. My name's Edith Hammer. My husband and I are thinking of moving here, and I was just wondering what draws people from out of town to Preston's Ferry. We're avid bird-watchers, so we like the proximity to the wildlife refuge, but there's not much else to recommend a relocation."

"I came here hoping to find a job," Lila answered, uneasy with the question.

"From up north?"

"Yes, north." She grasped the stroller handle and pushed forward, but the woman stepped in her path.

"That's funny, 'cause I heard you came from south of here."

Lila opened and closed her mouth, too surprised to think.

Edith Hammer's eyes narrowed to slits of steel.

A hand touched Lila's shoulder and she jumped.

Twelve

"This little lady is new to town," Bill said, giving her shoulder a squeeze.

Sinking under his comforting touch, Lila blew out a breath. Bill's sudden appearance made her feel protected, as if he were standing guard. Emboldened, she stiffened her spine. So what if Edith Hammer's expression was that of someone who refused to be deterred? Preston's Ferry was filled with nosy people and, so far, she'd been able to deflect their probing. This woman was simply one more hurdle in her quest for freedom.

"I doubt she can help with your questions about our town, but I could," Bill assured her. "If you folks come to the ESAW meeting, you'd get your answers on the alien thing too."

Edith's smile seemed forced. "I assume ESAW is the reason you wear that charming foil hat?"

"They're protection as well as our signature. Flyers for the meeting have been posted around town for days now." He pulled a sheet of paper from his bag of tricks and handed it to her. "I mentioned it to the fella I met at your trailer door Saturday, but he didn't seem too interested."

"That was my brother. He thought you were joking," she said dryly. "And we've been scour—er—walking the wildlife refuge, so I haven't seen the flyers."

"Couldn't help but see the plates on your trailer," Bill continued. "Whereabouts in the state are you from?"

"Here and there," she said, giving the handwritten notice a fleeting once-over.

"What brought you to town?"

"We're avid ornithologists. The bird sanctuary near the bridge is one of the best on the East Coast."

"I see." Bill rocked back on his heels. "So, is this a vacation for you?"

"Not that it's any of your business, but we're tying the trip to my husband's profession."

He raised a brow, seemingly undaunted by her tight-lipped expression. "What line of work is he in?"

"Edward—my husband—is a freelance writer for several travel magazines," answered Edith, her nostrils flaring. "He's thinking of doing a piece on the eastern shore, maybe featuring your Founders' Day celebration."

Bill rescued the foil hat Rick had thrown on the floor and set it back on the toddler's head. "Sounds to me like you're as curious about outer space as you are about birds. I hand-design these hats, three for five dollars, and they're guaranteed to keep UFO jockeys from messin' with your brain."

"Tell me again why you think the area is being visited by extraterrestrials," the woman goaded, "and maybe I'll buy one."

Lila took the opportunity to slip from the store. Their topic of conversation was too close for comfort. Edith Hammer seemed to be on a fact-finding mission, either about the town or aliens or both. Questions on Preston's Ferry made sense if the woman planned to help her husband research a travel article, but why, Lila wondered, would Edith be so curious about spacemen?

One thing was certain, Bill's interest in the occupants of the Windcruiser was a lucky break. He wouldn't let Edith or her companions bully any of the townsfolk, herself included.

She jostled the stroller over a section of uneven sidewalk and headed for home. Harley had dawdled on the way to the store, turning a ten-minute stroll into an hour trek while he'd asked questions that made her head spin. Then Millie had distracted her, and finally this altercation with Edith and Bill. It was almost time for Paul's lunch break. Once she prepared a meal, she would put the twins down for a nap and make a point of talking to Paul about their interaction.

After picking up the mail and newspapers from the box at the front walk, she steered the buggy to the rear of the house and entered through the back door. Teddy and Rick scuttled to the hall in search of their father and Lila followed. Voices from behind one of the closed examining rooms told her Paul was with a patient. Knowing it wouldn't do to intrude, she herded the twins to the stairs, where they scrambled ahead of her on their hands and knees.

Chortling with abandon, the toddlers took off toward the living room. Lila set the newspapers and mail on a corner of the kitchen table and sighed. From their still-explosive energy level, she guessed the boys weren't at all tired. Maybe a story or game after lunch would help them fall asleep faster, so she could take that pregnancy test this afternoon.

Paul heard the commotion in the hall, on the stairs, and overhead as running feet and shrieks of glee rattled the house. Lila and his sons were home. The racket reminded him that he'd had a hell of a morning. It might not have been so tiring if he'd gotten enough sleep, but the way he and his housekeeper had burned up the sheets last night, he could have slept until noon and not felt rested. If Harley hadn't sliced his thumb, he and Lila might have had time for a morning round or—

"That it, Dr. P? Can I get dressed now?"

Paul focused on Agnes Depew, his fifth patient of the day. She'd come in with one very irritated eye, which he'd diagnosed as conjunctivitis, commonly known as pink eye, and, to be on the safe side, had also given her a quick physical.

"Except for the eye infection you seem fine, so yes. It'll take a minute to find a sample of the drops I'm prescribing and write you a prescription."

He went to his makeshift lab and located the drug. After applying a dose to Agnes's infected eye, he removed his gloves and tossed them in the trash.

"I'm curious. Conjunctivitis is a highly contagious children's complaint." He sat on a stool and filled out a prescription. "Where have you been lately that might have put you in contact with the virus?"

The woman adjusted her blouse and returned her foil helmet to her gray curls. "Had the grandbabies over last weekend. Little Todd kept rubbin' his eyes, but I didn't think anything of it. He's in day care three times a week, so I guess I'd better call my daughter and warn her."

"You do that." Paul handed her the slip of paper along with the sample and a printed brochure on the care of her condition. "If she hasn't taken Todd to his pediatrician, tell her to make an appointment, and have the other children checked too."

He helped the older woman down from the table. Agnes, who barely flirted with five feet, held her aluminum cap in place with one hand as she tipped back her head and grinned at him. "Heard you did a fine job with Harley this morning."

"It was noth—" Paul rolled his eyes. "Who told you about the accident?"

"Millie, of course. She said things are going well with that new nanny of yours too." Agnes hobbled to the door. "Got an eyeful of the young lady on Saturday, when she pushed the twins past Eldora's beauty parlor. Looked like a keeper to me."

Paul escorted her to his office, filled out the required paperwork, and sent the woman on her way with no comment. He agreed that Lila was a "keeper" where his sons were concerned, but what was he supposed to do with her on a personal level?

The two of them could share a bed while Rick and

Teddy were babies, but eventually the boys would notice the intimacy. And what about Lila herself? She'd told him she didn't expect anything from their affair, but was she serious? If he explained that last night would be their one and only encounter, would she accept his decision or leave him high and dry?

His phone rang and he picked it up. "Dr. Anderson."

"It's Mother, dear. How are you?"

Paul settled back in his chair and prepared for the inquisition. "Fine, Mom. I take it you got my message?"

"I did, and I'm thrilled you found someone. I'll be down for the Founders' Day celebration with bells on. I already called the Seaside and made a reservation. I really do want to meet your new employee and give my unbiased opinion."

He grimaced. "That was fast work."

"It's what I do. Besides, I told you I thought the celebration sounded like fun. I can free up some of your time babysitting and get to know the woman who'll be taking care of the boys all at once."

"Lila and I will appreciate the break."

She waited a beat before asking, "Lila is a lovely name. Is she young or old?"

"You'll find out when you meet her." Paul sighed inwardly. "The weekend is going to be a zoo. Are you sure you want to . . . ?"

"Of course I do, but I'm not sure when I'm leaving Philadelphia. I'll check with you when I arrive, and I promise not to be underfoot."

After a few more minutes they said good-bye. He figured his mother would want final approval on the woman he hired, even if latent, but he hadn't thought it would happen this soon. Thank God she'd be sleeping at a B&B. He frowned. And what was he supposed to tell Lila? If his mother had an inkling of what was going on between them she'd have heart failure.

Or she'd be making wedding arrangements.

He shuffled through a stack of papers and stuffed the important ones in the envelope for his accountant. Peeking inside, he searched for the application he'd given Lila, then remembered he'd left it on the table upstairs and made a note to ask her for it. Aside from the fact that Lila was doing a great job with the twins, there was still so little he knew about her. Maybe, after she completed the form, he'd get a better handle on what had motivated her to answer his ad, not to mention one other thing that puzzled him.

She had been a virgin.

The undeniable fact raised his guilt quotient and piqued his curiosity at the same time. Lila had told him she was twenty-seven. Even though she appeared younger, she was a grown woman who'd made her own way in the world for several years. She was attractive and personable, as well as easy to talk to, even with her sometimes serious attitude. Unless she'd lived in a convent for most of her life, which he doubted, what reason was there for her to have waited this long to have sex?

She'd made it clear she wanted him in her bed from the get-go, almost as if he'd been specifically chosen for the task of deflowering her. Why had she picked him to be her first?

Paul shook his head at the antiquated term. These

days, women didn't get *deflowered*; they had sex with a boyfriend or significant other, often in high school and certainly before they graduated college. Yes, Lila had been a virgin, but she'd also been the aggressor. She'd worn that see-through nightgown openly in his presence, without an ounce of modesty or embarrassment, and practically sat on top of him on the sofa, even after he'd cowered in the corner.

He wasn't saying it was all Lila's fault they'd slept together; he'd had plenty of opportunity to walk away instead of muttering those feeble protests. It was just that she'd been so damned tempting. He'd been drawn to her as if he'd been drugged or bewitched. And since he didn't believe anything of the sort was possible, he was willing to shoulder half the responsibility for their reckless actions.

Still, if he could figure out what it was about her that had made him so enamored, he might be able to handle the situation better.

Scanning the desk, he took in the morning's paperwork. He didn't like to go more than a weekend without filling in the various insurance and Medicaid forms. If his patient load continued to increase, he'd soon be earning enough to buy a new computer for the office and hire a part-time secretary, which would give him more time to spend with his sons— and Lila.

He swallowed his surprise at the ease with which he'd just included his nanny in thoughts of his future. It had only been a few days since he'd hired the woman, and she was already a member of his family.

Annoyed his mind had created such a scenario, he

picked up a pen and began filling in the forms from his first patient of the morning.

Lila cornered Teddy and Rick when they ran to their room. Hoisting them both in her arms, she carried them to the kitchen and sat them in their high chairs. When it became obvious Paul was not joining them for the midday meal, she made vegetarian hot dogs and brought their plates to the table.

"Hmm, hot dogs," she said, taking a seat. "Rose said they're your favorite."

"Ha-da," said Rick. "Ha-da-dinna."

"Close enough," Lila answered, poking his tummy. "Now it's your turn. Hot dog," she pronounced slowly for Teddy.

Grinning through a mouthful of ketchup and almost-meat, Teddy kicked the underside of the table.

Lila sighed. "Okay, how about milk?" She handed Teddy his cup. "Can you say milk?"

Teddy accepted the cup and took a drink while Rick shouted, "Mik! Mik! Mik!"

She encouraged both boys to talk throughout the meal, then decided to make dessert more interesting. Taking a miniature box of raisins from the pantry, she thought their progress might go faster if she made a game out of the speech lesson. Rick received a raisin for each word he repeated, two if he noticeably improved his pronunciation. Teddy got a raisin for paying attention, two if he gave any type of audible response.

All too soon the raisins were gone, and Teddy was no closer to talking.

Lila wracked her brain while she wrestled the twins from their chairs and cleaned the kitchen. Millie had suggested that the best way to reach Paul was through his children. Since it was imperative he allow her in his bed until she became pregnant, and she hadn't as yet found time to take the test, she needed to prove she was doing a good job. If his ardor cooled, he might fire her, and that would end all hopes of conception.

She turned and gazed at Rick and Teddy, who were busy stacking the pots and lids they'd pulled from a cupboard next to the stove. They were good-natured, handsome babies who would make her—make any mother proud. Just like her and Rila, each had his own unique personality and temperament. She enjoyed Rick because he took charge of every situation and made sure his brother was included, as her sister had done for her. And she understood Teddy, because he seemed so eager to please and content to follow, exactly as she had been as a child.

If she were their mother, she would see to it Rick learned to control his temper and be patient. And she would make certain Teddy came out from behind his brother's shadow and started to think and speak for himself.

Lila's stomach fluttered as she imagined the child she and Paul might create. She had no doubt their baby would be intelligent with a pleasing disposition. He would be tall and sturdily built, of course, and his hair would be either red or gold, or a combination of colors, while his eyes might be blue or green. He would have his father's strong chin, broad forehead, and—

Stopping the thought from going any further, she rubbed at her temples. She had a goal, a personal mission to conceive a child. Paul Anderson was merely an end to that goal, and it was important she remember it whenever her mind wandered to things that could never be.

Focusing on the present, she keyed in on Teddy's now-familiar frown of concentration. Scooping him up, she raced to Paul's bathroom, whisked off the toddler's coveralls and Pull-Up diaper, and sat him on the potty chair.

"Stay right there until you take care of business," she warned. Rick stood in the doorway wide-eyed and watchful.

"I'll be right back."

In less than ten seconds she returned with a book. Sitting on the bathroom floor, she pulled Rick onto her lap and began to read a story out loud in hopes of keeping both boys interested long enough for Teddy to complete his job. When he finished, he squirmed in place.

"Okay," she said, setting Rick aside. "Let's take a look."

Teddy stood and peered into the potty, which encouraged Rick to do the same. Lila squatted down and joined in the inspection. The boys giggled and she grinned at each in turn as a sense of accomplishment surged through her system. Lifting him in her arms, she gave Teddy a hug. "See what you did? That means you're a big boy, like your daddy."

Teddy kicked his legs, his smile wide. Lila took care of him and the potty, then pulled down Rick's pants and sat him on the chair. "Your turn," she said, hoping he'd get the idea. Grabbing a diaper off the top of the toilet tank, she laid Teddy on the floor while she continued to praise both boys. Unfortunately, Rick didn't take the hint.

"That's all right," she told the older twin. "Your time will come. Besides, everyone needs to be first at something, and this it Teddy's feat. He's earned both of you a special treat."

After changing Rick's diaper, she led the boys into her room and sat them on her bed. Then she went to her dresser and removed the personal item she'd brought from home. The travelers had been warned against carrying anything that might prove detrimental to their mission or be used against them if caught, but this was a special toy, the one thing she would have to remind her of home when she was alone. And it only worked if Lila herself activated it, so she didn't see the harm.

Climbing between them, she lay back on the mattress while the twins spent a few moments crawling over her chest and stomach. Eventually, they each settled in the crook of an arm. Lila inhaled their scent and closed her eyes at the twist her heart took with their snuggling.

"When I was about your age, this was my favorite plaything," she began, holding up a shiny golden ball. "My father gave it to me when my psychic gift came to light, and I used it to hone my skill as a telekinetic."

Teddy grabbed for the colorful orb and she let him touch it. "It's very light, perfect for a child who's learning how to make inert objects move, don't you think?"

Rick reached out and giggled. "Bah. Bah."

"You sound like a sheep, silly." Lila tossed the globe in the air. "Say ball, and I'll let you hold it."

Letting his temper show, Rick grunted and kicked his legs.

"That won't work with me, young man. Say ball."

"Bah."

"Ball."

"La!"

"Yes, I'm Li-*la*, and this is a ball. But you may not touch it until you say its name."

"Ball," chirped Rick, his baby voice ringing true.

Lila's heart jumped. "Yes! Ball. That is so good, Rick. How about you?" She turned to Teddy. "Can you say ball?"

The toddler gave a toothy grin.

She sighed. "Okay, your brother did his part, and I won't go back on my word." Lowering the toy, she handed it to Rick, who immediately tried to bite it. "Oh, no," she said, rescuing the object. "Now pay attention."

Concentrating, she balanced the ball on the palm of her hand. Slowly, it began to sparkle, filling with a light Lila called up in her mind. Then the golden globe quivered in response to her mental suggestion. Soon she had it rising and falling in place, repeating one of the first exercises she'd been able to accomplish with the training tool.

Teddy and Rick squealed their delight and she encouraged the dance, sending tiny rays of energy arcing into the room. In moments the ball rose high, shimmering and bobbing above the bed. Lila breathed deeply, stretching her psychic muscles. It had been a while since she'd practiced her special gift, but as she focused, her talent came back full force, until she felt as if she were one with the globe, soaring through the room on an exhilarating mental ride.

"Keep your eye on the ball," she instructed sleepily. She eased the object to a stop, controlling its flight so that it hovered directly overhead.

Worn out by the busy day, Lila closed her eyes. She was getting used to this new planet and the people who resided on it, but she still missed her home and her family. Between last night with Paul, her early morning walk with Harley, meeting Millie, Bill, and Edith Hammer, and her time spent with the twins, she was exhausted.

As the comforting familiarity of her kinetic ability hummed within her, the one thing left of her old life lulled her into a peaceful, easy slumber.

Paul climbed the stairs, ready to end his day. He'd managed to wade through his paperwork, but it hadn't been easy. Questions about Lila and what a background check might discover, coupled with their impulsive actions in bed, had wormed their way into his thoughts so many times it was a miracle he'd been able to concentrate. If he'd made an error with his patient forms because of it, some bureaucratic paper pusher would return everything in a month or so and demand he do it all over again. Until then he'd mail the stuff out and hope for the best.

The apartment was quiet, so he assumed the boys were asleep. Lila would be napping too, if she felt as beat as he did. He'd look in on his sons after lunch, but not their nanny. Seeing her the way she'd appeared this morning, curled around a pillow with a soft smile on her lovely face, would only enhance the memory of a night he'd been trying hard to forget.

Yawning, he checked the refrigerator and found a package of hot dogs. Resisting the urge to read the label, he popped two in the microwave and retrieved buns and mustard. He didn't want to prejudge the food by studying the ingredients list, and knowing Lila and her vegetarian requirements, the franks had to be nutritious. It didn't matter what they were composed of, as long as they tasted okay.

When the microwave dinged, he slid the "meat" onto buns, added a squirt of spicy mustard, and sat down to his meal. To distract himself from further thoughts of Lila, he opened his mail as he ate, setting aside bills and tossing out circulars. Then he caught up on the news. After perusing the *Virginia Pilot,* he read the *Eastern Shore News,* the small local publication he'd used to advertise for a nanny/housekeeper, as well as the opening of his practice.

Turning to page two of the eight-page newspaper, he spied a photo topped with a caption printed in bold: *LOCAL MEN ON THE HUNT FOR ALIENS.* Paul recognized Bill Halverson immediately, smack in the center of the group picture of six older gents, each with an almost fierce expression on his face and an identical aluminum foil hat on his head.

The article went on to describe the Eastern Shore Alien Watch, hereafter referred to as ESAW, and its purpose, adding that each man was a district commander responsible for directing local meetings, spreading the word, and leading the search for one or more aliens they believed had landed on the remote eastern shore of Virginia.

Paul shook his head. The senior citizens of this town definitely had too much time on their hands. He didn't mean to trivialize their many plights. Memory and health issues, Social Security, family isolation, and lack of proper food and shelter were concerns every American would face someday, himself included. Older folks were his bread and butter, but thanks to a few new housing developments, younger couples were moving in and adding to the town's mix of citizens. Which was a good thing, because if he had to examine too many more geriatrics wearing one of those ludicrous tinfoil beanies, he was going to bust a gut.

He hadn't realized the extent of Bill's zeal until today, when three of the five patients he'd seen this morning came in wearing the hats. And the group had clout, if they were able to get themselves recognized by the local rag. Then again, so little happened on the peninsula that anything from an oyster roast to a frog infestation was considered newsworthy. Aliens had to be a step up from both of those nonevents.

He even gave the want ads a close going over, until he realized it was an excuse to kill time. Like it or not, he had to face Lila and inform her his mother was coming for a visit, as well as talk to her about his concerns.

After folding the paper, he tossed the junk mail in the trash and left the rest on the counter. In the bedroom, he slipped on a clean T-shirt and jeans, and checked himself out in the mirror. He'd forgotten to shave, but the shadow of beard gave him a slightly intimidating edge he thought he might need when he reminded the nanny of the ground rules. He didn't plan on frightening her, but he did want to appear formidable and decisive when he told her they couldn't sleep together while his mother was here.

When he peeked into Teddy and Rick's room and found their cribs empty, a ripple of worry jarred his system. Cocking his head, he listened for a clue to their whereabouts, but all he heard was silence. Where the heck had they gone to?

Crossing the living area, he went to Lila's closed bedroom door, hesitated a moment, then rapped on the panel. The gentle force of his knock pushed the door inward. Peering through the gap, he took in the drawn shade and almost spartan bedroom, which sounded another warning tremor. Though Lila had arrived with little but the clothes on her back, she'd shopped in town, yet there was nothing personal on her dresser top, no sign of an attempt to make the place her own.

Had he kept her so busy she hadn't found time to make herself at home? Or was there no need for her to settle in, because she wasn't planning to stay?

Flattening his palms, he opened the door and stepped into the darkened room. A feeling of calm washed over him when he spotted his sons, sound asleep against Lila's sides. Maybe they'd been frightened or restless, and she'd brought them to her bed to quiet them. Whatever the reason, they were safe and at peace.

Thirteen

Lila drifted back to consciousness. Aware that something wasn't quite right, she *felt* rather than saw a figure at the side of her bed. Shifting into full alert, she kept her eyes closed and her body relaxed while she linked with the entity.

Paul, she intuited, noting the rapid beating of her heart. How long had he been standing there?

When she realized that her mind had stayed in tune with her childhood toy while she slept, she gently guided the sphere down the final short distance to her chest.

Stretching, she breathed deep as she observed Paul through shuttered lids. With his arms crossed and his guarded expression, he appeared intense and forbidding. It didn't help that one eyebrow was raised and his beard-shadowed jaw seemed locked in place.

The globe rolled onto the coverlet and she ignored the movement. Opening her eyes, she held a finger to her lips and inched from between the boys. Nothing unusual would happen if they woke and played with the ball. She hoped her nonchalant attitude would keep any suspicions Paul might have formed at bay.

Gazing at each child in turn, Lila smiled inside as Teddy encircled the sphere and pulled it near, while Rick snuggled closer to his brother. The toy held remnants of her mental energy, and it warmed her to see them drawn to it as if it were the center of their universe. Determined not to disturb their nap, she stepped into the hall. If Paul expected an explanation, he would have to wait until they were in another part of the house.

She walked through the living area and into the kitchen, assessing the force of his footsteps as he trailed behind. Whenever she used her kinetic gift, it heightened her other, less-developed psychic senses, sharpening her ability to read the beings around her. She wasn't sure of the reason for Paul's warring emotions, but a cup of tea and a few cookies might help to diffuse the tension. At the sink, she filled two mugs with water, placed them in the microwave and set the timer, then hunted for tea bags in an upper cupboard.

"Lila, we need to talk." He stood at the far end of the counter with his hands stuffed in his pockets.

"If it's about the boys and I taking a nap together—"

"I don't have a problem with it, but I've read that kids need to stay in their own beds for a variety of reasons: stability, structure, a sense of private space—that kind of thing. I don't want it to become a habit."

"They weren't tired, but I was," she continued, subtly reminding him of the evening they'd shared. Filled with nervous energy, she crossed to the pantry, found a box of cookies, and brought it to the table. "And they were exceptionally good this morning."

The microwave stopped and she removed the cups, set them on saucers, and added tea bags, aware he was following her every move with a steely-eyed stare. She'd been so pleased by Teddy's progress that her childhood toy had seemed the perfect way to show approval. If Paul wasn't upset about finding them in her room, it had to be the ball—a topic she didn't care to explore.

"Teddy made great strides today. He actually—"

"We can talk about the boys later." Moving past her, Paul sat in his chair. "It's more important we discuss what happened between us last night." After dunking his tea bag a few times, he set it on the saucer and added a drop of milk to his cup. "I've thought about it until I can't see straight, and I don't think we should make lo—have sex—again."

Lila's heart fell to her feet. Gathering her composure, she studied his rigid shoulders and determined frown as she added sugar to her drink. Unless she was pregnant, they had to have intercourse a second time, maybe even a third and fourth. Perhaps if she appealed to him logically—

"You didn't enjoy what we did?"

Paul sipped his tea in order to stifle a groan. Enjoy was such a mild word, it hardly covered the gamut of emotions their intimacy had conveyed. "That's not the point," he muttered.

"Then I was a disappointment? You expected . . . more?"

Too much *more* and he'd have died on the spot. It wouldn't be a lie if he told Lila she was the most exciting woman he'd ever encountered, in bed or out of it, or that she tempted him on so many levels he'd wanted to spend the entire day with her. But it wouldn't help with this discussion.

"You were far from a disappointment," he assured her, hoping to erase the insecurity in her voice. "But I keep thinking our being personally involved is a bad idea. I'm your employer and I don't want to be accused of taking advantage. Besides, my mother is coming for a visit—"

She opened and closed her mouth. "Your mother?"

"Yeah. Mom lives in Philadelphia. Dad died about a year ago. Most of the time, she does a good job of minding her own business, but if she sees the two of us together in an intimate scenario or hears gossip—"

Paul's gut twisted when Lila leaned into the table and gazed at him through dewy eyes. All he'd wanted was an honest, simple exchange, one where he could say what he had to and be done with it. The last thing he'd expected was tears.

"You don't want me to meet your mother?"

"Of course I do, but I don't think it's a good idea she knows about how we spend our—spent last night. Word travels like the wind in this town." He sat back and made a conscious effort to soothe. "You were a virgin, Lila, and I'm honored I was your first, but we have to put things in perspective."

Sniffing loudly, she blew her nose in a napkin. "You think what we did was wrong?"

"Not wrong exactly." At a loss, he ran a hand through his hair. Her soulful expression reminded him of a kicked puppy. Could he screw up this discussion any worse? "I don't mean to pry, but I have to ask. Why did you choose me?"

Shrugging, she dabbed at her eyes. "I didn't like the direction my life had taken and thought it was time to forge a new path, break out of my shell, and do something . . . different."

"And part of the new path was losing your virginity?"

"Not exactly." Instead of meeting his gaze, she busied herself by sorting through the box of cookies. "When we met, I sensed we had a connection, and I hoped you felt the same."

Paul had felt it, all right. *Don't grope the nanny* had been a joke at first, then a serious warning, and finally, a rule he'd broken. If he were a child, he'd be punished, at the very least grounded for what he'd done. Lucky for him, he was an adult. He had the right to rescind the rule altogether. After listening to Lila, it was beginning to sound like a damn good idea.

"I've been trained in science, but in my profession it's important I'm a people person too. I have to understand human nature in order to treat my patients," he said, echoing the words his father had given when Paul graduated from medical school. "Your actions were surprising." He raised a brow. "You didn't want me to wear a condom."

Her face grew red, and he knew he'd touched a nerve.

"There's no need. My getting pregnant won't be a problem," she answered in a quiet voice.

"You're confusing me," Paul continued. "You were a virgin, but you're on the pill?"

"I'm confused too. I didn't expect to be so drawn to you after a single meeting; nor did I think my method of birth control would be open to discussion. Was it wrong of me to act on my feelings?"

The fact that she was skirting the issue barely registered. Melanie had told him he was so isolated by his drive to succeed that no woman in her right mind would want a relationship with him. The idea that someone as lovely as Lila longed to be in his arms resonated in the most male part of his brain—and his anatomy.

"It's not wrong to have a particularly strong sexual reaction to a person, but it isn't always right to do the first thing that pops into your head about it." Great, now it sounded as if he were giving a psychiatric consultation. "I sensed there was something between us too, but you're my sons' nanny and a potential patient. It's a dicey combination."

"But I'm not a patient yet," she reminded him. "And I waited until I found a man I thought was worthy of me before I decided to be intimate." She rubbed at her nose. "I'm sorry I've made this so difficult."

Her words, accompanied by a pathetic-sounding sigh, caused him to smile. "Don't apologize for being honest—it's a refreshing trait. I'm just trying to figure out where you're coming from."

"I'm not coming *from* anywhere. I wanted to have a pleasant physical moment with a man I was attracted to, and I hoped my first time would be special. I thought that type of no-strings experience was what huma—men enjoyed. Or do I have it totally backwards?"

Paul drained his tea, using the time to consider her logic. Every word she spoke was correct, and if he wasn't such an old-fashioned kind of guy, they'd make sense. He set his cup in the saucer. Hell, what was he thinking? They did make sense.

He was a single man, she was a single woman, and they shared a sexual chemistry that spontaneously combusted from across a room. What was his problem?

"Okay." The word shot from his mouth before he had a chance to think twice.

Lila tugged at her ear, shock registering in her eyes. "Okay?"

Her nervous habit had him grinning. He'd felt like a creep for the past few minutes, sending mixed signals that made her cry while she held herself together and spoke with honesty and calm. It was strangely comforting to know he was capable of catching her off guard by agreeing to see things her way.

"Yeah, okay. I'm willing to have a no-strings-attached relationship with you. My only request is that we cool it while my mother is here."

"And how long might that be?"

"She'll probably be on her way home by Saturday night. There's just one detail that needs to be made perfectly clear."

"And that would be . . . ?"

"Teddy and Rick. The moment I sense what we're doing affects them adversely, it's over."

* * *

Bill waited until Edith Hammer and her companions, carrying full backpacks and carting a canoe on the top of their Jeep, climbed into their car and drove from sight. At loose ends since his wife had started her dinner shift at the restaurant, he'd spent the day selling foil hats and memberships to ESAW. If his calculations were correct, they'd picked up twenty-seven new members today. Later, he would call Eustace Carter and give him the good news.

Taking a casual stroll through the parking lot, he sidled to the rear of the Windcruiser. After surveying the cement factory, which appeared vacant for the evening, and making sure the vicinity was deserted, he got on his hands and knees and inched under the huge vehicle. Inspecting the pipes, hoses, and myriad sections of metal tubing running a maze on the underside of the trailer, he decided everything looked on the up and up.

Backing out, he bumped his bottom against an immovable object and froze in mid-crawl. Glancing between his thighs, he spotted a pair of tree-trunk-sized jeans-clad legs that led to worn sneakers, and blew out a breath. If it had been Chief Gibson's spit-polished uniform shoes, he'd have been in trouble for sure.

"Whatcha lookin' at?"

Oh, hell! Just what I don't need.

Scrambling to his feet, Bill brushed off his plaid walking shorts and pulled up his knee socks, noting his left sandal had a frayed strap that would soon need replacing.

"Did you lose something? 'Cause maybe I could help you find it."

Bill squared his shoulders and turned. "Hey, Harley. How's the thumb?"

The gentle giant's face split into a grin as he held up his bandaged paw. "It's fine. Hardly hurts at all. Dr. P is a good doctor."

"That he is," said Bill, resting his backside against the trailer. "So what brings you over here? I thought you were supposed to spend a couple of days recuperating at the S&B."

"I am—I mean, I was. But it's boring, layin' around and doin' nothing in the storeroom. Millie said it was okay if I took a walk, so I decided to go to the beach, but I saw you over here and thought you might want company."

"Lucky me," muttered Bill.

"Me too," said Harley, pointing to his head. "I'm wearing my hat, like you told me to, so my brain don't get sucked out."

"Smart fella," said Bill. Holding on to his own foil helmet, he bent at the waist and checked under the Windcruiser a second time.

"Did you find what you were looking for?"

"I wasn't exactly *looking* for anything, just checking out whatever's new in town."

"You searching for them a-lee-uns?" asked Harley, his face suddenly grim.

"You might say that," said Bill. "Why?"

"Because I could help." Harley's expression brightened. "I know every inch of town, and the faraway places too. I get around."

"Is that so?"

"Uh-huh. I see . . . things."

For a moment Bill thought the man was going to

tell him he saw *dead people,* like in that damned ghost story he'd watched a couple of years back. "What sort of things?" he asked instead, positive he'd be sorry he posed the question.

"The folks who live in this trailer. I don't care much for them," Harley confided. "That hammer lady is mean."

No kidding. "Really? And where were they when you saw them? 'Cause if it was here in town—"

"Not so much around town, but they go to the wildlife refuge a lot," Harley continued. "I go there too, 'cause I want to look at the birds."

"Well, that makes sense, son, seeing as those folks are birders too. The mister is a travel writer."

"Yeah, but they don't act like any of the bird-watchers I ever saw before," said Harley, shaking his head. "They have boxes that remind me of those things on TV, sorta like the equipment people use when they're in a cave or the desert. And they don't use their binoculars to watch the birds."

Bill stopped tapping his foot and focused on Harley's information. "Equipment people use around rocks? What are you talking about? Can you describe it to me?"

Harley bit at his bottom lip, then used his hands to form a square. "A box, and it has a cord attached to it with a microphone thingy at the other end. And when they hold it out, it crackles and buzzes, kinda like a radio that's out of tune or my toaster when I get a knife caught in the slots."

A box that crackled and buzzed with a cord and a microphone attached?

"Are you talking about that thing they use for detecting radiation? A Geiger counter?"

"I dunno." Harley shrugged. "Maybe."

"Was it nighttime or daytime when you saw them?"

"It was after supper, but it wasn't real dark. They were carrying flashlights and a couple of other things. They even got out of their canoe and mucked through the swamp. Got bit bad by the skeeters, 'cause I heard 'em cussin' about the stings." He held up his good arm as if it were a trophy. "I used bug spray, so I only got one bite. See?"

"That was real smart of you," Bill praised, his brain shooting into hyper-drive. "Anything else?"

"I was hiding behind a stand of cattails, so it was hard to see, but I think they were collecting water. The one man took lots of pictures, but the other fella kept using the box."

"And what was the woman doing?"

"She was real bossy, kinda like my mama used to be when she wanted the garden weeded. Kept staring through her binoculars while she told them to go here and do that, as if they were kids." Harley sighed. "I really miss my ma."

"I'm sure you do," said Bill, trying to put the pieces together. Eustace had pinpointed the UFO landing somewhere south of Preston's Ferry, but after a group powwow they'd decided no self-respecting alien would land in the swampy miasma and stay there. That's why they were getting the word out for folks to keep watch in the towns along Route 13. Now he wondered if ESAW had dropped the ball. "Did you see anything else suspicious out there, Harley? Maybe something those birders missed?"

"Me? Nah. But guess what? Lila's thinking about marrying me, so I won't be lonely anymore. Isn't that great?"

Taken aback, the older man smiled. "I wouldn't count on it, Harley. I think she's sweet on Dr. P."

Harley's shoulders drooped. "Do you think so?"

"Well, she does take care of his boys, and she'd make a good mama for them," said Bill, still ruminating on Harley's information.

"Maybe if I got the boys to like me, Lila would too."

"Sounds good to me," answered Bill, not quite focused on the question. Scratching the side of his head, he made an executive decision as district leader of ESAW. "How'd you like to make a bit of money, son, doing what you've already been doin'? Only you got to promise to report directly to me, and not tell a soul about what you see?"

"You gonna pay me for helpin' in the ESAW booth on Founders' Day?"

" 'Fraid not. That has to be volunteer. But I do need you to do some reconnoitering."

"Recon . . . ?"

"Reconnoitering. It means take a look around, report back to me on what you see or hear with them birders."

"Oh. Then I'd work for you instead of Millie?"

"Just until your thumb heals," added Bill. "Since you aren't supposed to use your hand, my job would be perfect. All you have to do is keep your eyes open and your mouth shut."

Paul sat on the sofa, listening to the happy sounds coming from the twins' bedroom. Lila had cooked a great meal, some sort of vegetable and rice casserole with a salad on the side, and dished out more chocolate ice cream. Then she'd given Teddy and Rick a bath and read them a story, which had enabled him to catch the last few innings of a ball game on the television—something he hadn't done since he'd taken full custody of his sons.

Now Lila was singing them some nonsensical-sounding song with a pleasing melody and strange, almost foreign words. Oddly, the song's meaning didn't matter as much as her soothing tone. Her gentle, harmonious voice seemed to work magic on his mind. Whether she read out loud or sang, the compelling cadence always held him in thrall.

Closing his eyes, he let the tune carry him back over the past twenty-four hours. He and Lila had started out last evening on this very sofa and continued on through the night. If Harley's accident hadn't interrupted their morning, they might have begun the day in the same invigorating manner.

Thoughts about their earlier conversation had filtered through his brain on and off during the afternoon, but the strangest experience was one he'd yet to ask her about. Now he figured it had been a figment of his overtired mind. He had to be wrong about what he'd seen when he found Lila and his sons napping together.

The golden sphere that he'd thought had been hovering above her breasts had not happened—it had only appeared that way. The sphere had to have been resting on her chest.

Now that he was certain he had it straight, he anticipated the evening to come. He'd told Lila he was willing to explore a no-strings affair and she had agreed.

The wait was killing him.

The singing stopped and Paul realized the apartment was quiet, as if the absence of Lila's voice had removed all the life from his home. He shook his head. If he didn't know better, he'd think the woman had hypnotized him. Hell, she'd already mesmerized his sons. Rick's temper had mellowed since her arrival, and Teddy had done something pretty darned amazing as well. According to Lila, he'd used the potty for the first time.

She's doing what you hired her to do, buddy, sang a telling voice in his head.

He couldn't argue with his own logic. But he could wonder what kind of spell Lila had woven around him. Because every time he envisioned her he grew hard as a steel spike. In fact, it was all he could do not to march into the boys' bedroom, drag her out by her gorgeous red hair, toss her onto his bed, and do things to her he'd only dreamed were possible between a man and a woman.

As if stepping from his thoughts, the door opened and Lila entered the living room. Framed in the doorway, she looked self-assured and serene, but her hands were knotted in front of her, a sure sign she was as nervous about their decision as he was.

Then she smiled, and he saw the sunrise over the Chesapeake.

"Teddy and Rick are asleep. I'm going to take a shower."

"Uh—okay," he stuttered.

She licked at her lower lip. "Would you care to join me?"

Paul couldn't remember the last time he'd moved so fast. Trotting after her, he realized he was acting like a hormone-riddled adolescent and frowned. What if someone had an emergency and rang his bell? Everyone in town knew he and Lila shared the house. If no one answered the door, it would set tongues wagging for a week. His mother would hear the rumor and he'd have to spend the weekend digging himself out of a very deep hole. Caught up in the disappointing thought, he bumped smack into Lila when she turned to face him at the bathroom door.

"Oops, sorry," he mumbled. "I—um—maybe this isn't such a bright idea. If someone had an emergency and rang the bell, I wouldn't hear it in there."

Looking pensive, she wrinkled her nose. "Does that happen very often?"

"Uh, no, not really."

"Then why don't we give it a try?"

Paul swallowed down his next protest. He had to be ten times stupid to keep finding reasons for them to stay apart. He opened his mouth and Lila placed two fingers on his lips.

"Come on. We'll be quick."

But not too quick, he hoped. Because the idea of exploring every inch of her silky skin under a spray of steamy water had suddenly stripped him of his voice.

Tugging his T-shirt over his head, he followed her into the bathroom and almost walked into the doorframe. She giggled at his eager motions and bent to adjust the taps while he shrugged out of his jeans and underwear.

Turning, her face flushed red when she spotted his penis all ready for action. "I didn't expect—I mean, I didn't think—does that hurt?"

He closed the distance between them until they were a mere breath apart. "Not right now, but it will if I don't get inside of you in the next ten seconds."

Her expression turned to sunshine again, and together they removed her clothes and hopped into the tub. Paul whipped the shower curtain closed and they were enveloped in a warm, wet cocoon of sensuality. Clasping Lila's jaw, he inched closer, brushing his lips against hers. She rose on tiptoe and twined her arms around his neck, moving her pelvis against his groin. Paul moaned and pulled her to his chest.

Drowning in sensation, Lila broke the kiss. She squirted shower gel on a washcloth and soaped his chest, running the nubby cloth over his stomach and down to his engorged shaft.

He rested his forehead against hers and groaned. "Keep this up and I'm going to die a happy man."

Lila smiled. No one on her planet had told her how wonderful love play could be—or how good it felt to have a strong man melt to putty in her hands. "Turn around and I'll do your back."

His muscles clenched under her seeking fingers, and she grew bold. It seemed that once Paul Anderson made a decision about something, he forged ahead full speed. Now that he'd decided they could have an intimate relationship, he was more than willing to do his part to make it special for both of them.

She scrubbed his broad shoulders and lower, to the curve of his spine, circling the washcloth over his taut buttocks and the backs of his thighs. Then she ran her hands around his lean hips to his front and found the object of their pleasure.

Paul grabbed at her wrists and spun to face her. "Okay, that's about all the torture I can stand. It's your turn." Taking the cloth from her, he began a leisurely massage of her breasts, paying careful attention to her nipples as he worked the fabric up and over each mound.

He replaced the cloth with his lips and Lila's vision clouded as she sagged against him. "That feels wonderful."

Paul backed her against the tile wall. "Think you can handle a little more?"

Gazing into his eyes, she nodded.

Parting her legs, he delved into the center of her thighs, using his fingers to manipulate the hidden part of her he now knew so well.

Lila cried out at the exquisite sensation, moving to the rhythm of his hand. He settled between her legs and nudged her feet onto the sides of the tub. "Hold on to my shoulders and move closer," he ordered, his voice as steamy as the spray.

She did as he asked, and he set his hands on her waist and eased her up until the tip of his penis inched into her center.

"Now wrap your legs around my waist and hang on. I'll do all the rest."

Lila obeyed without question. He lowered her onto his rigid shaft while he slid upward at the same time, thrusting his body inside of her in one swift motion. Then he pressed her into the tile wall and captured her mouth with his as he began a steady pumping. The movement turned frantic when she clutched his head and deepened the kiss, opening her lips and encouraging his tongue to mimic the action of his hips.

Paul kept his hands under her bottom, anchoring her in place as he pistoned into her, their mouths fused as if they were one being.

Lila arched back to accept him more fully and he groaned in her mouth. Relentless in his movement, he sucked at her tongue as he ground into her until the pleasure built to an almost painful need. Then the world exploded and she stiffened as he took her over the edge.

As if suspended in time, neither moved. Finally, still deep inside of her, Paul raised a knee and let her rest on his thigh. "You okay?" he asked, his breath a rasp of desire.

She managed a weak nod. "Barely."

"Well, catch your breath," he murmured. Bending low, he licked a droplet of water beading over her nipple. "Because I want you to come again, only this time I want to take the ride at your side."

Fourteen

Lila snuggled under the covers, too content to do more than yawn. Paul's gentle breathing tickled the back of her ear, while his thighs cupped her possessively from behind. Even in sleep, his erection nudged at her bottom, reminding her of the words they'd whispered and the passion they'd shared several times during the night.

Shimmering pink-gray light seeped from around the window shade, bringing with it a memory of her old planet with its two suns and double moon. Often the colors of each sun blended to a brilliant fiery orange at daybreak, while the conjoined moons shone an intense turquoise at night. Knowing it was a sight she would never again see filled her with a profound sadness.

Someday in the future, the Elders would contact the people here, and thank them for the male children the select men had helped create with their women. But that wouldn't happen until her world knew for certain the bold experiment was a success. In the meantime, the travelers were expected to focus on their goal. If everything went as her world planned, all would meet the mother ship and return home as heros.

The burden of her own plan weighed twofold heavy on her heart. Not only was she betraying her people and her sister by being here; she was betraying Paul, as well. He trusted her to take care of his sons. He was a good father, a healer, and a genuinely decent man. He made her quiver with anticipation and weep with joy all at the same time. What would he think of her if he knew how many times she'd lied?

What would he say if he found out she was not of his world?

A wave of homesickness struck. She resided in Preston's Ferry now, a town overrun with alien hunters and strangers in huge vehicles who asked pointed questions. Questions that could bring to light a situation fraught with danger for both herself and the child she hoped to carry. All of the travelers were faced with such a challenge, but she had the most to lose. If she was discovered, there would be no help from her people, no emergency rescue.

No aid for a traitor.

The Elders had chosen the United States because of its advanced technology and continued interest in space exploration, but Americans were on par with the rest of Earth's inhabitants when it came to assessing those from a foreign planet. She'd sat through enough informational sessions to believe the data: the people of Earth were an uncivilized race, not ready to accept freely any friendship offered by beings from another solar system.

Thoughts bombarded her senses. She would have several more opportunities to conceive before all was lost, but the longer she remained in Preston's Ferry, the more certain her chances of detection. She couldn't leave until she became pregnant, then she would be forced to disappear. After her jewels were gone, she would still need a career here, a way to earn a living for herself and her child.

She consoled herself with the idea that until then, she could spend time in Paul's bed and, if she closed out the negative thoughts, pretend they were a couple with a future.

Dreaming about it now, while tucked in the safety of his arms, Lila realized the moment she left would be the most miserable of her existence. That she'd become so attached to Teddy and Rick she sometimes forgot she wasn't their birth mother was understandable, but she'd also done something utterly reckless and undeniably stupid.

She had lost her heart to her sister's target. She was in love with Paul Anderson.

"Hey, why the sigh?" Paul's arm tightened around her waist. "Are you starting to regret our decision?"

Never! she wanted to shout, but kept the urge in check. "I was thinking about the twins, wondering what we could do to pass the time today."

"What did you have in mind?"

"Rose invited us to come visit whenever we wanted, so I thought that a possibility. Then there's the beach, unless it's too cold."

"Both stellar ways to spend a spring day." He nuzzled the nape of her neck, warming her insides with a sizzle of desire. "What would make you happy?"

Staying here with you, forever. "I'm not the important one. It's the boys who need stimulation."

He moved his hand to her breast and palmed her nipple. "This boy has an idea that will keep us both *stimulated* for a while. . . ."

Bolstered by his teasing words, Lila turned in his arms and touched her mouth to his, hoping to convey the feelings in her heart. "Do you think we have time?"

"There's always time for a morning wake-up call," he said, catching her chin between his teeth.

She nestled a leg between his knees and moved closer in his embrace. Paul grazed her neck, sucked gently on the pulse point in her throat, then inched his way to the breast he'd been tormenting. Capturing a rigid nipple in his teeth, he bit down with just enough intensity to jolt her to her toes. Cupping the aching mound, he suckled at the sensitized nub until Lila moaned her pleasure.

He responded by parting her feminine folds with his free hand. Locating the swollen button that ached for his touch, he expertly circled the target with his fingertips, stroking until he brought her to mindless submission.

Lila gasped for breath as she rolled to her back and opened her thighs. Looming over her, Paul studied her face with an almost fierce expression as he settled into her center and thrust upward, possessing her completely. Dipping his head, he found her other breast and began to suckle in rhythm with the motion of his hips.

Wrapping her legs around his waist, she arched off the bed. Paul came to his knees and sat on his heels while his hands moved to her back and supported her on his thighs. Surging into her, he joined their mouths as he'd done their bodies, using his tongue to drive her to a greater frenzy.

With her hands on his shoulders for leverage, Lila rode the strength of his muscular legs, raising and lowering herself with his every thrust until they rocked in perfect harmony. Driven to near madness, she crested the wave of passion until she could stand it no longer and gave herself up to a shattering release.

In seconds, Paul clutched her to his chest and followed her spiral with a heated moan of surrender.

Panting, they fell to the mattress, still fused from breasts to hips. He rested his forehead against hers and together they fought for breath. Unable to speak, Lila ran her fingers through his thick golden hair, biting her lower lip to keep from revealing her emotions. Every time they made love was more exciting than the last, each incredible experience a treasure to be stored in her heart.

She felt a rumble deep in his chest and focused on his smoky blue eyes. "Did I do something amusing?"

"No, it's me," he said with a shake of his head. "Being with you makes me grateful you were so relentless in your arguments. Right now"—he kissed the tip of her nose—"I'm very happy I let myself be talked into this. Thank you."

Lila had no idea how to respond. Paul still

sounded as if he were here only because of her superior powers of persuasion; not because he desired her in the same way she did him.

"I'm going to shower and get dressed. It's early, so you can probably catch a few more winks." He slid off her and stood at the side of the bed. "I'll see you later. If it's a light day, I might even join you and the boys for lunch."

He walked from the room, leaving her to ponder her predicament.

Lila opened her eyes. The gray light she'd observed earlier was now golden, a sure sign of the late hour. Paul had meant well letting her sleep in, but if she didn't get out of bed soon, she would be up to her ears in demanding little boys with dirty diapers.

She swung her legs over the mattress and stood. Without warning, the room swam around her. Dropping back to the bed, she heaved a breath. Since landing here, she'd felt no ill effects from the unfamiliar food or water. Why was the room spinning? Why did her stomach feel as it had when she'd first entered Earth's atmosphere in her traveling pod?

Inhaling another deep breath, she pressed trembling fingers to her temples and ordered her queasy stomach to calm. Perhaps she'd contracted what earthlings sometimes referred to as a *bug*. Though her world had eradicated all forms of illness, this planet still teemed with diseases, some serious but much of it mild and nonthreatening. She only hoped that her species' close physiological makeup to a human would garner the identical earthly reaction to one of those simple and short-lived viruses.

Taking a third stabilizing breath, she stood on wobbly legs and forced herself into action. It didn't matter what ailed her, because the twins needed her. She had to begin the day. Moving slowly, she pulled fresh clothes from the dresser and half stumbled into the bathroom. After taking a quick shower, she dressed. Intent on drying her hair, she stood in front of the mirror.

And froze in place.

Blinking, she bent over the sink and peered at her face. Tilting her head from side to side, she gave another series of blinks, hoping to clear her vision of what could only be an illusion. Straightening, she continued to gaze at her reflection.

Brilliant green eyes stared back at her, their color such a shock it threatened to stop her heart. Their hue was deeper than spring grass, more arresting than the glow on the traffic signals she'd seen on the main highway, and brighter than the emeralds in the bracelet on her wrist.

What had happened to her eyes?

The question rattled in her skull, until the answer jumped out at her and caused her to plop onto the commode. Enveloped in happiness, her love for Paul crested in a great wrenching wave. She sniffed as the tears welled. Clutching her belly, she smiled until her lips ached.

She'd never heard what would happen to her physically if she became pregnant, probably because no woman of her race had ever carried a half-human child, but there could be no other reason for the strange phenomenon.

She was pregnant with Paul's baby.

Her hands shook as she walked to her room, opened her dresser drawer, and removed her backpack. After finding the small disk needed to confirm her suspicion, she slipped it into the clasp on her bracelet and pressed the back hard against the underside of her wrist, exactly as Rila had demonstrated when she'd explained about the test. The disk read her temperature and other pertinent bodily functions and combined the data with her heart rate to elicit a chemical reaction that would lead to a positive or negative result.

Lila counted to ten, then flipped open the clasp. If she was pregnant with a girl, the glow would be red; green meant she carried a boy. Smiling, she cradled her wrist to her breast, taking in the disk's emerald light. She had attained her goal. She could leave Preston's Ferry and start a new life with a child of her own.

Still in shock, she stowed the disk and returned to the bathroom to finish preparing for the day. A shriek sounded from the other side of the apartment, turning Lila to stone. Rick and Teddy were half-brothers to the son she carried. When she left, they would remain with their father. Her boy would never know his true family, just as she would never see her sister or her parents again.

A second series of shouts spurred her to action. She had to think, but she also had to care for her charges. Once she changed and fed the twins, she would find something for them to do while she thought out her next move. She'd waited a lifetime for this day. Now that it was here, she had to proceed with caution.

She had to make sure she didn't arouse suspicion by simply disappearing into thin air. She had to formulate the rest of her plan.

Paul sat at the kitchen table while Lila puttered at the stove. She'd darkened the room and set the table with flowers and a single lit candle, then served a plate of cheese and crackers, which he assumed was an effort to make their dinner time special. But instead of chatting about her day, she was strangely quiet.

His patient load had been surprisingly heavy, so he'd never joined her and the twins for lunch. By the time he'd caught a break and come upstairs, Rick and Teddy were in their cribs and their nanny was napping in her room. Lila had looked so beautiful and at peace, it had taken all his self-control not to climb into her bed and wake her with a kiss.

The rest of the afternoon had passed in a blur, but he'd been aware of Lila's every move. He knew exactly when she'd come downstairs to put clothes in the washer and dryer, and when she'd taken them out. He'd even found himself listening for her footsteps overhead while he'd sat in his office and taken care of paperwork. The urge to spend time with her was so compelling, he'd escorted Harley to the door immediately after his exam and locked it, then raced to the second floor because he knew she was waiting.

Lila brought a basket of garlic bread, one of his favorite foods, to the table. Snagging a piece, he flashed a smile, but she ignored him and headed back to the stove. Seconds later, she set down his plate, and he inhaled the tangy scent of tomato sauce and cheese.

"You made lasagna. It smells great."

She served Teddy and Rick, then brought over her own dinner and sat without comment. One taste of the filling surrounded by creamy cheese and firm noodles had him puzzled. "I'm not sure I want to know, but what's in this?" he asked, still trying to charm her with a smile.

Busy cutting Rick's food, Lila didn't meet his gaze. "Rose gave me the recipe. It's vegetarian Italian sausage."

Paul did his part by helping Teddy guide a forkful of lasagna to his mouth. "So you saw her today?"

"Yes, this morning at the S&B." She added a scoop of salad to each boy's plate, then passed the bowl to Paul.

"Sounds as if you and the twins had a busy day."

"Pretty much the same as we do every day," she answered, keeping her eyes on the table. "I went for a walk with Harley. I hope you don't mind, but I let him push the buggy. He was very careful."

"Was he wearing his foil beanie?"

"Yes, and I wore one too."

At her admission, Paul couldn't resist teasing. "Did you, now?"

"I bought it from Bill, and I don't wear it often, but whenever he sees me without it he reminds me, so I figured it was easier to just put it on."

"Has Bill been pestering you about that meeting he's holding tomorrow night?" He reached for his glass of red wine. "Because you don't have to go."

"I want to go," said Lila, pushing the food on her plate from side to side.

"Please don't tell me you believe that claptrap about an alien landing in the wildlife refuge."

She set down her fork. "Bill is a friend. I want to hear what he has to say."

"Then I'll come with you." Paul sipped his wine. It might be fun listening to those old geezers, and it wouldn't hurt for him to take a more active part in the community, especially since a good chunk of the money raised at the celebration was earmarked for a portable X-ray machine for his office. "The ESAW meeting is supposed to come to order after the town finalizes the details of Founders' Day. Very clever of Bill to arrange it so he has a built-in audience. He'll probably try to lock the doors and hold everyone captive."

Lila worried her lower lip as she spooned lasagna into Rick's open mouth. She'd been so tired this afternoon, she hadn't been able to think straight. Wearing sunglasses all day, avoiding eye contact with Paul, and serving dinner by candlelight was all she'd managed to come up with for a cover. Even though her eyes were still a bright green, she intended to go to both the Founders' Day and ESAW meetings in order to keep tabs on rumors about the alien landing and garner information about her fellow travelers.

She decided she couldn't leave until after the festival, when Paul's mother would be here to take care of the twins. By then she'd have an idea that would take her far away from Preston's Ferry and the man and boys she had come to love. But she didn't want Paul to get too involved in the propaganda he was sure to hear from Eustace Carter when he spoke at Bill's meeting.

"I don't see why you need to attend the ESAW meeting. Just because I'm interested doesn't mean you have to waste a night hearing their thoughts."

Paul set his glass on the table. "If it's important to you, I want to be there. If nothing else, it should be good for a laugh."

"It might not finish until late," she warned, hoping to dissuade him. "It's important the boys stick to their schedule and get to bed at a reasonable hour."

"Not a problem." He grabbed a second piece of garlic bread. "I'll call Ashley and ask if she's free to babysit. You remember her? She took our dinner order at Croakers."

Lila recalled Ashley all too well. Though barely past puberty, the young woman had designs on Paul. She wasn't about to allow the curvy, blond-haired cashier anywhere near her man—or the twins, she quickly amended.

"You have to get up early the next morning—"

"Not a problem. If I get tired, I can close the office and catch a nap." He took another sip of wine. "How about if I promise not to laugh? Then can I stay?"

Lila stared at her plate, still filled with lasagna. She'd had no appetite today, and Paul's latest request wasn't helping to calm her rebellious stomach. "I'm not sure Ashley is the right person to watch the boys. I'd prefer someone older and more responsible."

His blue eyes twinkling in the flickering light, Paul leaned back in his chair. "Now you're starting to sound like me. How about I ask Rose's mother?

I'm sure she'll be at the Founders' Day thing, but I doubt she's into ESAW. Maybe she'd be willing to walk the boys home and put them to bed while we stay and listen to Bill."

His sensible suggestion stripped Lila of further argument. "All right, but only Mrs. Sweeney, no one else." She stood and cleared the table, then took out ice cream and bowls. Before she could fill the dishes, she felt Paul's presence behind her.

"Dinner was great." He stepped close to her backside and ran his hands over her arms. "But I get the feeling something's wrong. You've been quiet."

Warmed by his concern, she melted against him. "I'm tired. I think I might be coming down with a—a bug."

"Uh-oh." He wrapped his arms around her from behind. "That's not good. How about I finish in here and put the boys to bed? You can take a shower and call it a night."

She turned and rested her head on his chest, reveling in the comfort of his embrace. He was so thoughtful and caring, while she was a liar and a thief. Soon she would be stealing his child.

"Are you sure you don't mind?" she asked, practically asleep on her feet.

"Nope. I've been doing this for a while, and Teddy and Rick have survived." He kissed the top of her head. "Go on, get some rest. We'll see you in the morning."

"And then me and Lila walked the boys to the beach and she let me push the stroller," said Harley. He had been dogging Bill's steps as the two of them sneaked around the back of the deserted building. "I tell you, it was a mighty fine day for both of us. I just know she's thinking about marrying me."

Bill gave the man a stern glance from over his shoulder. "How many times do I have to tell you, son, she's sweet on the doc. Use what little sense the good Lord gave you and stop thinking about her that way."

He crouched low and continued his duckwalk to the rear of the Windcruiser. After close observation, he'd deduced that the three birders had stayed inside the trailer tonight, and he was determined to hear what they were talking about, even at the cost of detection.

"But Bill—"

"Hush, now," he hissed, raising his hand. "If you can't keep quiet, you're gonna hafta go home. This is important." He flattened himself against the trailer and signaled Harley to do the same, then held a finger to his lips.

Harley did as he was told and Bill sighed his relief. He should have thought twice before taking the soft-headed man-child into his confidence, but there was no way he could be in two places at once. Having Harley follow the birders into the swamp while he kept in touch with Eustace, enrolled new members in ESAW, and encouraged folks to stay for the meeting was the best he could manage. Now the boy was blathering about him and Lila and a happily-ever-after, when it would never happen.

He cast Harley a warning glare, then reached into his pocket and pulled out his latest purchase. The compact gizmo had been touted as a genuine secret agent listening device. He'd bought it from a mail-order catalogue doing business out of New York City, and the company guaranteed its merchandise to be one hundred percent accurate. It had cost a pretty penny, nearly fifty bucks, but he'd tried it out on Ellen's bridge group and knew it worked as advertised.

"What's that?" asked Harley, his voice hushed.

"A Super Ear Sound Enhancer. Now be quiet."

"Oh," said Harley, as if he knew what Bill was talking about.

Bill stuck the suction cup on the window and placed the miniature receiver in his ear, then adjusted the dial on a rectangular box no bigger than a pack of cigarettes. The Windcruiser shifted and he jumped, as did Harley. Catching his breath, he motioned Harley to settle down. Intent on his mission, he played with the volume control until he heard a man's voice.

"How about we leave tomorrow and head north? There's only one newcomer in town, and she looks to be harmless."

"I say we stay until after the Founders' Day celebration," answered a masculine voice Bill dubbed number two. "There's supposed to be several hundred visitors. Maybe we'll get lucky and glean a bit of info from the crowd."

"It's a possibility, but I think we're wasting our time with the woman," continued the first voice.

"I don't agree," said Edith Hammer.

"You're not serious," the first man scoffed. "She's too attractive to be an alien."

"Yeah, well, I heard from Frank over in Texas that

the person they're investigating isn't what anyone expected either. Our suspect appears a tad too naïve if you ask me, and it seems as if she actually enjoys hanging out with the town idiot instead of normal people."

Bill gave a sidelong glance at his companion, who was busy picking dirt off his bandage, and felt suddenly contrite at the way he always talked down to Harley. Maybe it was time he treated the boy a little better.

"What if the extraterrestrial is doing something sneaky, like inhabiting a body? Say that crazy old biddy on the bicycle?" suggested voice number one.

"According to our man in Texas, that doesn't seem to be the MO. These aliens don't take over human bodies because they don't need to. He suspects the invaders look exactly like us—or so close to it everyone is fooled," said Edith. "He reported that their primary looks and acts like a normal human being. Theirs is a woman too, by the way, and she wears a bracelet that sounds a lot like the one on our suspect's wrist."

Bracelet? Bill thought he might start to hyperventilate.

"So what's the latest theory?" asked number one.

"Now that Lucas Diamond is missing—"

"Diamond is missing?" voice number two broke in. "How in the hell did the chief disappear?"

"That's still under investigation. Peggy and Martin Maddox think they have things under control."

"Maddox is back?" chimed number one. "That will throw a monkey wrench in the works."

"Seems he wanted to come out of retirement

when he realized what was happening, and the president agreed. Anyway, our people are handling it. Scuttlebutt is the interlopers landed singly at each site at almost the exact same time. Nine touchdowns across the country, with one alien at each drop," explained Edith. "The consensus is they're all women."

Bill adjusted the tuner. Had they just said the aliens were females? Evil spacemen, sending women to do their dirty work.

"I gather our men will have an easier time of it, now that Diamond's gone?" said voice number two.

"Of course," replied Edith. "And if they're reading the data correctly, we're all going to be very rich very soon."

"I like the sound of that," said the first voice. "Have we received any information on those water samples or goo we collected?"

"Yes. Unfortunately, the report doesn't help," answered Edith. "The slime we sent in has the same composition as they detected at the Texas site, so it will probably be identical everywhere—harmless proteins and amino acids in a plasma-based compound with about ten percent of a substance that doesn't register on any of our charts."

The trailer bounced as if someone inside were walking around, and Bill jumped again. His jerky reflexes pulled the suction cup off the window, which in turn popped the receiver from his ear, forcing him to scramble for the device. He flattened a hand on Harley's chest and pressed him against the trailer. The Windcruiser rocked in place, then settled back on its wheels. He heard the rumble of voices and waited, then inched the suction cup back onto the window.

There was the sound of shuffling papers, then the second voice spoke again. "You're right. This tells us nothing."

"We still need to be careful," cautioned Edith. "That crazy fool selling tinfoil headgear is suspicious of us."

Voice number one gave a bark of laughter. "That old fart couldn't find his wanker in a wind storm. He's more interested in making money than capturing aliens, just like Carter and the other members of that fly-by-night group."

"Don't be so sure about Carter," cautioned Edith. "I hear he's still got friends in high places."

"So," began voice number two, "what's next?"

"We could snatch her off the street the next time she goes out, but she's always with those kids," said number one. "Even though they're young, they'd make a racket."

Kids! Bill swallowed down the lump rising in his chest. After Rose, the only female who escorted kids around town was Lila . . . and she always wore a fancy-looking bracelet.

"I don't think we need to go that far just yet," said Edith. "I have an idea that might produce results, provided you two can—"

Harley tapped his shoulder and Bill jumped a foot.

"Can I listen?" Harley asked.

Bill gave his head an emphatic shake, which once again pulled out the receiver. Cursing silently, he jammed the earpiece back in just as Edith said, "At least one of us will be in a better position to get information. If I don't learn anything, we still have the ESAW meeting and the actual Founders' Day event. Between the three, we may glean enough to justify bringing her in for questioning."

Bill's heart hammered so loudly he thought for sure they'd hear it in the trailer. He couldn't—no—he wouldn't believe they were talking about his little friend Lila. She'd signed on with ESAW the very first time they'd met, and she was a damn fine caretaker to those two boys. She was sweet on Dr. P, for criminy sake. And Dr. Anderson was too smart a fella to be taken in by an alien.

And what was Edith's idea?

He adjusted the dial on the Super Ear, but all he got was static. Suddenly a high-pitched beep shattered his eardrum. Ripping the receiver from his ear, he stuffed it into his pocket. The sound of the television seeped through the window of the Windcruiser and Bill knew he was through for the night.

Fifteen

Lila felt the brush of cool lips on her forehead, then a warm hand caressed her cheek. Opening her eyes to slits, she gazed at Paul, crouched beside her bed, his face wreathed in worry as he stared intently.

"How do you feel?" he asked, his voice filled with concern.

She took in the dim room and sensed it was early. The last thing she remembered was dragging herself to bed immediately after dinner. Had she truly slept the night away?

"What time is it?" she muttered, keeping her eyes at half mast.

"Just before seven. The boys are snoozing. I'm going to make coffee and toast. Can I bring you a tray?"

She rolled to her side and surveyed the rumpled covers and indentation in the pillow next to her. "Did you sleep here last night?"

Standing, he stuffed his hands in his pockets and stared at the floor. "I didn't want you to be sick and not make it to the bathroom. I hope it was okay."

"It was very thoughtful," she assured him, a grin tugging at the corners of her mouth. "I'm feeling better."

"You're certain? Because I could phone Rose and ask her to come over or—"

"I'm fine. Really," Lila answered, not positive it was the truth. Her stomach had wavered when he mentioned food; she couldn't think of a single thing that might stay down after she swallowed it. "I'll be even better after I take a shower and put on clean clothes."

"Do you need help with . . . ?"

"No. I'm good," she insisted, certain she didn't want his assistance in the bathroom or anywhere else at the moment. She had no idea if her eye color was back to normal, and she needed time to compose herself. "You go ahead. I'll call if I have a problem."

Paul tucked his shirt into the waistband of his pants as he continued his careful scrutiny of her person. Finally, he nodded. "I'll be in the kitchen if you change your mind."

He walked from the room and Lila sighed. Moving to the opposite side of the bed, she placed her head on his pillow and breathed in his potent masculine scent. Maybe she would take the pillow cover with her when she left, just to have a reminder of his presence. Besides Paul's child, there would be precious little she would have to remember him by.

She realized she had to get moving or he would be back to check on her, and edged to the side of the mattress. So far, so good. Standing, she inhaled a ragged breath and waited for her knees to stop wobbling and her nerves to calm. Stepping to the dresser, she removed fresh clothing and underwear and slowly made her way to the bathroom. Leaning over the sink, she peered into the mirror, only to be met with the same jewel-toned eyes she'd seen yesterday.

Dismayed, she took a quick shower, letting the cleansing water ease her mind and sooth her wounded spirit. She still had sunglasses to hide behind, and she could always stay inside and keep the twins busy with her energy ball. There was no need for her to go out until tonight. With so many people expected at the meeting, she doubted anyone would notice the dark glasses or her pale face.

Staring again at her eyes, she remembered that some humans wore contact lenses to correct their vision. Would Paul believe she suddenly had need of them? What if she told him she'd worn them all along, and had used up her last pair of clear lenses, which required her to switch to the tinted ones?

A knock on the door startled her. "You doing okay in there?" asked Paul.

"I'm fine." She sat on the commode. "Are the boys awake?"

"Yes, but they're still in their cribs. Are you sure you can handle them?"

Inhaling through her nose, she exhaled through her mouth. "Positive."

"Okay. I'll be in my office if you need me."

Lila waited until his footsteps echoed in the distance before she stood and made a second inspection of her face. Her skin was the color of a paper napkin, the dark circles under her eyes emphasizing their unusual color. No wonder Paul had seemed so concerned; she was a fright.

"La! La! La!"

Rick and Teddy were waiting for her. Perhaps she would pass the time working on their speech. If she could give Paul one gift upon leaving, it would be Teddy saying daddy. It was such a small thing, when compared to what he'd given her, but it was all she had.

"Good morning," she said, walking into their room.

She sniffed the air and realized they had yet to do their morning business. Rushing to Rick, she scooped him from his crib, carried him to the bathroom, and whisked off his pajamas and diaper. Then she sat him on the potty chair.

"Stay there and do something productive while I get your brother," she ordered, heading back to their bedroom.

By the time she returned with Teddy, Rick had risen to the challenge. Lila praised him and quickly sat Teddy down while she cleaned and dressed Rick. After a few seconds, the younger twin met with success as well. Elated by their progress, she hoisted a child in each arm and began to dance around the apartment.

Her joy turned to tears as she realized this might be the only accomplishment the three of them would ever share. She wouldn't be here to see them take their first ride on a bicycle, or help them learn to read and write. She would miss their first day of school, and the good grades they were sure to receive. She wouldn't be able to guide Rick in controlling his temper, or comfort Teddy when his feelings were hurt.

She was going to miss so much in their lives.

Teddy patted her face, his lips puckered in a frown.

"No, no, don't cry," Lila told him when she saw the tears well in his bright blue eyes. "It's going to be all right. I'll find a way to come back and visit, honest I will."

She brought them into the kitchen and assembled their breakfast. She even managed to drink a cup of tea and nibble at a slice of toast with peanut butter. After tossing the remains in the trash, she glanced out the window and acknowledged the day was too beautiful to spend inside. She had sunglasses and the twins loved it in the yard.

She guided the boys down the stairs, through the lab, and into the play area, where she gazed at the clear blue sky and inhaled the fresh, sea-scented air. Teddy and Rick scrambled to the sandbox and Lila took a seat on the swings, where she was able to monitor their play and still give them the freedom to be themselves.

From the corner of her eye, she saw Paul standing at the back door, his expression almost wistful. After a time, he left and she sniffled. Hormones, she told herself, wiping her teary eyes. She'd been warned that pregnant women of her species were very much like earthwomen in this respect, and often were ruled by the infernal compounds. This inner longing to be near Paul and his children, her regret at having to leave, even her change in eye color were all a part of the chemicals bubbling through her system.

The sensitive reaction to her charged emotions would fade soon, and she would be overcome with a feeling of euphoria that would last well into her pregnancy. Until then, she'd be at the mercy of her hormones.

She wasn't sure how much time passed before she raised her head and locked gazes with a man standing at the rear gate.

Paul heard footsteps overhead moving in a rhythm he couldn't quite put his finger on. Accompanied by peals of childish laughter and a woman's muffled voice, the odd patter warmed his ears as the footwork escalated, then faded. The idea that Lila was well enough to roughhouse with the boys washed over him in a calming wave. He hoped she was correct about feeling better. If she did have a bug, he imagined another afternoon nap and a second night's rest would have her back to her old self by tomorrow.

He recalled her earlier exhaustion, which had seemed mental as well as physical. She'd been so tired, she hadn't even twitched when he'd first slipped into bed beside her. He'd had no intention of suggesting they have sex. His only goal had been to offer comfort, but when she'd turned and nestled against his chest, it felt so right, so perfect, he too had fallen into a deep and peaceful void.

Lila's lack of energy was a worry, but Paul found himself more concerned with the dark circles ringing her eyes than her need to sleep. He'd wondered throughout dinner why she kept avoiding his gaze, and now that he'd gotten a good look at her in the pale light of morning, he understood why. Her clear green eyes had heightened in color, turning to the brilliant tones of the emeralds in her bracelet.

Puzzled by the phenomenon, he frowned. He had no clue what type of virus would cause such an odd symptom, but the color only seemed quirky when compared to her waxen complexion. He wasn't going to worry about it unless his phone started ringing with frantic locals complaining of extreme exhaustion and an eerie eye color change as well. Lila hadn't said, but maybe she wore contacts and hadn't needed them until fatigued.

He did his usual check of the examining rooms and made sure the lab area was straightened. After a few minutes, he answered his first call of the day, and listened patiently while Agnes Depew let him know her conjunctivitis was on the mend. Moments later he received a second call, this one from his accountant, phoning to let Paul know he planned to visit sometime at the end of the month. David hoped to get in a little fishing and, in between, go over the books. In the meanwhile, he was still waiting for the paperwork on Paul's new employee.

Paul recalled bringing the employment application upstairs, setting it on the kitchen table, and asking Lila to fill it out. She'd probably put it somewhere, then got hit with that bug and forgotten it existed. After assuring David he would take care of it, he made a mental note to remind her as soon as he was certain she was on the mend.

A few minutes passed before he heard the twins

and Lila clatter down the stairs and out the back door. He didn't think she'd be foolish enough to take the boys for a buggy ride, but he wanted to make sure, so he headed for the porch. Using the door for a shield, he peeked into the yard and saw his sons toddling toward the sandbox. Teddy plopped down and immediately concentrated on filling the rear of a dump truck with sand, while Rick worked on doing the same to his bucket. Dressed in clean clothes and wearing lightweight jackets, they seemed healthy and content.

Telling himself he was merely standing guard while he made sure Lila could handle his rambunctious sons, Paul stared at her copper-colored hair waving in the breeze. A pair of sunglasses covered the top half of her pale face, while her khaki slacks and oversized navy blue sweater made her look almost matronly. His brow arched at the ironic thought. He knew firsthand that hidden underneath those plain tailored clothes was the arousing form of a sexy young woman.

A memory of the time they'd spent in bed zeroed straight to the area below his belt. Paul shook his head. Lila was so much more than a dynamite body with a throaty laugh and a wonderfully sensual nature. She was caring and warm and kind. She'd become the ideal substitute mother for his sons, just as he'd hoped she would. The day she'd walked into his office had been one of the luckiest in his life. The night they'd first shared a bed—

He shook his head. If he didn't curtail his wayward thoughts, his mother was going to read him as easily as she had when he'd lived at home. He'd never been able to pull anything over on her, especially when it had to do with his love life. She'd even suspected something was wrong between him and Melanie before he'd realized it himself. He and Lila were going to have to act cool and distant toward each other whenever his mom was around or they were toast.

Without conscious effort, a question formed in Paul's mind—one he couldn't ignore. What did Lila mean to him, really?

He refused to believe she was a convenience, a simple way for him to relieve sexual tension and find adventure between the sheets. If that were the case, why did he think about her when he was supposed to be concentrating on his patients or taking care of paperwork? And why had he felt the need to lie next to her last night, not to take advantage but to offer solace and assistance?

He smiled. He'd even promised to attend that ridiculous space invaders meeting Bill kept pushing, just so she wouldn't have to sit in the fire hall alone. That had to mean she was more than a bed partner.

But how much more?

As if on cue, his sensible inner voice—the one that had warned him *don't grope the nanny*—made its presence known and posed another, more serious question: What did *he* mean to Lila?

His pride joined forces with a healthy dose of male ego as he considered all he had to offer a woman. The world's greatest lover came to mind, and he stifled a laugh. Since Lila had no one to compare him to, fat little that would mean to her.

An excellent provider? He glanced around his office with its mismatched furniture and bare-bones living area above. If he still resided in Baltimore, maybe, but even here, at the tip of nowhere, this décor was sadly lacking.

A good father? He liked to think he'd improved his parenting skills, but would that matter in the type of relationship they'd developed?

He blew out a breath. It couldn't be his looks—Lila wasn't that shallow. And he'd given up his workaholic ways and indifferent attitude, as well. But was that enough to interest her in something more?

The front door opened before he finished the thought, and he walked into the waiting room to greet his first patient—a tall, thin woman wearing a pinched expression.

"I'm looking for the doctor," she said, her mouth stern.

"You've found him," answered Paul. "Are you here for a checkup, or do you have a specific problem?"

"I heard you might have need of a part-time receptionist, and thought I'd stop by to see about the job."

The phone rang and he moved to answer it, but the woman beat him to the punch. Assessing her efficient, no-nonsense manner, he let her handle the call.

"Good morning, Dr. Anderson's office. How may I help you?"

She picked up one of his business cards, read it, and set it back in the holder. "His hours today are nine-to-five . . . one moment and I'll check." She ran a bony finger down a page in the appointment book. "Eleven will be fine. Your name and home number?"

She jotted the information on a message pad and set the phone in its cradle. "A Mr. Mervin Taylor will be here at eleven. It seems he has a severe cough that will not be tamed with over-the-counter medication."

The door opened and Dora Gibson walked in, followed closely by her police-chief husband. It was obvious from the way she clutched her reddened arm to her ample chest that she was in a great deal of pain.

"The wife burned herself pretty bad this morning while fixing her breakfast tea, Doc," said the chief. "Thought you could take a look-see."

The phone rang again and the woman behind the desk snatched at the receiver. "Dr. Anderson's office. One moment, please."

Paul glanced at Dora, then back to the woman. "I can't pay much in the way of a salary, and I'm not doing well enough to offer benefits."

"That's fine, because I'm not sure how long I'll be in town. I'm just looking to make some pocket money." She held out her free hand. "My name is Edith Hammer."

Lila adjusted her sunglasses as Bill let himself in through the back gate. He stopped to greet Teddy and Rick, dumped a few shovels of sand into the bucket and truck, then removed the plastic wrapper from two lollipops and handed one to each boy.

She imagined the mess—sticky hands and faces coated with grit and other bits of yard matter—and grimaced. They would need a bath *before* lunch, but Bill's gesture was kind. She'd deal with the mess later.

Wearing his aluminum helmet and dressed in his usual outfit—plaid shorts, striped shirt, patterned knee socks, and sandals—Bill hunched forward and strode to the swing set with his hands in his pockets.

"Mind if I sit a spell?"

She wasn't feeling friendly, but he didn't know that. "Go right ahead."

He perched on the vacant, adult-sized swing and glanced around the yard. "Nice morning."

"Yes, it is."

He sat sideways and gave her a penetrating stare. "You're looking a bit under the weather this morning."

She focused on the twins. "I'm just tired."

"Got to take care of yourself. Those little guys can be a handful," said Bill.

Resting his elbows on his knobby knees, he gazed at his hands. A breeze kicked up off the bay and whistled through the yard, ruffling the hair at her nape, and Lila crossed her arms against the sudden chill.

"Looks like rain," Bill continued. "Smells like it too."

She sniffed the damp air. "I guess."

"Glad the weather's coming in today, so it'll be outta here by Friday."

"Friday? What's going to happen on Friday?"

"That's right," said Bill, dragging the toe of his sandal in the dirt. "You never been to a Founders' Day celebration, have you?"

"No, but I've seen the advertisements in the paper." Food stands, game tents, arts and crafts, music, and a face-painting booth for the children, all of it guaranteed to be fun. "It sounds exciting."

"Usually is. Friday's the day the fellas from the rental company in Florida drive up with the rides. We got a Ferris wheel coming and one of them Tilt-A-Whirl things, plus a merry-go-round for the youngsters. Takes just about every able body in town to put it all together."

"Then the hammering I heard earlier was—"

"Setup phase of booth construction. The men work off a plan we use every year. There'll be so much noise tomorrow your ears will hope to fall off." He swiveled his head. "You going to work Dr. P's booth?"

Paul had mentioned she could bring the boys and help him pass out pamphlets for the different types of tests offered at his practice. If his mother agreed to sit with Rick and Teddy while they napped, it might be productive for her to join Bill at his ESAW booth in the afternoon.

"I was, unless you're asking for my assistance."

He cocked his head to glance at her fully. "Only if you ain't adverse to telling folks about the evils of an alien invasion."

Lila twisted her fingers together. "Will I have to say such a thing if I work the booth?"

"If they ask," said Bill. "Besides, everyone knows aliens are the most heinous creatures in the galaxy. Don't you agree?"

Lila worried the inside of her cheek. Her people were peaceful; each of the travelers had been warned to use their energy stones only if attacked. This was a chance for her to strike a small, almost invisible blow for her world, and put in a good word for their mission.

"Since I have yet to see any negative impact of an alien visit firsthand, I'm not sure."

"Then you don't believe they're here?" Bill asked.

"I didn't say that. But I don't automatically want to agree that if they are, they have evil intentions."

He squirmed on the swing. "Other than wanting to take over the world, what reason do you think they'd have for being here?"

"Friendship?" suggested Lila. "An exchange of technology?" She unclenched the fingers she'd knotted in her lap. "Maybe they need something the Earth—we—have and they don't think it's safe to simply reveal themselves and ask for it."

Bill's lips flattened to a thin line. "You mean they want our natural resources, our minerals, and the like?"

"Not necessarily." She cleared her throat, searching for a simple explanation for her planet's life-threatening problem. "But suppose beings from another world have visited Earth—our planet—many times over the centuries, and each time have been greeted with threats of destruction? So this time they came in secret because—"

"Because why?" Bill's voice turned brittle. "Why can't they just come right out and announce they're here, then tell us their intentions?"

"Fear?" Lila licked at her lower lip. "Remember Roswell? And don't forget about Area Fifty-one.

Just this week, one of the television news stations announced that the current president approved a measure to continue the secrecy procedures set in place there before he went to those peace talks."

He snorted his disbelief. "Hadn't heard that one, but I have been wondering about Roswell. You think all that stuff really happened?"

"I know—I mean, yes, I think Roswell happened, and a lot of other incidents as well." Lila figured she might as well list what she knew was public knowledge here on Earth, in case Bill decided to check her facts. "Have you seen any of the cave drawings your—our—archaeologists discovered, or read up on crop circles? Do you recall 1978, when the astronaut Gordon Cooper wrote a letter to the United Nations and supplied pictures of a group of UFOs he'd taken from his spacecraft?"

Bill scratched his head, causing his foil hat to list to the right. "Don't recall that one."

"And what about one of your own presidents' opinions? Ronald Reagan believed you—we—had been visited by beings from another world. He even advocated a government study, but no one took him up on it."

"He did?" Bill raised a bushy brow. "Hey, now, you couldn'ta been more than a baby when Reagan was in office. How come you know so much?"

Lila trained her eyes on the ground, not wanting to meet his quizzical gaze. "I studied the history—I went to school to learn about it."

"Is that so?"

"Yes, that's so." Realizing she sounded as belligerent as the Earth people she'd just complained about, she softened her tone. "I've always been fascinated by the concept of interplanetary travel."

"Then how come you didn't say so when we first met?" Bill jutted his chin. "You and me have talked plenty about ESAW and what they stand for."

"I was new to town, I guess, and didn't want people to think I was . . . odd." Surely he'd sympathize with that excuse. "But I'm telling you now."

Bill rubbed his jaw, his gray eyes scanning her face as if seeing her for the first time. "I know how that feels."

Lila fought the smile creeping up from inside. For some reason she had yet to fathom, sitting here and talking to Bill about her view of aliens was more a challenge than a threat. He was a nice man, and he seemed to genuinely care about her ideas and beliefs. It wasn't his fault he believed most of the misinformation the people of Earth touted of aliens.

"I could tell you more, if you're interested."

"I don't know about that," he answered, narrowing his gaze. "I mean, who's to say what you know is the truth?"

"Some of it is well documented," said Lila, fiddling with her bracelet. She knew better than to overwhelm Bill by going on the attack. The travelers had been warned to never reveal their mission, even under pain of exposure or death. "But it's difficult to make an informed decision without all the facts."

"That's a mighty nice piece of jewelry you're wearing," he said, abruptly changing the focus of the conversation.

"Thank you. It was a—a gift."

"Looks like an expensive present to me."

"I guess so, but I wear it more for the sentimental value than anything else. It reminds me of where I—my home."

"Miss your family, do ya?"

She placed her palms on her thighs. "I do. But I have Teddy and Rick to keep me company." *For a short while longer.*

"They're cute little fellas, and Dr. P's a good man. People in town would be upset if anything happened to him or his sons."

"I agree," she said, though it almost sounded as if Bill were giving her a warning.

The shriek of the noon fire whistle shattered the calm, and Bill stood. "Guess it's time for me to go home and make lunch. You still coming to the meeting tonight?"

"Of course. I wouldn't miss it."

"Maybe you'd like to tell folks what you just told me? Could make people see things in a different light, I'd expect."

Lila had no intention of spouting her views at an open forum, especially with Mr. Carter in attendance, but it was nice to know Bill was at least thinking about her idea.

"I'm afraid I'm not a very good public speaker," she said. "I have to prepare lunch for the boys. I thought I'd serve it out here on the back porch—sort of like a . . ." She tugged at her earlobe, searching for the word. "Picnic."

"Nice day for it. What you gonna make?"

"Cheese sandwiches, with lettuce and tomato?"

"Maybe with a little mustard on the bread, and some potato chips on the side?"

"Could be." Lila grinned. "But I need someone to watch the twins while I get things ready. Would you be interested in the job?"

Bill gazed at Teddy and Rick, still playing in the sandbox. "Them younguns look a might . . . gritty. I suppose I could turn on the back hose and water 'em down while you did the cooking."

"I suppose you could," she said, pleased Bill had thought of the idea. She was on the porch before she heard him call her name. "Yes?" she asked, turning to face him.

"Do me a favor and bring down the twins' ESAW hats—yours too. I'd hate to have those aliens suck up all the knowledge you got stored away in that brain of yours."

She nodded. "See you in a few minutes."

Sixteen

*Wh*ack! Whack! Whack!

"The Preston's Ferry Founders' Day meeting will now come to order."

Mayor Hickey and all four members of the town council sat at a table at the front of the fire hall assembly room. When the mayor, a dapper older man with bright blue eyes and an engaging smile, banged his gavel, Lila pushed her sunglasses to the bridge of her nose and sat at attention.

Unfortunately, she seemed to be the only one impressed with the man's commanding tone.

Paul was listening to Rose, who sat next to him chattering about Sally. Bill and his ESAW cronies stood in a rear corner, planning strategy, Lila guessed, for their own meeting. Most of the other citizens were holding gossip sessions on everything from the upcoming celebration to the number of times someone should be allowed to win at the local bingo game in one night.

"Order!" The mayor banged the gavel two more times. "Bill, you and your space buddies take it outside or sit down. The rest of you folks can continue your yammering after the meeting." He waited patiently until he had everyone's attention. "First item of business is the Founders' Day building committee. Frank, you want to bring us up to speed?"

A middle-aged man with a shock of dark hair shot with silver stood and informed everyone things would be done exactly as they had been done the previous year. An assignment sheet would be posted on a bulletin board at the back of the room detailing the jobs and chairpersons.

The mayor then called on a variety of people, who discussed the needs of various committees. Some spoke about the timetable for manning the different stands and asked for volunteers, while Lila alternately rocked the stroller and handed Teddy, Rick, and Harley, who'd taken a seat next to her, cookies. In between, she kept an eye on Bill, who had his gaze glued to the rear door.

"Psst, Lila?" Harley tapped her knee. "How come you're wearing sunglasses inside?"

Paul had asked her the same question a few minutes earlier, and she'd given her only logical answer, which she passed along to Harley. "I think that virus made my eyes sensitive to the light. Dark glasses help soften the glare."

"Why do you keep lookin' at Bill?"

Teddy started to fuss, so she picked him up and sat him on her knee. "I was hoping to see his friend, Mr. Carter, before the meeting started. Do you know him?"

"One time, when he came to Bill's house."

"Can you let me know when he gets here?" Rick made tired-toddler noises, and she jiggled the stroller.

Paul leaned over and hoisted both boys onto his lap. "Did you ask Mrs. Sweeney if she'd bring Teddy and Rick home and put them to bed?" He scanned the room as if looking for the woman.

"She'll be here at eight," said Lila. "Are you sure you don't want me to take one of the twins?"

"Nah. But are you sure you feel well enough to stay for both meetings?"

Lila wanted to be home, snuggled next to Paul in bed, but that wasn't something she could say out loud, even in a whisper. "I'm sure. But I won't mind if you leave early."

He grinned and her heart thumped in double time. "I want to be wherever you want to be. Besides, they haven't brought up the X-ray machine yet."

Paul was counting on the town council to find the money needed for the expensive piece of equipment. He told her he'd already attended one meeting in which he'd given a cost estimate of both a new and used machine. Tonight the council was supposed to render an opinion on how much cash they would allow for the purchase.

Mayor Hickey thumped his gavel and Paul tensed beside her.

"Our next item is the distribution of profits from Founders' Day. As you know, in the past we've used the money to replace the flags hanging on the lamp-posts on Main Street, put in new flower beds at the city park, and rebrick the walkway leading to the municipal building. We've also bought a third computer for the town's recordkeeping and accounting system, as well as the software." The mayor scratched his head with the gavel. "Danged costly, that software stuff, and now the whole thing has to be linked. I think they call it networking."

The statement took the crowd off on a tangent about computers. From the intense and sometimes boisterous comments, it was obvious technological advancement was frowned upon by a faction of Preston's Ferry's citizens.

Mayor Hickey again rapped the gavel. "This topic has already been talked to death. We need the computers so we can hook into the county system. If we don't, there'll be hell to pay with the tax collection and city services. Those of you who don't like it, write to the governor. We got something more important to discuss."

Paul gave Lila a wink. "This is it. The amount will tell me whether I'll be ordering a new machine or a refurbished one."

"Now that we have a doctor in town—"

Polite applause filled the room, and Paul nodded.

"We can all rest easy knowing we'll be getting decent medical care without having to drive thirty miles or expect the fire department to get us to the ER in an emergency. Dr. Anderson has asked the council for several pieces of medical equipment to assist him in his job, and we have agreed that the first item purchased be an X-ray machine. After paying our expenses, we'll be able to give him five thousand dollars to be used at his discretion."

"Crap," muttered Paul. He raised his hand at the exact moment the mayor raised the gavel. "Mayor Hickey. I have something to say."

"Order! Order!" The mayor gave the evil eye to the rowdy crowd, and waited until everyone settled down before saying, "Dr. Anderson, you may have the floor."

Paul shot Lila a determined look, then stood. "I'm pleased that you're still willing to buy X-ray equipment, but if you'll check the minutes of the meeting I had with the town council when they hired me, you'll see that the amount offered is several thousand dollars shy of what was agreed on."

The mayor turned to the council and the three men and one woman went into a huddle. Mary Krebbs shuffled papers, then tapped a finger to a page and passed it around the table.

The mayor scratched his head as he turned. "You sure those machines cost as much as you say?"

"If we're talking new, yes. If we can only afford used, I'll call a few contacts," answered Paul.

Mayor Hickey stood at attention and waited for the room to quiet. "Any chance we could buy the machine on credit?"

Paul shrugged, jostling the twins in his arms. "Possibly. I'd have to look into it."

"Then please do," said the mayor, raising his gavel.

"Hang on. I'm not finished." Paul passed Teddy to Harley, then handed Rick to Lila, and walked to the center aisle. "I moved here fully aware of Preston's Ferry's monetary shortcomings, but I expect to receive the items I was promised. One of them was help with my boys and, as you know, I had to secure that on my own. Lila is doing a fine job, and I'm grateful to those of you who've been kind to her since her arrival."

Lila smiled up at him and he continued. "What I will not let you renege on is your promise of adequate medical equipment. New flags for the main drag and petunias for the town hall are fine, but they're secondary to basic health care."

He went on to explain in passionate detail the other things needed to turn his office into more than a treatment center for bruises and sniffles. And it was in that moment Lila realized she would always love him, not only because he'd given her a child, but because he was strong and kind. And intent on doing what was right.

When he finished, even the mayor was applauding. "Okay, Dr. Anderson. We hear you. If you make up a list of necessary items, prioritized, of course, and a cost estimate, we'll take it into consideration. The committee's going to meet again one week after the celebration to decide on the distribution of funds, and we'll see what we can do."

Paul returned to his seat. "Let's see if they follow through," he whispered.

The mayor took a minute to adjourn the meeting. Bill walked to the front of the room and Lila's heart skipped in her chest.

"The first meeting of the Eastern Shore Alien Watch will begin in five minutes," said Bill. "I ask that all interested parties remain seated."

* * *

"Sorry, Lila, I got so caught up listening to Dr. P, I forgot to tell you." Harley leaned close. "The man standing next to Bill is Eustace Carter."

Lila patted his hand. "I already figured that out."

Paul settled the twins in the stroller. "Eleanor Sweeney is at the back door waiting for the boys. Stay here and save my seat. I'll give her a few instructions and be right back."

His comments barely registered as Lila concentrated on the tall, lean man talking to Bill. Eustace Carter had thinning dark hair, a prominent chin, and deep-set eyes perched above a beaked nose. She assumed his overly large foil hat was meant to impress, as well as intimidate. The two men were embroiled in what looked to be a serious conversation, with each of them intent on taking control.

Paul returned to his seat. "Eleanor and the twins are on their way home. Did I miss anything?"

"No." Lila pulled her silver helmet out from under the chair. Setting it on her head, she braced for his reaction.

"Take me to your leader," Paul deadpanned, then his lips twitched. "Or your television set. How many channels can you receive on that thing?"

Before she could think of a snappy comeback, Edith Hammer and two male companions sat directly in front of them. Turning in her chair, Edith gave her an insincere smile as she stared first at Harley's then Lila's foil crown.

"Dr. Anderson. Ms. Shore."

"Edith, I didn't realize you two knew each other." Paul's gaze darted from one woman to the other. "I forgot to mention it, Lila, but Mrs. Hammer started work as my receptionist today."

Shifting her attention to Paul, Edith introduced her companions. "This is my husband Edward and my brother Vernon. Since we're thinking of settling in Preston's Ferry, we decided it might be smart to attend any function that gave us a flavor of the town. This meeting sounded too good to miss."

Edith continued the small talk while Lila did her best to make sense of Paul's announcement. After lunch, she'd put the boys down for a nap and straightened the apartment, then taken the opportunity to rest. Hours later, she'd woken refreshed and found that Paul had cared for his sons and prepared dinner. She'd been quiet during the meal and avoided direct eye contact with Paul, but they had talked, mostly about his mother's visit and their need to be discreet. She'd done the dishes while he readied Teddy and Rick for tonight, and they'd left for the meeting. Not once had he mentioned hiring Edith.

She understood he had no obligation to discuss the details of his office with her, and even if Paul told her there was little she could have said to deter him from giving the woman a job. Edith's presence brought a distinct feeling of unease to her stomach, but short of declaring her mistrust there was no real reason on which to base her objection.

Though his decision was a shock, she had a more important concern at the moment. Training her gaze on the table at the front of the room, Lila watched four older gentlemen organize, staple, and fold sheets of paper while Bill and Mr. Carter engaged in a tug-of-war over Mayor Hickey's gavel. When Bill yanked the mallet end and wrested the gavel to his chest, Eustace crossed his arms and glared.

Whack! Whack! Whack!

Bill beamed a victorious smile as he rapped his prize and surveyed the audience. "Evening, folks, welcome to Preston's Ferry's first public meeting of the Eastern Shore Alien Watch. I'm Bill Halverson, district commander of the southern end of the shore, and I'll be chairing tonight's event."

The townsfolk applauded, Harley being the most enthusiastic.

"I'd like to begin by introducing the man in charge of our organization and the other chairmen." He proceeded to name Carter and the gentlemen still folding papers.

Reclaiming control, Eustace stepped forward. "I can see from the silver headwear we have a goodly number of members in the audience. As it stands, ESAW's ranks are close to six hundred. First off, I'm going to bring you up to date on what we've accomplished." He scrutinized his list, then read off the points. "Number one: we did a town-by-town canvass and spread word of the alien landing, thereby alerting the shore's citizens of a possible danger to their persons. Number two: we recruited members and instructed them to report any suspicious activity to their district commanders. To date, we have received and investigated over a dozen questionable incidents which, I am pleased to report, had nothing to do with the aliens."

After another smattering of applause, he continued. "Last, and most important, we heard from a reputable source who works at the NASA station on Wallops Island. He informed me—off the record, of course—that there are representatives of a government agency in our area trying to steal our thunder. My source admits that a highly classified team is here carrying out the investigation, but won't admit they suspect an alien invasion. Which tells me the danged government is running a cover-up, just like they did with Roswell."

An invasion? Lila wanted to question Eustace on where ESAW got its information, but knew it wouldn't do to make an enemy of the man or the membership. Besides, if she opened her mouth, Bill might decide to put her on the spot about what they'd discussed that morning—not something she wanted to do in front of Paul or Edith and her buddies.

Someone in the crowd asked why the government was keeping things secret, and Eustace said, "The boys in Washington want to trap the aliens for their own gain, maybe use them for illicit experimentation or confiscate their weaponry. Unlike our group what comes right out with our goal: find, apprehend, and bring news of their arrival to every citizen."

"Sounds serious," said Paul in an amused tone. "Good thing you're a member and not a suspect."

Hoping to mask her fear, Lila tossed him a tepid grin. If the situation wasn't so dire, she might be able to laugh at his irreverent humor, but she'd caught Edith's almost imperceptible flinch when Eustace mentioned a secret government agency, which only heightened Lila's suspicions.

"Right now, we figure at least one alien spacecraft landed on the peninsula, probably in the wildlife refuge. We expect they're headed north to the capital, where they will join forces with others of their kind. In the meantime, we've amassed a few stories from around the country, just to let you know we're not the only ones who've been alerted to this invasion."

"Just curious," said the mayor. "But does anyone have an idea what these aliens look like?"

"Not exactly, but we do have an assortment of reports," said Carter. "Go ahead, boys."

The men sitting at the table stood and passed out what they'd been working on, a publication titled the *ESAW Review*. Lila opened hers and scanned the first headline and story.

WOMAN GIVES BIRTH TO THREE-EYED BABY IN NEVADA DESERT

Just six days after claiming she was impregnated by a three-eyed alien, a local woman gave birth in her hometown of Needles, Nevada. Officials have taken the woman and child under protective custody until the claim can be validated, but those who have seen the baby agree there is definitely something unworldly about the infant's bulging forehead, where it is suspected the third eye is concealed.

The item brought a smile to her lips. Though she'd heard of a race of four-eyed beings, she doubted there were any three-eyed species roaming the galaxies. She scanned the headlines that followed.

ALIENS ACCOST FLORIDA MAN HUNTING GATORS

MONTANA RANCHER SAYS ALIENS
MUTILATED AND KILLED STEER
IN BIZARRE MIDNIGHT RITUAL

CAMPERS IN PENNSYLVANIA MOUNTAINS
SURPRISED BY ALIEN
LOOKING FOR LOVE CONNECTION

The stories covered six pages, each one growing more absurd as they continued. Some were accompanied by a photo so out of focus it was difficult to tell if the picture correctly depicted the subject of the article in question. Her people would never harm an animal, and none of the women would approach a group of men when they each had one particular target, so Lila knew none of them had a toehold in reality.

"I'll take questions from the audience," Carter said after a moment. "Anyone seen anything odd happen around town?"

Lila held her breath, waiting for Edith to speak, but the woman only smiled smugly at her companions. The crowd murmured, but no one made a comment. Finally someone asked, "So what's the next step on our agenda?"

"A march," answered Eustace, thumbing his suspenders.

The attendees muttered as one. Even Bill seemed surprised. Eustace held up his hands. "They had the Million Woman March; the Million Man March; the Veterans' March, even Rolling Thunder, so why not ESAW? We may not number in the millions, but we got the right to be heard. It's time the government stopped hiding the truth from its citizens, and this alien invasion is the perfect incident to make them accountable. This coming Sunday we're heading out, hundreds strong, and we're gonna pick up support along the way. We'll drive straight up the eastern shore, cut over on Route 50, cross the Bay Bridge, and roll into the capital. We'll search for the aliens along the way and bring them in when we find them."

The hair at the back of Lila's neck rose.

"If we don't get a handle on the creature, we'll camp on the Mall and demand Washington tells us what's going on."

Headed for home, Paul kept pace beside Lila as he scanned the froth of dark clouds covering the yellow half moon that hung low over the bay. The prediction for two days of precipitation, then clear skies and balmy temperatures had heartened the festival's planning committee. They'd have to get ready for Founders' Day in the rain, but lousy weather would be worth it, if it guaranteed a prosperous fair. High attendance meant bigger profits for the city coffers, which translated into more money for Paul's X-ray machine, a fact that had taken his mind off of Lila for a short while.

Now that they were alone, he was again concerned with her almost palpable discomfort. He didn't want to pry, but it was obvious from her serious expression and hesitant attitude there was something on her mind. She'd been quiet at dinner, and distant when he informed her of his decision to hire Edith Hammer. After Carter shared his plans for a march on the capital, she'd turned pale and commented only to Harley.

"You and Harley had a lot to talk about during the meeting," he said in an attempt to lift Lila's spirits. "Don't tell me the two of you plan to trap an alien so you can become a headline in that newsletter."

Lila hugged her chest as if warding off a chill. "We were just talking. Harley's a nice man, but he doesn't always understand the way things are. As long as his hand is bandaged, he can't work, so he has nothing to do."

Because the last thing he wanted was to give the town gossips another rumor to chew on, Paul fought the urge to drape an arm over her and pull her near. "Millie's afraid he'll get in trouble if he's bored, so I gave him permission to do small tasks. I'll be removing his stitches next week. After that, he can go back to work full-time." He shrugged out of his windbreaker and slipped it over her shoulders. "Maybe you should buy a jacket."

"Summer's coming." She slid her arms through the sleeves and zipped the zipper. "I won't need a coat until the fall."

"It still gets cool when the wind blows in off the Chesapeake." When she didn't answer, he said, "I could give you an advance on your next paycheck. You might want some cash for the festival. The local craftsmen will have lots of handmade items for sale."

"Thank you, but no. I have a little left," she answered, her voice low.

Unhappy with her answer, Paul didn't know what to say. He thought he'd made it clear she had the job, so an advance wasn't a problem. They rounded the corner and went through the back gate to the rear porch, where he opened the door and let Lila enter the house first. Eleanor greeted them as they walked into the kitchen.

"How was the meeting?" she asked.

"Entertaining," said Paul. "That guy running ESAW had an answer for everything." He waited while the older woman put on her sweater. "How did things go with Teddy and Rick?"

"Just fine. Little Teddy even used the potty chair. The boy's a smart one, even if he doesn't say much."

Paul's chest swelled with the compliment. "Do you want me to drive you home?"

"Nope. I brought an umbrella, and I have a flashlight. Preston's Ferry's streets are about as safe as it gets."

"Then I gather you're not taken with the rumor of the town being home to an alien?"

Eleanor fisted her hands on her hips. "Lord, no, though a booth featuring a visitor from another planet might bring more folks to the Founders' Day celebration. And what if there was an alien living among us? If it minded its own business and contributed to the welfare of our citizens, I doubt anyone in town would care, except Bill and his buddies. All God's creatures have a right to life as long as they don't harm others is my thought." She glanced at Lila, who was peering into the refrigerator. "Heard you were a might under the weather, missy. Feeling any better?"

Lila kept her gaze averted as she poured a glass of milk. "I am, and thank you for asking."

"It's supposed to rain tomorrow. Do you want to bring the boys to my house in the morning? I'll call Rose and we can have coffee while the twins play with Sally."

"I'd like that," Lila said.

"I'm on the corner of Peach and Plum, the big white house with black shutters. Come around ten and you can help me make signs for the food booths." She ambled to the stairs and disappeared from view as she called a pleasant farewell. "I'll be sure to close and lock the back door, so you don't need to worry. Good night."

Paul turned to see Lila eating a banana. "You must be feeling better if you have your appetite back."

She swallowed, her gaze darting to the fruit bowl. "I'm sorry, I should have asked if you want something. I could make tea or—"

"Don't worry about me." He crossed the worn linoleum and stood in front of her, hoping to put her at ease. "Why don't I make the tea while you get ready for bed?"

She placed the remainder of the banana on the counter, then edged to the stove and picked up the kettle. "It's my job, and I'm not tired."

"You do realize I—we—want you to stay?" Reaching around, Paul covered her hand with his and set the kettle on the burner, then grabbed Lila's elbow and tugged until she faced him. "You've become so much more than an employee to us, Lila. The nanny position is yours, for as long as the boys need you."

She stared at the buttons on his shirt. "I figured as much. Thank you."

He sighed. "Then what else is wrong? Is there something you're not telling me about your condition?" She stiffened and tried to pull away, but he held her tight. "What's really bothering you?"

"Nothing's bothering me, exactly. There's just so much going on in town, and your mother is coming, and—"

He brushed a lock of hair from her forehead. "Forget about my mother for a minute. Let's talk about your eyes."

Lila jerked up her chin, her expression a cross between defiance and relief. "I . . . um . . . I guess I should have—"

Hit full force with her emerald gaze, Paul saw that his guess had been correct. "I was aware contacts came in colors, but that green is something else. You're not as pale as this morning, but the contacts stand out against your skin." He grinned. "You didn't really believe that I'd disapprove of you not having twenty-twenty vision did you? Heck, half the people I know wear them."

"They do? I mean, I know they do. It's just that I ran out of the clear ones, and these were all I had left. I thought maybe they were a little too much, and you'd be displeased."

"Not a chance. They'll just take getting used to." Paul enfolded her in his arms and rubbed the curve of her back. "It's no big deal. The shore is isolated, but the folks who live here are pretty knowledgeable about what the real world has to offer."

"You think so?"

"In this town? When half the population is willing to explore the possibility of an alien landing in the wildlife refuge? Trust me, most people are going to be so involved in Founders' Day preparations they'll comment and go about their business." He gave her a squeeze of reassurance. "Wear the sunglasses if it makes you more comfortable, but don't hide from me and the boys. If the color bothers you, order the clear ones online. I'll even let you use my credit card."

Seconds passed before she pulled away and gazed at him through a shimmer of tears. "Really?"

"Really." He stared into her shining eyes. "The only thing you have to concentrate on is getting better."

She matched his smile with one of her own. "I hope so. I don't mind answering questions, but Edi—I mean, some people just want to pry."

"I got the impression you weren't too crazy about Edith," he said, zeroing in on another possible reason for her uneasy attitude. "If her presence bothers you, I'll simply tell her I can't afford her. It's important that you're happy here."

"You'd do that for me?"

"Of course I would." Bending to her lips, he kissed her, absorbing her lush curves as they molded to the wall of his chest. Once his mother was gone, he'd take the time to logically examine the feelings for Lila pooling inside of him. Until then, he'd show her in whatever way he could how much she meant to him.

Wrapping her arms around his neck, she responded with her usual warmth and trust. Her body melted against his while she seemed to inhale him into her very center, returning the kiss until they were both gasping for air.

Pulling back, Paul sighed into her open mouth and thrust his tongue into her heat, offering assurance while at the same time telling her how much he cared. To his delight, Lila hitched a leg around his hip, enabling him to nestle his arousal into the notch of her thighs.

Raising her up, he sat her on the counter. "Still hungry?" he asked, inching his lips to the pulse point of her throat.

"Only for you," she answered, running her fingers through his hair.

He nibbled at the tender spot under her ear. "I don't want to take advantage, especially while you're recuperating." He moaned as he bit gently on her earlobe.

She caught his jaw with trembling hands and raised his head so their gazes locked. "I'm recovered enough to know that I want you beside me in bed. Please, make love to me."

Lila's sweetly plaintive words seduced his senses. The past two evenings had taken a hefty toll on his good intentions. Still wary of admitting to the emotions behind his longing, he only knew that he wanted to lie beside her skin to skin, breath to breath, heartbeat to heartbeat. They might not get another chance to do so until after his mother left town, an idea that made him shudder.

"Thank God you're on the mend, because I wasn't sure I'd make it through another night without touching you," he rasped. "Want to know a secret?"

She smiled. "Of course."

"That very first day, when you walked into my office, I thought about the two of us in bed, even though I knew it was wrong."

Lila stilled in his arms. "You think what we're doing is wrong?"

"I did. Now I'm not so sure." He rested his forehead against hers. "Times like this, I think fate decided to drop you in my lap, sort of like a cosmic reward. You came into our lives at the exact time the boys and I needed you most. But I'm worried we're taking more than our fair share of your attention. If this isn't what you want, just tell me. It'll be difficult, but I'll find the willpower to leave you be."

Her expression turned soft, her eyes dreamy. "If you made sleeping together a part of my cure, there'd be no need to feel guilty."

Grinning, he lifted her off the counter, cupped her bottom, and walked them through the kitchen and living room, into his bedroom, where he stopped at the foot of his bed.

Lila wiggled her hips against his erection, and he growled low in his throat. "Seems to me you're feeling better already."

"Better, but not completely. In fact, it may take an extra dose of whatever my physician prescribes to get the job done."

He sat her on the bed, stepped back, and began to undress. "Then I guess we'd better get started."

Seventeen

Lila woke to find Paul gone and the house quiet. She remembered his plan to go for an early morning run and supposed that's where he was, even though rain pattered against the windowpane and the light peeking in from around the shades looked gray. His energy level amazed her, especially since he'd worn her out last night before they'd fallen asleep in each other's arms.

They'd made love twice, and both encounters had left her reeling. Paul's actions had been so intense she'd thought he would never get enough of her, while he'd encouraged her to indulge solely in her own pleasure. She had taken full advantage, touching and tasting him as if she could imprint herself on his skin. No matter what happened to separate them, she would always have the memory for comfort.

Thoughts of all that had transpired since her arrival in Paul's home bombarded her senses. She'd learned enough about this planet to make living here possible. She'd met Teddy and Rick, little boys who had carved a permanent place in her heart. And she'd fallen in love with Paul.

But there were negatives to consider. This house had been infiltrated by Edith Hammer, and ESAW was intent on marching to the capital with an alien—no, with *her*—in tow. Add the fact that Paul's mother was coming to visit, and Lila suspected her head might explode. How had her simple plan to make a new life become so complicated?

She understood why she'd lost her heart to Teddy and Rick, but how could she have been so foolish as to fall in love with Paul? Caring for the Anderson men was a foolish error that kept her off guard, when she needed to concentrate on the dangers that seemed to lurk around every corner.

Would she ever be free of ESAW and the group Eustace Carter had said were searching for her?

Rolling to her side, she cradled her stomach. At least one thing in her world was secure and on schedule. She and Paul had created a child. That single bright spot would have to sustain her for the rest of her life.

It was important she stay positive. Paul had given her a logical reason for the change in eye color. If he accepted it, so would everyone else. She could avoid speaking to Edith or anyone connected with ESAW, and join in the Founders' Day festivities as planned. After the festival, she would lose herself in the departing throng, catch a ride over the bridge, and find shelter. There she'd sell a jewel from her bracelet and use the money to further her disappearance.

Paul would be angry that she'd left him without help for his sons, but eventually he would accept her defection.

He and the boys would forget she'd ever existed.

The harsh thought brought an unfamiliar tightness to her chest, and she swallowed down a lump of regret. Even though he'd plied her with words of promise, it was obvious Paul was ashamed of her. He didn't want his mother or anyone else in Preston's Ferry to know he and his housekeeper were involved. He'd made it clear from their first night together they had no personal future. It would be easy for him to erase her from his mind, while she lived the rest of her life with the proof of her love. Their son.

Lila almost envied the other travelers who were returning home. They were disciplined and strong. Intent on their duty, they'd accepted their fate, well aware they had to go back without the father of their child. She imagined there was a flaw inside of her, some inner weakness that had allowed her to fall in love with a man who didn't belong to her. It must have been apparent in one of the many psychological tests she'd taken that she would fail at this task as she had so many others.

Standing, she headed for the bathroom, where she checked her eyes. Paul had said that humans who met her for the first time would take the bright tone in stride and assume she was wearing contacts. Perhaps, as her pregnancy progressed, her eyes would fade to their original hue and she'd no longer need to remember the excuse.

Rick sang his usual morning wake-up call and she

readied the boys, amusing them with teasing chatter as she brought them into the kitchen and settled them in high chairs. Her stomach rumbled for attention and she started breakfast, positive she could devour a double portion of everything in the refrigerator.

Rick banged the table with his fork while Teddy grinned and grabbed for his milk. She served the twins before fixing a meal for herself and Paul. Absorbed in eating their food, neither child noticed when she sniffed back a tear. Not only did she love these mischievous miniature humans; in a moment of weakness, she'd promised them she would someday find a way to return. Would she be able to keep her word?

Lost in thought, she didn't realize Paul had finished his run until he strode into the kitchen. After wiping his face with a paper towel, he poured a cup of coffee.

"Breakfast smells great," he commented, carrying his drink to the table.

The sight of him damp with rain, his wet clothes clinging to his muscular body, caused Lila's breath to hitch. Tears threatened to overflow like a raging river. It took all her self-control to keep from brushing a glistening tendril of hair from his forehead as she set down his plate. Not only had she come to think of Teddy and Rick as her own; Paul had become her friend, her lover . . . her man.

"Are you still going to Eleanor's house?" he asked, taking a bite of his omelet.

"As soon as I straighten the kitchen, I'll put the

twins in the stroller and walk over," she answered. "Mrs. Sweeney needs help making signs for the festival, and it will be a healthy social interaction for the boys to play with Sally."

"You're worried about their *social interaction*?" Grinning, he showed Rick how to hold his fork. "I'd be happy if they just learned to eat like civilized human beings. Right now, I'd even settle for Teddy making a noise that sounded half human."

"Playing with other children will help them to develop those skills," Lila reminded him.

He cut into a sausage, chewed, and swallowed. "You know, this fake meat stuff isn't half bad." He watched the boys eagerly consume their smaller but identical meals. "The guys like it too."

"You have Rose to thank. She's responsible for all my recipes," said Lila, sitting down to eat. But before she could taste the fragrant eggs and cheese, her empty stomach churned a warning. Shuddering, she pushed the plate away. "Aren't you supposed to work on building your booth today?"

Paul helped Teddy spear a last piece of egg and guide it to his mouth. "Yes, now that I know for certain Mrs. Hammer will watch the office. If you tell me what time you want to come home for lunch, I'll take a break and pick you up." Leaning into the table, he spread a spoonful of jam on his toast. "Is there a reason you're not eating?"

"I'm not hungry," she countered, annoyed that her appetite seemed to have a mind of its own.

"Funny how your desire for food comes and goes. I hope last night didn't cause a relapse."

Lila caught his cocky grin and felt her cheeks grow warm. "I'm sure it's just a leftover symptom of the virus. I ate after the meeting, remember?"

"I'd hardly call half a banana a meal."

Her sudden blush told Paul she recalled the fantastic night they'd shared. He too doubted that great sex was the reason her hunger meter spiked from high to low without reason, but he enjoyed seeing her cheeks flush pink with the suggestion.

Besides, as a general practitioner it was his duty to see to her health, not only because he was worried about her, but in case other patients exhibited similar symptoms. Lila's virus had him puzzled. If it had been a simple twenty-four-hour bug, it would be gone by now. He ticked off a mental list of her complaints: a roller-coaster appetite; a too-pale complexion; the unusual need for sleep—

He gulped down the last of his coffee as the obvious answer skirted the edges of his brain. When they'd first been intimate Lila had told him there was no need for protection, and like a typical sex-obsessed male he'd believed her. The moment he discovered she was a sexual innocent, he should have realized she might not know how to prevent a pregnancy.

Needing a few seconds for the idea to sink in, he stood and walked across the kitchen. After pouring a second round of coffee for himself, he filled Lila's mug.

"Thank you," she said politely, dabbing at Rick's mouth with a napkin.

Paul set the carafe on the warmer, propped his backside against the counter, and watched as she coaxed Teddy into eating the last of his sausage. Though her blush had faded and she was again pale, her skin seemed to glow from within. If Lila was pregnant, it couldn't be more than a few days. It was too early for her to use one of those over-the-counter tests. Short of quizzing her about the regularity of her monthly cycle or giving her an exam, there was little he could do but wait.

"Besides your unpredictable appetite, is there anything else bothering you? Something you think is insignificant, so you've forgotten to tell me?" he asked, hoping she would volunteer the information.

She nibbled at her lower lip. "I don't think so. Why?"

Okay. Either he was overreacting or Lila was an award-winning actress. He might be wrong, and her symptoms were simply a coincidence.

"Just making sure. Promise you'll tell me if you notice anything odd. Some strains of flu are so severe they sneak up and knock you on your butt before you know it. I don't want your problem to get that far."

She stood and began clearing the table. "I promise. Now let me finish in here. You have to change and meet with whoever is building your booth, and the boys and I have to get to Mrs. Sweeney's." She flashed a teasing grin. "Unlike some doctors I know, I don't have today off."

Balancing an open umbrella on her shoulder, Lila wheeled the twins home. She'd spent a productive morning at Eleanor's working alongside Rose in the construction of signs for the Founders' Day food booths. Without sunshine, there'd been no need to wear dark glasses, so when the women asked about her eyes, she'd done as Paul suggested and told them she was wearing colored contact lenses. Being trusting souls, Rose and her mother had accepted her explanation, then gone on a tangent about modern medical techniques and how Eleanor hoped to someday have Lasik surgery to correct her vision.

Lila's heart had lightened when she realized she hadn't once needed to tug her earlobe to activate either the memory or translator chips. That meant her condition was having the desired effect on her system, and her heightened hormone levels were reacting properly with the implants. If there were no other surprises associated with her pregnancy, her physiology would be so close to human no one would be able to tell she was an alien unless they performed DNA testing.

Rose had shared a new recipe, one Lila wanted to make for tonight's dinner, so she steered the stroller into the Shop and Bag. After locating the proper ingredients, she met Harley and Millie at the checkout counter.

"What happened to your eyes?" Harley asked, bagging her items with his good hand as they traveled the conveyor belt.

Inspecting Lila's face, Millie handed her the receipt. "You're wearing colored contacts, I'll bet."

Before Lila could answer, she heard a voice at her side. "Oh, really? Did you just get them?"

Turning, she locked gazes with Edith Hammer.

"It's not as if there's an optometrist in this town who can order them for you," the woman continued.

"You can buy them on the Internet. I know because my niece did just that," said Millie. "Only hers are purple as a pansy, not a pretty green like Lila's."

Lila had never seen Paul's computer, but Edith didn't need to know that. "I've always worn contacts, but I used the last of my clear ones. All I had left were these," she said smoothly, sliding into Millie's explanation without missing a beat.

"Well, I like 'em. They remind me of grass in the springtime," said Harley, tucking her parcel into the stroller's carryall. "I saw Dr. P a while ago working on his booth. He says he's gonna take out my stitches next week."

"I know," Lila answered. She turned to Edith. "I thought you were watching the office this morning."

Edith raised her beaked nose in the air. "I'm on my lunch break."

"Well, the boys and I are going home. See you later." Lila headed outside. Thanks to Harley, Millie, Eleanor, and Rose, the contact lens story would soon be all over town, which would eliminate further prying questions. If Edith tried to make more out of it, she doubted anyone would care.

By the time she unloaded the boys from the stroller, herded them upstairs, and wrestled them out of their damp clothing, Lila was exhausted. Ready to nap, she was too tired to argue when Rick scampered into her bedroom and went straight to her night table.

"Ball! La, ball!" He scooped up the toy she'd used

to entertain them a few days earlier and held it to his chest.

"Yes, ball. How about you, young man?" she asked Teddy. "Can you say ball?"

At her inquiry, Teddy ran to her bed and tried to hop on board. Thinking to again use the toy as a teaching tool, she joined them and cuddled them near. Concentrating, she sent the golden orb on another merry dance of circles and dips. When the toy dropped low over Teddy's outstretched hands, she said, "Ball, Teddy. Say the word and you can have it."

"Ball," cried Rick.

She let him hold the shiny object for a few seconds before she again sent it hovering out of reach. In between Rick's garbled words and Teddy's giggles, they played the game until Lila's eyes drooped. Just as she was about to shut down her mental powers, she heard a single syllable echo in the air.

"Ball."

Turning, she found Teddy grinning from ear to ear. "Ball, la-la. Ball."

Too surprised to speak, Lila blinked

"La-la, ball," he said again, reaching for the toy.

She mentally guided the toy into his hands, then leaned toward him and kissed his baby-soft cheek. "You are a clever boy, keeping those lovely words to yourself all this while." Paul would be overjoyed—speechless—shocked. She knew, because those same feelings were flooding her system this very moment. "Can you say ball again? Or repeat my name? Say Lila."

He clutched the object in his pudgy hands. "La-la. Ball."

Convinced no more important words were ever spoken, she sniffled back a round of tears. Frustrated at her illogical reaction to such a joyous moment, she imagined an army of hormones marching through her veins while she spouted like a broken faucet for the next several months. At this rate, she'd go through a box of tissues a day. Then an idea popped into her brain, and she hopped off the mattress and ran into Paul's room, where she retrieved a framed photo from his dresser.

Scooting back into bed, she held it aloft. "Here's a picture of the two of you with your father. Daddy, Rick, and Teddy." She sent it floating overhead. "Can you say daddy?"

"Da-da." Rick grabbed for the photo and she let him hold it a few seconds.

"Your turn," she said to Teddy. "Say daddy and you can have the picture."

Teddy screwed his face in concentration.

"Come on, it's easy," Lila coaxed. She passed Rick the ball and moved the picture until it hovered above Teddy. "Daddy or da-da, either one will do."

Eyes alight, Teddy said, "Da-da. La-la, da-da."

They played the game for what felt like hours, while Lila alternated the ball and the picture between the boys. Rick's speech improved, while Teddy began to say his brother's name as well, though it came out sounding very close to " 'Ick."

Finally worn out by the task, the twins snuggled next to her while she shifted her mental energy to idle. She settled the picture over her thighs, and the ball floated mere inches from her chest as she drifted to sleep.

* * *

Tired, wet, and pretty much sick of Founders' Day already, Paul checked his messages with Edith, sent her home, and dragged himself up the stairs. He'd worked the day away on his own booth and a few others. In between, he'd taped several smashed fingers, put an arm in a sling, and sent Ernie Yothers to the hospital to get his ankle X-rayed. Thinking to save himself from falling, the eighty-three-year-old had jumped from the fourth rung of a toppling ladder and ended up landing on the mayor. Ray Hickey was merely bruised, but Ernie had turned his foot when he fell. Paul suspected a torn tendon, but old bones were brittle, so he'd prescribed a visit to the hospital ER.

It was too bad about Ernie, but the accident enabled Paul to see the bright side: it reinforced the plea he'd made at the town meeting. Preston's Ferry needed an X-ray machine.

He'd also had to contend with Harley, who had followed him around like a lost puppy most of the afternoon. The giant had held an umbrella over their heads while he babbled his excitement over the news that Bill had promised Harley he could march to Washington as the district commander's right-hand man. To top it off, Paul had been informed that the Founders' Day committee had expanded the duties of his booth and turned it into a first-aid stop. By doing so, there would be a place for medical emergencies at both ends of Main Street, one at the town fire station and the other in his area. He wasn't looking forward to the business.

He filled a glass with tap water, drank it down in

one long swallow, and scanned the kitchen. At just past five, the two hot dogs he'd eaten for lunch were a distant memory to his grumbling stomach. He'd hoped to find the comforting aroma of home cooking, and maybe a snack of cheese and crackers, anything filling to stave off hunger until he got cleaned up, but the idea didn't look promising.

The only saving grace to his hectic day was that the chaos had kept his mind from Lila and her possible condition. Now that he was here, he could ask her a few more questions and try to figure out if his suspicion was true.

He grabbed a banana from the fruit bowl and finished it off in three bites, recalling what little he remembered of the time line of a healthy pregnancy. If everything went well, Lila would probably have a couple more months of funky eating habits and exhaustion before the second trimester brought a return of her normal energy level and good humor. Once the holidays passed and the new year began, she'd start feeling out of sorts, maybe a bit cranky, until . . .

Counting the months in his head, Paul grinned. Come February, he might be a father again. And if that were true, this time he would work his damnedest to do it right.

He tugged off his damp shirt as he walked to his bedroom. Peeking in the twins' room on his way to the bath, he found their beds empty and figured they'd crashed with Lila, as they had the other day. After a quick shower, he headed for her bedroom, smiling when he heard the sound of giggles.

Stopping at the door, he inhaled a deep breath.

Why hadn't he figured it out before now? It didn't matter if Lila was pregnant or not. He cared for her, and he was pretty certain she cared for him. He'd been an idiot, thinking they could have a no-strings affair when it was obvious they had the makings of an excellent relationship.

The inner battle he'd waged about never again getting involved with a woman died a quick death when he thought about the pluses of living with Lila. He'd told himself he wouldn't remarry because he'd thought getting hitched would be another round of daily arguments, uncomfortable moments, and even more miserable nights. He and Melanie had fought until indifference quietly took over their lives. He just couldn't imagine that happening with Lila.

For one thing, he doubted she would let a tiff fester until it ate away at their understanding. Nor would she allow him to neglect her in bed, as Melanie had accused him of doing. Lila would make him live up to his responsibilities as a husband and father. Not that he'd need any prodding. Since the day she'd walked into his life, things had seemed brighter, the boys happier, his world more orderly and calm.

All he had to do was get through this weekend. Once his mother meet Lila and saw how wonderful she was, how content and healthy her grandsons were, she would have to agree Lila was perfect. His mother had never made a secret of her wish for her only son to remarry. Heck, she'd probably be the one to suggest he and his nanny do that very thing.

Smug, now that he'd become a man with a plan, he inched open her door and peered inside. The touching scene almost made him run and find his camera. Eyes closed, Lila was fast asleep with her back to the door, while a twin sat on either side of her. Too engrossed in the game they were playing to notice him, the boys batted a golden ball over her sleeping form.

The very one he thought he'd seen hovering the last time she'd napped with the twins. The one he'd forgotten to ask her about.

He rubbed his eyes, positive they were playing tricks on him. Teddy and Rick were agile, but not co-ordinated enough to toss a ball so lightly. Or with one hand. And no kid could make it float from side to side.

He stepped inside, and Rick saw him. Breaking into a grin, he stood on the unstable mattress, scrambled over Lila, and fell into his brother, who immediately began to cry. The ball dropped some-where in the middle of their sprawl as Lila rolled to-ward the tangle of arms, legs, and tears.

"What's wrong?" she asked, her tone soft and sleepy. "Did you have a bad dream?" She drew both children near. "It's okay, I'm here," she cooed. "You're safe."

Choking on a combination of suspicion and ten-derness, Paul cleared his throat. There had to be a simple explanation for what he'd just witnessed. "I'm afraid it was my fault."

Lila jumped at the sound of his voice. Eyes wide, she gazed at him. "You startled me." Juggling the boys, she sat one on each knee. "Look, it's Daddy. What do you say we show him our surprise?"

Paul ran a hand through his hair. "Sorry to cause such a commotion, but I opened the door and Rick saw me. He got excited and climbed over you, then fell on Teddy, and—"

"A chain reaction of disaster followed." She wiped at Teddy's tears. "They're fine now. And once they quiet down, we—they have something special to show you."

"Lila, they were playing with a ball, and it looked sort of strange—"

Setting the boys on their feet, she twisted around and searched for the object, now wedged under a pillow. "This ball?"

"Uh . . . yeah. That's the one. Where did it come from?"

"It's mine—I've had it since I was a child. I carry it with me for sentimental reasons." She tossed it in the air and it dropped neatly into Rick's upraised hands. "We've been practicing. As you can see, it's really improved their eye-to-hand coordination."

"I'll say." Visions of his boys with pro baseball or basketball careers swam before Paul's eyes, almost, but not quite, numbing him to what he'd seen. She was going to think him crazy, but he had to sort it out. "I know this will sound nutty, but it looked to me as if the ball were actually . . . um . . . cooperating."

"Cooperating?"

"You know—moving. On its own."

Rick dropped the toy and grabbed at his crotch.

"Oh-oh." Lila shot to her feet. "Potty time. You take Teddy to your bathroom, I'll get Rick to mine." She caught the boy by his underarms and jogged across the room. "Hurry!"

Paul did as ordered, praising Teddy when the toddler lived up to expectations. Lila was right about one thing: practice did make perfect, at least with the twins' potty-training. And she hadn't laughed when he'd told her what he *thought* he'd seen.

After adjusting clothes and Pull-Ups, he swung his son in his arms and walked into the hall, still pondering the incident. Inanimate objects did not move by themselves. They didn't do anything unless propelled by a human being. Then again, he'd had a rough day. He was hungry and tired and—

"Time for our surprise," said Lila when they met in the living room. Squatting, she set Rick down, then held out her hands. Paul placed a bouncing Teddy on his feet and the little guy ran to her. She knelt between them, encircling a boy at each side.

"Do I need to sit for this surprise?" he asked.

"It might be a good idea. How about right there on the sofa? And don't say a word until we're through. There's no guarantee we'll have luck on our first try."

He did as she suggested, taking in the heightened color in her cheeks, her huge smile, and gleaming eyes. His sons stared at her adoringly, and Paul swore his heart did a flip inside his chest. God, they were as in love with Lila as he was.

Before he had the time to dissect the mind-numbing thought, she spoke.

"Okay, Rick, who's this?" She pointed to Teddy.

" 'Eddy," said Rick.

"And who am I?" She thumbed her chest.

"La-la."

"And who's that?" she asked, nodding at Paul.

Paul waggled his fingers. "Hey, guy."

Eighteen

Lila tucked the twins into bed for the night, closed their door, and walked to the sofa. Picking up the remote, she flipped through channels until she found a news station. After watching for half an hour, she heaved a sigh. There were no stories on alien sightings, UFOs, or any other type of suspected cosmic activity in the United States or anywhere on Earth. Maybe she'd been right about those articles in the *ESAW Review*. Her fellow travelers were safe, and well on their way to accomplishing their mission.

But if Edith suspected what she was and tried to convince others, how would those people react? More importantly, what would Paul think?

She doubted she could escape a third round of interrogation on the energy orb, especially if Rick and Teddy clamored for more of the ball's tricks. Paul was a logical human, grounded in science. If he thought hard enough about her change of eye color and her "self-propelled" toy, he might believe what they said about her.

Still, using the toy had been worth discovery, because it had encouraged Teddy to speak. The incredulous expression on Paul's face when he'd heard his son's first words would be imprinted forever on her heart. Watching their familial play had given her great joy, but had also summoned a great sorrow. The knowledge that her own son would never share special times with his father had brought a fresh stream of tears that caused her to race from the room and bury herself in dinner preparations. The impromptu party had continued throughout their meal, with Paul encouraging the boys to repeat dozens of ordinary words, sometimes with hilarious success. He'd included her in the game, as well, telling Teddy and Rick how lucky they were to have such a brilliant and caring nanny.

Unfortunately, he'd left on an emergency shortly after dinner. A patient had called complaining of chest pains, and Paul had grabbed his jacket, kissed each of them good-bye, and run from the house with a terse, "Don't wait up."

Since then, she'd given the twins their bath, read them a story, and conducted another speech lesson, this time without the energy orb. Now that they were snug in their cribs and there was nothing of importance on the news, it was time she readied herself for bed. The first thing she did when she arrived in her room was stow the ball in her backpack. Even though she was the only one who could activate it, she didn't want to risk Paul seeing it again.

The thought of staying awake for his return was

tempting, but she had no clue as to when he would be home. Imagining him beside her, holding her safe in his arms, she drifted off peacefully on a wave of longing . . .

A noise woke Lila from her light doze. First she heard footsteps on the lower floor, then a more deliberate creaking on the stairs. The sounds from the kitchen became familiar, and she realized Paul was home. In her mind, she followed him as he checked the house, looked in on his sons, crossed the living room, and opened her door. Her breath caught in her throat when she saw him at the foot of her bed, undressing in the moonlight, his imposing form outlined in a pool of liquid silver. Then he was lying beside her under the covers.

"It's me," he whispered. "You still up?"

"Hm-mm," she said drowsily, smiling when he spooned his body against her. "Is everything okay?"

"Sort of." Paul slipped an arm underneath her and pulled her into his chest. "Maude Pelter is in the hospital."

"Oh, no. What happened? Is she all right?"

"Probably, but you never know with someone that old. After I examined her, I called the firehouse and woke the guy on duty. They sent their emergency vehicle and I followed them to Shore Memorial."

"You were gone a long time. I thought maybe—"

"I had to stay with her. Maude has no relatives. When they wheeled her into CCU, she looked so frail and worn I thought she might need a friend. Then she clutched my sleeve and I . . ." He sighed against her ear. "I know she's a pain in the ass, but I couldn't leave her, not until I was sure she'd been stabilized."

Lila turned in his embrace and lay her head on his chest. "That was very kind of you."

"I'm her doctor, and I wouldn't be a very good one if I didn't do my duty. I'll have to get to the hospital early in the morning to check her condition. I want to set her up with a cardiology consult, so I'll need to talk with a specialist."

Lila hugged him tight. "I wasn't worried, but we missed you. The house is too quiet when you're gone."

"I'm fine. Just dead on my feet." He kissed the top of her head. "I'm sorry I didn't get to tell you how grateful I was for today before I left."

"For today?"

"You know, because of Teddy. It was such a shock to finally hear him speak, I sort of lost it. Then we ate dinner and I got involved with the boys and forgot to say thanks. The twins and I will never be able to repay you for all you've done. You deserve a raise."

Lila's heart took a header to her toes. Did he think she cared for them only because she expected to be paid? "He's a bright boy. All he needed was a little coaxing. It helps to make a game out of the exercises for both of them."

"Still, it might have been months before I figured that out and found the time to try it myself." He cupped her breast with his hand and palmed the nipple. "There's so much I want to talk to you about, so much I have to tell you." Yawning, he nuzzled her ear. "I don't know where to begin."

Not sure what to say, she welcomed his touch. She'd rather they made love than discuss the reasons they should put a halt to their affair, or hear for the thousandth time that what they were doing was wrong. If they were intimate, she could remember this moment and all the others she'd spent in his arms, when she knew only love and contentment.

She smoothed the hardened wall of his chest with her fingertips. "Maybe we should wait until after the Founders' Day festivities? It's late, and you said you had to make an early trip to the hospital." She bit her lower lip. "And your mother is coming, remember?"

When he didn't answer, she frowned. It was obvious from the number of times he'd mentioned the woman that he valued her opinion. Lila would never see her again after this weekend, but she did want to make a good impression.

"What's your mother like?"

His chest rumbled and she thought he was laughing. "Is she going to find me amusing?"

Glancing up at Paul's serene expression, she realized the rumble was a soft snore.

Lila corralled the twins inside the rectangle of tables that made up Paul's booth. With only one day left before Founders' Day, the sun had split through the rain clouds, which sent everyone scurrying outside to do as much as they could in preparation for the festival. Because of a heavy appointment scheduled, Paul had no time to organize the boxes holding promotional trinkets and pamphlets he'd been given by a number of pharmaceutical companies, so Lila had volunteered for the job.

The sound of friendly chatter mingled with the pounding of hammers and the whine of motors in use for all manner of construction. Several women were decorating the quilting booth adjacent to Paul's in red, white, and blue streamers. Behind her, Mary Lou washed the front windows of the Clothes Closet. Across the street, vendors dressed the food booths and tables that would, she'd been told, hold award-winning edibles. Chancing the weather, a few brave workers had hung cardboard signs with a list of offerings and prices.

Adjusting her sunglasses, Lila scanned Paul's space with its red-and-white-striped canvas awning and dark blue table skirt, and decided there wasn't much more she could do to embellish a medical information booth that would double as a first-aid station. Squatting, she used a black marker to label the contents of each box. To her right, the twins sat on the sidewalk with toys. Rick played with a plastic fire truck, loudly imitating the squeal of a siren. Still experimenting with his voice, Teddy seemed fascinated by a gadget that made animal sounds.

"The cow says moo," announced the toy when Teddy pulled its string.

He giggled. "Moo. Moo-moo-moo!"

"That's right," Lila agreed, grinning when he again drew out the cord. Now that he'd started talking, words flowed from his rosebud lips like water from a broken dam. She ran a hand over his golden curls, then did the same to Rick, ignoring the pain she felt at the thought of leaving them.

Almost finished with her chore, she considered sitting and joining in their fun. Then the concrete vibrated and she stood. In the distance, she caught sight of two huge trucks rounding the corner onto Main Street. A crowd gathered as the vehicles pulled to a stop at the vacant lot next to the cement factory.

Earlier, when she'd left home with the boys, Lila had overheard Edith complain to Paul about being inconvenienced. Since the lot was the only space in town large enough to hold the rides, every inch of pavement was needed to set up the carousel, Tilt-A-Whirl, and Ferris wheel. Mayor Hickey had ordered the Hammers to relocate to an out-of-the-way area for the weekend. Millie had given them permission to park the Windcruiser next to the grocery's loading dock, but they weren't happy about the surprise move.

The fact that Edith worked in the bottom floor of her home still had Lila uneasy, but knowing Paul was there to make certain the woman stayed in the reception area gave her a small sense of security. If he kept Edith occupied with office duties, she would be too busy to snoop.

"Tuck! Tuck!"

Lila heard Rick's clamor right before he scampered between the boxes and scooted under the table skirting, with Teddy on his heels. Vaulting over the obstacle, she landed on her feet and grabbed hold of each boy's jacket, anchoring them in place. "Oh, no, you don't. If you want to see the trucks, I'll take you. Then we'll go home for lunch."

Both boys shrieked in protest. Rick fell to the sidewalk, stiffening his arms and legs, while Teddy plopped on his bottom and wailed. She wrestled them into the stroller and strapped them in place amid a barrage of screeches. Then she took a step back, folded her arms, and glared.

"We're not moving until you stop your tantrum."

Teddy sniffled, his lower lip quivering. It took longer for Rick to calm down, but he finally did the same. Kneeling beside the carriage, Lila swiped at their damp cheeks, soothing their wounded egos with words of comfort.

"Hey, you two, cool your jets. I heard the racket all the way at my office."

Startled by Paul's voice, Lila placed a hand over her heart. He stood smiling, with Harley at his side. "What are you doing here? I thought you had patients scheduled this morning."

"I do. But the sound of trucks emptied my waiting room. Seems that setting up the rides is a city-wide event. The men who deliver them need help, and everyone else gets to watch. How about if I give the boys a tour of the truck while you take a few minutes to inspect some of the other booths? Might as well kill some time, since my next patient is on the setup committee."

Paul pulled Teddy from the stroller and lifted him atop his shoulders, while Harley did the same with Rick. She pushed the carriage and followed them until they crossed the street, then propped a shoulder against the side of the Shop and Bag to continue her vigil. A woman in the throng chatted with Teddy, jiggling his foot. Paul held a conversation with an older couple, his expression interested, as if he'd known them his entire life. Mayor Hickey walked to Paul and shook his hand, then tugged on each of the twins' legs.

The scene touched Lila's heart. Paul and his sons fit perfectly in Preston's Ferry. They belonged, while she did not. But oh, how she wished she did.

"It figures you'd forget to wear your hat." Bill Halverson magically appeared at her side and sat a foil crown on Lila's head. "How many times do I have to tell you, don't venture outside unless you're wearing it?"

Lila pushed her sunglasses up onto her nose. A breeze blew in from the bay and she clamped her hand on the hat to anchor it in place. "I have a lot on my mind." She nodded at the trucks and men milling around the parking lot. "How long does it take to assemble the rides?"

"They'll probably be at it right on through the night, even if the rain starts up again." Following her gaze, Bill zeroed in on Paul. "Heard about what Dr. P did for Maude. Staying with her until he knew she was gonna be okay was a nice touch. He's quite a doctor."

"I know," said Lila, holding back tears.

"Good dad too. He seems a very understanding man."

"You think so?" she said, sniffing.

"He'd make a fine husband for some upstanding young woman—no matter where she came from."

"He would," she agreed. "I only wish . . ." Coming to her senses, she attempted a smile. "I meant to compliment you on the meeting. It went well, didn't it?"

"Eustace thinks so." Bill gave her a hard stare. "But I'm not sure. Saw you reading the newsletter. What did you think of those articles?"

Lila raised a brow. "Do you want the truth?"

"Wouldn't have asked if I didn't."

Clearing her throat, she told herself this was merely a continuation of the discussion they'd had in the backyard—not a way for Bill to interrogate her. "I thought every one was a figment of someone's overzealous imagination. I watched the news several times this week, and I haven't seen a thing to corroborate any of the articles."

He folded his arms. "That's exactly what I was thinking. Made me wonder if ESAW is on the right track." He shifted his gaze to the Windcruiser. "What's your take on that Hammer woman and her friends?"

Lila's chest tightened. "I try not to think of her. You know she showed up at Paul's office and asked for a job as his receptionist?"

"That I do. But I'm talking about the way she and her buddies darn near jumped out of their chairs when Eustace mentioned those covert groups he'd heard about." Bill leaned closer. "Don't repeat this to a soul, but I spied on them a time or two and I think they're here to make trouble."

Lila's skin grew clammy, her hands damp. "Trouble?"

He cocked his head. "For you."

"Me?" Her breath rasped in her throat. "What gave you the idea they want to make trouble for me?"

"Because of who—what you are," he said softly. She grabbed her bracelet and Bill covered her hand. "I know what—who you are, Lila, but you can rest easy. I'm not planning to do a thing about it, leastways not until you and I talk a bit more."

Lila checked the street. It was bad enough she and Bill were holding hands. If she took off running everyone would notice. "You aren't going to call Mr. Carter?"

Shaking his head, he released her. "Heck, no. But I do want to know your reason for being here." He smiled. "I never thought I'd live to meet an alien or call one a friend, but that's what you've become. I want to help, if you'll let me."

"If you know, then Edith does too." She took a step back. "I have to leave—I have to—"

"Don't go packing your bags just yet. They sounded interested but uncertain—though they did talk about your bracelet." He tugged on his chin. "I'd keep it out of sight, and if anyone asks, don't let them get too close, just in case they've a mind to *borrow* it."

"Tuck! La-la, tuck!"

Harley walked toward them with Rick bouncing on his shoulders. "How come you two are hiding back here? Don't you want to watch them unload the horses? Dr. P says I can take the boys on a ride tomorrow."

"We're coming," said Bill. Grasping the stroller in one hand, he pulled Lila along by her elbow, guiding her across the street and straight to Paul's side. "Say, Doc, if you're out here, who's minding the store?"

Holding Teddy by the ankles, Paul swung around. "Thought you would have heard by now. I have a receptionist. Edith Hammer is manning the office."

Bill squeezed her arm so hard she thought it might snap off. "Alone?"

"Well, yeah. But I should probably get back and

see if my next patient has shown. And it's lunchtime. I'm sure the boys are hungry. I know I am."

Narrowing his eyes, Bill frowned. "Then we won't keep you. Harley, put that little fella in his buggy and come with me. We got to get to work on those carnival gizmos."

Paul and Harley strapped the boys in place while Bill drew his eyebrows together. Glancing at Lila, he jerked his chin in the direction of Paul's office. "We'll talk later."

Paul laid Teddy in his crib, while Lila did the same with Rick. He'd spent the afternoon seeing patients, several of whom had received minor injuries during the setup phase of the rides. The men were still hard at work on the Ferris wheel, which someone had mentioned was "acting peculiar," but he couldn't stay to help. Now that he and Lila had cared for the twins, it was time to pay another visit to Maude.

"I hate leaving you alone again," he said as he closed the boys' bedroom door.

"It's all right. I can watch television or read. I might even keep tabs on the construction. I ran an experiment while Teddy and Rick were napping and found that if I crane my neck out the window on the far right I have a fairly clear view of the parking lot."

He walked to her side and drew her into his arms. "Just don't hang out too far. The last thing I need is a page from the ER telling me they've admitted another of my patients."

"I won't fall out." She squeezed his middle. "Besides, you're the one I worry about—in bed at midnight and awake at dawn for the past few days. You're not getting enough rest."

"I'm fine. Once this weekend is over, I'll be able to relax." Gazing down at her, he waggled his eyebrows. "If I can talk Mom into taking the twins home for a visit, we might even get to spend a little quality time together."

Lila's eyes opened wide. "You'd let your mother take Teddy and Rick away?"

He kissed the tip of her nose, amused that she'd ignored his sexual innuendo. "Why wouldn't I? She was thrilled to have them while I spent a week moving here. She's a very 'with it' grandmother. Believe me, if she heard you casting aspersions on her parenting abilities, she'd be miffed."

"I'm not doubting her skills, it's the boys I'm thinking of. Will she cook their favorite foods or play the Speak-and-Say game?" She stabbed a finger in his chest with each question. "Will she read them a story every night? Does she know that Teddy likes to sleep with Pooh, and wants him under the covers, or—"

Paul grabbed the digit threatening to poke a hole in his lung. "She'll play with them all day long. Mom's had a lot of time on her hands since Dad died. If I don't let her bring them home, she'll probably kidnap them anyway."

"Kidnap them!"

His lips twitching, he guided Lila to the sofa and dragged her onto his lap. "I'm joking. She knows she can't keep them long before I'll start to howl." Nuzzling the soft skin behind her ear, he whispered, "In the meantime, we'll get a chance to be alone. We have to talk, and it's been darn hard to find a few free minutes lately."

She sighed against his chest. "I know."

Paul cupped her jaw. Tilting her head, he kissed her, drinking in her sweetness. If he could, he'd sit here all night and say the things he'd been thinking for the past twenty-four hours. He loved her. It had taken a night of soul-searching, but he now knew he wanted them to make a life together. Lila needed to know that, if she was pregnant, he approved, and would care for both her and their baby. But he wanted to tell her in a more romantic setting, after a nice dinner with music and candlelight and a bottle of wine.

Drowning in the taste of her, he gulped for air. "I have to go." He breathed in the scent of oranges. "You've been in the baking cupboard again," he said with a laugh. "I remember the first time you smelled like this."

"I hoped you might." She kissed the underside of his jaw. "I'll try to wait up for you."

"That would be nice, but you need rest, especially now that you're—uh—you have a busy weekend planned." He maneuvered them to their feet. "Don't get too concerned about meeting Mother. She's going to love you as much as I do." He gave her a quick kiss good-bye. "I have to go."

Lila plopped back on the sofa and placed her head in her hands while she listened to Paul's fading footsteps. Had he just said he loved her? The idea was wonderful . . . amazing . . . impossible.

Could her life get any more confusing?

Minutes passed while she sat like stone, unable to

move. Then she heard the front buzzer. Racing down the stairs, she hoped there hadn't been an accident at the amusement ride site, because her medical skills were minimal.

"Who is it?" she asked through the door.

"I'm looking for Paul Anderson," the voice returned.

"Dr. Anderson isn't here."

"Then you're the nanny?" The woman's voice rose as the doorknob rattled. "Let me in, please."

"Is this a medical emergency?"

"Hardly. I'm Mrs. Anderson. Paul's mother."

Lila thought her heart had stopped. She needed this complication like she needed an eleventh toe. She was still trying to absorb Paul's last words, and now his mother had arrived. Before she could speak, she heard shuffling sounds. Great, she'd been so rude she'd frightened the woman away. Wending her way to the stairs, she heard noise at the back door, then footsteps. Perhaps Paul had forgotten his medical bag. What would he say when he learned she'd scared off his mother?

She walked to the lab area and stumbled against a body heading with purpose into the hallway. Disentangling herself, Lila switched on the light. Before her stood a diminutive blond-haired woman with a familiar dimple in her chin. Dressed in jeans and an expensive-looking sweater, the blue-eyed burglar wore a frown of suspicion on her bright red lips.

"Mrs. Anderson?" Lila asked, but she already knew the answer.

"Yes, and call me Tricia." The woman appraised her slowly, stopping at Lila's eyes for several seconds before continuing her inspection. When finished, she held out her hand. "You must be Lila. Paul told me a little about you, but it looks as if he skipped a few of the more pertinent details. I'm pleased to meet you."

Lila accepted her greeting, clasping the small palm in her larger one. "I'm sorry about the mix-up at the door. Paul—Dr. Anderson's gone, and I have to be careful who I let in."

Tricia smoothed her navy and white sweater over slim hips. "I understand. If Paul complains, tell him I used my key. He's such a fuss pot, so like his father."

Paul? A fuss pot?

"Where did you say he was?" Tricia asked.

"He has a patient at the hospital. He said you wouldn't be here until tomorrow morning. Did he know you were arriving tonight?"

Tricia forged past her, calling an answer over her shoulder. "He should have, since I phoned and left a message with his receptionist. Unpleasant woman," she muttered as she disappeared from view.

Lila placed two fingers on each temple and took a deep breath, hoping to stem the beginnings of a headache. Either Edith had forgotten to inform Paul, or he'd been too busy for the change in plans to register. Gathering her composure, she climbed the steps, and arrived to see Tricia gazing around the kitchen as if conducting a crime scene inspection.

The woman walked to the sink and filled the teakettle. After setting it on the burner, she continued into the living room. Lila peered around a corner and watched her slowly open the door to the boys' bedroom and go inside. Seconds later, she tiptoed out and detoured to the bathroom. The kettle whistled and Lila rushed to the stove, still reeling from surprise.

She assembled tea, milk, and sugar and brought everything to the table, then arranged cookies on a plate. Tricia's footsteps echoed from the far side of the apartment and Lila imagined her going from room to room as she checked out the terrain.

Had she remembered to put away the clothes Paul had tossed over the foot of her bed last night?

Sitting down, Lila recalled one of her training classes before the final travelers had been chosen. The Elders had installed every candidate in a room and sat them face-to-face with a supposed human. Each traveler had undergone rapid-fire questioning, very much, she suspected, like what was about to happen to her in the next few minutes.

Finally, Tricia arrived in the kitchen. "The boys are fast asleep. I noticed a box of Pull-Ups on the changing table. Are you the one responsible for that little miracle?"

"Um—yes—though it wasn't too difficult."

Adding milk to her cup, Tricia stirred the brew, then raised her brilliant blue eyes. "So, Lila, tell me, where do you come from? I find it hard to imagine a young, attractive woman would want to live in a backwater town such as Preston's Ferry. What kind of position did you hold before this one?"

"I worked at a child care center," she answered politely. "Paul was kind enough to give me a trial period before he hired me permanently."

"The boys can be a handful." Tricia sipped her

tea. "Did you babysit as a teenager or help your mother with brothers and sisters?"

"I'm a twin," she said in return. "When I met Rick and Teddy, I knew immediately I could relate to them."

"They're such happy boys, aren't they? It's hard to imagine them not getting along with people. Paul's the same—warm, friendly, outgoing. Sometimes he's too kind for his own good." She bit daintily into a cookie.

Lila felt her cheeks warm. If the woman knew how well she and Paul were getting along, she'd probably haul her grandsons from their beds and carry them off tonight.

"There's just one teensy thing I need to ask," said Tricia, her smile shrinking. "How long have you and my son been sleeping together?"

Nineteen

The morning of the festival dawned bright and clear. Paul had returned home during the night and slipped into bed beside her, but they hadn't talked. Glancing at his empty pillow, Lila recalled that she hadn't even had time to inform him of his mother's visit before the buzzer had rung and he'd tossed on jeans and a shirt, and raced to answer the door.

Minutes later, she heard his voice and Tricia's raised in friendly chatter. The sound of Paul's shower mingled with the rattle of pots and pans, and she envisioned the woman fixing breakfast for her son and grandchildren. Soon, an enticing aroma scented the air, then Rick's morning shout wrenched at her maternal instincts, almost coercing her from the bed. Sadly, Lila thought it best not to intrude on what was sure to be a family affair. Besides, she had to get used to waking without them.

Dejected, she pulled the covers over her head.

Even now, she imagined Tricia Anderson advising her son to fire his impertinent housekeeper.

Last night, when the woman had asked her nosy question, Lila had been close to speechless, but at least she hadn't burst into tears. Instead, she'd gathered her composure and said, "I don't think that's any of your business, Mrs. Anderson." Upon hearing the succinct response, Tricia had walked from the house without uttering a word.

Rather than face the woman at such an early hour, Lila continued her cowardly retreat until the house grew quiet. Certain the foursome had left to put the finishing touches on the first-aid booth, she breathed easier. It would have been nice if Paul had looked in on her and informed her of his plans, but his inattention was probably for the best. He was with his family. The break would be clean.

She padded to the bathroom, showered, and dressed in her best pair of pants, a shirt, and sweater. Grateful for the privacy, she sorted through her clothes and shoved the most serviceable into her backpack. Sniffing back tears, she ate a light breakfast while she thought about her day. She was committed to assisting Paul in the morning, and working with Bill for the afternoon. Instead of returning to the house and all its memories, she would leave the tote bag with Bill and retrieve it on her way out of town.

Before she went downstairs, she remembered her sunglasses and aluminum hat. Let Tricia Anderson see her wearing the tinfoil crown, she thought. It would give her one more reason to convince Paul he had to fire his nanny.

After pinning the hat to her head, she locked the back door, even though Edith wasn't scheduled to come in. When she and Paul had returned to the house yesterday, they'd found Edith sitting at her desk filling out paperwork, but that didn't mean she hadn't snooped before they'd arrived.

Rounding the corner onto Main Street, Lila stared in awe. Yesterday's rush of activity hadn't prepared her for the wondrous scene that ran the six-block length of town. Men standing guard at wooden blockades directed traffic away from an avenue awash with pedestrians. Walking the pavement, she dodged racing children, couples pushing strollers, quick-stepping adults, and older citizens using canes and walkers. The lines for booths selling tickets for food, beverages, and rides seemed to stretch forever; those selling merchandise were the same.

To her left, in the once-vacant lot, gaily painted horses galloped in place to a rousing swirl of music as the carousel enticed the crowd to take a ride. Passengers screamed with delight or fright, she wasn't sure which, as the Tilt-A-Whirl spun and dipped. The centerpiece of the display, an enormous wheel with basketlike appendages, slowed to a stop in order to board another group of smiling patrons.

Lila knew of no such event on her planet, though she supposed there had been something similar long ago. Paul intimated the festival would be a small affair, but to her it was larger than life, a feast for the eyes, a joy to the senses. One more thing about Preston's Ferry that would be forever imprinted on her heart.

She found Bill's booth and hid her backpack under an empty carton while he talked to customers. Distracted on all sides, it took her some time to travel to the far end of the strip, where Paul's booth was located. People milled around the display, sorting through pamphlets and token giveaways from various pharmaceutical companies. Paul stood to one side, using a blood pressure cuff to monitor a young woman with four energetic children hovering around her.

"I'd say you've added about twenty extra points for each of these little hellions, Sue," he said, grinning. "My best advice is cut back on your salt intake and try to make a little time for yourself each day. Robbie and Andy are in school, so I'd take an hour nap every afternoon when Angela and Candy go down. If you can't sleep, put your feet up and breathe deep for a while. And send Hal to me if he's not giving you a hand with the housework. I'll set him straight."

Sue tucked a packet of information into her purse and gathered her children. "Thanks, Dr. P. I'll call to make that appointment on Monday."

When Paul raised his head, he locked gazes with Lila, and his expression morphed from friendly to flustered. "Hey, you're here. I was hoping you'd sleep in."

"I did—sort of." She scanned the area. "Where are the twins . . . and your mother?"

He clasped her elbow, guiding her around the tables and into the center of the booth. "There's a miniature petting zoo by the rides, and a series of eastern shore artisans across the street and up a block, closer to the beach. She could be at either place or somewhere in between. You never know with Mom."

Lila pulled a box of sample pain relievers from underneath the table and refilled a basket. "Did she tell you we met?"

"She mentioned it, and I'm sorry she barged in unannounced. I haven't seen Edith yet, but when I do I'll remind her I need to get all my messages, not just those she deems important."

Lila simply nodded. Soon she'd be rid of Edith, and Paul's mother, and Bill and Harley, and the twins, and everyone else who complicated her existence . . .

"Lila, is something wrong?"

She shook her head and felt the tears well. Turning away, she brushed at her cheeks. He touched her shoulder and she shrugged. "I'm just a little overwhelmed."

"Mom is taking the boys to her house after dinner. I have a volunteer coming to help at lunchtime, so you can work the ESAW booth with Bill while I give Mom a hand packing my car. She's leaving hers with us, because it's easier than changing out the car seats."

Lila stifled a sob. Once the twins were gone, she might never see them again. She sucked in a breath. "That's fine."

To distract herself, she passed out pamphlets to adults and miniature coloring books and crayons to their children. Paul taught her how use the blood pressure cuff and take a pulse. In between, she smiled until her cheeks ached. She didn't realize it was time for lunch until she heard a cheerful voice.

"Hey, Dr. P, I'm here. Want to show me what to do?"

Lila glanced over her shoulder and found Ashley somebody-or-other, the pretty girl from the restaurant, hip to hip with Paul while gazing at him with admiration. They put their heads together for instruction, and the young woman colored pink when he praised her for catching on so quickly.

This was Paul's helpmate? While she had to sit with Bill!

Without warning, Tricia and the boys stood in front of her. "La! La-la!" chanted Teddy and Rick.

Tricia raised a finely arched brow. "I must admit, Lila, you've made quite an impression on my grandsons. Every other word they've shouted this morning has been your name."

Lila slid sideways through the table opening and crouched next to the stroller. "I've missed you." She kissed each of them on a rosy cheek. Unable to stop herself, she enfolded them in her arms and held them until they squirmed. While Paul and Tricia discussed their plans, she leaned closer and whispered, "Always remember that I love you."

"It's time to get the twins lunch, and put them down for a nap. Then we can pack the car," said Tricia.

Paul glanced at Ashley. "If there's an emergency the fire station can't handle, send someone to the house." He nodded at Lila. "Come on, I'll walk you to Bill's booth and make sure you have something to eat while you work. If you get tired, come home and nap with the boys." Paul halted at the ESAW tables. "I'll stop by to see you on my way back."

She was about to tell him she would take care of herself when Harley stepped to her side. "Hey, Lila, I'm going to get lunch. Bill gave me money."

"Food is just what Lila needs," said Paul, handing Harley a few dollars. "How about getting her something too?"

"She's in good hands, Dr. P," added Bill. "We'll see to it she's taken care of."

Lila ate french-fried potatoes smothered in gooey yellow cheese, then Harley brought her a sticky pink froth of sugar on a paper cone. Later in the afternoon he served her a waffle covered with ice cream and strawberries, then a plate of crispy cookies drenched in powdered sugar. Bolstered by her revitalized appetite, Lila handed out ESAW newsletters and helped Bill form tinfoil hats, which he sold mostly to children under the age of ten.

At five o'clock Paul returned with his sons. "Okay, Harley. I've closed for the day. You ready to escort the boys to a ride?"

"I want to take 'em on the Ferris wheel. Is that okay?"

Paul peered at the parking lot, where the huge machine was circling smoothly. "Only if the seats have safety straps as well as a bar. Let me check it out first. If I don't think it's safe, it'll have to be the merry-go-round."

Lila couldn't bear to watch the twins and Paul leave, but at the same time she couldn't look away. She was so engrossed in her emotional tug-of-war, she didn't notice Tricia standing beside her until the woman cleared her throat.

"I owe you an apology," Tricia began politely. "I've discussed it with Paul, and it seems you're just what he needs in his life. Can you ever forgive me for being rude?"

She forced a smile. Paul had defended her to his mother, a thought that made her happy and strangely sad at the same time. "There's nothing to forgive. Just promise you'll take good care of the twins." *Don't let them forget me.* "And keep them safe."

"Of course. In the meanwhile, I hope you and my son find time to talk. I'll see you when I bring the boys home."

Lila waited until Tricia crossed the street and disappeared in the crowd. With Paul occupied, this was the perfect time to disappear.

As if reading her mind, Bill moved to block her exit. "You're leaving." It wasn't a question, but a statement

"I have to go," she answered, bending to retrieve her bag. "If I stay, Paul and the boys will be in danger."

"Ain't no call for that, Lila. There's got to be a way we can work things out so you and them are protected."

Words caught in her throat. She focused on his weathered face and knew instantly that Bill was aware of her plans. "It's better this way. Just don't tell Eustace or anyone else about me until after the march. Please?" She sighed. "I never meant to cause any harm."

His eyes shining, Bill sniffed. "I wish we had

more time to talk. I have a ton of questions about . . ." He drew a circle in the air over his head.

"Maybe someday I'll come back and answer them." She leaned forward and kissed his papery cheek. "You've been a good friend. I'm going to miss you."

Turning, she slipped through the masses, intent on getting to the main parking lot a few streets over, where she hoped to beg a ride from a stranger. At the Shop and Bag, she stopped and gave the Ferris wheel a final look of longing. Harley sat in the bottom basket, with a twin harnessed on each side. The wheel moved forward, then halted to take on another round of passengers. In the distance, the sun was setting, casting a pinky-orange glow over the town. The streetlights flickered on, as did those illuminating the parking lot. Paul stood at the foot of the huge machine, his head tipped up as he watched his sons, who were bouncing with excitement next to Harley.

Just one time around, Lila thought. *One last glimpse of them, and I'll go.*

The wheel jerked, then the motor revved and chugged until their basket lifted another quarter of a circle. A few seconds passed before the wheel began to move in an erratic round of fits and starts.

Lila furrowed her brow. Something was wrong.

Paul walked to the operator and gestured at Harley's basket. The man shook his head and continued to tug on the lever as if everything were fine, but people in the crowd were now paying attention. Chief Gibson ambled over, then Mayor Hickey. Paul took them aside, and they approached the operator as a unit.

By this time, Harley and the twins were at the very top of the loop. A gust of wind skittered across the bay, swinging them in place as the entire wheel shuddered. Lila peered at Harley. Instead of holding on to the boys, he was rocking back and forth, as if he could make the wheel move.

Another heavy breeze swept in from the Chesapeake, causing the crowd to point. "Harley, sit still," shouted Chief Gibson.

Paul began to pace as he barked orders to the operator, but nothing he said seemed to help. Finally, the mayor marched to the fire station and spoke to one of the men.

Harley panicked, calling to Paul as his terror grew. The twins began to cry, their wails sending a shock wave over the throng. A siren bleated a series of warnings as the ladder truck rolled slowly across the street, deliberately parting the crowd. After maneuvering the huge contraption to the base of the Ferris wheel, the firemen positioned the ladder and cranked it skyward. A chorus of disappointment filled the air when the ladder fell a good dozen feet from its destination.

Lila glanced around her. Hidden alongside the grocery store, and with everyone's attention focused on the unfolding emergency, she swallowed her fear and concentrated. Aside from working with the energy orb, she'd had little practice with her skills here on Earth. With her eyes on the still running motor, she gave it a mental order. In her mind, she saw the cogs turn and the gear pulleys inch forward. The wheel began to rotate in reaction to her vision.

Harley wrapped an arm around each twin when he realized they were moving. The man in charge released the lever and held up his hands, indicating he'd lost control of the machine, but no one seemed to notice. The wheel inched around the circle in increments, until their basket slid smoothly to the bottom. By this time, Paul had pushed the operator aside and raced up the ramp. Grabbing his sons, he gathered them in his arms and carried them off as Harley trotted behind.

Lila stayed put, mentally urging the wheel forward until each basket emptied of its riders. Finally, she willed the motor to disengage. Not until the machine gave a huge shudder and came to a full stop did she turn to leave.

"I don't understand," said Paul, watching while Bill collected the last of his newsletters and foil. "What do you mean, Lila's gone?"

"Lila's not gone," said Harley.

Bill threw both men a frown of pity. "She didn't say where she was going, but it's been over two hours. Why'd you wait so long to come for her?"

Paul raked both hands through his hair. "After that fiasco with the Ferris wheel, it was all I could do to think straight. First I had to calm Mom down, then we fed the twins and loaded them in the car. I figured Lila would come home when she was through here." He glanced up and down the street, where vendors were packing their supplies and closing shop. "Did she say where she was going?"

"Nope," said Bill, averting his gaze.

"Why is it I get the feeling there's something you're not telling me?"

Jutting his jaw, Bill stretched to his full height. "I promised her I wouldn't say anything. I gave my word."

"You gave your—" Stepping back, Paul held him temper in check. "Listen, this isn't about your word. This is the woman I love we're discussing. Now tell me what you know."

"I love Lila too," chimed Harley. "Even though she said she won't marry me. But she didn't leave."

Ignoring Harley's chatter, Paul stuffed his hands in his pockets. "Just tell me where she went. I want to take her to dinner tonight."

"The woman you love, huh?" Bill shook his head. "If I tell, you aren't gonna believe me, so why should I bother? Besides, it's obvious she didn't trust you, or she would of told you herself."

"She doesn't trust me?"

"Not the way a woman and man should have faith in each other, she doesn't." He folded his arms and returned Paul's scowl. "Probably because of that smart-assed attitude of yours whenever you heard us talkin' about aliens. I saw you at the meeting making jokes and acting like we were all nutty as a jar of Skippy, Lila included. Don't give a woman a warm fuzzy feeling knowing her man don't believe in her, I'll bet."

"This isn't about aliens, you fool. This is about Lila," Paul shot back. Damn the old codger for making this so difficult.

Bill hitched up a corner of his mouth. "That's what I'm trying to tell you, Doc. It's the same damned thing."

Paul opened his mouth, but no sound came out. It

felt as if someone had dropped a bowling ball on his shoulders and rammed his head into his chest. Bill was just being Bill, he told himself, slightly off center and contrary as a one-legged rooster.

"You're not making any sense."

"See, I knew that's what you'd say." The old man swiveled his head and took in the now-deserted street. "Think on it a minute, and see if you can put the pieces together." He nodded to Harley. "Come on, son. You can sleep at my house tonight. We got to leave for the march at the crack of dawn."

Paul followed Bill's gaze. Empty booths sat like ghostly arches in the moonlight. The cleanup crew would be out early to finish the tear-down. And he would be alone. Without his sons. Without Lila.

Harley tagged behind his mentor. "Can we pick up Lila on the way?"

"I don't see how, since she's left town."

"That's what I've been trying to tell you. She hasn't."

Paul jerked back to reality. Jogging to Harley, he grabbed his arm and spun him in place. "What the hell are you saying?"

"Hang on a second, Doc," said Bill. "Harley, do you know were Lila is?"

Harley nodded. "I think so."

"Well, spit it out," demanded Bill.

"I saw her with that hammer lady, right after I got off the Ferris wheel."

"That *hammer* lady? Does he mean Edith? My receptionist?"

Bill pulled at his lower lip. "Where did they go?"

"To the trailer. I saw the lady push Lila inside. I

haven't been watching the whole time, but the trailer's still there."

Lila shifted, trying to find a comfortable position. Her wrists were taped together in front of her, and she sat on a hard-backed chair in a far corner of the Windcruiser. Up front, Edith and her partners in crime whispered as they huddled around some kind of tracking device. They'd been at it since right after they'd hustled her inside and strapped her to the chair. If Edith hadn't been holding a gun the entire time, Lila might have used her mental powers, but she was afraid something would go wrong to hurt her baby.

"Excuse me," she shouted, sick of being ignored. "Would someone mind telling me what's going on?"

Not one of her captors paid attention.

"Excuse me!" Jumping in place, she managed to set the chair rocking.

Edith peered over her shoulder. "Stop that or I'll—"

Lila stiffened her spine. "Or you'll what?" She rocked a few more times, hoping to lure Edith near. "Shoot me? Go ahead. What are you waiting for?"

Edith spoke to the men, then stormed toward Lila with her gun raised. "I told you to be quiet."

"Why are you keeping me here? I haven't hurt you. I haven't hurt anyone."

"Poor little fool," the woman responded through gritted teeth. "You're not even bright enough to deny it."

"Deny what?" Lila challenged.

"That you're an alien."

"You have no proof," countered Lila.

"How about I pry out those so-called colored contacts you claim to be wearing?" Edith threatened.

Lila jerked backward and the woman sneered a victory. "I checked the apartment and didn't find a container of saline or a storage case. No normal human being's eyes would turn color overnight the way yours did." She lifted a shoulder. "And let's not forget that I was standing behind you when the Ferris wheel stalled. You have powers that go above and beyond those of a regular person."

"If that's so, why haven't I used them on you?"

Edith glared. "I haven't figured that one out yet, but I will." She waved the gun. "Just because you're worth big money doesn't mean I won't shoot you in the foot."

Lila gulped. "Big money?"

"The finder's fee on your head is plenty, and we can double it if we make a deal with a newspaper or magazine conglomerate for the story and pictures. We're just waiting to contact our partners and arrange a meeting." She gave Lila an icy stare. "Now sit still and shut up."

Greed, Lila reminded herself, was a huge motivator on Earth. Humans seemed to thrive on it, no matter the reason. "I have jewels in my ears and on my wrist." She raised her taped hands. "You can have them if you let me go."

"Are they real?"

"Yes, and they're big. See?"

Edith bent closer, inspecting Lila's ears. With an ugly grin, she snatched first one diamond stud, then the other, and tucked them into her shirtfront pocket.

"Lift your hands and let me have a look at that bracelet I've heard so much about," Edith ordered.

Lila complied. If she could get them to remove the duct tape, she could manipulate an energy chip into the clasp and—

A knock at the door startled everyone. Edith's henchmen looked at her, waiting for orders. She pointed the gun at Lila and held a finger to her lips. "Who's there?"

"It's me. Harley. The mayor says to move the trailer."

"It's the town idiot," Edith hissed. "Get rid of him."

One of the men sidled to the door. "We'll do it in the morning. Go away."

If all earthmen had as much brainpower as her captors, thought Lila, this planet would never conquer outer space.

"Nu-uh. Millie says so too. She's expecting a delivery in the morning. There's no room for it with you here."

The man inched open the door. "I said we'd do it—"

The panel crashed inward, throwing him into the lap of the guy still seated at the computer. His head low, Harley barreled forward and slammed into Edith. The gun flew from her hand and landed at Lila's feet as Bill and Paul hurtled in right after.

"Paul! The gun!" Lila shouted.

Paul dived on the weapon, lurched to his feet, and aimed. The two men at the desk scrambled to a stand, cowering as Bill waved a baseball bat over their heads.

Moaning, Edith staggered onto the sofa, while Harley clambered to his hands and knees.

With the gun still pointed at the kidnappers, Paul knelt next to Lila. "Are you all right, sweetheart? Did they hurt you or the baby?"

He knew about the baby? "I'll be better when you get this tape off my wrists and ankles. How did you find me?"

Harley crawled next to Paul. "I saw the hammer lady push you inside. Bill told Dr. P you left, but I knew better." He reached into his overalls and pulled out a pocketknife. "Will this help?"

Paul stuck the gun in the waistband of his jeans, then carefully slit the tape at Lila's wrists and ankles. "Bill, how you doing back there?"

"Doing fine, but you might want to hurry. This computer gizmo is squawking up a storm."

Paul glanced over his shoulder. "I'd say you have the answer to your problem right there in your hands."

Bill stared at the bat and grinned. Hauling the Louisville Slugger over his shoulder, he let it rip into the tracking system. The two henchmen fell to their knees in a hail of shattering glass.

"I'll have you arrested for interfering with a government field operation in progress," protested Edith, half rising from her seat. "Let us go this minute—"

Lila stood and leaned into Paul. "The boys. Tell me they're safe with your mother."

"They left a while ago. I came looking for you and—"

"I—I don't know how to thank you," she said above Edith's screeching. "I'm so sorry I have to go—"

"Just a second, I can't hear you over all that racket." He walked to Bill and handed him the gun. Bill passed the bat to Harley, and Paul said, "Think you can shut them up while I talk with Lila?"

"No problem."

"Do you know what you're doing? She's the biggest discovery of the century, possibly the millennium," whined Edith. "She's worth millions, maybe billions—"

"Get your butt over here, and quit yer yapping," snapped Bill, waving the gun threateningly in her direction. "You're starting to get on my nerves."

Paul returned to Lila's side and drew her near, then kissed her until she melted into his chest.

"I went crazy when I thought you'd left me," he rasped against her ear.

"I'm so sorry. I didn't mean for you to—" She sucked in a breath. "I wanted to leave before you found out about everything."

Paul stepped back and frowned, a steely glint in his eyes. "I just want to know one thing—what the hell is going on?"

Twenty

*P*aul tried to control his temper, but it was damned difficult. If he hadn't been so worried about Lila, Bill's ridiculous story would have had him laughing out loud. Now that he was in the trailer, he realized the part about her being in danger was true. As for the rest of it? He hadn't meant to sound so angry or crude, but come on . . . an alien?

Unclenching his jaw, he found himself drawn to her emerald eyes. He'd thought her a bit irrational when she was worried that he'd object to her wearing contacts, but he'd attributed her concern to the virus. Exactly when had the color change occurred? And when had that employment application disappeared?

About the same time I thought she might be pregnant, came the obvious answer.

As if reading his mind, Lila's shoulders sagged, and he pulled her hard into his chest. He didn't give a damn about her eyes or anything else. All he knew was that he needed her by his side. "Don't ever disappear like that again. If anything happened to you . . ." He brushed her forehead with his lips. "I love you, Lila. I should have told you sooner."

"You love me?"

Paul wrapped his arms around her and hugged her hard. "More than I ever thought I could love a woman. I was a fool for not saying the words the second I knew them to be true."

"How can you love me?" she muttered against his shirtfront. "All you ever seemed concerned about was the way our involvement would look to outsiders. You said we couldn't be together, that no one could know—"

"I was wrong. And when I figured out about the baby, it helped to get my feelings straight."

Leaning back, Lila gazed at him. "The baby? How did you find out about the baby?"

Despite the situation, he grinned. "I'm a doctor, remember? And it's fine—"

She wrenched from his embrace and shoved at his chest.

"No, wait! It's better than fine." He caught her hands before she smacked him again. "It's fantastic— it's mind-blowing—it's the best thing that's happened to me since the twins were born." He glanced over his shoulder to find Bill, Harley, and their three prisoners listening to every word. "I love you and I love our child," he whispered.

"You're being honest?"

"Yes, I'm being honest." He lowered his voice another decibel. "I can't imagine what proof this woman has for her outlandish charges, but it can't be enough to warrant what she's done to you. We'll go to the authorities and have her arrested. We'll—"

Sighing, Lila plopped back into her chair, and he squatted in front of her, still holding her hands. "We'll get through it, I swear."

"You have no idea what you're saying." Her voice wavered. "I'm not sure if she's telling the truth about working for the government, but one thing's certain, she's been looking for me. If she takes me to the authorities, they'll find the proof."

Paul caught her chin between two fingers and raised her head until they were eye to eye. "You're serious about this? Bill hasn't gone insane along with Mrs. Hammer and her pals?"

She blinked, and a fat tear rolled down her cheek. "I'm from another world, just like Bill said. And I have to leave here before more people like Edith find me."

"You expect me to believe you're an alien?"

She pursed her lips. "I do."

Oh, hell. He was in love with a woman who thought she was from another planet. If the situation wasn't so dire, he'd have the beginnings of a best-selling science fiction novel.

"That's a tough one." He blew out a breath. "You're asking me to take a lot on faith."

"I'd believe you if you came to my planet," she countered.

Paul cringed inside. He was a doctor, not some hero from a Steven Spielberg film. But when he'd seen Lila tied to that chair his love for her had superseded every promise he'd ever made. Now she was asking him to throw away his common sense and take her word for something so fantastic—so bizarre—

"I'll give it my best shot, but I need a little help—just to erase the questions. Is that too much to expect?"

Before she answered, Bill gave a loud cough. "Hey, there, missy. You got anything to beef up your argument? Not for me, of course, since I know one hundred percent you are what—who you say you are. But this idea is all new to Dr. P. I imagine it's quite a shock."

Lila's gaze swept the inside of the trailer. Drawing her brows together, she concentrated on the computer desk. Seconds passed, then an object rose from atop a pile of papers. Every person in the room was riveted on the pencil as it floated through the air and stopped in front of Paul, who caught it in his trembling fingers.

He shook his head. "The ball hovering over your bed?"

"I didn't lie, not really. It is a childhood toy, but it's also a training tool for my telekinetic abilities."

"Did you see what she just did? Are you listening to what she's saying?" Edith shouted, taking a step forward. "She's admitted she's a creature from another planet. Let me go, so I can take her into custody—"

Bill thrust the gun in her face. "Hush, woman, or I'll ask Lila to treat you the way she did that pencil, and move you someplace nice and peaceful—like the swamp."

Still trying to come to grips with what he'd just witnessed, Paul ignored the bickering. "You can make things move—with your mind?"

"It's a talent some of my people have."

"The stuck Ferris wheel? You rescued Harley and the boys—and all those others?"

One corner of her mouth lifted in a sad smile. "I'm sure the operator would have figured it out eventually, but I couldn't leave knowing the twins might be trapped there."

He nodded toward Edith. "And that's when she found you? And dragged you here?"

"I knew they'd been watching me, and I didn't want to put you or the boys in danger. I'm not supposed to use my powers unless threatened, but I love Teddy and Rick. It didn't matter when I thought they were in trouble."

"Isn't that sweet," scoffed Edith. "It'll be a nice story to sell to the tabloids. I can see the headline now: ALIEN SAVES CHILDREN TO RISK EXPOSURE. DETAILS INSIDE. It makes me want to puke."

Scanning the room, Paul spotted the roll of duct tape and threw it at Harley. "Bill, think you and your deputy can put this to good use?"

"You got it, Doc."

Facing Lila, he cupped her elbows. "How about you start by telling me why you're here?" He raised a brow. "I can't believe I'm going to ask this, but where were you going? Do you have to rendezvous with your . . . um . . . ship?"

Lila worried her lower lip. "It's a bit more complicated than that. Officially, I'm not here. I'm a stowaway."

"You stowed away on a spaceship to Earth?" *Only his Lila.* "Now, that's original."

"It's also forbidden. But I have no intention of going back. My planet is stifling. Restrictive. It lacks freedom of choice, of color, of beauty. I refuse to return, even though my sister and family, my entire world, will never forgive me for leaving—"

"You really have a twin?"

"Of course. I wouldn't lie about family," she said with a huff. "I told the truth whenever I could."

"Okay, okay. Don't get upset."

"Ah, folks. We're in the middle of something here. I think we need to figure out our next move."

Lila and Paul turned as one. Harley had used the duct tape to bind Edith and her companions the same way they'd wrapped Lila. Only he'd covered their mouths, as well.

"Bill's right. We need a plan," said Paul. "Do you have any other . . . um . . . tricks up your sleeve?"

"Maybe. I'll have to experiment and see what I can do."

"Experiment?" Paul swallowed hard. "Please don't do anything that could harm you—or our baby."

"I wouldn't." She held up the wrist wearing the bracelet. "This isn't mine, so it's not programmed for me specifically, but I know how to use it. Unfortunately, there's no guarantee it will do what it's supposed to."

"Not programmed for you? Then who is it programmed for?" He narrowed his gaze. Could that fancy bit of jewelry actually be a weapon, like a ray gun or— "It's not a bomb, is it?"

She sighed. "You watch too much of the Sci-Fi Channel. It's more like a mentally enhanced computer, but it's set to my sister's psychic impulses. I'm hoping that because we're identical it will work for me, too, but I have yet to try it out to be sure."

"Do you think this is the right time to practice?"

Lila studied the bracelet, her gaze intent. "Don't worry. It should only do what I suggest." After removing one of the diamonds, she placed it into the underside of the catch, snapped the circle shut, and closed her eyes. "Thinking good thoughts might help."

"Mmm-mmm!" Edith squeaked from behind the duct tape.

Lila's expression of concentration never wavered. Edith continued to shriek. Then, in the middle of her tirade, her voice simply stopped.

Paul's gaze darted from Lila to Edith and back again as he waited for Lila to open her eyes. When she did, he followed her as she walked toward the trio. Mouths open, Bill and Harley stepped aside to let them pass. Stopping in front of Edith, Lila stared and he did the same. The woman and her friends were still. Very still. In fact, they were frozen in place, each face set in a rock-hard grimace of fear.

Harley inched his way between them, then leaned forward and poked at Edith's cheek. "Wow! Lila turned her into a statue."

Bill waved the gun in front of Edith and her cohorts, who now resembled deer caught in the headlights of an oncoming semi. He tapped the gun on the nearest man's head and a dull *thunk* echoed in the trailer. "My, my, my." Grinning, he swung around. "That's some trick, Lila girl."

Paul ran his hand across Edith's terror-filled eyes

and gave a low whistle. "How the heck did you do that?"

"With the energy stone and my mind. Unless directly attacked, it's all we're allowed to use for protection. I'm not sure how long it will last, but they're not hurt, just locked in place."

"Locked. In place." He rapped on one of the men's foreheads. "I guess so. But this one is staring at me, and he doesn't look happy."

"The way I understand it, the subjects can breathe, hear, and see, but they can't move until the effects of the stabilizer wear off. I have no idea how long that might be." She grabbed his arm. "I don't want them hurt, but I need to get away. I have to go where no one can find me or my baby. I have to—"

Paul drew his brows together as her words washed over him. What the hell had she just said? "You're not going anywhere. I won't let you."

"But—"

He ran a hand through his hair, then focused on the human statuary. "I've got an idea. Bill, Harley, are you with us?"

Harley tore his gaze from Edith. "Are we gonna help Lila?"

"If my memory is correct, we are."

"If it's for Lila, then I want to help."

Paul glanced at Bill.

The older man snorted. "I'm insulted you'd even have to ask."

Crammed inside Tricia's small convertible, Lila sat in the passenger seat and gazed at Paul. Right now they were waiting in front of Bill's house, while the old gent was inside talking to his wife and packing a bag. Then they were driving to Harley's trailer, where they'd dropped him a few minutes ago, so he could pack a bag as well.

Lila clutched her backpack to her chest, relieved she'd remembered to grab it before they'd raced from the Windcruiser. She'd also reclaimed her earrings from Edith's pocket and put them back in her ears. The diamonds were worth a lot of money. She wasn't about to give that woman a penny.

With his jaw set and his eyes focused straight ahead, Paul drummed his fingers on the steering wheel. "You never did say why you were here. And leave out the business about your sister. There's no way I'll believe she's more beautiful or compassionate than you."

At his compliment, Lila's heart beat a rapid little tap dance in her chest. "Everyone loves Rila. She's perfect."

He turned, his eyes shining in the light from the street lamp. "She can't be more perfect than you. And don't forget, I'm still trying to get used to the idea of—well—you know. One space woman is enough for any man."

"I'm not a spacewoman. I'm a woman who comes from another planet. Except for the obvious differences in our gender, my body's physical composition is so close to yours it would be impossible to detect the disparity without DNA testing."

"Uh-huh." Paul leaned back in his seat, his expression weary. "How about you tell me the rest in simple sentences, and start at the beginning?"

She twisted her fingers into a knot. "I came here

as one of nine women whose sole goal is to complete a mission that will ensure our planet's future. It's a matter of life or death for my people."

"And the mission is . . . ?"

She inhaled, trying to ease into the answer, but no matter how many ways she formed her response, it sounded harsh and self-serving. "Each of us had to become impregnated by a human male." When he didn't comment, she untangled her fingers and turned to face him. "Even though I knew I was staying, I felt it was my duty to complete the mission—to prove to myself I'd have succeeded had I been chosen."

"That part was important, I take it?"

"Very. I wasn't . . . I didn't have . . ." She sucked in a breath. "All my life, I had a hard time fitting in. Nothing I ever did, no career I tried, felt right to me except caring for children, but there are none on our planet now. Going on this mission was my chance to have a child of my own, and a way to get out from under my sister's shadow at the same time."

He continued to stare at the car ceiling. "So having sex with me was an experiment? A step you needed to fulfill your own agenda?"

"Yes. At least, it was until I met you. After we slept together, everything changed." She focused on her hands. "I fell in love with you."

Paul swiveled his head and gave her a hard stare. "You say you love me, yet you were going to abandon me—us? You were going to take away my child?" His lips thinned. "You were willing to walk out of our life?"

"To keep you safe!" She ran a hand across her

eyes. "Knowing I had to leave you and the twins was killing me, but there was no other way. I'm an alien. According to your world, I'm nothing more than a—a creature to be hunted down and captured—something to be put on exhibition or dissected in the name of science. Can you love me, knowing I'm not like the rest of your species? Can you love our child, knowing he's only half human?"

Reaching out, Paul swept a thumb over her damp cheek. "I guess you don't have much faith in me, if you think I toss out words like 'I love you' with so little commitment."

She clutched at his wrist, kissed his palm. "I'm sorry I doubted you." She snuggled her face into his hand. "Can you ever forgive me?"

"I can do better than that," he whispered. "I can love you forever. Marry me and be my wife, the mother of my sons. The mother of all my children."

Leaning forward, he brushed her lips with his, and Lila folded against him as everything she'd been through faded, until there was nothing in her world but this moment. This man.

"You're mine, Lila. Forever. And when this is over, we're coming back here to live as a family."

Drawing away, she sighed as she caught his lop-sided grin. "Why are you smiling?"

Paul's chuckle bounced off the car windows. "I can see the title of my first best-seller now. *I Was an Alien's Love Slave.*"

"That is not funny. My world needs your sperm, and this seemed the only logical way to get it."

"Our sperm? What's wrong with yours—er—theirs? The men on your planet, I mean."

"Generations ago, our scientists became experts at altering DNA, and used the technology to create designer babies. The procedure didn't affect the females, but it made each new wave of males weak, until they became either impotent or sterile. They tried to develop a reversal drug, but nothing worked, so they went on a search for fresh sperm."

"Why didn't your people simply sneak into one of our sperm banks and make a withdrawal?"

"The Elders no longer felt they could trust the job to a test tube. They wanted to start from square one, and asked for female volunteers—"

"And you were the first one in line?" He raised a brow. "Pretty brave thing to do, if you ask me."

"Not so courageous. I was unhappy with my life and saw it as a way to escape."

"Why and how was I chosen?"

"When they first started the search, our scientists placed several of their own in sperm banks around the country, and they took samples. Every candidate was investigated thoroughly. They know your IQ, your medical history, each plus and minus on your DNA chain. You're all pluses, by the way."

"Tricia will be happy to hear that," he answered wryly.

Lila couldn't resist smiling. "You have an abnormally high quantity of sperm carrying the XY chromosome, as do the rest of the men who were targeted."

"So where are the other women who came down with you?"

"I can only hope they've found their match and become pregnant. They're each scheduled to meet the mother ship in a few weeks and return carrying a healthy male baby."

Paul brought her hand to his mouth and kissed it. "I'm very happy you were miserable on your planet, otherwise we might never have found each other."

Fate, she decided, was a wonderful thing. She'd met a man who loved her, despite the fact that she'd dragged him into an ugly situation. If only she could predict what would happen to her, to any of them once they left town.

"Now tell me exactly where you're from."

"Can you read an interstellar map?"

"Try me and we'll find out."

Lila fiddled with her bracelet. "I have to use one of my locater stones, but that's okay, because as I said I have no intention of ever locking on to the mother ship and going home."

"Does it have anything to do with your mental abilities, like what you used to move the ball and the Ferris wheel?"

"Not exactly." It was dark, but she could see the gleam of his teeth and guessed he was smiling.

"Teddy and Rick must have loved playing with it."

"I thought about leaving it here, but they wouldn't have been able to do anything with it."

"They need you, Lila, not a toy. You're their mother now, and the mother of my child. It's a boy, I take it?"

"Yes, a boy. And now that Edith and her contacts know about me, we're in danger."

"Speaking of Edith, who do you think she is?"

Lila frowned. "I'm not sure. At first I thought she was from your government, but now I wonder."

"She didn't make much sense, did she?" He shrugged. "We can't worry about it now, not when we have to protect you until we get things ironed out."

"Does that mean you have a plan?"

"I do." Paul's expression grew thoughtful. "First off, I'm hoping the duct tape holds for longer than your living statue trick. Chief Gibson was more than willing to do as I asked and padlock the door to the Windcruiser. I imagine he's towing it and their Jeep to the middle of the wildlife refuge right now. Then he's going to slash all the tires. The trailer will be mired in the swamp, so it's going to take Edith and her pals a while to get out and find transportation. And even if they manage to locate a car, they don't know I've traded vehicles with Tricia. That should buy us enough time."

"To do what?"

"Talk to a friend of mine."

"You have a friend?"

"An old college buddy who went to work for the government after graduation. When I met him at our ten-year reunion a few months back, he was pretty secretive, but there was a rumor going around that he had a high-level job with the space agency. He wouldn't confirm it, but I got the impression he was an important guy. Now show me where you come from."

Lila removed a green stone, set it in place, and pressed the clasp, then called up a mental picture of the universe. A dazzling hologram appeared on the windshield in front of them, filled with hues of pink, blue, gold, and every color in between. Tiny planets twirled against a backdrop of sparkling stars. Comets and meteors flashed and died in milliseconds, while other celestial bodies orbited myriad galaxies at a mesmerizing rate of speed.

Paul ran a hand across his eyes, then whistled. "That is amazing. Kind of reminds me of a movie I once saw."

Pleased she'd impressed him, she pointed to a planet. "This is your solar system. If we work outward from your sun you can see Mercury, Venus, Mars . . . Once we get to here"—she touched a dense cluster of stars—"it gets tricky. This is what your world calls the Milky Way. We're beyond it by several million miles. Right . . . here."

"Jeez. How long did the trip take? How did you get here, by the way?"

"How well do you understand astrophysics?"

He barked out a laugh. "Okay, I get the idea. It's all going to be clear as mud." He squinted at the planet she'd pointed to. "But damn, that's far."

"It was a journey of several months. Our spacecraft is out there hovering, undetectable by your instruments, waiting to pick up the others at a specific time and place."

"As long as they don't come looking for you." He shifted in his seat. "I'm sorry I didn't believe you, but I meant what I said. No one is going to separate us." He inched across the console and drew her hands to his chest. "I don't have a ring or anything, and I know this is a poor excuse for a proposal, but I love you—will you marry me?"

A spot of warmth blossomed in Lila's chest, then expanded outward until it felt as big as the sun, and so hot she thought it might set both of them on fire. Meeting him halfway, she sighed out the words, "Yes, I'll marry you," before she placed her lips against his.

Paul drew her to him in a way that made her completely secure. He meant every word he said. He loved her and he was going to find a way to keep them together.

He would make everything right.

The back door opened and the interior light flashed on, instantly dousing the mood.

"Stop the mushy stuff and get rolling," muttered Bill. Then he saw the star map. "Woo-ee. Now, that is a pretty sight. Show me where you're from."

Lila gave him an abbreviated lesson. "I'm going to shut the map down so Paul can drive. Please don't mention this to Harley or he'll pester until I do it all over again."

"Shoot, we have to find the boy and get moving. It's a half hour to Eustace's house."

"We're not going to Mr. Carter's." Paul threw the car into gear and pulled onto the road.

"Why in blazes not?" Bill sputtered.

"Paul knows someone," answered Lila.

"Knows someone?" The older man didn't waste a moment tapping him on the shoulder. "Who you taking us to, Doc?"

Paul glanced at him in the rearview mirror. "Someone I'm fairly certain will know how to get Lila out of this mess."

"You know someone in the government?"

"Not just someone. I was best man at the guy's

wedding. Trust me, if anyone can tell us what to do, it'll be him."

"So where are we going?" Bill asked again.

"Washington, D.C." Paul turned left at the light and headed north on Route 13. "We have to find Lucas Diamond."

Epilogue

Washington, D.C.

Lucas slammed open the parking garage door. He'd been an idiot, a fool for not putting the pieces together sooner. He deserved to be fired for his inability to control his raging hormones. If his suspicion was correct, he'd almost blown the find of the century for nothing more than a few nights of horizontal recreation.

Scanning the dimly lit area, he spotted his quarry in the distance, walking briskly toward the exit. What arrogance, to think he'd be dumb enough to search the lobby while she made her escape from down here.

Heading toward her, he spun in place at the sound of squealing tires. A mid-sized black sedan, its high beams blinding, swung around the corner and screeched to a halt at her side. Two men jumped out, grabbed her arms, and pinned her to the car.

Drawing his gun, Lucas took off at a sprint. He couldn't risk firing, but he could intimidate. "Stop!" He crouched and aimed the weapon. "Let her go! Now!"

Ignoring his command, they used the woman as a shield while they tried to wrestle her into the rear seat. She kicked like a karate expert, whirled free, and dived for cover, surprising him with her strength and agility.

He used the scuffle to get closer, and attacked the thugs from behind. One swift whack with the butt of his revolver had the first guy face down on the cement. The shorter, stockier man turned and plowed a fist into his gut. Lucas let go of the gun, stumbled, and came up swinging. Three punches later, the second man was stretched out next to his pal.

Bending down, he picked up his weapon, then searched their suit pockets. When he came up empty, he panned the garage. *Where the hell was she?* He heard a scuffling noise and duckwalked toward a row of cars. Lucky for him the sedan's lights were still on, illuminating all but the farthest corners of the garage.

Moving with stealth, he came up behind her and wrapped an arm around her waist. "Going somewhere?"

She struggled, her heart beating against his forearm like a trapped bird. He hauled her upward in a punishing grip, and she rammed an elbow in his ribs. Inhaling a painful breath, he asked, "Is that any way to treat someone who just saved your life?"

Her shoulders sagged, her body went limp. Had she fainted? He loosened his arm. To his dismay, she jerked away and took off running. Cursing, Lucas zigzagged between parked cars, vowing never again to underestimate her.

Lucas jumped into motion, vaulted over a low-slung sports car, and tackled her to the ground. She thrashed beneath him, and damn if the squirming didn't bring his arousal to full mast. Too bad for her he was smarter now. No more would he be swayed by a hot body and even hotter sex.

She expelled a gasp of air and stilled. Willing his erection to take a hike, he whispered, "Those thugs won't stay unconscious forever. How about I take you back there and hand you over?"

A scant second passed before she shook her head.

"That's what I thought," Lucas mumbled. "Okay, swear you won't run, and I'll let you up."

It took a bit longer for her to nod a yes.

Lucas rolled to his side and came to his feet, his free hand still gripping her upper arm. Slowly, she rose to her knees, collecting her tote bag as she stood. He hauled her against his side and dragged her along until he found the vehicle he was looking for. Good thing Martin had decided to stay at the same hotel. Clutching her tightly, he tucked the gun in his waistband, squatted next to the Humvee's rear wheel well, and fumbled until he found his prize. The ex-director hadn't changed the hiding spot of his spare key.

"Get in." He thrust her none to gently into the passenger seat, then trotted to the driver's side, slid behind the wheel, and slammed the door. Activating the childproof locks with one hand, he started the engine with the other.

At three A.M. the garage was deserted. He steered slowly past the black sedan and memorized the license number, then headed for the exit. Pulling down the visor, he found the parking ticket and passed it to the sleepy-eyed attendant along with a ten-dollar bill. "I'm in a hurry. Do me a favor and add the charges to my tab."

Turning into the street, he clutched the wheel in a death grip. "Put on your seat belt."

She obeyed without a word.

He didn't have a clue what question to ask first. Where did she come from? What had brought her and the others here? Where had she been heading when she'd left him? Who were those men? Did they know her true identity, or had they meant it to be a random snatch? Telling himself the last thought was unlikely—the coincidence factor was just too damned high—Lucas gave a sidelong glance and caught her staring through narrowed eyes.

He was a patient man, but her belligerent manner pissed him off. This was his country, damn it. His job. His dream. No matter where she came from, she had no right to use him and walk away.

She sighed loud and long. "Where are you taking me?"

He fought the urge to gloat. Just because he had her in custody didn't mean he'd won. Somebody knew who—what—she was and they wanted in. "I'll make a deal with you—a question for a question."

She gave a strangled laugh. "And I suppose you want to go first" came her angry retort.

"I think I earned that right ten minutes ago, don't you?"

He took her silence for agreement, and figured he should have bargained for honesty first. There was so much Lucas wanted to know, but what guarantee did he have that she'd tell him the truth? Logic reminded him that he couldn't go wrong if he started at the beginning.

He meant to choose his words carefully, but she'd had him so tied in knots he blurted the first sentence that formed on his lips. "Just who the hell are you?"

*Keep your resolution to get more passion
with these irresistible love stories coming
in January from Avon Romance!*

Sin and Sensibility by Suzanne Enoch

An Avon Romantic Treasure

Lady Eleanor Griffin's overprotective brothers fully intend to choose her bridegroom, and Eleanor knows she might as well enjoy herself now, before a man dull enough to satisfy them appears. But when she meets her brothers' best friend, her idea of enjoyment takes a whole new turn, and her brothers' wishes are the last thing on her mind . . .

The Protector by Gennita Low

An Avon Contemporary Romance

After a covert mission goes awry, Navy SEAL Jazz Zeringue has no doubts he'll be rescued, but he's certainly surprised when his savior turns out to be the mysterious and beautiful agent Vivi Verreau. Vivi doesn't trust him and is trying very hard not to like him, but they'll have to work together if they're to escape from dangerous enemy territory alive.

Seducing a Princess by Lois Greiman

An Avon Romance

Having set out to avenge a great wrong, William Enton, third baron of Landow, finds himself with nowhere to turn in the most lawless part of Darktowne. Then a vision appears from the dirty alleyways, a woman who seems to know him at once. But she is the princess of thieves, and nothing is as it seems, including the woman he is quickly coming to love.

What an Earl Wants by Shirley Karr

An Avon Romance

Desperate for employment, Josephine Quincy dresses as a secretary would—as a man—and lets her new employer, the rakish Earl of Sinclair, make his own assumptions. But he is no fool, and just when she thinks her game is up, she realizes she has a bargaining chip she never dreamed of—the powerful Earl's attentions . . . and perhaps he in turn is gaining possession of her heart.

REL 1204

Discover Contemporary Romances at Their Sizzling Hot Best from Avon Books

WANTED: ONE PERFECT MAN　　by Judi McCoy
0-06-056079-7/$5.99 US/$7.99 Can

FACING FEAR　　by Gennita Low
0-06-052339-5/$5.99 US/$7.99 Can

HOT STUFF　　by Elaine Fox
0-06-051724-7/$5.99 US/$7.99 Can

WHAT MEMORIES REMAIN　　by Cait London
0-06-055588-2/$5.99 US/$7.99 Can

LOVE: UNDERCOVER　　by Hailey North
0-06-058230-8/$5.99 US/$7.99 Can

IN THE MOOD　　by Suzanne Macpherson
0-06-051768-9/$5.99 US/$7.99 Can

THE DAMSEL IN THIS DRESS　　by Marianne Stillings
0-06-057533-6/$5.99 US/$7.99 Can

**SINCE YOU'RE LEAVING ANYWAY,
TAKE OUT THE TRASH**　　by Dixie Cash
0-06-059536-1/$5.99 US/$7.99 Can

A DATE ON CLOUD NINE　　by Jenna McKnight
0-06-054928-9/$5.99 US/$7.99 Can

THE THRILL OF IT ALL　　by Christie Ridgway
0-06-050290-8/$5.99 US/$7.99 Can